I0635990

*"He had scrambled into the field
and fetched it for her"*

—Colonel Quaritch

Colonel Quaritch, V.C.

A TALE OF COUNTRY LIFE

BY

H. RIDER HAGGARD

WITH FRONTISPIECE

Wildside Press
PO Box 45
Gillette, NJ 07933-0045
www.wildsidepress.com

CONTENTS.

1—Vol. 8

CONTENTS.

COLONEL QUARITCH, V.C.

CHAPTER I.

HAROLD QUARITCH MEDITATES.

THERE are some things and faces which, when felt or seen for the first time, project themselves upon the mind like a sun image on a sensitive plate and there remain unalterably fixed. To take the case of a face—we may never see it again, or it may become the companion of our life, but there the picture is just as we *first* knew it, the same smile, the same look, un-altering and unalterable, reminding us in the midst of change of the absolutely indestructible nature of every experience, act, and aspect of our life. For that which has been, is, since the past knows no change and no corruption, but lives eternally in its frozen and completed self.

These are somewhat large words to be born of small matter, but they rose up spontaneously in the mind of a soldierly-looking man who was leaning, on the particular evening when this history opens, over a gate in an Eastern country lane, staring vacantly at a ripe field of corn.

He was a peculiar and rather battered looking individual, apparently over forty years of age, and yet bearing upon him that unmistakable stamp of dignity and self-respect which, if it does not exclusively belong to, is yet one of the distinguish-ing attributes of the English gentleman. In face he was ugly, no other word can express it. Here were not the long mus-tache, the almond eyes, the aristocratic air of the colonel of fiction—for our dreamer was a colonel. These were—alas! that the truth should be so plain—represented by rather

1

scrubby, sandy-colored whiskers, small but rather kindly blue
eyes, a low broad forehead, with a deep line running across
it from side to side, something like that to be seen upon the
bust of Julius Cæsar, and a long thin nose. One good feature, however, he did possess, a mouth of such sweetness and
beauty that, set, as it was, above a very square and manly-
looking chin, it had the air of being ludicrously out of place.
" Umph," said his old aunt, Mrs. Massey (who had just died
and left him what she had), on the occasion of her first introduction to him five-and-thirty years before, " Umph ! Nature
meant to make a pretty girl of you, and changed her mind
after she had finished the mouth. Well, never mind, better
be a plain man than a pretty woman. There, go along, boy,
I like your ugly face."

Nor was the old lady peculiar in this respect, for plain as
the countenance of Colonel Harold Quaritch undoubtedly was,
people found something very taking about it, when once they
got used to its rugged air and stern regulated expression.
What that something was it would be hard to define, but perhaps the nearest approach to the truth would be to describe
it as a light of purity which, notwithstanding the popular idea
to the contrary, is to be found quite as often upon the faces
of men as upon those of women. Any person of discernment
in looking at Colonel Quaritch must have felt that he was in the
presence of a good man, not a prude or a milksop, but a man
who had attained to virtue by thought and struggle that had
left their mark upon his face, a man whom it would not be
well to tamper with, and one to be respected by all, and feared
of evil-doers. Men felt this, and he was popular among those
who knew him in his service, though not in any hail-fellow-
well-met kind of way. But among women he was not popular.
As a rule they both feared and disliked him. His presence
jarred upon the frivolity of the lighter members of their sex,
who dimly realized that his nature was antagonistic, and the
more solid ones could not understand him. Perhaps this was
the reason why Colonel Quaritch had never married, had never
even had a love affair since he was five-and-twenty.

And yet it was of a woman's face that he was thinking as he
leaned over the gate and looked at the field of yellowing corn,
undulating like a golden sea beneath the pressure of the wind.

Colonel Quaritch had twice in his life been at Honham before the present time, when he had come to abide there for
good and all, once ten, and once five years ago. His old
aunt, Mrs. Massey, had a place in the village—a very small
place—called Honham Cottage, or Molehill, and he had on
those two occasions been down to stay with her. Now, Mrs.
Massey was dead and buried, and had left him the property,
and he had given up his profession, in which he had no
further prospects, and come to live at Honham. This was
his first evening in the place, for he had arrived by the last
train on the previous night. All day he had been busy trying
to get the house a little straight, and now, thoroughly tired of
the task, he was refreshing himself by leaning over a gate.
It is, though a great many people will not believe it, one of
the most delightful refreshments in the world.

And then it was, as he leaned over the gate, that the image
of a woman's face rose before his mind as it had been continually rising for the last five years. It was five years since
he had seen it, and those five years he had spent in India and
Egypt, that is, with the exception of six months which he had
passed in hospital, as the result of an Arab spear thrust in
the thigh. It had risen before him in all sorts of places and
at all sorts of times—in his sleep, in his waking moments, at
mess, out shooting, and even once in the hot rush of battle.
He remembered it well—it was at El Teb. It happened that
stern necessity forced him to shoot a man with his pistol.
The bullet cut into the spine of his enemy, and with a few
convulsions he died. He watched him die, he could not help
doing so, there was some fascination in following the act of
his own hand to its dreadful conclusion, and indeed conclusion
and commencement were very near together. The terror of
the sight, the terror of what in defence of his own life he had
been forced to do, revolted him even in the heat of the fight,
and then, even then, over that ghastly, agony-distorted face,
another face had spread itself like a mask, blotting it out
from view—that woman's face. And now again it re-arose,
inspiring him with the rather recondite reflections as to the
immutability of things and impressions with which this do-
mestic record opens.

Five years is a good stretch in a man's journey through the

world.   Many things happen to us in that time.   If a thoughtful man were to set to work to record all the impressions that
impinge upon his mind during that period, he would fill a
library with volumes, the mere tale of its events would furnish
a shelf.   And yet how small they are to look back upon.   It
seemed but the other day that he had been leaning over this
very gate, and had turned to see a young girl dressed in black,
with a spray of honeysuckle stuck in her girdle, and a stick
in her hand, walking leisurely down the lane.   There was something about the girl's air that had struck him while she was
yet a long way off—a dignity and a grace, and a set of the
shoulders, and then as she came nearer he saw the soft dark
eyes and the waving brown hair that contrasted so strangely
and effectively with the pale and striking face.   It was not a
beautiful face, for the mouth was too large, and the nose was
not as straight as it might have been, but there was a power
about the broad brow, and a force and solid nobility stamped
upon the features which had impressed him strangely.   Just as
she arrived opposite to where he was standing, a gust of wind,
for there was a stiff breeze, had blown the lady's hat off, taking it right over the hedge, and he, as in duty bound, had
scrambled into the field and fetched it for her, and she had
thanked him with a quick smile and a lighting up of the
brown eyes, and then passed on with a bow.

Yes, with a little bow she had passed on, and he had
watched her departing down the long level drift, till she melted into the stormy sunset light, and was gone.   When he returned to the cottage he had described her to his old aunt,
and asked who she might be, to learn that her name was Ida
de la Molle, which sounded like a name out of a novel, the
only daughter of the old squire who lived at Honham Castle.
And then next day he had departed to India, and saw Miss
de la Molle no more.

And now he wondered what had become of her.   Probably
she was married; so striking a person would be almost sure
to attract the notice of men.   And, after all, what could it
matter to him.   He was not a marrying man, and women as
a class had little attraction for him; indeed he disliked them.
It had been said that he had never married, and never even
had a love affair since he was five-and-twenty, and this was

true enough. But though he was not married, he once, before he was five-and-twenty, had very nearly taken that step. It was twenty years ago now, and nobody quite knew the history, for in twenty years many things are fortunately forgotten. But there was a history, and a scandal, and the marriage was broken off almost on the very day before it was to have taken place. And after that it leaked out in the neighborhood—it was in Essex, near Romford—that the young lady, who by the way was a large heiress, had gone off her head, presumably with grief, and been confined in an asylum, where she was presumed still to remain.

Perhaps it was the thinking of this one woman's face, the woman he had once seen walking down the drift, her figure limned out against the stormy sky, that led him to think of the other face, the face hidden in the madhouse. At any rate, with a sigh, or rather a groan, he swung himself round from the gate and began walking homeward at a brisk pace.

The drift that he was following was known as the mile drift, and had in ancient times formed the approach to the gates of Honham Castle, the seat of the ancient and honorable family of De la Molle (sometimes written "Delamol" in history and ancient writings). Honham Castle was now nothing but a ruin, with a manor-house built out of the wreck on one side of the square, and the broad way that led to it from the high-road which ran from Boisingham,* the local country town, was a drift or grass lane.

Colonel Quaritch followed this drift till he came to the high-road, and then turned to the left. A few minutes' walk brought him to a drive opening out of the main road on the left as he faced towards Boisingham. This drive, which was some three hundred yards long, led up a rather sharp slope to his own place, Honham Cottage, or Molehill, as the villagers called it, a title calculated to give a keen impression of a neat spic-and-span red brick villa with a slate roof. As a matter of fact, however, it was nothing of the sort, being a building

---

* Said to have been so named after the Boissey family, whose heiress, a De la Molle, married in the fourteenth century. As, however, the town of Boisingham is mentioned by one of the old Saxon chroniclers, this does not seem very probable. No doubt the family took their name from the town or hamlet, not the town from the family.

of the fifteenth century, as a glance at its massive flint walls was sufficient to show. In ancient times there had been a large abbey at Boisingham, two miles away, which, as the records show, in the fifteenth century suffered terribly from an outbreak of the plague. After this the monks obtained by grant from the De la Molle of the day ten acres of land, known as the Molehill, and so named either on account of its resemblance to a molehill, of which more presently, or after the family. On this elevated spot, which was supposed to be particularly healthy, they built the little house now known as Honham Cottage, whereto to fly when next the plague should visit them.

And as they built it, so, with some slight additions, it had remained to this day, for in those ages men did not skimp their flint and oak and mortar. It was a beautiful little spot, upon the flat top of a swelling hill, which comprised the ten acres of grazing-ground originally granted, and was, wonderful to say, to this day the most magnificently timbered piece of ground in the country side. For on the ten acres of grass land there were over fifty great oaks, some of them pollards of the most enormous antiquity, and others which had originally, no doubt, grown very close together, fine upstanding trees with a wonderful length and girth of bole. This place old Mrs. Massey, Colonel Quaritch's aunt, had bought nearly thirty years before, when she became a widow, and now it had, together with a modest income of two hundred a year, passed to him under her will.

Shaking himself clear of his sad thoughts, Harold Quaritch turned round at his own front door to contemplate the scene. The long, single-storied house stood, as has been said, at the top of the rising land, and to the south and west and east commanded as beautiful a view as is to be seen in that county. There, a mile or so away to the south, situated in the midst of grassy grazing-grounds, flanked on either side by still perfect towers, frowned the massive gateway of the old Norman castle. Then, to the west, almost at the foot of the Molehill, the ground broke away in a deep bank clothed with timber, which led the eye down by slow descents into the beautiful valley of the Ell. Here the silver river wound its gentle way through lush and poplar-bordered marshes, where the cattle stand knee-deep in

flowers; past quaint old wooden mill-houses, through Boisingham Old Common, windy looking even now, and brightened
here and there with a dash of golden gorse, till it was lost in
the picturesque cluster of red-tiled roofs that marked the
ancient town. Look which way he would, the view was lovely, and equal to any to be found in the eastern counties, where
the scenery is fine enough in its own way, whatever people,
whose imaginations are so weak that they require a mountain
and a torrent to excite them into activity, may choose to say
to the contrary.

Behind the house to the north there was no view, and for
a good reason, for here in the very middle of the back garden
rose a mound of large size and curious shape, which completely shut the landscape out. What this mound, which may perhaps have covered half an acre of ground, was, nobody had
any idea. Some learned folk said that it was a Saxon tumulus, a presumption to which its ancient name, " Dead Man's
Mount," seemed to give color. Other folk, however, yet
more learned, declared that it was an ancient British dwelling,
and pointed triumphantly to a hollow at the top, wherein the
ancient Britishers were supposed to have moved, lived, and
had their being, which must, urged the other party, have been
a very damp one. Thereon the late Mrs. Massey, who was a
British dwellingite, proceeded to show with much triumph
how they had lived in the hole, by building a huge mushroom-
shaped roof over it, and thereby turning it into a summer-
house, which, owing to unexpected difficulties in the construc-
tion of the roof, cost a great deal of money. But as the roof
was slated, and as it was found necessary to pave the hole
with tiles and cut surface drains in it, the result did not clearly prove its use as a dwelling-place before the Roman conquest. Nor did it make a very good summer-house. Indeed,
it now served as a store-place for the gardeners and for rubbish generally.

CHAPTER II.

THE COLONEL MEETS THE SQUIRE.

SUDDENLY, as Colonel Quaritch was contemplating these various views and reflecting that on the whole he had done well to come and live at Honham Cottage, he was startled by a loud voice saluting him from about twenty yards' distance, with such a peculiar vigor that he fairly jumped.

"Colonel Quaritch, I believe," said, or rather shouted, the voice from somewhere down the drive.

"Yes," answered the colonel, mildly, "here I am."

"Ah, I thought it was you. Always tell a military man, you know. Excuse me, but I am resting for a minute, this last pull is an uncommonly stiff one. I always used to tell my dear old friend, Mrs. Massey, that she ought to have the hill cut away a bit just here. Well, here goes for it," and after a few heavy steps the visitor emerged from the shadow of the trees into the sunset light which was playing on the terrace before the house.

Colonel Quaritch glanced up curiously to see who the owner of the great voice might be, and his eyes lit upon as fine a specimen of humanity as he had seen for a long while. The man was old, as his white hair showed, seventy perhaps, but that was the only sign of decay about him. He was a splendid man, broad and thick and strong, with a keen, quick eye, and a face sharply chiselled, and clean-shaved, of the stamp which in novels is generally known as aristocratic, a face that, in fact, showed both birth and breeding. Indeed, as clothed in loose tweed garments and a gigantic pair of top-boots, his visitor stood there, leaning on his long stick and resting himself after breasting the hill, Harold Quaritch thought to himself that he had never seen a more perfect specimen of the typical English country gentleman—as the English country gentleman used to be.

"How do you do, sir, how do you do? My name is De la Molle. My man George, who knows everybody's business except his own, told me that you had arrived here, so I thought that I would walk round and do myself the honor of making your acquaintance."

"That is very kind of you," said the colonel.

"Not at all. If you only knew how uncommonly dull it is down here you would not say that. The place isn't what it used to be when I was a boy. There are plenty of rich people about, but they are not the same stamp of people. It isn't what it used to be in more ways than one," and the old squire gave something like a sigh, and thoughtfully removed his white hat, out of which a dinner napkin and two pocket handkerchiefs fell to the ground, in a fashion that reminded Colonel Quaritch of the climax of a conjuring trick.

"You have dropped some—some linen," he said, stooping down to pick the mysterious articles up.

"Oh, yes, thank you," answered his visitor, "I find the sun a little hot at this time of the year. There is nothing like a few handkerchiefs or a towel to keep it off," and he rolled the mass of napery into a ball, and, cramming it back into the crown, replaced the hat on his head in such a fashion that about eight inches of white napkin hung down behind. "You must have felt it in Egypt," he went on—"the sun, I mean. It's a bad climate, that Egypt, as I have good reason to know," and he pointed again to his white hat, which, as Harold Quaritch now observed for the first time, was encircled by a broad black band.

"Ah, I see," said he; "I suppose that you have had a loss."

"Yes, sir, a very heavy loss."

Now Colonel Quaritch had never heard that Mr. De la Molle had more than one child, Ida De la Molle, the young lady whose face had remained so strongly fixed in his memory, although he had scarcely spoken to her on that one occasion five long years ago. Could it be possible that she had died in Egypt. The idea sent a tremor of fear through him, though of course there was no real reason why it should. Deaths are so common.

"Not—not Miss De la Molle?" he said, nervously, adding, "I had the pleasure of seeing her once, a good many years ago, when I was stopping here for a few days with my aunt."

"Oh, no, not Ida, she is alive and well, thank God. Her brother James. He went all through that wretched war which we owe to Mr. Gladstone, as I say, though I don't know what your politics are, and then caught a fever, or, as I think, got touched by the sun, and died on his way home. Poor boy! He was a fine fellow, Colonel Quaritch, and my only son, but very reckless. Only a month or so before he died I wrote to him to be careful always to put a towel in his helmet, and he answered, in that flippant sort of way that he had, that he was not going to turn himself into a dirty-clothes bag, and that he rather liked the heat than otherwise. Well, he's gone, poor fellow, in the service of his country, like many of his ancestors before him, and there's an end of him."

And again the old man sighed, heavily this time.

"And now, Colonel Quaritch," he went on, shaking off his oppression with a curious rapidity that was characteristic of him, "what do you say to coming up to the Castle for your dinner. You must be in a mess here, and I expect that old Mrs. Jobson, whom my man George tells me you have got to look after you, will be glad enough to be rid of you for to-night. What do you say—take the place as you find it, you know. I know that there is a leg of mutton for dinner if there is nothing else, because, instead of minding his own business, I saw George going off to Boisingham to fetch it this morning. At least, that is what he said that he was going for; just an excuse to gossip and idle, I fancy."

"Well, really," said the colonel, "you are very kind; but I don't think that my dress clothes are unpacked yet."

"Dress clothes! Oh, never mind your dress clothes. Ida will excuse you, I dare say. Besides, you have no time to dress. By Jove, it's nearly seven o'clock; we must be off if you are coming."

The colonel hesitated. He had intended to dine at home, and, being a methodical-minded man, did not like altering his plans. Also he was, like most old military men, very punctilious about his dress and personal appearance, and objected to going out to dinner in a shooting-coat. But, all this notwithstanding, a feeling that he did not quite understand, and that it would have puzzled even an American novelist to analyze—something between restlessness and curiosity, with a dash of magnetic attraction thrown in—got the better of his scruples, and he went.

"Well, thank you," he said, "if you are sure that Miss De la Molle will not mind, I will come. Just allow me to tell Mrs. Jobson."

"That's right," halloaed the squire after him. "I'll meet you at the back of the house. We had better go through the fields."

By the time that the colonel, having informed his house-keeper that he should not want any dinner, and hastily brushed his not too luxuriant locks, had reached the garden that lay behind the house, the old gentleman was nowhere to be seen. Presently, however, a loud halloa from the top of the tumulus-like hill announced his whereabouts.

Wondering what the old gentleman could be doing up there, Harold Quaritch walked up the steps that led to the summit of the mound, and found him standing at the entrance to the mushroom-shaped summer-house, contemplating the view.

"There, colonel," he said, "there's a perfect view for you. Talk about Scotland and the Alps. Give me a view of the valley of Ell from the top of Dead Man's Mount on an autumn evening, I never want to see anything finer. I have always loved it from a boy, and always shall so long as I live—look at those oaks, too. There are no such trees in the country that I know of. The old lady, your aunt, was wonderfully fond of them. I hope "—he went on in a tone of anxiety— "I hope that you don't mean to cut any of them down."

"Oh, no," said the colonel, "I should never think of such a thing."

"That's right. Never cut down a good tree if you can help it. I'm sorry to say, however," he added, after a pause, "that I have been forced to cut down a good many myself. Queer place this, isn't it," he continued, dropping the subject of the trees, which was evidently a painful one to him. "Dead Man's Mount is what the people about here call it, and that is what they called it at the time of the Conquest, as I can prove to you from ancient writings. I always believed that it was a tumulus, but of late years a lot of these clever people have been taking their oath that it is an ancient British dwelling, as though ancient Britons, or any one else for that matter, could live in

a kind of drain-hole. But they got on the soft side of your
old aunt—who, by the way, begging your pardon, was a wonderfully obstinate old lady when once she got an idea into her
head—and so she set to work and built this slate mushroom
over it, and one way or another it cost her two hundred and
fifty pounds. Dear me! I shall never forget her face when
she saw the bill," and the old gentleman burst into a Titanic
laugh, such as Harold Quaritch had not heard for many a long
day.

"Yes," he answered, "it is a queer spot. I think that I
must have a dig at it one day."

"By Jove," said the squire, "I never thought of that. It
would be worth doing. Halloa, it is twenty minutes past
seven, and we dine at half-past. I shall catch it from Ida.
Come on, Colonel Quaritch; you don't know what it is to
have a daughter—a daughter when one is late for dinner is a
serious thing for any man," and he started off down the hill
in a hurry.

Very soon, however, he seemed to forget the terrors in store,
and strolled along, stopping now and again to admire some
particular oak or view; chatting all the while in a discursive
manner, which, though it was somewhat aimless, was by no
means without its charm. He was a capital companion for
a silent man like Harold Quaritch, who liked to hear other
people talk, though some people found him a somewhat tire-
some one.

In this way they got down the slope, and, passing through a
couple of wheat fields, came to a succession of broad meadows,
somewhat sparsely timbered, through which the footpath ran
right up to the grim gateway of the ancient castle, which now
loomed before them, outlined in red lines of fire against the
ruddy background of the sunset sky.

"Ay, it's a fine old place, colonel, isn't it?" said the squire,
catching the exclamation of admiration that broke from his
companion's lips, as a sudden turn brought them into line with
the Norman ruin. "History—that's what it is; history in
stone and mortar; this is historic ground, every inch of it.
Those old De la Molles, my ancestors, and the Boisseys before
them, were great folk in their day, and they kept up their
position well. I will take you to see their tombs in the church

yonder on Sunday. I always hoped to be buried beside them, but I can't manage it now, because of the act. However, I mean to get as near to them as I can. I have a fancy for the companionship of those old barons, though I expect that they were a roughish set in their lifetime. Look how squarely those towers stand out against the sky. They always remind me of the men who built them—sturdy, overbearing fellows, setting their shoulders against the sea of circumstance and caring neither for man nor devil till the priests got hold of them at last. Well, God rest them, they helped to make England, whatever their faults. Queer place to choose for a castle, though, wasn't it, right out in an open plain."

" I suppose that they trusted to their moat and walls, and the hagger at the bottom of the dry ditch," said the colonel. " You see there is no eminence from which they could be commanded, and their archers could sweep all the plain from the battlements."

" Ah, yes, of course they could. It is easy to see that you are a soldier. They were no fools, those old crusaders. My word, we must be getting on. They are hauling down the Union Jack on the west tower. I always have it hauled down at sunset," and he began walking briskly again.

In another three minutes they had crossed a narrow by-road, and were passing up the ancient drive that led to the castle gates. It was not much of a drive, but there were still some half dozen of old pollard oaks that had no doubt stood there before the first Boissey, from whose family, centuries ago, the De la Molles had obtained the property by marriage with the heiress, had got his charts and cut the first sod of his moat.

Right before them was the gateway of the castle, flanked by two great towers, and that, with the exception of some ruins, was, as a matter of fact, all that remained of the ancient building, which had been effectually demolished in the time of Cromwell. The space within, where the keep had once stood, was now laid out as a flower-garden, while the house, which was of an unpretentious nature, and built in the Jacobean style, occupied the south side of the square, and was placed with the back to the moat.

" You see, I have practically rebuilt those two towers," said the squire, pausing underneath the Norman archway. " If I

had not done it," he added, apologetically, "they would have
been in ruins now ; but it cost a pretty penny, I can tell you.
Nobody knows what stuff that old flint masonry is to deal
with, till he tries it.   Well, it will stand now for many a long
day.   And here we are "—and he pushed open a porch door
and then passed through a passage into a kind of oak-panelled
vestibule, which was hung with tapestry originally taken, no
doubt, from the old castle, and decorated with coats of armor,
spear-heads, and ancient swords.

And here it was that Harold Quaritch once more beheld
the face that had haunted his memory for so many months.

CHAPTER III.

THE TALE OF SIR JAMES DE LA MOLLE.

" Is that you, father?" said a voice, a very sweet voice, but
one of which the tones betrayed the irritation natural to a
healthy woman who has been kept waiting for her dinner.
The voice came from the recesses of the dusky room in which
the evening gloom had gathered deeply, and, looking in its
direction, Harold Quaritch could see the outline of a tall form
sitting in an old oak chair with its hands crossed.

" Is that you, father? Really it is too bad to be so late for
dinner—especially after you blew up that wretched Emma last
night because she was five minutes after time. I have been
waiting so long that I have almost been asleep."

" I am very sorry, my dear, very," said the old gentleman,
apologetically, " but—hullo! I've knocked my head; here,
Mary, bring me a light."

" Here is a light," said the voice, and at the same moment
there was a sound of a match being struck.

In another moment the candle was alight, and the owner
of the voice had turned round with it, holding it in such a
fashion that its rays surrounded her like an aureole—showing Harold Quaritch that same face of which memory had
never left him. There was the same powerful broad brow,
the same nobility of look, the same brown eyes and soft waving hair. But the girlhood had gone out of it, the face was
now the face of a woman, who knew what life was, and had
not found it too easy. It had lost some of its dreaminess, he
thought, though it had gained in intellectual force; as for the
figure, it was much more admirable than the face, which was,
strictly speaking, not a beautiful one. The figure, however,
was undoubtedly beautiful; indeed, it is doubtful if many
women could show a finer. Ida De la Molle was a large,
strong woman, and there was about her a swing and a lissom

grace which is very rare, and as attractive as it is rare. She was now nearly six-and-twenty years of age, and not having begun to wither in accordance with the fate which overtakes nearly all unmarried women after thirty, was at her very best. Harold Quaritch, glancing at her well-poised head, her perfect bust and arms (for she was in evening dress), and her gracious form, thought to himself that he had never seen a nobler-looking woman.

"Why, my dear father," she went on as she watched the match burn up and held it to the candle, "you made such a fuss this morning about the dinner being punctually at 7.30, and now it is eight o'clock and you are not dressed. It is enough to ruin any cook," and she broke off for the first time, perceiving that her father was not alone.

"Yes, my dear, yes," said the old gentleman, "I dare say I did. It is human to err, my dear, especially about dinner on a fine evening. Besides, I have made amends and brought you a visitor, our new neighbor, Colonel Quaritch. Colonel Quaritch, let me introduce you to my daughter, Miss De la Molle."

"I think that we have met before," said Harold, in a somewhat nervous fashion, as he stretched out his hand.

"Yes," answered Ida, taking it, "I remember. It was in the long drift, five years ago, on a windy afternoon, when my hat blew over the hedge and you went to fetch it."

"You have a good memory, Miss De la Molle," said he, feeling not a little pleased that she should have recollected the incident.

"Evidently not better than your own, Colonel Quaritch," was her ready answer. "Besides, one sees so few strangers here that one naturally remembers them. It is a place where nothing happens—time passes, that is all."

Meanwhile the old squire, who had been making a prodigious fuss with his hat and stick, which he managed to send clattering down the flight of stone steps, departed to get ready, saying in a kind of roar, as he went, that Ida was to order in the dinner, as he would be down in a minute.

Accordingly she rang the bell, and told the maid to bring in the soup in five minutes and to lay another plate. Then, turning to Harold she began to apologize to him.

"I don't know what sort of a dinner you will get, Colonel Quaritch," she said; "it is so provoking of my father, he never gives one the least warning when he is going to ask any one to dinner."

"Not at all—not at all," he answered, hurriedly. "It is I who ought to apologize, coming down on you like—like—"

"A wolf on the fold," suggested Ida.

"Yes, exactly," he went on earnestly, "and in this coat, too."

"Well," she went on laughing, "you will get very littl to eat for your pains, and I know that soldiers always like good dinners."

"How do you know that, Miss De la Molle?"

"Oh, because of poor James and his friends whom he used to bring here. By the way, Colonel Quaritch," she went on, with a sudden softening of the voice, "you have been in Egypt, I know, because I have so often seen your name in the papers; did you ever meet my brother there?"

"I knew him slightly," he answered. "Only very slightly. I did not know that he was your brother, or indeed that you had a brother. He was a dashing officer."

What he did not say, however, was that he also knew him to have been one of the wildest and most extravagant young men in an extravagant regiment, and as such had to some extent shunned his society on the few occasions when he had been thrown in with him. Perhaps Ida, with a woman's quickness, divined from his tone that there was something behind his remark; at any rate she did not ask him for particulars of their slight acquaintance.

"He was my only brother," she continued; "there never were but us two, and of course his loss was a great blow to me. My father cannot get over it at all, although—" and she broke off suddenly and rested her head upon her hand.

At this moment, too, the squire was heard advancing down the stairs, shouting to the servants as he came.

"A thousand pardons, my dear, a thousand pardons," he said, as he entered the room; "but—well, if you will forgive particulars, I was quite unable to discover the whereabouts of a certain necessary portion of the male attire. Now, Colonel Quaritch, will you take my daughter? Stop, you don't know

the way—perhaps I had better show it to you with the
candle."

Accordingly he advanced out of the vestibule, and, turning
to the left, led the way down a long passage till he reached
the dining-room. This apartment was, like the vestibule, oak
panelled, but the walls were mostly decorated with family and
other portraits, including a very curious painting of the castle
itself, as it was before its destruction in the time of Cromwell.
This painting was executed on a massive slab of oak, and conceived in a most quaint and formal style, being relieved in the
foreground with stags at graze and woodeny horses, that must,
according to any rule of proportion, have been about half as
large as the gateway towers. Evidently, also, it was of an
older date than the present house, which is Jacobean, having
probably been removed to its present position from the ruins
of the old castle. Such as it was, however, it gave a very good
idea of what the ancient seat of the Boisseys and De la Molles
had been like before the Roundheads had made an end of its
glory. The dining-room itself was commodious, though not
large. It was lighted by three narrow windows which looked
out upon the moat and bore a considerable air of solid comfort. The table, which was of extraordinary solidity and
weight, made of black oak, was matched by a sideboard of the
same material and apparently of the same date, both pieces of
furniture being, as Mr. De la Molle informed his guest, relics
of the old castle.

On this sideboard were placed several pieces of very massive ancient plate, on each of which was rudely engraved three
falcons *or*, the arms of the De la Molle family, one piece, indeed, a very ancient salver, bearing those of the Boisseys—a
ragged oak, in an escutcheon of pretence—showing thereby
that it dated from the De la Molle who in the time of Henry
the Seventh had obtained the property by marriage with the
Boissey heiress.

As the dinner, which was a very simple one, went on, the
conversation having turned that way, the old squire had his
piece of plate brought by the servant-girl to Harold Quaritch
for him to examine.

"It is very curious," he said; "have you much of this, Mr.
De la Molle?"

"No, indeed," he said; "I wish I had. It all vanished in the time of Charles the First."

"Melted down, I suppose," said the colonel.

"No, that is the odd part of it. I don't think it was. It was hidden somewhere—I don't know where—or perhaps it was turned into money and the money hidden. But I will tell you the story, if you like, as soon as we have done dinner."

Accordingly, as soon as the servant had moved the cloth, and, after the old fashion, placed the wine upon the naked wood, the squire began his tale, of which the following is the substance:

"In the time of James I. the De la Molle family was at the height of its prosperity, that is, so far as money goes. For several generations previous the representatives of the family had withdrawn themselves from any active participation in public affairs, and, living here at small expense upon their lands, which were at that time very large, had amassed a quantity of wealth which, for the age, might fairly be called enormous. Thus, Sir Stephen de la Molle, the grandfather of the Sir James who lived in the time of James I., left to his son, who was also named Stephen, a sum of no less than twenty-three thousand pounds in gold. This Stephen was a great miser, and tradition says that he trebled the sum in his lifetime. Anyhow, he died rich as Crœsus, and abominated alike by his tenants and by the country side, as might be expected when a gentleman of his name and fame degraded himself, as this Sir Stephen undoubtedly did, to the practice of usury.

"With the next heir, Sir James, however, the old spirit of the De la Molles seems to have revived, although it is sufficiently clear that he was by no means a spendthrift, but, on the contrary, a careful man, though one who maintained his station, and refused to soil his fingers with such base dealings as it had pleased his uncle to do. Going to court, he became, perhaps on account of his wealth, a considerable favorite with James I., to whom he was greatly attached, and from whom he bought a baronetcy. Indeed, the best proof of his devotion is, that he on two occasions lent large sums of money to the king which were never repaid. On the accession of Charles I., however, Sir James left court under circumstances which were never quite cleared up. It is said that, smarting

under some slight which was put upon him, he made a somewhat brusque demand for the money which he had lent to
James. Thereon the king, with sarcastic wit, congratulated
him on the fact that the spirit of his uncle, Sir Stephen de
la Molle, whose name was still a byword in the land, evidently
survived in the family. Sir James turned white with fury,
bowed, and without a word left the court, nor did he ever return thither.

"Years passed, and the civil war was at its height. Sir
James had as yet steadily refused to take any share in it. He
had never forgiven the insult put upon him by the king, for
like most of his race, of whom it was said that they never forgave an injury, and never forgot a kindness, he was a perti-
nacious man. Therefore he would not lift a finger in the king's
cause. But still less would he help the Roundheads, whom he
hated with a singular hatred. So time went, till at last, when
he was sore pressed, Charles, knowing his great wealth and
influence, brought himself to write a letter to this Sir James,
appealing to him for support, and especially for money.

"'I hear,' said the king in his letter, 'that Sir James de la
Molle, who was aforetime well affected to our person and
more especially to the late king, our sainted father, doth stand
idle, watching the growing of this bloody struggle, and lifting
no hand. Such was not the way of the race from which he
sprang, which, unless history doth greatly lie, hath in the past
been each found at the side of their kings striking for the
right. It is said to me also, that Sir James de la Molle doth
thus place himself aside, blowing neither hot nor cold, because
of some sharp words which we spake in heedless jest many a
year that's gone. We know not if this be true, doubting if a
man's memory be so long, but if so it be, then hereby do we
crave his pardon, and no more can we do. And now is our
estate one of grievous peril, and sorely do we need the aid of
God and man. Therefore, if the heart of our subject Sir
James de la Molle be not rebellious against us, as we cannot
readily credit it to be, we do implore his present aid in men
and money, of which last it is said he hath large store, this
letter being proof of our urgent need.'

"These were, as nearly as I can remember, the very words
of the letter, which was written in his own hand, and show

pretty clearly how hardly he was pressed. It is said that when he read it, Sir James, forgetting his grievance, burst into tears, and, taking paper, wrote hastily as follows, which last he certainly did, for I have seen the letter in the Museum.

"'*My Liege*,—Of the past I will not speak. It is past. But since it hath graciously pleased your majesty to ask mine aid against the rebels who would overthrow your throne, rest assured that all I have is at your majesty's disposal, till such time as your enemies are discomfited. It hath pleased Providence to so prosper my fortunes that I have stored away in a safe place, till these times be past, a very great sum in gold, whereof I will at once place ten thousand pieces at the disposal of your majesty, so soon as a safe means can be provided of conveying the same, seeing that I had sooner die than that these great moneys should fall into the hands of the rebels to the furtherance of an evil cause.'

"Then the letter went on to say that the writer would at once buckle to and raise a troop of horse among his tenantry, and that if other satisfactory arrangements could not be made for the conveyance of the moneys, he would bring them in person to the king.

"And now comes the climax of the story. The messenger was captured, and Sir James's incautious letter taken from his boot, as a result of which he, within ten days' time, found himself closely besieged by five hundred Roundheads under the command of one Colonel Playfair. The castle was but ill-provisioned for a siege, and in the end Sir James was driven by sheer starvation to surrender. No sooner had he obtained an entry, than Colonel Playfair sent for his prisoner, and to his astonishment produced to Sir James's face his own letter to the king.

"'Now, Sir James,' he said, 'we have the hive, and I must ask you to lead us to the honey. Where be these great moneys whereof you talk herein. Fain would I be fingering these ten thousand pieces in gold, the which you have so snugly stored away.'

"'Ay,' answered old Sir James, 'you have the hive, but the secret of the money you have not, nor shall you have it. The ten thousand pieces in gold is where it is, and with it is much more. Find it if you may, colonel, and take it if you can.'

"'I shall find it by to-morrow's light, Sir James, or otherwise—well, or otherwise you die.'

"'I must die—all men do, colonel; but if I die the secret dies with me.'

"'This shall we see,' answered the colonel, grimly, and old Sir James was marched off to a cell, and there closely confined on bread and water. But he did not die the next day, nor the next, nor for a week, indeed.

"Every day he was brought up before the colonel and questioned as to where the treasure was, under the threat of immediate death, not being suffered meanwhile to communicate by word or sign with any one, save the officers of the rebels, and every day he refused, till at last his inquisitor's patience gave out, and he was told frankly that if he did not communicate the secret he would be shot at dawn the following day.

"Old Sir James laughed, and said that shoot him they might, but that he consigned his soul to the devil if he would enrich them with his treasures, and then asked that his Bible might be brought to him that he might read therein and prepare himself for death.

"They gave him the Bible and left him. Next morning, at the dawn, a file of Roundheads marched him out into the courtyard of the castle, and here he found Colonel Playfair and his officers waiting.

"'Now, Sir James, for your last word. Will you reveal where the treasure lies, or will you choose to die?'

"'I will not reveal,' answered the old man. 'Murder me if ye will. The act is worthy of holy Presbyters. I have spoken and my mind is fixed.'

"'Bethink you,' said the colonel.

"'I have thought,' he answered, 'and am ready. Slay me and seek the treasure. But one thing I ask. My young son is not here. In France hath he been this three years, and nought knows he of where I have hid this gold. Send to him this Bible when I am dead. Nay, search it from page to page. There is nought therein save what I have writ here upon this last sheet. It is all I have left to give.'

"'The book shall be searched,' answered the colonel, 'and if nought is found therein it shall be sent. And now, in the name of God, I adjure you, Sir James, let not the love of lucre stand between you and your life. Here I make you one last offer. Discover but to us the ten thousand pounds whereof you speak in this writing,' and he held up the letter to the king, ' and you shall go free—refuse, and you die.'

" ' I refuse,' he answered.

" ' Musketeers make ready,' shouted the colonel, and the file of men stepped forward.

" But at that moment there came up so furious a squall of wind, together with dense and cutting rain, that for a while the execution was delayed. Presently it passed, and the wild light of the November morning swept out from the sky, and revealed the doomed man kneeling upon the sodden turf, with the water running from his white hair and beard, and praying.

" They called to him to stand up, but he would not, and continued praying. So they shot him on his knees."

" Well," said Colonel Quaritch, " at any rate he died like a gallant gentleman."

At that moment there was a knock at the door, and the servant came in.

" What is it ?" asked the squire.

" George is here, please, sir," said the girl, " and says that he would like to see you."

" Confound him," growled the old gentleman; " he is always here about something or other. I suppose it is about the Moat Farm. He was going to see Janter to-day. Will you excuse me, Quaritch ? Ida will tell you the end of the story if you care to hear any more. I will join you in the drawing-room."

CHAPTER IV.

THE END OF THE TALE.

As soon as her father had gone, Ida rose and suggested that if Colonel Quaritch had done his wine they should go into the drawing-room, which they accordingly did. This room was much more modern than either the vestibule or the dining-room, and had a general air and flavor of nineteenth-century young lady about it. There were the little tables, the draperies, and the photograph frames, and all the hundred and one knick-knacks and odds-and-ends, by means of which a lady of taste makes a room lovely in the eyes of brutal man. It was a very pleasant place to look upon, this drawing-room at Honham Castle, with its irregular recesses, its somewhat faded colors illuminated by the soft light of a shaded lamp, and its general air of feminine dominion. Harold Quaritch was a man who had seen much of the world, but had not seen much of drawing-rooms, or, indeed, of ladies at large. They had not come in his way, or if they had come in his way he had avoided them. Therefore, perhaps, was he the more susceptible to such influences when he came in contact with them. Or perhaps it was the presence of Ida's gracious self which threw a charm about the place that added to its natural attractiveness, as the china bowls of lavender and rose leaves added perfume to the air. Anyhow, it struck him that he had never seen a room which conveyed to his mind such an idea of gentle rest and refinement.

"What a charming room!" he said, as he entered it.

"I am glad you think so," answered Ida; "because it is my own territory, and I arrange it."

"Yes," he said, "it is easy to see that."

"Well, would you like to hear the end of the story about Sir James and his treasure?"

"Certainly; it interests me very much."

"It positively *fascinates* me," said Ida, with emphasis.

"Listen, and I will tell you. After they had shot old Sir James they took the Bible off him, but whether or no Colonel Playfair ever sent it to the son in France is not known.

"The story is all known historically, and it is known that, as my father said, he asked that his Bible might be sent, but nothing more. This son, Sir Edward, never lived to return to England. After his father's murder, the estates were seized by the Parliamentary party, and the old castle, with the exception of the gate towers, razed to the ground, partly for military purposes, and partly in the long and determined attempt that was made to discover old Sir James's treasure, which might, it was thought, have been concealed in some secret chamber in the walls. But it was all of no use, and Colonel Playfair found that, in letting his temper get the better of him and shooting Sir James, he had done away with the only chance of finding the money that he was ever likely to have, for to all appearance the secret had died with its owner. There was a great noise about it at the time, and the colonel was degraded from his rank in reward for what he had done. It was presumed that old Sir James must have had accomplices in the hiding of so great a mass of gold, and every means, by way of threats and promises of reward—which at last grew to half of the total amount that should be discovered—was taken to induce these to come forward if they existed, but without result. And so the matter went on, till after a few years the whole thing died away and was forgotten.

"Meanwhile the son, Sir Edward, who was the second and last baronet, led a wandering life abroad, fearing or not caring to return to England now that all his property had been seized. When he was two-and-twenty years of age, however, he contracted an imprudent marriage with his cousin, a lady of the name of Ida Dofferleigh, a girl of good blood and great beauty, but without means. Indeed, she was the sister of George Dofferleigh, who was a cousin and companion in exile of Sir Edward's, and, as you will presently see, my lineal ancestor. Well, within a year of this marriage, poor Ida, my namesake, died, with her baby, of fever, chiefly brought on, they say, by want and anxiety of mind, and the shock seems to have turned her husband's brain. At any rate, within three or four months of her death, he committed suicide. But before he did so, he formally executed a rather elaborate will, by which he left all his estates in England, 'now unjustly withheld from me contray to law and natural right by the rebel pretender Cromwell, together with the treasure hidden thereon or elsewhere, by my late murdered father, Sir James de la Molle,' to John Geoffrey Dofferleigh, his cousin, and the brother of his late wife, and his heirs forever, on condition only of his assuming the name and arms of the De la Molle family, the direct line of which became extinct with himself. Well, of course, this will, when it was executed, was to all appearance so much waste paper, but within three years from its execution Charles II. was King of England.

"Thereon John Dofferleigh produced the document, and on assuming the name and arms of De la Molle actually succeeded in obtaining the remains of the castle and a considerable portion of the landed property, though the baronetcy became extinct. His son it was who built this present house, and he is our direct ancestor, for though my father talks of them as though they were—it is a little weakness of his—the old De la Molles were not our direct male ancestors."

"Well," said Harold, "and did Dofferleigh find the treasure?"

"No, ah, no; nor anybody else; the treasure has vanished. He hunted for it a great deal, and he did find those pieces of plate which you saw to-night, hidden away somewhere, I don't know where, but there was nothing else with them."

"Perhaps the whole thing was nonsense," said Harold, reflectively.

"No," answered Ida, shaking her head, "I am sure it was not; I am sure the treasure is hidden away somewhere to this day. Listen, Colonel Quaritch—you have not heard quite all the story yet—I found something."

"You—what?"

"Wait a minute and I will show you;" and going to a cabinet in the corner, she unlocked it and took out a despatch box, which she also unlocked.

"Here," she said, "I found this. It is the Bible that Sir James begged might be sent to his son, just before they shot him, you remember," and she handed him a small brown book. He took it and examined it carefully. It was bound in leather, and on the cover was written in large letters, "Sir James de la Molle, Honham Castle, 1611." Nor was this all. The first sheets of the Bible, which was one of the earliest copies of the authorized version, were torn out, and the top corner was also gone, having to all appearance been shot off by a bullet, a presumption that a dark stain of blood upon the cover and edges brought near to certainty.

"Poor fellow," said Harold, "he must have had it in his pocket when he was shot. Where did you find it?"

"Yes, I suppose so," said Ida, "in fact, I have no doubt of it. I found it when I was a child in an old oak chest in the basement of the western tower, quite hidden up in dust and rubbish and bits of old iron. But look at the end and you will see what he wrote in it to his son, Edward. Here, I will show you," and, leaning over him, she turned to the last page of the book. Between the bottom of the page and the conclusion of the final chapter of Revelations there had been a small blank space densely covered with crabbed writing in faded ink, which she read aloud. It ran as follows:

" 'Do not grieve for me, Edward, my son, that I am thus suddenly and wickedly done to death by rebel murderers, for nought happeneth but according to God's will. And now farewell, Edward, till we shall meet in heaven. My moneys have I hid and on account thereof I die unto this world, knowing that not one piece shall Cromwell touch. To whom God shall appoint, shall all my treasure be, for nought can I communicate.'

"There," said Ida, triumphantly, "what do you think of that, Colonel Quaritch? The Bible, I think, was never sent to his son, but here it is, and in that writing, as I solemnly believe," and she laid her white finger upon the faded characters, "lies the key to wherever it is that the money is hidden, only I fear that I shall never make it out. For years I have puzzled over it, thinking that it might be some form of acrostic, but I can make nothing of it. I have tried it all ways. I have translated it into French, and had it translated into Latin, but still I can find out nothing—nothing. But some day somebody will hit upon it—at least, I hope so."

Harold shook his head. . " I am afraid," he said, " that what has remained undiscovered for so long will remain so till the end of the chapter.   Perhaps the old Sir James was hoaxing his adversaries ?"

" No," said Ida, " for if he was, what became of all the money ?   He was known to be one of the richest men of his day, and that he was rich one can see from his letter to the king.   There was nothing found after his death, except his lands, of course.   Oh, it will be found some day, twenty centuries hence probably, much too late to be any good to us," and she sighed deeply, while a pained and wearied expression spread itself over her handsome face.

" Well," said Harold, in a doubtful voice, " there may be something in it.   May I take a copy of that writing ?"

" Certainly," said Ida, laughing, " and if you find the treasure we will go shares.   Stop, I will dictate it to you."

Just as this process was finished and Harold was shutting up his pocketbook, in which he put the fair copy he had executed on a half-sheet of note-paper, the old squire came into the room again.   Looking at his face, his visitor saw that his interview with " George " had evidently been anything but satisfactory, for it bore an expression of exceeding low spirits.

" Well, father, what is the matter ?" asked his daughter.

" Oh, nothing, my dear, nothing," he answered, in melancholy tones.   " George has been here, that is all."

" Yes, and I wish he would keep away," she said, with a little stamp of her foot, " for he has always some bad news or other."

" It is the times, my dear, it is the times ; it isn't George. I really don't know what has come to the country."

" What is it ?" said Ida, with a deepening expression of anxiety.   " Something wrong about the Moat Farm ?"

" Yes ; Janter has thrown it up after all, and I am sure I don't know where I am to find another tenant."

" You see what the pleasures of landed property are, Colonel Quaritch," said Ida, turning towards him with a smile which did not somehow convey a great sense of cheerfulness.

" Yes," he said, " I know.   Thank goodness I have only the ten acres that my dear old aunt left to me.   And now," he added, " I think that I must be saying good-night.   It is half-past ten, and I expect that old Mrs. Jobson is sitting up for me."

Ida looked up in remonstrance, and opened her lips to speak, and then, from some reason that did not appear, changed her mind and held out her hand. "Good-night, Colonel Quaritch," she said; "I am so pleased that we are going to have you as a neighbor. By the way, I have a few people coming to play lawn-tennis here to-morrow afternoon, will you come too?"

"What," broke in the squire, in a voice of irritation, "more lawn-tennis parties, Ida? I think that you might have spared me for once—with all this business on my hands, too."

"Nonsense, father," said his daughter, with some acerbity. "How can a few people playing lawn-tennis hurt you? It is quite useless to shut one's self up and be miserable over things that one cannot help."

The old gentleman collapsed with an air of pious resignation, and meekly asked who was coming.

"Oh, nobody in particular. Mr. and Mrs. Jeffries—Mr. Jeffries is our clergyman, you know, Colonel Quaritch—and Dr. Bass and the two Miss Smiths, one of whom he is supposed to be in love with, and Mr. and Mrs. Quest, and Mr. Edward Cossey, and a few more."

"Mr. Edward Cossey," said the squire, jumping off his chair; "really, Ida, you know that I detest that young man, that I consider him an abominable young man; and I think that you might have shown more consideration for me than to have asked him here."

"I could not help it, father," she answered, coolly. "He was with Mrs. Quest when I asked her, so I had to ask him too. Besides, I rather like Mr. Cossey; he is always so polite, and I don't see why you should take such a violent prejudice against him. Anyhow, he is coming, and there is an end of it."

"Cossey, Cossey," said Harold, throwing himself into the breach, "I used to know that name." It seemed to Ida that he winced a little as he said it. "Is he one of the great banking family?"

"Yes," said Ida, "he is one of the sons. They say he will have half a million of money or more when his father, who is very infirm, dies. He is looking after the branch banks of his house in this part of the world, at least nominally. Really, I fancy that Mr. Quest manages them; certainly he manages the Boisingham branch."

"Well, well," said the squire, "if they are coming, ? pose they are coming. At any rate, I can go out walkin; you are going home, Quaritch, I will walk with you. I a little air."

"Colonel Quaritch, you have not said if you will come to my party to-morrow yet," said Ida, as he stretched out his hand to say good-by.

"Oh, thank you, Miss De la Molle; yes, I think I can com^ though I play tennis atrociously."

"Oh, we all know that. Well, good-night. I am so very pleased that you have come to live at Molehill; it will be s nice for my father to have a companion," she added as a afterthought.

"Yes," said the colonel, grimly, "we are almost of an age; good-night."

Ida watched the door close, and then leaned her arm on the mantelpiece, and reflected that she liked Colonel Quaritch very much, so much that even his not very beautiful physiognomy did not repel her—indeed, rather attracted her than otherwise. "Do you know," she said to herself, "I think that that is the sort of man that I should like to marry. Nonsense," she added, with an impatient shrug—"nonsense, you are nearly six-and-twenty, altogether too old for that sort of thing. And now there is this new trouble about the Moat Farm. My poor old dad! Well, it is a hard world, and I think that sleep is about the best thing in it." And with a sigh she lighted her candle to go to bed, then changed her mind and sat down to await her father's return.

CHAPTER V.

" I DON'T know what is coming to this country ; I really don't, and that's a fact," said the squire to his companion, after they had walked some paces in silence. " Here is this farm, the ,oat Farm. It fetched twenty-five shillings an acre when I was a young man, and eight years ago it used to fetch thirty-five. Now I have reduced it and reduced it to fifteen, just in order to keep the tenant. And what is the end of it? Jan-er—he's the tenant—gave notice last Michaelmas ; but that stupid owl, George, said it was all nothing, and that he would continue at fifteen shillings when the time came. And now to-night he comes to me with a face as long as a yard-arm, and says that Janter won't keep it at any price, and that he does not know where he is to find another tenant, not he. It's quite heartbreaking, that's what it is. Three hundred acres of good, sound, food-producing land, and no tenant for it at fifteen shillings an acre. What am I to do?"

" Can't you take it in hand and farm it yourself?" asked Harold.

" How can I take it in hand? I have one farm of a hundred and fifty acres in hand as it is. Do you know what it would cost to take over that farm," and he stopped in his walk and struck his stick into the ground. " Ten pounds an acre, every farthing of it—and say a thousand for the covenants—about four thousand pounds in all. Now where am I to get four thousand pounds to speculate with in that way, for it is a speculation, and one which I am too old to look after myself, even if I had the knowledge. Well, there you are, and now I'll say good-night, sir. It's getting chilly, and I have felt my chest for the last year or two. By the way, I suppose I shall see you to-morrow at this tennis-party of Ida's. It's all very well for Ida to go in for her tennis-parties, but how can I think of such things with all this worry on my hands. Well, good-night, Colonel Quaritch, good-night," and he turned and walked away through the moonlight.

Harold Quaritch watched him go and then stalked off home, reflecting, not without sadness, upon the drama which was opening up before him, that most common of dramas in these days of depression, the break-up of an ancient family through causes beyond control. It required far less acumen and knowl-edge of the world than he possessed to make it clear to him that the old race of De la Molle was on its last legs. This story of farms thrown up and money not forthcoming pointed its own moral, and a sad one it was. Even Ida's almost child-ish excitement about the legend of the buried treasure showed him how present to her mind must be the necessity of money; and he fell to thinking how pleasant it would be to be able to play the part of the fairy prince and step in with untold wealth between her and the ruin which threatened her family. How well that old squire would become a great station, fitted as he was by nature, descent, and tradition, to play the solid part of an English gentleman of the good-fashioned kind. It was pitiful to think of a man of his stamp, forced by the vile exigencies of a narrow purse to scheme and fight against the advancing tide of destitution. And Ida, too—Ida, who was equipped with every attribute that can make wealth and pow-er what they should be—a frame to show off her worth and state. Well, it was the way of the world, and he could not mend it; but it was with a bitter sense of the unfitness of things that he, with some little difficulty—for he was not yet fully accustomed to its twists and turns—found his way past the swelling heap of Dead Man's Mount and round the house to his own front door.

He entered the house, and having told Mrs. Jobson that she could go to bed, sat down to smoke and think. Harold Quar-itch was, like many solitary men, a great smoker, and never did he feel the need of the consolation of tobacco more than he did this night. A few months ago, when he had retired from the army, he found himself in a great dilemma. There he was, a hale, active man of three-and-forty, of busy habits and regular mind, suddenly thrown upon the world without occupation. What was he to do with himself? While he was asking himself this question and waiting blankly for an answer which did not come, his aunt, old Mrs. Massey, departed this life, leaving him heir to what she possessed—it might be three hundred a year in all. This, added to his pension and the little that he owned independently, put him beyond the necessity of seeking further employment. So he had made up his mind to come to reside at Molehill, and live the quiet, somewhat aimless life of a small country gentleman. His reading, for he was a great reader, especially of scientific works, would, he thought, keep him employed, seeing that in addition to reading he was a thorough sportsman, and an ardent, though owing to the smallness of his means necessarily not a very extensive, collector of curiosities, and more particularly of coins.

At first, after he had come to his decision, a feeling of infinite rest and satisfaction had taken possession of him. The struggle of life was over for him. No longer would he be obliged to think and contrive and toil, henceforth his life would slope gently down towards the inevitable end. Trouble lay in the past, now rest and rest alone awaited him, rest that would gradually grow deeper and deeper as the swift years rolled by him, till it was swallowed up in that almighty peace to which, being a simple and religious man, he had looked forward from childhood as the end and object of his life.

Foolish man and vain imagining! Here, while we draw breath, there is no rest. We must go on continually, on from strength to strength, or weakness to weakness; we must always be troubled about this or that, and must ever have this to desire and that to regret. It is an inevitable law within whose attraction all must fall; yes, even the purest souls, cradled in their hope of heaven; and the most swinish, wallowing in the mud of their gratified desires.

And so our hero had already begun to find out. Here, before he had been forty-eight hours in Honham, a fresh cause of troubling had arisen. He had seen Ida De la Molle again, and after an interval of between five and six years had found her face yet more charming than he had before. In short he had fallen in love with it, and, being a sensible man, he did not conceal this fact from himself. Indeed, the truth was that he had been in love with her for all these years, though he had never looked at the matter in that light. At the least the

pyre had been gathered and laid, and did but require the
touch of the match to burn up merrily enough. And now
this was supplied, and at the first glance of Ida's eyes the
magic flame began to hiss and crackle, and he knew that nothing short of a convulsion or a deluge would put it out.

Men of the stamp of Harold Quaritch generally pass through
three stages with reference to the other sex. They begin in
their youth by making a goddess of one of them, and finding
out their mistake. Then for many years they look upon
woman as the essence and incarnation of evil and a thing no
more to be trusted than a jaguar. Ultimately, however, this
folly wears itself out, probably in proportion as the old affection fades and dies away, and is replaced by contempt and regret that so much should have been wasted on that which was
so little worth. Then it is that the danger comes, for then a
man puts forth his second venture, puts it forth with fear and
trembling, and with no great hope of seeing a golden Argosy
sailing into port. And if it sinks or is driven back by adverse
winds and frowning skies, then there is an end of his legitimate
dealings with such frail merchandise.

And now he, Harold Quaritch, was about to put forth this
second venture, not of his own desire or free will indeed, but
because his reason and judgment were overmastered. In short,
to put it briefly, he had fallen in love with Ida De la Molle
when he first saw her five years ago, and was now in the process of discovering the fact. There he sat in his chair in the
old half-furnished room, which he proposed to turn into his
dining-room, and groaned in spirit over this portentous discovery. What had become of his fair prospect of quiet years
sloping gently downwards, and warm with the sweet drowsy
light of afternoon. How was it that he had not known those
things that belonged to his peace ? And probably it would
end in nothing; was it likely that such a splendid young woman as Ida would care for a superannuated army officer, with
nothing beyond four or five hundred a year and a Victoria
Cross, which he never wore, to recommend him. Probably if
she married at all she would try to marry some one who would
assist to retrieve the fallen fortunes of her family, which it was
absolutely beyond his power to do. Altogether the outlook
did not please him, as he sat there far into the watches of the

night, and sucked at his empty pipe. So little did it please him, indeed, that when at last he rose to find his way to bed up the old oak staircase, the only imposing thing in Molehill, he had almost made up his mind to give up the idea of living at Honham at all, to sell the place and emigrate to Vancouver's Island or New Zealand, and thus place an impassable barrier between himself and that sweet, strong face, which somehow seemed to have acquired a touch of sternness since last he had looked upon it.

Ah, wise resolutions of the quiet night, whither do you go to in the garish light of day? To heaven, perhaps, with the mist-wreaths and the dew-drops.

When the squire got back to the castle, he found his daughter still sitting up in the drawing-room.

"What, not gone to bed, Ida?" he said.

"No, father, I was going, and then I thought that I would wait to hear what all this was about Janter and the Moat Farm. It is best to get it over."

"Yes, yes, my dear—yes, but there is not much to tell you. Janter has thrown up the farm after all, and George says that there is not another tenant to be had for love or money. He tried one man, who said that he would not have it at five shillings an acre, as prices are."

"That is bad enough in all conscience," said Ida, pushing at the fireirons with her foot. "What is to be done?"

"What is to be done?" answered her father, irritably. "How can I tell you what is to be done? I suppose that I must take the place in hand, and that is all."

"Yes, but that costs money, does it not?"

"Of course it does, it costs about four thousand pounds."

"Well," said Ida, looking up, "and where is all that sum to come from. We have not got four thousand pounds in the world."

"Come from? Why, I suppose that I must borrow it on the security of the land."

"Would it not be better to let the place go out of cultivation," she answered, "rather than risk all that sum of money?"

"Go out of cultivation! Nonsense, Ida, how can you talk like that? Why, that strong land would be ruined for a generation to come."

"Perhaps it would, but surely it would be better that it should be ruined than that we should be. Father, dear," she said, appealingly, laying one hand upon his shoulder, "do be frank with me, and tell me what our position really is. I see you wearing yourself out about business from day to day, and I know that there is never any money for anything, scarcely enough to keep the house going; and yet you never tell me what we really owe, and I think I have a right to know."

The squire turned impatiently. "Girls have no head for these things," he said, "so what is the use of talking about it?"

"But I am not a girl; I am a woman of six-and-twenty; and, putting other things aside, I am almost as much interested in your affairs as you are yourself," with determination. "I cannot bear this sort of thing any longer. I see that abominable man, Mr. Quest, continually hovering about here like a bird of ill-omen, and I cannot stand it; and I tell you what it is, father, if you don't tell me the whole truth at once I shall cry," and she looked as if she meant it.

Now the old squire was no more impervious to a woman's tears than any other man, and of all Ida's moods, and they were many, he most greatly feared that rare one which took the form of tears. Besides, he loved his only daughter more dearly than anything in the world except one thing, Honham Castle, and could not bear to give her pain.

"Very well," he said, "of course if you wish to know about these things, you have a right to. I have wished to spare you trouble, that is all; but as you are so very imperious, the best thing that I can do is to let you have your own way. Still, as it is rather late, if you have no objection I think that I had better put it off till to-morrow."

"No, no, father. By to-morrow you will have changed your mind. Let us have it now. I want to know how much we really owe, and what we have got to live on."

The old gentleman hummed and hawed a little, and after various indications of impatience at last began:

"Well, as you know, our family has for some generations depended upon the land. Your dear mother brought a small fortune with her, five or six thousand pounds, but that was, with the sanction of her trustees, expended upon improve-

ments to the farms and to this house. Well, for many years
the land brought in about two thousand a year, but somehow
we always found it difficult to keep within that income. For
instance, I found it necessary to repair the gateway, and you
have no idea of the expense in which those repairs landed me.
Then your poor brother James cost a lot of money, and always
would have the shooting kept up in such an extravagant way.
Then he went into the army, and Heaven only knows what he
cost me there. Your poor brother was very extravagant, my
dear, and well, perhaps I was foolish; I never could say him
no. And that was not all of it, for when the poor boy died
he left fifteen hundred pounds of debt behind him, and I had
to find the money, if it was only for the honor of the family.
Of course you know that we cut the entail when he came of
age. Well, and then these dreadful times have come upon
the top of it all, and, upon my word, at the present moment I
don't know which way to turn," and he paused and drummed
his finger uneasily upon a book.

"Yes, father, but you have not told me yet what it is that
we owe."

"Well, it is difficult to answer that all in a minute—perhaps
twenty-five thousand on mortgage, and a few floating debts."

"And what is the place worth?"

"It used to be worth between fifty and sixty thousand
pounds. It is impossible to say what it would fetch now.
Land is practically a drug in the market. But things will
come round, my dear. It is only a question of holding on."

"Then if you borrow a fresh sum in order to take up this
farm, you will owe about thirty thousand pounds, and if you
have to pay five per cent., as I suppose you do, you will have
to pay fifteen hundred a year in interest. Now, father, you
said that in the good times the land brought in two thousand
a year, so, of course, it can't bring in so much now. Therefore,
by the time that you have paid the interest, there will be
nothing, or less than nothing, left for us to live on."

Her father winced at this cruel and convincing logic.

"No, no," he said, "it is not so bad as that. You jump
to conclusions; but really, if you do not mind, I am very tired,
and should like to go to bed."

"Father, what is the good of trying to shirk the thing just

because it is disagreeable?" she asked, earnestly. "Do you suppose that it is more pleasant to me to talk about it than it is for you? I know that you are not to blame about it. I know that poor dear James was very thoughtless and extravagant, and that the times are crushing. But to go on like this is only to go to ruin. It would be better for us to go to live in a cottage on a couple of hundred a year than to try to keep our heads above water here, which we cannot do. Sooner or later these people, Quest, or whoever they are, will want their money back, and then, if they cannot have it, they will sell the place over our heads. I believe that man Quest wants to get it himself—that is what I believe—and set up as a country gentleman. Father, I know it is a dreadful thing to say, but we ought to leave Honham."

"Leave Honham," said the old gentleman, jumping up in his agitation, "what nonsense you talk, Ida! How can I leave Honham? It would kill me at my age. How can I do it? And, besides, who is to look after the farms and all the business? No, no, we must hang on and trust to Providence. Things may come round, something may happen, one can never tell in this world."

"If we do not leave Honham, then Honham will leave us," answered his daughter, with conviction. "I do not believe in chances. Chances always go the wrong way against those who are looking for them. We shall be absolutely ruined, that is all."

"Well, perhaps you are right, perhaps you are right, my dear," said the old gentleman, wearily. "I only hope that my time may come first. I have lived here all my life, and I know that I could not live anywhere else. But God's will be done. And now, my dear, go to bed."

She leaned down and kissed him, and as she did so saw that his eyes were filled with tears. Not trusting herself to speak, for she felt for him too deeply to do so, she turned away and went, leaving the old man sitting there with his gray head bowed upon his breast.

CHAPTER VI.

LAWYER QUEST.

THE day following the conversation described in the last chapter was one of those glorious autumn mornings which sometimes come as a faint compensation for the utter vileness and bitter disappointment of the season which in this country we dignify by the name of summer. Notwithstanding his vigils and melancholy of the night before, the squire was up early, and Ida, who between one thing and another had not had the best of nights, heard his loud cheery voice shouting about the place for "George."

Looking out of her bedroom window, she soon perceived that functionary himself, a long, lean, powerful-looking man, with a melancholy face and a twinkle in his little gray eyes, hanging about the front steps. Presently her father emerged in a brilliant but ancient dressing-gown, his white locks waving on the breeze.

"Here, George! Where are you, George?"

"Here I be, sir."

"Ah, yes; then why don't you say so? Here I have been shouting myself hoarse for you."

"Yes, squire," replied the imperturbable George, "I have been standing here for the last ten minutes, and I heard you."

"You heard me? then why the dickens didn't you answer?"

"Because I didn't think that you wanted me, sir. I saw that you hadn't finished your letter."

"Well, then, you ought to. You know very well that my chest is weak, and yet I have to go halloaing all over the place after you. Now look here, have you got that fat pony of yours here?"

"Yes, squire, the pony is here, and if it is fat it isn't for the want of movement."

"Very well, then, take this letter," and he handed him an

epistle sealed with a tremendous seal—"take this letter to Mr. Quest at Boisingham, and wait for an answer. And look here, see you are about the place at eleven o'clock, for I expect Mr. Quest to see me about the Moat Farm."

"Yes, sir."

"I suppose that you have heard nothing more from Janter, have you?"

"No, squire, nothing. He means to get the place at his own price or chuck it."

"And what is his price?"

"Five shillings an acre. You see, sir, it's this way. That army gent, Major Boston, as is agent for all the College lands down the valley, he be a poor weak fool, and when all these tenants come to him and say that they must either have the land at five shillings an acre or go, he gets scared, he dew, and down goes the rent of some of the best meadow land in the country from thirty-five shillings to five. Of course it don't signify to him not a halfpenny, the College must pay him his salary all the same, and he don't know no more about farming, nor land, nor northing, than my old mare minder. Well, and what comes of it. Of course every tenant on the place hears that those College lands are going for five shillings an acre, and they prick up their ears and say they must have their land at the same figger; and it's allowing to that Boston varmint, who ought to be kicked through every hole on the place and then drowned to dead in a dyke."

"Yes, you're right there, George; that silly man is a public enemy, and ought to be treated as such; but the times are very bad, with corn down to twenty-nine—very bad."

"I'm not saying that they ain't bad, squire," said his retainer, his long face lighting up; "they are bad, cruel bad, bad for everybody. And I'm not denying that they are bad for the tenants, but if they are bad for the tenants they are wus for the landlord. It all comes on his shoulders in the long run. If men find that they can get land at five shillings an acre that's worth twenty, why it isn't in human nature to pay twenty; and if they find that the landlord must go as they drive him, of course they'll lay on the whip. Why, bless you, sir, when a tenant comes and says that he is very sorry, but he finds he can't pay his rent, in nine cases out of ten, if you could just look at that man's bank-book, you'd find that the bank was paid, the tradesmen were paid, the doctor's paid, everybody's paid before he thinks about his rent. Let the landlord suffer, because he can't help himself; but Lord bless us, if a hundred pounds was overdue to the bank it would have the innards out him in no time, and he knows it. Now as for that varmint, Janter, to tell me that he can't pay fifteen shillings an acre for the Moat Farm is nonsense. I only wish I had the capital to take it at the price."

"Well, George," said the squire, "I think that if it can be managed I shall borrow the money and take the farm on hand. I am not going to let Janter have it at five shillings an acre."

"Ah, sir, that's the best way. Bad as times are, it will go hard if I can't make the interest and the rent out of it too. Besides, squire, if you give way about this farm, all the others will come down on you. I'm not saying a word agin your tenants, but where there's money to be made you can't trust no man."

"Well, well," said the squire, "perhaps you are right and perhaps you ain't. Right or wrong, you always talk like Solomon in all his glory. Anyway, be off with that note, and let me have the answer as you get back. Mind you don't go loafing and jawing about down in Boisingham, because I want my answer."

"So he means to borrow the money if he can get it," said Ida to herself as she sat, an invisible auditor, doing her hair by the open window. "George can do more with him in five minutes than I can in a week, and I know that he hates Janter. I believe Janter threw up the farm because of his quarrelling with George. Well, I suppose that we must take our chance."

Meanwhile George had mounted his cart and departed upon the road to Boisingham, urging his fat pony along as though he meant to be there in twenty minutes. But so soon as he was well out of reach of the squire's shouts, and sight of the Castle gates, he deliberately turned up a by-lane and jogged along for a mile or more to a farm, where he had a long fabulation with a man about thatching some ricks. Thence he quietly made his way to his own little place, where he proceeded to comfortably get his breakfast, remarking to his wife that he was of opinion that there was no hurry about the squire's letter, as "laryers" wasn't in the habit of coming to office at eight in the morning.

Breakfast over, the philosophic George quietly got into his cart, the fat pony having been tied up outside, and leisurely drove into the picturesque old town which lay at the head of the valley. All along the main street he met many acquaintances, and with each he found it necessary to stop and have a talk, indeed with two he had a modest half-pint. At length, however, his labor o'er, he arrived at Mr. Quest's office, which, as all the Boisingham world knows, is just opposite the church, of which Mr. Quest is one of the churchwardens, and which was but two years ago beautifully restored, mainly owing to his efforts and generous contributions. Driving up to the small and quiet-looking doorway of a very unpretentious building, George descended and knocked, whereon a clerk opened the door, and in answer to his inquiries informed him that he believed Mr. Quest had just come over to the office.

In another minute he was shown into an inner room, of the ordinary country-office stamp, and there at the table sat Mr. Quest himself.

Mr. Quest was a man of about forty years of age, rather under than over, with a pale ascetic cast of face, and a quiet and pleasant, though somewhat reserved, manner. His features were in no way remarkable, with the exception of his eyes, which seemed to have been set in his head owing to some curious error of nature. For whereas his general tone was dark, his hair in particular being jet black, these eyes were gray, and jarred extraordinarily upon their companion features. For the rest, he was a man of some presence and with the manners of a gentleman.

"Well, George," he said, "what is it that brings you to Boisingham? A letter from the squire. Thank you. Take a seat, will you, while I look through it. Umph, wants me to come and see him at eleven o'clock. I am very sorry, but I can't manage that any way. Ah, I see, about the Moat Farm. Janter told me that he was going to throw it up, and I advised him to do nothing of the sort, but he is a dissatisfied sort of a fellow, Janter is, and Major Boston has upset the whole country-side by his very ill-advised action about the College lands."

" Janter is a warmint, and Major Boston, begging his pardon,

for the language, is an ass, sir. Anyway, there it is, Janter
has thrown up, and where I am to find a tenant between now
and Michaelmas I don't know ; in fact, with the College lands
going at five shillings an acre there ain't no chance.

"Then what does the squire propose to do—take the land
in hand ?"

"Yes, sir, that's it; and that's what he wants to see you
about."

"More money, I suppose," said Mr. Quest.

"Well, yes, sir. You see there will be the covenants to
meet, and then the farm is three hundred acres, and to stock
it proper means nine pounds an acre quite, on this here heavy
land."

"Yes, yes, I know, a matter of four thousand more or less;
but where is it to come from, that's the question ? Cossey's
do not like land now, any more than other banks do. However, I'll see my principal about it. But, George, I can't possibly get up to the Castle at eleven. I have got a churchwarden's meeting at a quarter to, about that west pinnacle, you
know. It is in a most dangerous condition, and, by the way,
before you go I should like to have your opinion, as a practical
man, as to the best way to deal with it. To rebuild it would
cost a hundred and twenty pounds, and that is more than we
see our way to at present, though I can promise fifty, if they
can scrape up the rest. But about the squire. I think that
the best thing I can do will be to come up to the Castle to
lunch, and then I can talk over matters with him. Stay, I will
just write him a note. By the way, you would like a glass of
wine, wouldn't you, George ? Nonsense, man, here it is in the
cupboard ; a glass of wine is a good friend to have handy
sometimes."

George, who, like most men of his stamp, could put away
his share of liquor and feel thankful for it, drank his glass of
wine while Mr. Quest was engaged in writing his note, wondering meanwhile what made the lawyer so civil to him. For
George did not like Mr. Quest. Indeed, it would not be too
much to say that he hated him. But this was a feeling that
he never allowed to appear ; he was too much afraid of the
man for that, and in his own way too much devoted to the old
squire's interests to run the risk of imperilling them by the

exhibition of any aversion to Mr. Quest. He knew more of
his master's affairs than anybody living, unless it was, perhaps, Mr. Quest himself, and was aware that the lawyer held
the old gentleman in a bondage that could not be broken.
Now, George was a man with many faults. He was somewhat sly, and, perhaps, within certain lines, at times capable
of giving the word honesty a liberal interpretation. But he
had one conspicuous virtue ; he loved the old squire as a
Highlander loves his chief, and would almost, if not quite,
have died to serve him. Indeed, as it was, his billet was no
easy one, for Mr. De la Molle's temper was none of the best
at times, and when things went wrong, as they pretty frequently did, he was exceedingly apt to visit his wrath on the head
of the devoted George, saying things to him which he should
not have said. But his retainer took it all in the day's work,
and never bore malice, continuing in his own pigheaded sort
of way to labor early and late to prop up his master's broken
fortunes. Indeed, had it not been for George's contrivings
and procrastinations, Honham Castle and its owner would have
parted company long before.

CHAPTER VII.

EDWARD COSSEY, ESQUIRE.

AFTER George had drunk his glass of wine and given his opinion as to the best way to deal with the dangerous pinnacle on the Boisingham church, he took the note, untied the fat pony, and ambled off back to Honham, leaving the lawyer alone. As soon as he was gone Mr. Quest threw himself back in his chair—an old oak one, by the way, for he had a very pretty taste in antiquities and a positive mania for collecting them—and plunged into a brown study.

Presently he leaned forward, unlocked the top drawer of his writing-table, and extracted from it a letter addressed to himself, which he had received that very morning. It was from the principals of the great banking firm of Cossey & Sons, and dated from their head office in Mincing-lane. It ran as follows:

"(Private and confidential.)

"DEAR SIR,—We have considered your report as to the extensive mortgages which we hold upon the Honham Castle estates, and have given due weight to your arguments as to the advisability of allowing Mr. De la Molle time to give things a chance of righting. But we must tell you that we can see no prospect of any such solution of the matter, at any rate for some years to come. All the information that we are able to gather points to a further decrease in the value of land rather than to a recovery. The interest on the mortgages in question is moreover a year in arrear, probably owing to the non-receipt of rents by Mr. De la Molle. Under these circumstances, much as it grieves us to take action against Mr. De la Molle, with whose family we have had dealings for five generations, we can see no alternative to foreclosure, and hereby instruct you to take the necessary preliminary steps to bring it about in the usual manner. We are, presuming that Mr. De la Molle is not in a position to pay off the mortgages, quite aware of the risks of a forced sale, and shall not be astonished if, in the present unprecedented condition of the land market, such a sale should result in a loss, although the sum recoverable does not amount to half the valuation of the estates, which was undertaken at our instance about twelve years ago on the occasion of the first advance. The only alternative, however, would be for us to enter into possession of the property or to buy it in. But this would be a course totally inconsistent with the usual practice of the bank; and, what is more, our confidence in the stability of landed property is so utterly shattered by our recent experiences that we cannot burden ourselves by such a course, preferring to run the risk of an immediate loss, which, however, we hope that the historical character of the property and its great natural advantages as a residential estate will avert, or, at the least, minimize.

"Be so good as to advise us by an early post of the steps you take in pursuance of these instructions. We are, dear sir, your obedient servants,

"COSSEY & SON.

"W. Quest, Esq.

"P. S. We have thought it better to address you direct in this matter, but of course you will communicate the contents of this letter to Mr. Edward Cossey, and, subject to our instructions, which are final, act in consultation with him."

"Well," said Mr. Quest to himself, as he folded up the sheet of paper, "that is about as straight as it can be put. And this is the time that the old gentleman chooses to ask for another four thousand. He may ask, but the answer will be more than he bargains for."

He rose from the chair and began to walk up and down the room in evident perplexity. "If only," he said, "I had twenty-five thousand, I would take up the mortgages myself and foreclose at my leisure. It would be a good investment at that figure, even as things are, and, besides, I should like to have that place. Twenty-five thousand, only twenty thousand, and now when I want it I have not got it. And I should have had it if it had not been for that tiger, that devil Edith. She has had more than that out of me in the last ten years, and still she is threatening and crying for more, more, more. Tiger; yes, that is the name for her, her own name, too. She would coin one's vitals into money if she could. All Belle's fortune she has had, or nearly all, and most of my savings, and now she wants another five hundred, and she will have it, too.

"Here we are," and he drew a letter from his pocket written in a bold but somewhat uneducated woman's hand. It ran:

"DEAR BILL,—I've been unlucky again and dropped a pot. Shall want £500 by the first of October. No shuffling, mind; money down; but I think that you know me too well to play any more larks. When can you

tear yourself from the lovely Mrs. Q., and come and give your E—— a look? Bring some tin when you come, and we will have times.
"Thine, THE TIGER."

"The Tiger, yes, the Tiger," he gasped, his face working with passion and his gray eyes glinting as he tore the epistle to fragments, and threw them down and stamped on them. "Well, be careful that I don't one day cut your claws and paint your stripes. By Heaven, if ever a man felt like murder, I do now. Five hundred more, and I haven't five thousand clear in the world. Truly, we pay for the follies of our youth! It makes me mad to think of those fools Cossey & Son forcing that place into the market just now. There's a fortune in it at the price. In another year or two I might have recovered myself, that devil of a woman might be dead—and I have several irons in the fire, some of which would be sure to turn up trumps. Surely there must be a way out of it somehow. There's a way out of everything if only one thinks enough, but the thing is to find it," and he stopped in his walk opposite to the window that looked upon the street, and put his hand to his head.

As he did so he caught sight of the figure of a tall gentleman strolling idly towards the office door. For a moment he stared at him blankly, as a man does when he is trying to catch the vague clew to a new idea. Then, as the figure passed out of his view, he brought his fist down heavily upon the sill.

"Edward Cossey, by George!" he said, aloud. "There's the way out of it, if only I can work him, and unless I have made a strange mistake I think I know the way."

A couple of minutes afterwards a tall, shapely young man, of about twenty four or five years of age, came strolling into the office where Mr. Quest was sitting, to all appearance hard at work at his correspondence. He was dark in complexion, and decidedly distinguished looking in feature, with large dark eyes, dark mustache, and a pale, somewhat Spanish-looking skin. Young as the face was, it had, if observed closely, a somewhat worn and worried air, such as one would scarcely expect to see upon the countenance of a gentleman born to such brilliant fortunes, and so well fitted by nature to do them justice, as was Mr. Edward Cossey. For it is not every young

man with dark eyes and a good figure who is destined to be the
future head of one of the most wealthy private banks in England, and to inherit in due course a sum of money in hard
cash variously estimated at from half a million to a million
sterling. Such, however, was the prospect in life that opened
out before Mr. Edward Cossey, who was now supposed by his
old and eminently business-like father to be in process of ac-
quiring a sound knowledge of the provincial affairs of their
house by attending to the working of their country branches
in the eastern counties.

"How do you do, Quest?" said Edward Cossey, nodding
somewhat coldly to the lawyer and sitting down. "Any
business?"

"Well, yes, Mr. Cossey," answered the lawyer, rising re-
spectfully, "there is some business, some very serious business."

"Indeed," said Edward, indifferently, "what is it?"

"Well, it is this, the house has ordered a foreclosure on the
Honham Castle estates—at least it comes to that—"

At the sound of this intelligence Edward Cossey's whole
demeanor underwent the most startling transformation—his
languor vanished, his eye brightened, and his form became instinct with active life and beauty.

"What the deuce!" he said, and then paused. "I won't
have it," he went on, jumping up, "I won't have it. I am
not particularly fond of old De la Molle, perhaps because he
is not particularly fond of me," he added, rather drolly, "but
it would be an infernal shame to break up that family and
sell the house under them. Why, they would be ruined. And
then there's Ida—Miss De la Molle, I mean—what would become of her? And the old place, too. After being in the
family for all these centuries, I suppose it would be sold to
some confounded counter-skipper or some retired thief of a
lawyer. It must be prevented at any price—do you hear,
Quest?"

The lawyer winced a little at his chief's contemptuous allusion, and then remarked, with a smile, "I had no idea that you
were so sentimental, Mr. Cossey, or that you took such a lively
interest in Miss De la Molle," and he glanced up to observe
the effect of his shot.

Edward Cossey colored. "I did not mean that I took any particular interest in Miss De la Molle," he said; "I was referring to the family."

"Oh, quite so, though I am sure I don't know why you shouldn't. Miss De la Molle is one of the most charming women that I ever met, I think the most charming, if I except my own wife, Belle," and he again looked up suddenly at Edward Cossey, who, for his part, colored for the second time. "It seems to me," went on the lawyer, "that a man in your position has a most splendid opportunity of playing knight-errant to the lovely damsel in distress. Here is the lady with her aged father about to be sold up and turned out of the estates which have belonged to her family for generations; why don't you do the generous and graceful thing, like the hero in a novel, and take up the mortgages?"

Edward Cossey did not reject this suggestion with the contempt that might have been expected, on the contrary he appeared to be turning the matter over in his mind, for he drummed a little tune with his knuckles and stared out of the window.

"What is the sum?" he said, presently.

"Five-and-twenty thousand, and he wants four more, say thirty thousand."

"And where am I going to find thirty thousand pounds to take up a bundle of mortgages which will probably never pay a farthing of interest? Why, I have not got three thousand I can come at. Besides," he added, recollecting himself, "why should I interfere in it?"

"I do not think," answered Mr. Quest, ignoring the latter part of the question, "that with your prospects you would find it difficult to get thirty thousand pounds or twice thirty thousand pounds. I know several who would consider it an honor to lend the money to a Cossey, if only for the sake of the introduction—that is, of course, provided the security was of a legal nature."

"Let me see the letter," said Edward.

Mr. Quest handed him the document conveying the commands of Cossey & Son, and he read it through twice.

"The old man means business," he said, as he returned it; "that letter was written by him, and when he has once made up his mind it is useless to try and stir him. Did you say that you were going to see the squire to-day ?"

" No, I did not say so, but, as a matter of fact, I am. His man, George—a shrewd fellow, by the way, for one of these bumpkins—came with a letter asking me to go up to the Castle, so I shall get round there to lunch. It is about this fresh loan that the old gentleman wishes to negotiate. Of course I shall be obliged to tell him that, instead of giving a fresh loan, we shall have to serve a notice on him."

" Don't do that just yet," said Edward, with decision. " Write to the house and say that their instructions shall be attended to. There is no hurry about the notice, though I don't see how I am to help in the matter. Indeed, there is no call upon me."

" Very well, Mr. Cossey. And now, by the way, are you going to the castle, this afternoon ?"

" Yes, I believe so, why ?"

" Well, I want to get up there to luncheon, and I am in a fix. Belle will want the trap to go there this afternoon. Can you lend me your dog-cart to drive up, and then perhaps you would not mind if she gave you a lift this afternoon."

" Very well," answered Edward, " that is if it suits Mrs. Quest. Perhaps she may object to carting me about the country."

" I have not observed any such reluctance on her part," said the lawyer, dryly, " but we can easily settle the question. I must go home to get some plans before I attend the vestry meeting about that pinnacle. Will you step across with me and we can ask her ?"

" Oh, yes," he answered. " I have nothing particular to do."

And, accordingly, as soon as Mr. Quest had made some small arrangements, and given particular directions to his clerks as to his whereabouts for the day, they set off together for the lawyer's private house.

CHAPTER VIII.

MR. QUEST'S WIFE.

MR. QUEST lived in one of those ugly but comfortably-built old red brick houses which abound in almost every country town, and which give us the clearest possible idea of the want of taste and love of material comfort that characterized the gross age in which they were built. This house looked out on to the market-place, and had a charming old walled garden at the back, famous for its nectarines, which, together with the lawn-tennis court, was, as Mrs. Quest would say, almost enough to console her for living in a town. The front door, however, was only separated by a little flight of steps from the pavement upon which the house abutted.

Entering into a large, cool-looking hall, Mr. Quest paused, and asked a servant who was passing where her mistress was.

"In the drawing-room, sir," said the girl; and, followed by Edward Cossey, he made his way down a long panelled passage till he reached a door on the left, which he opened quickly and passed through into a charming, modern-looking room, handsomely and even luxuriantly furnished, and lighted by French windows opening on to the walled garden.

A little lady dressed in some black material was standing at one of these windows, her arms crossed behind her back, and absently gazing out of it. At the sound of the opening door she turned swiftly, her whole delicate and lovely face lighting up like a flower in a ray of sunshine, the lips slightly parted, and a deep and happy light shining in her violet eyes. Then, all in an instant, it was instructive to observe *how*, instantaneously, her glance fell upon her husband (for the lady was Mrs. Quest), and her entire expression changed to one of cold aversion, the light fading out of her face as it does from a November sky, and leaving it cold and hard.

Mr. Quest, who was a man who saw everything, saw this also, and smiled bitterly.

"Don't be alarmed, Belle," he said, in a low voice; "I have brought Mr. Cossey with me."

She flushed up to the eyes, a great wave of color, and her breast heaved; but before she could answer, Edward Cossey, who had stopped behind to wipe some mud off his shoes, entered the room, and politely offered his hand to Mrs. Quest, who took it coldly enough.

"You are an early visitor, Mr. Cossey," she said.

"Yes," said her husband, "but the fault is mine. I have brought Mr. Cossey over to ask you if you can give him a lift up to the Castle this afternoon. I have to go up there to lunch, and have borrowed his dog-cart."

"Oh, yes, with pleasure, but why can't the dog-cart come back for Mr. Cossey."

"Well, you see," put in Edward, "there is a little difficulty; my groom is sick, but there is really no reason why you should be bothered. I have no doubt that a man can be found to bring it back."

"Oh, no," she said, with a shrug, "it will be all right; only you had better lunch here, that's all, because I want to start early, and go to an old woman's at the other end of Honham about some fuchsia cuttings."

"I shall be very happy," said he.

"Very well, then, that is settled," said Mr. Quest, "and now I must get my plans and be off to that vestry meeting. I'm late as it is. With your permission, Mr. Cossey, I will order the dog-cart as I pass your rooms."

"Certainly," said Edward, and in another moment the lawyer was gone.

Mrs. Quest watched the door close, and then sat down in a low arm-chair, and, resting her head upon the back, looked up with a steady, inquiring gaze, full into Edward Cossey's face.

And he, too, looked at her and thought what a beautiful woman she was, in her own way. She was very small, rounded in her figure almost to stoutness, and possessed the tiniest and most beautiful hands and feet. But her greatest charm lay in the face, which was almost infantile in its shape, and delicate as a moss-rose. She was exquisitely fair in coloring;

indeed, the darkest things about her were her violet eyes, which in some lights looked almost black in contrast with her white forehead and waving auburn hair.

Presently she spoke.

" Has my husband gone ?" she said.

" I suppose so. Why do you ask ?"

" Because from what I know of his habits I should think it very likely that he is listening behind the door," and she laughed faintly.

" You seem to have a good opinion of him."

" I have exactly the opinion of him that he deserves," she said, bitterly ; " and my opinion of him is, that he is one of the wickedest men in England."

" If he is behind the door he will enjoy that," said Edward Cossey. " Well, if he is all this, why did you marry him ?"

" Why did I marry him ?" she answered, with passion ; " because I was forced into it, bullied into it, starved into it. What would you do if you were a defenceless, motherless girl of eighteen, with a drunken father who beat you—yes, beat you with a stick—apologized in the most gentlemanlike way next morning, and then went and got drunk again ? And what would you do if that father were in the hands of a man like my husband, body and soul in his hands, and if between them pressure was brought to bear, and brought to bear until at last—there, what is the good of going on with it—you can guess the rest."

" Well, and what did he marry you for ; your pretty face ?"

" I don't know ; he said so ; it may have had something to do with it. I think it was my ten thousand pounds ; for once I had a whole ten thousand pounds of my own ; my poor mother left it me, and tied it up so that my father could not touch it. Well, of course, when I married, my husband would not have any settlements, and so he took it, every farthing."

" And what did he do with it ?"

" Spent it upon some other woman in London—most of it. I found it out ; he gave her thousands of pounds at once."

" Well, I should not have thought that of him," said he, with a laugh.

She paused a moment and covered her face with her hand, and then went on : " If you only knew, Edward, if you had the faintest idea what my life was till a year and a half ago, when I first saw you, you would pity me and understand why I am bad and passionate and jealous, and everything that I ought not to be. I never had any happiness as a girl—how could I in such a home as ours—and then almost before I was a woman I was handed over to that man. Oh, how I hated him, and what I endured !"

" Yes, it can't have been very pleasant."

" Pleasant—but there, we have done with each other now—we don't even speak much except in public, that's my price for holding my tongue about the lady in London, and one or two other little things—so what is the use of talking of it ? It was a horrible nightmare, but it has gone. And then," she went on, fixing her beautiful eyes upon his face, " then I saw you, Edward, and, for the first time in my life, I learned what love was, and I think that no woman ever loved like that before. Other women have had something to care for in their lives, I never had anything till I saw you. It may be wicked, but it's true."

He turned slightly away, and said nothing.

" And yet, dear," she went on, in a low voice, " I think it has been one of the hardest things of all—my love for you. For, Edward," and she rose and took his hand and looked into his face with her soft eyes full of tears, " I should have liked to be a blessing to you and not a curse, and—and—a cause of sin. Oh, Edward, I should have made you such a good wife, no man could have had a better ; and I would have helped you too, for I am not such a fool as I seem ; and now I shall do nothing but bring trouble upon you, I know I shall. And it was my fault, too, at least most of it ; don't ever think that I deceive myself, for I don't ; I led you on, I know I did, I meant to—there ! Think me as shameless as you like, I meant to from the first. And no good can come of it, I know that, although I would not have it undone. No good can ever come of what is wrong. I may be very wicked, but I know that—" and she began to cry outright.

This was too much for Edward Cossey, who, as any man must, had been much touched by this unexpected outburst. " Look here, Belle," he blurted out on the impulse of the moment, " I am sick and tired of all this sort of thing. For more than a year my life has been nothing but a living lie, and I can't stand it, and that's a fact. I tell you what it is: I think we had better just take the train to Paris and go off at once, or else give it all up. It is impossible to go on living in this continual atmosphere of falsehood."

She stopped crying. " Do you really care for me enough for that, Edward ?" she said.

" Yes, yes," he said, somewhat impatiently ; " you can see I do, or I should not make the offer. Say the word, and I'll do it."

She thought for a moment, and then looked up again. " No," she said, " no, Edward."

" Why," he asked, " are you afraid ?"

" Afraid !" she answered, with a gesture of contempt; " what have I to be afraid of ? Do you suppose that such a woman as I am has any care for consequences ? We have got beyond that—that is, for ourselves. But we can still feel a little for others. It would ruin you to do such a thing, socially and in every other way. You know that you have often said that your father would cut you out of his will if you compromised yourself and him like that."

" Oh, yes, he would do that. I am sure of it. He would never forgive the scandal ; he has a hatred of that sort of thing. But I could get a few thousands ready money, and change our names and go off to some colony, or something."

" It is very good of you to say so," she said, humbly. " I don't deserve it, and I will not take advantage of you. You will be sorry that you made the offer by to-morrow. Ah, yes, I know it is only because I cried. No, we must go on as we are until the end comes, and then you can discard me ; for all the blame will follow me, and I shall deserve it, too, for I am older than you, you know, and a woman ; and my husband will make some money out of you, and then it will all be forgotten, and I shall have had my day and go my own way to oblivion, like thousands of other unfortunate women before me, and it will all be the same a hundred years hence, don't you see ? But, Edward, remember one thing, don't play me any tricks, for I am not of the sort to bear it. Have patience and wait for the end, for these things never last very long, and I shall never be a burden on you. Don't desert me or make me jealous, for I cannot bear it—I cannot, indeed—and I do not know what I might do—make a scandal, or kill myself or you—I'm sure I can't say what. You nearly set me wild the other day when you were carrying on with Miss de la Molle—ah, yes, I saw it all—I have suspected you for a long time, and sometimes I think that you are really in love with her. And now, sir, I tell you what it is, we have had enough of this melancholy talk to last me for a month. What did you come here for at all this morning, just when I wanted to get you out of my head for an hour or two and think about my garden? I suppose it was all a trick of Mr. Quest's, bringing you here. He has got some fresh scheme on, I am sure of it from his face. Well, it can't be helped, and since you are here, Mr. Edward Cossey, tell me how you like my new dress," and she posed herself and courtesied before him. " Black, you see, to match my sins and show off my complexion. Doesn't it fit well?"

" Charmingly," he said, laughing, in spite of himself, for he felt in no laughing mood ; "and now I tell you what it is, Belle, I am not going to stop here all the morning, and lunch, and all that sort of thing. It does not look well to say the least of it. The probability is that half the old women in Boisingham have got their eyes fixed on the hall-door to see how long I stay. I shall go down to the office and come back at half-past two."

" A very nice excuse to get rid of me," she said, " but I dare say you are right, and I want to see about the garden. There, good-by, and mind you are not late, for I want to have a nice drive round to the Castle. Not that there is much need to warn you to be in time when you are going to see Miss de la Molle, is there? Good-by, good-by."

CHAPTER IX.

THE SHADOW OF RUIN.

Mr. Quest departed to his vestry meeting with a smile upon his thin, gentlemanly-looking face, and with rage and bitterness in his heart.

"I caught her that time," he said to himself; "she can do a good deal in the way of deceit, but she can't keep the blood out of her cheeks when she hears that fellow's name. How she did color up to be sure! But she is a clever woman, Belle is—how well she managed that little business about the luncheon, and how well she fought her case when once she got me in a cleft stick about Edith and that money of hers, and made good terms too. Ah! that's the worst of it, she has the whip hand of me there; if I could ruin her she could ruin me, and it's no use cutting off one's nose to spite your face. But, ah, my fine lady," he went on, with an ominous flash of his gray eyes, "I shall have you yet. Give you enough rope and you will hang yourself. You love this fellow, I know that, and it will go hard if I can't make him break your heart for you. Bah! you don't know the sort of stuff men are made of. If only I did not happen to be in love with you myself I should not care. If— Ah! here I am at the church."

The human animal is a very complicated machine, and can conduct the working of an extraordinary number of different interests and sets of ideas, almost, if not entirely, simultaneously. For instance, Mr. Quest—seated at the right hand of the rector in the vestry-room of the beautiful old Boisingham church, and engaged in an animated and even warm discussion with the senior curate on the details of fourteenth-century church work, in which he clearly took a lively interest and understood far better than did the curate—would have been exceedingly difficult to identify with the scheming, vindictive creature whom we have just followed up the church path. But, after all, that is the way of human nature, although it may not be the way of those who try to draw it, and who love to paint the villain black as your hat, and the virtuous heroine so radiant that you begin to fancy you hear the whispering of her wings. Few people are altogether good or altogether bad; indeed, it is probable that the vast majority are neither good nor bad—they have not the strength to be either the one or the other. Here and there, however, one does meet with a spirit with sufficient will and originality to press the scale down this way or that, though even then the opposing force, be it good or evil, is constantly striving to bring the balance equal. Even the most wicked men have their redeeming points and their righteous instincts, nor are their thoughts continually fixed upon iniquity. Mr. Quest, for instance, one of the evil geniuses of this history, was, where his plots and passions were not immediately concerned, a man of eminently generous and refined tendencies. Many were the good turns, contradictory as it may seem, that he had done to his poorer neighbors; he had even been known to forego his bills of costs, which is about the highest and rarest exhibition of earthly virtue that can be expected from a lawyer. He was, moreover, eminently a cultured man, a reader of the classics in translations, if not in the originals, a man with a fine taste in fiction and poetry, and a really sound and ripe archæological knowledge, especially where sacred buildings were concerned. All his instincts, moreover, were towards respectability. His most burning ambition was to secure a high position in the county in which he lived, and to be classed among the resident gentry. He hated his lawyer's work, and longed to accumulate sufficient means to be able to give it the good-by and to indulge himself in an existence of luxurious and learned leisure. Such as he was he had made himself, for he was the son of a poor and inferior country dentist, and had begun life with a good education, it is true, which he chiefly owed, however, to his own exertions, but with nothing else. Had his nature been a temperate nature, with a balance of good to its credit to draw upon, instead of a balance of evil, he was a man who might have gone very far indeed, for in addition to his natural ability he had a great power of work. But unfortunately this was not the case, his instincts on the whole were evil instincts, and his passions—whether of hate or love or desire or creed—when they seized him did so with extraordinary violence, rendering him for the time being utterly callous to the rights or feelings of others, provided that he attained his end. In short, had he been born to a good position and large fortune, it is quite possible, providing always that his strong passions had not at some period of his life led him irremediably astray, that he would have lived virtuous and respected, and died in good odor, leaving behind him a happy memory. But fate had placed him in antagonism with the world, and yet had endowed him with a gnawing desire to be of the world, as it appeared most desirable to him; and then, to complete his ruin, fate had thrown him into temptations from which inexperience and the headlong strength of his passions gave him no opportunity to escape. It may at first appear strange that a man so calculating and whose desires seemed to be fixed upon such a material end as the acquirement of wealth which he coveted, by artifice or even fraud, should also nourish in his heart so bitter a hatred and so keen a thirst for revenge upon a woman who had been unfaithful to him as Mr. Quest undoubtedly did towards his beautiful wife. It would have seemed more probable that he would have left heroics alone and attempted to turn his wife's passion into a means of wealth and self-advancement; and this would no doubt have been so had his wife's estimate of his motives in marrying her been an entirely correct one. She had told her lover, it will be remembered, that her husband had married her for her money—the ten thousand pounds of which he stood so badly in need. Now, this was the truth to a certain extent, and a certain extent only. He had wanted the ten thousand pounds, in fact at the moment money was necessary to him. But, and this his wife had never known or realized, he had been, and still was, also in love with her. Possibly the ten thousand pounds would have proved a sufficient inducement to him without the passion, but the passion was none the less there. Their relations, however, had never been happy ones. She had detested him from the first, and had not spared to say so. No man with any refinement—and, whatever he lacked, Mr. Quest had refinement—could bear to be thus continually repulsed by a woman, and so it came to pass that their relations had always been of the most strained nature. Then when she at last had obtained the clew to the secret of his life, under threat of exposure she drove her bargain, of which the terms were complete separation in all but outward form, and virtual freedom of action for herself. This, considering the position, she was perhaps justified in doing, but her husband never forgave her for it. More than that, he determined, if by any means it were possible, to turn the passion which, although she did not know it, he was perfectly aware she bore towards his business superior, Edward Cossey, to a refined instrument of vengeance against her; with what success it will be one of the purposes of this history to show.

Such were, put as briefly as possible, the outlines of the character and aims of this remarkable and contradictory man, whose history, had he but possessed a sense of honor, might very probably have been painted in very different colors.

Within an hour and a half of leaving his own house, "The Oaks," as it was called, although the trees from which it had been so named had long since vanished from the garden, Mr. Quest was bowling swiftly behind Edward Cossey's powerful bay horse towards the towering gateway of Honham Castle. When he was within three hundred yards he pulled the horse up sharply, for he was a good whip and alone in the dog-cart, and paused to admire the view. "What a beautiful place!" he reflected to himself with enthusiasm, "and how grandly those old towers stand out against the sky. The old squire has restored them very well, too, there is no doubt about it; I could not have done it better myself. I wonder if that place will ever be mine. Things look black now, but they may come round, and I think I am beginning to see my way." And then he started the horse on again slowly, reflecting on the unpleasant nature of the business before him. Personally he rather liked and respected the old squire, and he certainly pitied him, though he would no more have dreamed of allowing his liking and pity to interfere with the prosecution of his schemes than an ardent sportsman would dream of not shooting pheasants because he had happened to take a friendly interest in their nurture. He had a certain gentlemanlike distaste to being the bearer of crushing bad news, for Mr. Quest disliked scenes, possibly because he had such an intimate personal acquaintance with them. While he was still wondering how he might best deal with the matter, he passed over the moat, and through the ancient gateway which he admired so fervently, and found himself in front of the hall door. Here he pulled up, looking about for somebody to take his horse, when suddenly the squire himself emerged upon him with a rush, his pen in his hand (for he had been writing letters) and his white hair waving in the breeze.

"Hullo, Quest, is that you?" he shouted, as though his visitor had been fifty yards off instead of five. "I have been looking out for you. Here, William! William!" (crescendo), "William!" (fortissimo); "where on earth is that boy? I expect that idle fellow, George, has been sending him on some of his errands instead of attending to them himself. Whenever he is wanted to take a horse he is nowhere to be found, and then it is 'Please sir, Mr. George'—that's what he calls him—'Please, sir, Mr. George sent me up to the Moat Farm, or somewhere, to see how many eggs the hens laid last week,' or something of that sort. That's a very nice horse you have got there, by the way, very nice indeed."

"It is not my horse, Mr. De la Molle," said the lawyer, with a faint smile, "it is Mr. Edward Cossey's."

"Oh! it's Mr. Edward Cossey's, is it?" answered the old gentleman, with a sudden change of voice. "Ah, Mr. Edward Cossey's? well, it's a very good horse anyhow, and I suppose that Mr. Cossey can afford to buy good horses."

Just then a faint cry of "Coming, sir, coming," was heard, and a long hobble-de-hoy kind of youth, whose business it was to look after the not extensive Castle stables, emerged in a great heat round the corner of the house.

"Now, where on earth have you been?" began the squire, in a stentorian tone.

"If you please, Mr. George—"

"There, what did I tell you?" broke in the squire. "Have I not told you time after time that you are to mind your own business, and leave 'Mr. George' to mind his? Now take that horse round to the stables, and see that it is properly fed."

"Come in, Quest, come in. We have a quarter of an hour before luncheon, and can get our business over," and he led the way through the passage into the tapestried and panelled vestibule, where he took up his stand before the empty fireplace.

Mr. Quest followed him, stopping ostensibly to admire a particularly beautiful suit of armor which hung upon the wall, but really to gain another moment for reflection.

"A beautiful suit of the early Stuart period, Mr. De la Molle," he said ; "I never saw a better."

"Yes, yes, that belonged to old Sir James, the one whom the Roundheads shot."

"What! the Sir James who hid the treasure ?"

"Yes. I was telling that story to our new neighbor, Colonel Quaritch, last night—a very nice fellow, by the way ; you should go and call upon him."

"I wonder what he did with it," said Mr. Quest.

"Ah, so do I, and so will many another, I dare say. I wish that I could find it, I'm sure. It's wanted badly enough nowadays. But that reminds me, Quest. You will have gathered my difficulty from my note and what George told you. You see this man, Janter, has—thanks to that confounded fellow, Major Bolton, and his action about those College lands— thrown up the Moat Farm, and George tells me that there is not another tenant to be had for love or money. In fact, you know what it is ; one can't get tenants nowadays, they simply are not to be had. Well, under these circumstances, there is, of course, only one thing to be done that I know of, and that is to take the farm in hand and farm it myself. It is quite impossible to let the place fall out of cultivation— and that is what would happen otherwise ; and if I were to lay it down in grass it would cost a considerable sum, and be seven or eight years before I got any return."

The squire paused and Mr. Quest said nothing.

"Well," he went on, "that being so, the next thing to do is to obtain the necessary cash to pay Janter his valuation and stock the place—about four thousand would do it; or, perhaps," he added, with an access of generous confidence, "we had better say five. There are about fifty acres of those low-lying meadows which want to be thoroughly bush drained—

bushes are quite as good as pipes for that stiff land; if they put in the right sort of stuff it don't cost half so much—but still it can't be done for nothing, and then there is a new wagon shed wanted, and some odds and ends; yes, we had better say five thousand."

Still Mr. Quest made no answer, so once more the squire went on.

"Well, you see, under these circumstances, not being able to lay hands upon the necessary capital from my private resources, of course I have made up my mind to apply to Cossey & Son for the loan. Indeed, considering how long and intimate has been the connection between their house and the De la Molle family, I think it right and proper to do so; indeed, I should consider it very wrong of me if I neglected to give them the opportunity of the investment "—here a faint smile flickered for an instant on Mr. Quest's face, and then went out —" of course they will, as a matter of business, require security, and very properly so, but as this estate is unentailed, there will fortunately be little difficulty about that. You can draw up the necessary deeds, and I think that, under the circumstances, the right thing to do would be to charge the Moat Farm specifically with the amount. Things are bad enough, no doubt, but I can hardly suppose it possible, under any conceivable circumstances, that the farm would not be good for five thousand pounds. However, they might possibly prefer to have a general clause as well, and if that is so, although I consider it quite unnecessary, I shall raise no objection to that course."

Then, at last, Mr. Quest broke his somewhat ominous silence.

"I am very sorry to say, Mr. De la Molle," he said, gently, 'that I can hold out no prospect of Cossey & Son being induced, under any circumstances, to advance another pound upon the security of the Honham Castle estates. Their opinion of the value of landed property as security has received so severe a shock that they are not at all comfortable as to the safety of the amount already invested."

Mr. De la Molle started when he heard this most unexpected bit of news, for which he was totally unprepared. He had always found it possible to borrow money, and it had never occurred to him that a time might perhaps come in this country when the land, which he held in almost superstitious veneration, would be so valueless a form of property that lenders would refuse it as security.

" Why," he said, recovering himself, " the total encumbrances on the property do not amount to more than twenty-five thousand pounds, and when I succeeded to my father, forty years ago, it was valued at fifty, and the castle and premises have been thoroughly repaired since then, at a cost of five thousand, and most of the farm buildings also."

" Very possibly, Mr. De la Molle, but, to be honest, I very much doubt if Honham Castle and the lands round it would now fetch twenty-five thousand pounds on a forced sale. Competition and Radical agitation have brought estates down more than people realize, and land in Australia and New Zealand is worth as much per acre as cultivated lands in England. Perhaps, as a residential property and on account of its historical interest, it might fetch more, but I doubt it. In short, Mr. De la Molle, so anxious are Cossey & Son in the matter, that I regret to have to tell you that, so far from being willing to make a further advance, the firm have formally instructed me to serve the usual six months' notice on you, calling in the money already advanced on mortgage, together with the interest, which, I must remind you, is nearly a year overdue, and this step I propose to take to-morrow."

The old gentleman staggered for a moment, and caught at the mantelpiece, for the blow was a heavy one, and as unexpected as it was heavy. But he recovered himself in an instant, for it was one of the peculiarities of his character that his spirits always seemed to rise to the occasion in the face of urgent adversity; in short, he possessed an extraordinary share of moral pluck.

" Indeed," he said, indignantly—" indeed, it is a pity that you did not tell me that at once, Mr. Quest; it would have saved me from putting myself in a false position by proposing a business arrangement which is not acceptable. As regards the interest, I admit that it is as you say, and I very much regret it. That stupid fellow, George, is always so dreadfully behindhand with his accounts that I can never get anything settled " (he did not state, and, indeed, did not know, that the reason that the unfortunate George was behindhand was that there were no accounts to make up; or, rather, that they were all on the wrong side of the ledger). "I will have that matter seen to at once. Of course, business people are quite right to consider their due, and I do not blame Messrs. Cossey in the matter, not in the least. Still, I must say that, considering the long and intimate relationship that has for nearly two centuries existed between their house and my family, they might—well—have shown a little more consideration."

"Yes," said Mr. Quest, "I dare say that the step strikes you as a harsh one. To be perfectly frank with you, Mr. De la Molle, it struck me as a very harsh one; but, of course, I am only a servant, and bound to carry out my instructions. I sympathize with you very much; very much indeed."

"Oh, don't do that," said the old gentleman. "Of course, other arrangements must be made; and, much as it will pain me to terminate my connection with Messrs. Cossey, they shall be made."

"But I think," went on the lawyer, without any notice of his interruption, "that you misunderstand the matter a little. Cossey & Son are only a trading corporation, whose object is to make money by lending it, or otherwise; at all hazards, to make money. The kind of feeling that you allude to, and that might induce them, in consideration of long intimacy and close connectiom in the past, to forego the opportunity of so doing, and even to run a risk of loss, is a thing which belongs to former generations, which, whatever their failings, were very often generous in their dealings, and allowed their business to be sometimes conducted upon personal rather than commercial principles. But the present is a strictly commercial age, and we are the most commercial of the trading nations. Cossey & Son move with the times, that is all; and they would rather sell up a dozen families which had dealt with them for two centuries than lose five hundred pounds, provided, of course, that they could do so without scandal and loss of general respect, which, where a banking-house is concerned, also means a loss of custom. I am a great lover of the past myself, and believe that our ancestors' ways of doing business were, on the whole, better and more charitable than ours, but I have to make my living, and take the world as I find it, Mr. De la Molle."

5

"Quite so, Quest; quite so," answered the squire, quietly. "I had no idea that you looked at these matters in such a light. Certainly the world has changed a good deal since I was a young man, and I do not think it has changed much for the better. But you will want your luncheon; it is hungry work talking about foreclosures." Mr. Quest had not used this unpleasant word, but the squire had seen his drift. "Come into the next room," and he led the way into the drawing-room, where Ida was sitting, reading the *Times*.

"Ida," he said, with an affectation of heartiness which did not, however, deceive his daughter, who knew how to read every change of her father's face, "here is Mr. Quest. Take him in to luncheon, my dear. I will come presently. I want to finish a note."

Then he returned to the vestibule, and sat down in his favorite old oak chair.

"Ruined!" he said to himself. "I can never get the money as things are, and there will be a foreclosure. Well, I am an old man, and I hope that I shall not live to see it. But there is Ida! Poor Ida! I cannot bear to think of it; and the old place, too, after all these generations! after all these generations!"

CHAPTER X.

IDA shook hands coldly enough with the lawyer, for whom she cherished a great dislike, not unmixed with fear. Many women are by nature gifted with an extraordinary power of intuition, which fully makes up for their deficiency in reasoning force. They do not conclude from the premises of their observation; they *know* that this man is to be feared, and that trusted. In fact, woman shares with the rest of breathing creation that self-protective instinct of instantaneous and almost automatic judgment, given to guard it from the dangers with which it is continually threatened at the hands of man's overmastering strength and ordered intelligence. Ida knew nothing to Mr. Quest's disadvantage; indeed, she always heard him spoken of with great respect; and, curiously enough, she liked his wife very much. But she could not bear the man, feeling in her heart that he was not only to be avoided on account of his own hidden qualities, but that he was, moreover, an active personal enemy.

They went into the old dining-room, where the luncheon was set, and while Ida allowed Mr. Quest to cut her some cold boiled beef, an operation in which he did not seem to be very much at home, she came to a rapid conclusion in her own mind. She had seen clearly enough from her father's face that his interview with the lawyer had been of a most serious character, but she knew that the chances were that she would never be able to get its upshot out of him, for the old gentleman had a curious habit of keeping such unpleasant matters to himself until he was absolutely forced by circumstances to reveal them. She also knew that her father's affairs were in a most critical condition, for that she had extracted from him on the previous night, and if any remedy was to be attempted it must be attempted at once, and on some heroic scale. Therefore she made up her mind to ask her *bete noir*, Mr. Quest, what the truth might be.

"Mr. Quest," she said, with some trepidation, as he at last triumphantly handed her the beef, "I hope that you will forgive me for asking you a plain question, and that, if you can, you will favor me with a plain answer. I know my father's affairs are very much involved, and that he is now anxious to borrow some more money; but I do not know quite how matters stand, and I want to hear the exact truth."

"I am very glad to hear you speak like that, Miss De la Molle," answered the lawyer, "because I was trying to make up my mind to broach the subject, which is a very painful one to me. Frankly, then, forgive me for saying it, your father is absolutely ruined. The interest on the mortgages is a year in arrear; his largest farm is just thrown upon his hands; and, to complete the tale, the mortgagees are going to call in their money or foreclose."

At this statement, which was almost brutal in its brief comprehensiveness, Ida turned as pale as death, as well she might, and dropped her fork with a clatter upon her plate.

"I did not realize that things were quite so bad," she murmured. "Then I suppose that the place will be taken from us, and we shall—shall have to go away."

"Yes, certainly, unless money can be found to take up the mortgages, of which I see no chance. The place will be sold for what it will fetch; and that, nowadays, will be no great sum."

"When will that be?" she asked.

"In about six or nine months' time."

Ida's lips trembled, and the sight of the food upon her plate became nauseous to her. A vision arose before her mind's eye of herself and her old father departing hand in hand from the Castle gates, behind and about which gleamed the hard wild lights of a March sunset, to seek a place to hide themselves, and the horror of it almost overcame her.

"Is there no way of escape?" she asked, hoarsely. "To lose this place would kill my father. He loves it better than anything in the world, his whole life is wrapped up in it."

"I can quite understand that, Miss De la Molle; it is a most charming old place, especially to anybody interested in the past. But, unfortunately, mortgagees are no respecters of feelings. To them land is so much property and nothing more."

"I know all that," she said, impatiently; "you do not answer my question," and she leaned towards him and rested her hand upon the table. "Is there no way out of it?"

Mr. Quest drank a little claret before he answered. "Yes," he said, "I think that there is, if only you will take it."

"What way?" she asked, eagerly.

"Well, though, as I said just now, the mortgagees of an estate as a body are merely a business corporation, and look at things from a business point of view only, you must remember that they are composed of individuals, and that individuals can be influenced if they can be got at. For instance, Cossey & Son are an abstraction and harshly disposed in their abstract capacity, but Mr. Edward Cossey is an individual, and I should say, so far as this particular matter is concerned, a benevolently disposed individual. Now Mr. Edward Cossey is not himself at the present moment actually one of the firm of Cossey & Son, but he is the heir of the head of the house, and of course has authority, and, what is better still, the command of money."

"I understand," said Ida. "You mean that my father should try to win over Mr. Edward Cossey. Unfortunately, to be frank, he dislikes him, and my father is not a man to keep his dislikes to himself."

"People generally do dislike those to whom they are crushingly indebted; your father dislikes Mr. Cossey because his name is Cossey, and for no other reason. But that is not quite what I meant—I do not think that the squire is the right person to undertake a negotiation of that sort. He is a little too outspoken and incautious. No, Miss De la Molle, if it is to be done at all you must do it. You must put the whole case before him at once—this very afternoon, there is no time for delay; you need not enter into details, he knows all about them—only ask him to avert this catastrophe. He can do so if he likes; how he does it is his own affair."

"But, Mr. Quest," said Ida, "how can I ask such a favor of any man. I shall be putting myself in a dreadfully false position."

"I do not pretend, Miss De la Molle, that it is a pleasant task for any young lady to undertake. I quite understand your shrinking from it. But sometimes one has to do unpleasant things and make compromises with one's self-respect. It is a question whether or no your family shall be utterly ruined and destroyed. There is, as I honestly believe, no prospect whatever of your father being able to get the money to pay off Cossey & Son, and if he did, it would not help him, because he could not pay the interest on it. Under these circumstances you have to choose between putting yourself in an equivocal position and letting events take their course. It would be useless for anybody else to undertake the task, and of course I cannot guarantee that even you will succeed; but I will not mince matters—as you doubtless know, any man would find it hard to refuse a favor asked by such a suppliant. And now you must make up your own mind. I have shown you a path that may lead your family from a position of the most imminent peril. If you are the woman I take you for, you will not shrink from following it."

Ida made no reply, and in another moment the squire came in to take a couple of glasses of sherry and a biscuit. But Mr. Quest, furtively watching her face, said to himself that she had taken the bait and that she would do it. Shortly after this a diversion occurred, for the clergyman, Mr. Jeffries, a pleasant little man, with a round and shining face and a most unclerical eyeglass, came up to consult the squire upon some matter of parish business, and was shown into the dining-room. Ida took advantage of his appearance to effect a retreat to her own room, and there for the present we may leave her to her meditations.

No more business was discussed by the squire that afternoon. Indeed, it interested Mr. Quest, who was above all things a student of character, to observe how wonderfully the old gentleman threw off his trouble. To listen to him energetically arguing away with the Rev. Mr. Jeffries as to whether or no it would be proper, as had hitherto been the custom, to devote the proceeds of the harvest festival collection (£1 18s. 3d. and a brass button) to the county hospital, or whether it should be applied to the repair of the woodwork in the vestry, was, under the circumstances, most instructive. The Rev. Mr.

Jeffries, who suffered severely from the condition of the vestry, at last gained his point by triumphantly showing that no patient from Honham had been admitted to the hospital for fifteen months, and that therefore the hospital had no particular claim on this particular year, whereas the draught in the vestry was enough to cut any clergyman in two.

"Well, well," said the old gentleman, "I will consent for this year, and this year only. I have been churchwarden of this parish for between forty and fifty years, and we have always given the harvest-festival collection to the hospital, and although under these exceptional circumstances it may possibly be desirable to diverge from that custom, I cannot and will not consent to such a thing in a permanent way. So I shall write to the secretary and explain the matter, and tell him that next year, and in the future generally, the collection will be devoted to its original purpose."

"Great heavens!" ejaculated Mr. Quest to himself. "And all the time the man must know that in all human probability the place will be sold over his head before he is a year older. I wonder if he puts it on or if he deceives himself. I suppose he has lived here so long that he cannot realize a condition of things when he will cease to live here and the place will belong to somebody else. Or perhaps he is only brazening it out." And then he strolled away to the back of the house and had a look at the condition of the outhouses, reflecting that some of them would be sadly expensive to repair for whoever came into possession here. After that he crossed the moat and walked through the somewhat extensive plantations at the back of the house, wondering if it would not be possible to get enough timber out of them, if one went to work judiciously, to pay for putting the place in order. Presently he came to a spot where there had been a line of very fine timber oaks, in a hedgerow, of which the squire had been notoriously fond, and of which he had himself taken particular and admiring notice in the course of the previous winter. The trees were gone. In the hedge where they had stood were a series of gaps like those in an old woman's jaw, and about upon the ground were littered remains of bark and branches and of fagots that had been made up of the brushwood. "Cut down this spring fell," was Mr. Quest's ejaculation; "poor old fellow, he must have been pinched before he consented to part with those oaks."

Then he turned and went back to the house, just in time to see Ida's guests arriving for the lawn-tennis party. Ida herself was standing on the lawn behind the house, which, bordered as it was by the moat and at the farther end by a row of ruined arches, was one of the most picturesque in the country, and a most effective setting to any young lady. As the people came they were shown through the house to the lawn, and here she was receiving. She was dressed in a plain, tight-fitting gown of blue flannel, which showed off her perfect figure to great advantage, and a broad-brimmed hat, which shaded her fine but somewhat dignified face. Mr. Quest sat down on a bench beneath the shade of an arbutus, watching her closely, and, indeed, if the study of a perfect English lady of the noblest sort has any charms, he was not without his reward. There are some women—most of us know one or two—who are born to hold a great position, and to sail across the world like a swan through meaner fowl. It would be very hard to say to what their peculiar charm and dignity is owing. It is not to beauty only, for though they have presence, many of these women are not beautiful, while some are even plain. Better not—this face has been so often described in different and non-accordant terms. Nor does it spring from native grace and tact alone; though these things must be present. Rather is it the reflection of a cultivated mind acting upon a naturally pure and elevated temperament, which makes these ladies conspicuous above the level of their sex, and fashions them in such kind that all men looking upon them and putting aside the mere charm of beauty and the natural softening of judgment in the atmosphere of sex, must recognize in them an equal mind, and a presence more noble than their own.

Such a woman was Ida de la Molle, and if any one doubted it, it was sufficient to compare her in her simplicity to the various human items by whom she was surrounded. They were a typical county society gathering, such as needs no description, and would not greatly interest if described. Some of them were good-tempered people, and some of them were bad-tempered and spiteful. For the most part they had a very good idea of their own value, and a somewhat exaggerated estimate of the position which they occupied in the eye of their little world. Their regard for their neighbors was, on the whole, largely regulated by what they believed to be the length of their respective purses, and for poverty they had a very real loathing and contempt which they scarcely thought it worth while to conceal. Their loves were few and shallow, and their hates and spites astonishingly bitter, considering how small were the eggs from whence they were hatched. The arts and sciences scarcely lived for them, or at the least formed no part of their inner life; they were too much concerned with what is material to soar to what is ideal. The girls were commonplace, hard and handsome, and much occupied with their matrimonial chances; the young men, what young men generally are before they have found their level; but they could all play lawn-tennis well, and chaff with a freedom and a delicate depth of local allusion that greatly puzzled Colonel Quaritch when he came to listen to it. Here and there, by way of shadow to the picture, was a good and earnest man, a clergyman probably, and here and there a woman whose face told the observer that she was meant for better things, had she not been forced by circumstances down this stony and unprofitable groove.

It was no wonder, then, that a woman like Ida de la Molle was *facile princeps* among such company, or that Harold Quaritch, who was poetically inclined for a man of his age, where the lady in question was concerned, should in his heart have compared her to a queen. Even Belle Quest, lovely as she undoubtedly was in her own way, paled and looked shop-girlish in face of her gentle dignity, a fact of which the latter was evidently aware, for although the two women were friendly, nothing would induce the latter to stand long near Ida in public. She would say to Edward Cossey that it made her look like a wax doll by a live child.

It was while Mr. Quest was still watching Ida with complete satisfaction, for she appealed to the artistic side of his nature, that Colonel Quaritch arrived upon the scene, looking, Mr. Quest thought, particularly plain with his solid form, his long thin nose, light whiskers, and square and massive chin. Also he looked particularly imposing in contrast to the youths and maidens and domesticated clergymen. There was a gravity, almost a solemnity, about his bronzed countenance and deliberate, ordered conversation, which did not, however, favorably impress the aforesaid youths and maidens, if a judgment might be formed from such samples of conversational criticism which Mr. Quest heard going on on the farther side of his arbutus.

CHAPTER XI.

WHEN Ida saw the colonel coming, she put on her sweetest smile and took his hand.

"How do you do, Colonel Quaritch?" she said. "It is very good of you to come, especially as you don't play tennis much; by the way, I hope you have been studying that cipher, for I am sure that it is a cipher."

"I studied it for half an hour before I went to bed last night, Miss De la Molle, and for the life of me I could not make anything out of it, and, what's more, I don't think that there is anything to make out."

"Ah," she answered with a sigh, "I wish there was."

"Well," he answered, "I'll have another go at it. What will you give me if I find it out?" he said, with a smile which lighted up his rugged face most pleasantly.

"Anything you like to ask and that I can give," she answered, with a tone of earnestness, which struck him as peculiar, for of course he did not know the tale that she had just heard from Mr. Quest.

Then, for the first time for many years, Harold Quaritch delivered himself of a speech that might have been capable of a tender and hidden meaning.

"I am afraid," he said, bowing, "that if I came to claim the reward I should ask for more even than you would be inclined to give."

Ida blushed a little. "We can consider that when you do come, Colonel Quaritch; excuse me, but here are Mrs. Quest and Mr. Cossey, and I must go and say how do you do."

Harold Quaritch looked round, feeling unreasonably irritated at this interruption to his little advances, and for the first time saw Edward Cossey. He was coming along in the wake of Mrs. Quest, looking very handsome and rather languid, when their eyes met, and, to speak the truth, the colonel's first impression was not a complimentary one. Edward Cossey was in some ways not a bad fellow, but, like a great many young men who are born with silver spoons in their mouths, he had many airs and graces, one of which was the affectation of treating older and better men with an assumption of off-handedness and even of superiority which was rather obnoxious. Thus while Ida was greeting Mrs. Quest, he was engaged in taking the colonel in in a way that irritated that gentleman considerably.

Presently Ida turned and introduced Colonel Quaritch, first to Mrs. Quest and then to Mr. Cossey. Harold bowed to each, and then strolled off to meet the squire, whom he noted advancing with his usual array of towels hanging out of his hat, and for a while he saw neither of them any more.

Meanwhile Mr. Quest had emerged from the shelter of his arbutus, and was going from one person to another, saying some pleasant and appropriate word to each, till at last he reached the spot where his wife and Edward Cossey were standing. Nodding affectionately at the former, he asked her if she was not going to play tennis, and then drew Cossey aside.

"Well, Quest," said the latter, "have you told the old man?"

"Oh, yes, I told him."

"How did he take it?"

"Oh, talked it off and said that of course other arrangements must be made. I spoke to Miss De la Molle too."

"Oh," said Edward, in a changed tone, "and how did she take it?"

"Well," answered the lawyer, putting on an air of deep concern (and as a matter of fact he really did feel sorry for her), "I think it was the most painful professional experience that I ever had. The poor woman was utterly crushed. She said that it would kill her father."

"Poor girl!" said Mr. Cossey, in a voice that showed his sympathy was of a very active order, "and how pluckily she is carrying it off too! look at her," and he pointed to where Ida was standing, a lawn-tennis bat in her hand, and laughingly arranging a "set" of married *versus* single.

"Yes, she is a good, plucky girl," answered Mr. Quest; "and

what a splendid woman she looks, doesn't she? I never saw
anybody who was quite such a lady—there is nobody to touch
her round here, unless," he added, meditatively, "perhaps it is
Belle."

"They are different types of beauty," answered Edward
Cossey, flinching.

"Yes, but equally attractive in their separate ways. Well,
it can't be helped, but I feel sorry for that poor girl, and the
old gentleman too—hullo, there he is."

As he was speaking the squire, who was walking past with
Colonel Quaritch, with the object of showing him the view
from the end of the moat, suddenly saw Edward Cossey, who
at once stepped forward to greet him, but to his surprise was
met by a cold and most stately bow from Mr. De la Molle, who
passed on without vouchsafing a single word.

"Old idiot!" ejaculated Mr. Quest to himself; "he will put
Cossey's back up and spoil the game."

"Well," said Mr. Cossey aloud, and coloring almost to his
eyes, "that old gentleman knows how to be insolent."

"You must not mind him, Mr. Cossey," answered Quest,
hastily. "The poor old boy has got a very good idea of himself—he is dreadfully injured because Cossey & Son are calling in the mortgages after the family has dealt with them for
so many generations; and he thinks that you have something
to do with it."

"Well, if he does, he might as well be civil. It does not
particularly incline a fellow to go out of his way to pull him
out of the ditch, just to be cut in that fashion; I have half
a mind to order my trap and go."

"No, no, don't do that; you must make allowances, you
must indeed; look, here is Miss De la Molle coming to ask
you to play tennis."

At this moment Ida arrived and took off Edward Cossey
with her, not a little to the relief of Mr. Quest, who began to
fear that the whole scheme was spoiled by the squire's unfortunate magnificence of manner.

Edward played his game, having Ida herself as his partner.
It cannot be said that the set was a pleasant one for the latter,
who, poor woman, was doing her utmost to bring up her courage to the point necessary to the carrying-out of the appeal, *ad*

misericordiam, which she had decided to make as soon as the game was over. However, chance put an opportunity in her way, for Edward Cossey, who had a curious weakness for flowers, asked her if she would show him her chrysanthemums, of which she was very proud. She consented readily enough, and they crossed the lawn, and, passing through some shrubbery, reached the greenhouse, which was placed at the end of the house itself. Here for some minutes they looked at the flowers just now bursting into bloom. Ida, who felt exceedingly nervous, was all the while wondering how on earth she was to broach so delicate a subject, when fortunately Mr. Cossey himself gave her the necessary opening.

"I can't imagine, Miss De la Molle," he said, "what I can have done to offend your father; he almost cut me just now."

"Are you sure that he saw you, Mr. Cossey—he is very absent-minded sometimes?"

"Oh, yes, he saw me, but when I offered to shake hands with him he only bowed in rather a crushing way and passed on."

Ida broke off a Scarlet Turk from its stem, and nervously began to pick the bloom to pieces.

"The fact is, Mr. Cossey—the fact is, my father, and indeed I also, are in great trouble just now about money matters, you know, and my father is very apt to be prejudiced—in short, I rather believe he thinks you may have something to do with his difficulties—but perhaps you know all about it."

"I know something, Miss De la Molle," said he, gravely, "and I hope and trust that you do not believe that I have anything to do with the action which Cossey & Son have thought fit to take."

"No, no," she said, hastily. "I never thought anything of the sort; but I know that you have influence—and, well, to be plain, Mr. Cossey, I implore of you to use it. Perhaps you will understand that it is very humiliating for me to be obliged to ask this, though you can never guess how humiliating. Believe me, Mr. Cossey, I would never ask it for myself, but it is my father—he loves this place better than his life; it would be much better he should die than that he should be obliged to leave it; and if this money is called in, that is what must happen, because the place will be sold over us. I believe he would go mad, I do indeed," and she stopped speaking and stood there before him, the fragment of the flower in her hand, her breast heaving with emotion.

"What do you suggest should be done, Miss De la Molle?" said Edward Cossey, gently.

"I suggest that—that—if you will be so kind, you should persuade Cossey & Son to forego their intention of calling in the money."

"It is quite impossible," he answered. "My father has ordered the step himself, and he is a hard man. It is impossible to turn him if he thinks he will lose money by turning. You see he is a banker, and has been handling money all his life, till it has become a sort of god to him. Really, I believe that he would rather beggar every friend he has than to lose five thousand pounds."

"Then there is no more to be said. The place must go, that's all," replied Ida, turning away her head and affecting to busy herself in removing some dried leaves from a chrysanthemum plant. Edward, watching her, however, saw her shoulders shake and a big tear fall like a raindrop with a splash on the pavement, and the sight, strongly attracted as he was and had for some time been towards the young lady, was altogether too much for him. In an instant, moved by an overwhelming impulse, and something not unlike a gust of passion, he came to one of those determinations which so often change the whole course and tenor of men's lives.

"Miss De la Molle," he said, rapidly, "there may be a way found out of it."

She looked up inquiringly, and there were tear stains on her face.

"Somebody might take up the mortgages and pay off Cossey & Son."

"Can you find any one who will?" she asked, eagerly.

"No, not as an investment. I understand that thirty thousand pounds are required, and I tell you frankly that as times are I do not for one moment believe the place to be worth that amount. It is all very well for your father to talk about land recovering itself, but at present, at any rate, nobody can see the faintest chance of anything of the sort. The probabilities are, on the contrary, that as the American competition in-

creases land will gradually sink to something like a prairie
value."

"Then how can the money be got if nobody will advance
it?"

"I did not say that nobody would advance it; I said that
nobody would advance it as an investment—a friend might
advance it."

"And where is such a friend to be found? He would be a
very disinterested friend who would advance thirty thousand
pounds."

"Nobody in this world is quite disinterested, Miss De la
Molle; or, at any rate, very few are. What would you give to
such a friend?"

"I would give anything and everything over which I have
control in the world, to save my father from seeing Honham
sold over his head," she answered, simply.

Edward Cossey laughed a little. "That is a large order,"
he said. "Miss de la Molle, I am disposed to try and find
the money to take up these mortgages. I have not got it,
and I shall have to borrow it; and, what is more, I shall have
to keep the fact that I have borrowed it a secret from my
father."

"It is very good of you," said Ida, faintly. "I don't know
what to say."

For a moment he made no reply, and, looking at him, Ida
saw that his hand was trembling.

"Miss De la Molle," he said, "there is another matter of
which I wish to speak to you. Men are sometimes put into
strange positions, partly through their own fault, partly by
force of circumstances, and when in those positions are forced
down paths that they would not follow. Supposing, Miss De
la Molle, that mine were some such position, and supposing
that owing to that position I could not say to you words which
I should wish to say—"

Ida began to understand now, and once more turned aside.

"Supposing, however, that at some future time the difficulties of that position of which I have spoken were to fade
away, and I were then to speak those words, can you, supposing all this—tell me how they would be received?"

Ida paused and thought. She was a strong-natured and

clear-headed woman, and she fully understood the position. On her answer would depend whether or no the thirty thousand pounds were forthcoming, and, therefore, whether or no Honham Castle would pass from her father and her race.

"I said just now, Mr. Cossey," she answered, coldly, "that I would give anything and everything over which I have control in the world to save my father from seeing Honham sold over his head. I do not wish to retract those words, and I think that in them you will find an answer to your question."

He colored. "You put the matter in a very business-like way," he said.

"It is best put so, Mr. Cossey," she answered, with a faint shade of bitterness in her tone; "it preserves me from feeling under an obligation. Will you see my father about these mortgages?"

"Yes, to-morrow. And now I will say good-by to you," and he took her hand, and with some little hesitation kissed it. She made no resistance and showed no emotion.

"Yes," she answered, "we have been here some time. Mrs. Quest will wonder what has become of you."

It was a random arrow, but it went straight home, and for the third time that day Edward Cossey reddened to the roots of his hair. Without answering a word he bowed and went.

When Ida saw it, she was sorry she had made the remark, for she had no wish to appear to Mr. Cossey (the conquest of whom gave her neither pride nor pleasure) in the light of a spiteful, or, worse still, of a jealous woman. She had indeed heard some talk about him and Mrs. Quest, but not being of a scandal-loving disposition it had not interested her, and she had almost forgotten it. Now, however, she saw that there was something in it.

"So that is the difficult position of which he talks," she said to herself; "he wants to marry me as soon as he can get Mrs. Quest off his hands. And I have consented to that, always provided that Mrs. Quest can be disposed of, in consideration of the receipt of a sum of thirty thousand pounds. And I do not like the man. It was not nice of him to make that bargain, though I brought it on myself. I wonder if my father will ever know what I have done for him, and if he will

appreciate it if he does.   Well, it is not a bad price—thirty
thousand pounds—it is a good figure for any woman in the
present state of the market."   And with a hard and bitter
laugh, and a prescience of sorrow to come lying at the heart,
she threw down the remains of the Scarlet Turk and turned
away.

CHAPTER XII.

GEORGE PROPHESIES.

IDA, for obvious reasons, said nothing to her father of her interview with Edward Cossey, and thus it came to pass that on the morning following the lawn-tennis party there was a very serious consultation between the faithful George and his master. It appeared to Ida, who was lying awake in her room, to commence somewhere about daybreak, and it certainly continued with short intervals for refreshment till eleven o'clock in the forenoon. First the squire explained the whole question to George at great length, and with a most extraordinary multiplicity of detail, for he began with his first loan from the house of Cossey & Son, which he had contracted a great many years before. All this while George sat with a very long face, and tried to look as though he were following the thread of the argument, which was not possible, for his master had long ago lost it himself, and was mixing up the loan of 1863 with the loan of 1874, and the money raised on the severance of the entail with both, in a way which would have driven anybody except George, who was used to this sort of thing, perfectly mad. However, he sat it through, and when at last the account was finished, remarked that things " sartainly did look queer."

Thereupon the squire called him a stupid owl, and having, by means of some test questions, discovered that he knew very little of the details which had just been explained to him at such portentous length, he, in spite of the protest of the wretched George, who urged that they "didn't seem to be gitting no forrader somehow," began and went through every word of it again.

This brought them to breakfast-time, and after breakfast George's accounts were thoroughly gone into, with the result that confusion was soon worse confounded, for either George

could not keep accounts or the squire could not follow them.
Ida, sitting in the drawing-room, could continually hear her
father's ejaculatory outbursts after this kind :

" Why, you stupid donkey, you've added it up all wrong,
it's nine hundred and fifty, not three hundred and fifty ;" followed by a " No, no, squire, you be a looking on the wrong
side—them there are the debits," and so on till both parties
were fairly played out, and the only thing that remained clear
was that the balance was considerably on the wrong side.

" Well," said the squire, at last, " there you are, you see.
It appears to me that I am absolutely ruined, and, upon my
word, I believe that it is a great deal owing to your stupidity.
You have muddled and muddled and muddled till at last you
have muddled us out of house and home."

" No, no, squire, don't say that—don't you say that. It
ain't none of my doing, for I've been a good servant to you if
I haven't had much book larning. It's that there dratted borrowing, that's what it is, and the interest and all the rest on
it, and though I says it as didn't ought, poor Mr. James—God
rest him !—and his free-handed ways. Don't you say it's me,
squire."

" Well, well," answered his master, " it doesn't much matter whose fault it is, the result is the same, George ; I'm ruined,
and I suppose that the place will be sold if anybody can be
found to buy it. The De la Molles have been here between
four and five centuries, and they got it by marriage with the
Boisseys, who got it from the Norman kings, and now it will
go to the hammer and be bought by a picture-dealer, or a
manufacturer of shoddy, or some one of that sort. Well,
everything has its end, and God's will be done."

" No, no, squire, don't you talk like that," answered George,
with emotion. " I can't bear to hear you talk like that. And
what's more it ain't so."

" What do you mean by that ?" asked the old gentleman,
sharply. " It is so ; there's no getting over it unless you can
find thirty thousand pounds, or thereabouts, to take up these
mortgages with. Nothing short of a miracle can save it.
That's always your way. ' Oh, something will turn up, something will turn up.' "

" Thin there'll be a miracle," said George, bringing down a

fist like a leg of mutton with a thud upon the table ; " it ain't
no use of your talking to me, squire. I knaw it, I tell you I
knaw it. There'll never be other than a De la Molle up at the
Castle while we're alive, no, nor while our children are alive
either. If the money's to be found, why, drat it, it will be
found. Don't you think that God Almighty is going to put
none of them there counter-jumpers into Honham Castle,
where gentlefolk have lived all these ginerations, because he
ain't. There, and that's the truth, because I knaw it, and so
help me God—and if I'm wrong it's a master one."

The squire, who was striding up and down the room in his
irritation, stopped suddenly in his walk, and looked at his retainer with a sharp and searching gaze upon his noble features.
Notwithstanding his prejudices, his simplicity, and his occasional absurdities, he was in his own way an able man, and an
excellent judge of human nature. Even his prejudices were,
as a rule, founded upon some good solid ground, only it was,
as a general rule, impossible to get at it. Also he had a share
of that marvellous instinct which, when it exists, registers the
mental altitude of the minds of others with the accuracy of
an aneroid. He could tell when a man's words rang true and
when they rang false, and, what is more, when the conviction
of the true, and the falsity of the false, rested upon a sub-
stantial basis of fact or error. Of course the instinct was a
vague, and from its nature an indefinable one, but it existed,
and in the present instance arose in strength. He looked at
the ugly, melancholy countenance of the faithful George with
that keen glance of his, and observed that for the moment it
was almost beautiful—beautiful in the light of conviction
which shone upon it. He looked, and as he looked it was
borne in upon him that what George said was true, and that
George knew it was true, although he did not know where the
light of truth came from, and as he looked half the load fell
from his heart.

" Hullo, George ! are you turning prophet in addition to
your other occupations ?" he said, cheerfully, and as he did so
Edward Cossey's splendid bay horse pulled up at the door and
the bell rang.

" Well," he added, as soon as he saw who his visitor was,
" unless I am much mistaken, we shall soon know how much

truth there is in your prophecies now, for here comes Mr. Cossey himself."

Before George could sufficiently recover from his recent agitation to make any reply, Edward Cossey, looking particularly handsome and rather overpowering, was shown into the room.

The squire shook hands with him this time, though coldly enough, and George touched his forelock and said, "Sarvant, sir," in the approved fashion. Thereon his master told him that he might retire, though he was to be sure not to go out of hearing, as he should want him again presently.

"Very well, sir," answered George, "I'll just step up to the Poplars. I told a man to be round there to-day, as I want to see if I can come to an onderstanding with him about this year's fell in the big wood."

"There," said the squire, with an expression of infinite disgust, "there, that's just like your way, your horrid cadging way; the idea of telling a man to be 'round about the Poplars' some time or other to-day, because you wanted to speak to him about a fell. Why didn't you write him a letter like an ordinary Christian, and make an offer, instead of dodging him round a farm for half a day like a wild Indian. Besides, the Poplars is half a mile off, if it's a yard."

"Lord, sir," said George, as he retired, "that ain't the way that folks in these parts like to do business, that ain't. Letter-writing is all very well for Londoners and other furriners, but it don't do here. Besides, sir, I shall hear you well enough up there. Sarvant, sir"—this to Edward Cossey—and he was gone.

Edward burst out laughing, and the squire looked after his retainer with a comical air.

"No wonder that the place has got in such a mess with such a fellow as that to manage it," he said, aloud. "The idea of hunting a man round the Poplars Farm like—like an Indian squaw. He's a regular cadger, that's what he is, and that's all he's fit for. However, it's his way of doing business, and I sha'n't alter him. Well, Mr. Cossey," he went on, "this is a very sad state of affairs, at any rate so far as I am concerned. I presume, of course, that you know of the steps which have been taken by Cossey & Son to force a foreclosure, for that is what it amounts to, though I have not as yet received the formal notice; indeed, I presume that those steps have been taken under your advice."

" Yes, Mr. De la Molle, I know all about it, and here is the notice calling in the loans," and he placed a folded paper on the table.

" Ah," said the squire, " I see. As I remarked to your manager, Mr. Quest, yesterday, I think that considering the nature of the relationship which has existed for so many generations between our family and the business firm of which you are a member, considering, too, the peculiar circumstances in which the owners of land find themselves at this moment, and the ruinous loss—to put questions of sentiment aside— that must be inflicted by such sale upon the owner of property, that more consideration might have been shown. However, it is useless to try to make a silk purse out of a sow's ear, or to get blood from a stone, so I suppose that I must make the best of a bad job—and," with a polite bow—" I really do not know that I have anything more to say to you, Mr. Cossey. I will forward the notice to my lawyers; indeed I think that it might have been sent to them in the first instance."

Edward Cossey had all this while been sitting on an old oak chair, his eyes fixed upon the ground, and slowly swinging his hat between his legs. Suddenly he looked up, and, to the squire's surprise, said quietly,

" I quite agree with you. I don't think that you can say anything too bad about the behavior of my people. A Shoreditch Jew could not have done worse. And look here, Mr. De la Molle, to come to the point and prevent misunderstanding, I may as well say at once that, with your permission, I am anxious to take up these mortgages myself, for two reasons: I regard them as a desirable investment even in the present condition of land, and also I wish to save Cossey & Son from the discredit of the step which they meditate."

For the second time that morning the squire looked up with the sharp and searching gaze he occasionally assumed, and for the second time his instinct, for he was too heady a man to reason overmuch, came into play and warned him that in making this offer Edward Cossey had other motives than those which he had brought forward. He paused to consider what they might be. Was he anxious to get the estate for himself? Was he put forward by somebody else? Quest, perhaps; or was it something to do with Ida? The first alternative seemed the most probable to him. But whatever was the lender's object, the result to him was the same, it gave him a respite. For Mr. De la Molle well knew that he had no more chance of raising the money from any ordinary source of investment than he had of altering the condition of agriculture.

"Hum!" he said, "this is an important matter, a most important matter. I presume, Mr. Cossey, that before making this definite offer you have consulted a legal adviser."

"Oh, yes; I have done all that, and am quite satisfied with the security—an advance of thirty thousand charged on all the Honham Castle estates at four per cent. The question now is if you are prepared to consent to the transfer. In that case all the old charges on the property will be paid off, and Mr. Quest, who will act for me in the matter, will prepare a simple deed charging the property for the round total."

"Ah, yes; the plan seems a satisfactory one, but of course in so important a matter I should prefer to consult my legal adviser before giving a final answer; indeed, I think that it would be better if the whole affair were carried out in a proper and formal way."

"Surely, surely, Mr. De la Molle," said the younger man with some irritation, for the old gentleman's somewhat magnificent manner rather annoyed him, which, under the circumstances was not unnatural—"surely you do not want to consult a legal adviser to make up your mind as to whether or no you will allow a foreclosure. I offer you the money at four per cent. Cannot you let me have an answer now, yes or no?"

"I don't like being hurried. I can't bear to be hurried," said the squire, pettishly. "These important matters require consideration, a great deal of consideration. Still," he added, observing signs of increased irritation upon Edward Cossey's face, and not having the slightest intention of throwing away the opportunity, though he would dearly have liked to prolong the negotiations for a week or two, if it was only to enjoy the illusory satisfaction of dabbling with such a large sum of money—"still, as you are so pressing about it, I really, speaking off-hand, can see no objection to your taking up the mortgages on the terms you mention."

"Very well, Mr. De la Molle. Now I have on my part one condition, and one only, to attach to this offer of mine, that is that my name is not mentioned in connection with it. I do not wish Cossey & Son to know that I have taken up this investment on my own account. In fact, so necessary to me is it that it should not be mentioned, that if it does transpire before the affair is completed I shall withdraw my offer, and if it transpires afterwards I shall call the money in. The loan will be advanced by a client of Mr. Quest's. Is that understood between us?"

"Hum!" said the squire, "I don't quite like this secrecy about these important matters of business, but still, if you make a point of it, why, of course I cannot object."

"Very good. Then I presume that you will write officially to Cossey & Son, stating that the money will be forthcoming to meet their various charges and the overdue interest. And now I think that we have had about enough of this business for once, so with your permission I will pay my respects to Miss De la Molle before I go."

"Dear me," said the squire, pressing his hand to his head, "you do hurry me so dreadfully—I really don't know where I am. Miss De la Molle is out; I saw her go out sketching myself. Sit down and we will talk this business over a little more."

"No, thank you, Mr. De la Molle, I have to talk about money every day of my life, and I soon have enough of the subject. Quest will arrange all the details. Good-by; don't bother to ring, I will find my horse." And with a shake of the hand he was gone.

"Ah!" said the old gentleman to himself when his visitor had departed, "he asked for Ida, so I suppose that is what he is after. But it is a queer sort of way to begin courting, and if she finds it out I should think that it would go against him. Ida is not the sort of woman to be won by a money consideration. Well, she can very well look after herself, that's certain. Anyway, it has been a good morning's work, but somehow I don't like that young man any the better for it. I have

it—there's something wanting.   He is not quite a gentleman.
Well, I must find that fellow George," and he rushed to the
front door and roared for "George," till the whole place
echoed and the pheasants crowed in the woods.

After a while there came faint answering yells of "Coming,
squire, coming!" and in due course George's long form became
visible, striding swiftly up the garden.

"Well," said his master, who was in high good-humor,
"did you find your man?"

"Well, no, squire—that is, I had a rare hunt after him, and
I had just happened of him up a tree, when you began to
halloa so loud that he went nigh to falling out of it, so I had
to tell him to come back next week or the week after."

"You happened of him up a tree?   Why, what the deuce
was the man doing up a tree—measuring it?"

"No, squire, I don't rightly know what he was after; but he
is a curious kind of a chap, and he said he had a fancy to
wait there."

"Good heavens! no wonder the place is going to ruin,
when you deal with men who have a fancy to transact their
business up a tree.   Well, never mind that; I have settled the
matter about the mortgages.   Of course somebody, a client
of Mr. Quest's, has been found without the least difficulty to
take them up at four per cent., and advance the other five
thousand too, so that there need be no more anxiety about
that."

"Well, that's a good job at any rate," answered George,
with a sigh of relief.

"A good job?   Of course it's a good job, but it is no more
than I expected.   It wasn't likely that such an eligible investment, as they say in the advertisements, would be allowed to
go begging for long.   But that's just the way with you: the
moment there's a hitch you come with your long face, and
your uneducated sort of way, and swear that we are all ruined,
and that the country is breaking up, and that there's nothing
before us but the workhouse, and nobody knows what."

George reflected to himself that the squire had forgotten
that not an hour before he himself had been vowing that they
were ruined, while he, George, had stoutly sworn that something would turn up to help them.   But his back was accus-

tomed to those vicarious burdens, nor, to tell the truth, did they go nigh to the breaking of it.

"Well, it's a good job anyway, and I thank God Almighty for it," said he, "and more especially since there'll be the money to take over the Moat Farm and give that warmint Janter the boot."

"Give him *what ?*"

"Why, kick him out, sir, for good and all, begging your pardon, sir."

"Oh, I see. I do wish that you would respect the queen's English a little more, George, and the name of the Creator too. By the way, the parson was speaking to me again yesterday about your continued absence from church. It really is disgraceful; you are a most confirmed Sabbath-breaker. And now you mustn't waste my time here any longer. Go and look after your affairs. Stop a minute, would you like a glass of port ?"

"Well, thank you, sir," said George, reflectively, "we have had a lot of talk and I don't mind if I do, and as for that there parson, begging his pardon, I wish he would mind his own affairs, and leave me to mind mine."

CHAPTER XIII.

EDWARD COSSEY drove from the Castle in a far from happy frame of mind. To begin with, the squire and his condescending way of doing business irritated him very much; so much that once or twice in the course of the conversation he was within an ace of breaking the whole thing off, and only restrained himself with difficulty from so doing. As it was, notwithstanding all the sacrifices and money risks which he was undergoing to take up these mortgages, and they were very considerable, even to a man of his great prospects, he felt that he had been placed in the position of a person who receives a favor rather than of a person who grants one. Moreover, there was an assumption of superiority about the old man, a visible recognition of the gulf which used to be fixed between the gentleman of family and the man of business who has grown rich by trading in money and money's worth, which was the more galling because it was founded on actual fact, and Edward Cossey knew it. All his foibles and oddities notwithstanding, it would have been impossible for any man of discernment to entertain a comparison between the half-bankrupt squire and the young banker, who would shortly be worth between half a million and a million sterling. The former was a representative, though a somewhat erratic one, of all that is best in the old type of Englishmen of gentle blood, which is now so rapidly vanishing, and, indeed, of the class to which, to a very large extent, this country owes her greatness. His very eccentricities were wandering lights, which showed unsuspected heights and depths in his character—love of country and his country's honor, respect for the religion of his fathers, loyalty of mind, and valor for the right. Had he lived in other times, probably, like some of the old Boisseys who were at Honham before him, he would have died in the

Crusades or at Cressy, or perhaps, more uselessly, for his king at Marston Moor, or like that last, but one of the true De la Molles, kneeling in the courtyard of his castle, and defying his enemies to wring his secret from him. Now no such opportunities are left to men of his stamp, and they are, perhaps as a consequence, dying out of an age which is unsuited to them, and indeed to most strong growths of individual character. In fact, it would be much easier to deal with a gentleman like the squire of this history if we could only reach down one of those old suits of armor from the walls of his vestibule, and put it on his back, and take that long two-handled sword which last flashed on Flodden Field from its resting-place beneath the clock, and at the end see him die as a loyal knight should do, in the forefront of his retainers, with the old war-cry of "*a Delamol—a Delamol*" upon his lips. As it is, he is an aristocratic anachronism, an entity unfitted to deal with the elements of our advanced, and in some ways emasculated, age. His body should have been where his heart was—in the past. What chance have such as he against the Quests of this polite era of political economy and bi-metalism?

No wonder that Edward Cossey felt his inferiority to this symbol and type of the things that no more are, yes, even in the shadow of his thirty thousand pounds. For here we have a different breed. Goldsmiths two centuries ago, then bankers from generation to generation, money-bees seeking for wealth and counting it and hiving it from decade to decade, till at last money became to them what honor is to the nobler stock—the pervading principle; and the clink of the guinea and the rustling of the bank-note stirred their blood as the clang of armed men and the sound of the flapping banner, with its three golden hawks flaming in the sun, was wont to set the hearts of the race of Boissey, of Dofferleigh, and of De la Molle beating to that tune to which England marched on to win the world.

"It is a foolish and vain thing to scoff at business and those who do it in the market-places, and to shout out the old war-cries of our fathers in the face of a generation which sings the song of capital, or groans in heavy labor beneath the banners of their copyrighted trade-marks; and, besides, who would buy our books (also copyrighted, except in America)

if we did?   Let us rise up and clothe ourselves, and put a tall
hat upon our heads, and greet the new Democracy with a big
big D.   And yet, in the depth of our hearts and the quiet of
our chambers (after the gas is turned down and the ladies
have gone to bed), let us sometimes cry to the old times and
the old men and the old ways of thought, let us cry "*Ave
atque vale!*—Hail and farewell!"   Our fathers' armor hangs
above the door; their portraits, which, whatever else they
may be, we now know are not "art," decorate the wall; and
their fierce and half-tamed hearts moulder beneath the stones
of yonder church.   Hail and farewell to you our fathers!
Perchance a man might have had worse company than he met
with at your boards, and even have found it not more hard to
die beneath your sword-cuts, fighting for some cause which
to you, at any rate, appeared to be good and grand, than to
be gently cozened to the grave by duly qualified practitioners
at two guineas a visit.

And the upshot of all this is that the squire was not altogether wrong when he declared, in the silence of *his* chamber,
that Edward Cossey was not quite a gentleman.   He showed
it when he allowed himself to be guided by the arts of Mr.
Quest into the adoption of the idea of obtaining a lien upon
Ida, to be enforced if convenient.   He showed it again, and,
what is more, he committed a huge mistake when, tempted
thereto by the opportunity of the moment, he made a conditional bargain with the said Ida, whereby she was placed in
pledge for the sum of thirty thousand pounds, well knowing
that her honor would be equal to the test, and that, if convenient to him, she would be ready to pay the debt.   I say
he made a huge mistake, for, had he been quite a gentleman,
he would have known that he could not have adopted a worse
road to the affections of a lady.   Had he been content to advance the money, and then by and by, though even that
would not have been gentlemanlike, have gently let it transpire what he had done at great personal expense and incon-
venience, her imagination might have been touched, and her
gratitude would certainly have been excited.   But the idea
of bargaining, the idea of purchase, which, after what had
passed, could never be put aside, would of necessity be fatal
to any hope of tender feeling.   Shylock might get his bond,

but of his own act he had debarred himself from the possibility of ever getting more.

Now Edward Cossey was not lacking in that afterglow of refinement which is left behind by a course of public-school and university education. No education can make a gentleman of a man who is not a gentleman at heart, for whether his station in life be that of a ploughboy or an earl, the gentleman, like the poet, is born, and not made. But it can, and does, if he be of an observant nature, give him a certain insight into the habits of thought and probable course of action of the members of that class to which he outwardly, and by repute, belongs. Such an insight Edward Cossey possessed, and at the present moment its possession was troubling him very much. His trading instincts, the desire bred in him to get something for his money, had led him to make the bargain, but now that it was done his better judgment rose up against it. For the truth may as well be told at once, although he would as yet scarcely acknowledge it to himself. Edward Cossey was already violently enamoured of Ida. He was by nature a passionate man, and, as it chanced, she had proved the magnet with power to draw his passion. But, as the reader is aware, there existed another complication in his life for which he was not perhaps entirely responsible. When still quite a youth in mind he had suddenly found himself the object of the love of a beautiful and enthralling woman, and he had, after a more or less severe struggle, yielded to the temptation, as, out of a book, many young men would have done. Now to be the object of the violent affection of such a woman as Belle Quest is no doubt very flattering and even charming for a while. But if that affection is not returned in kind, if, in short, the gentleman does not love the lady quite as warmly as she loves him, then in course of time the charm is apt to vanish, and even the flattery to cease to please. Also, when, as in the present case, the connection is wrong in itself, and universally condemned by society, the affection which can still triumph and endure on both sides must be of a very strong and lasting order. Even an unprincipled man dislikes the acting of one long lie such as an intimacy of the sort necessarily involves, and if the man happens to be rather weak than unprincipled, the dislike is apt to turn to loathing, some portion of which will certainly in time be reflected on to the partner of his ill-doing.

These are general principles, but the case of Edward Cossey offered no exception to them, indeed, it illustrated them very well. He had never been in love with Mrs. Quest; to begin with, she had shown herself too much in love with him to necessitate any display of emotion on his part. Her violent and unreasoning passion wearied and alarmed him; he never knew what she would do next, and was kept in a continual condition of anxiety and irritation as to what the morrow might bring forth. Too sure of her unaltering attachment to have any pretext for jealousy, he found it exceedingly irksome to be obliged to avoid giving cause for it on his side, which, however, he dreaded doing lest he should thereby bring about some overwhelming catastrophe. Mrs. Quest was, as he well knew, not a woman who would pause to consider consequences if once her passionate jealousy was really aroused. It was even doubtful if the certainty of her own ruin would check her. Her love was everything to her; it was her life, the thing she lived for, and rather than tamely lose it, it seemed extremely probable to Edward Cossey that she would not hesitate to face shame, or even death. Indeed, it was by means of this great passion of hers, and by its means only, that he could hope to influence her. If he could persuade her to release him by pointing out that a continuance of the intrigue must involve him in ruin of some sort, all might yet go well with him. If not, his future was a dark one.

This was the state of affairs before he became attached to Ida de la Molle, after which the horizon grew blacker than ever. At first he tried to get out of the difficulty by avoiding Ida, but it did not answer. She exercised an irresistible attraction over him. Her calm and stately presence was to him what the sight of mountain snows is to one scorched by continual heat. He was weary of passionate outbursts, tears, agonies, alarms, presentiments, and all the paraphernalia of secret love. It appeared to him, looking up at the beautiful snow, that if once he could reach it life would be all sweetness and light; that there would be no more thirst, no more fear, and no more forced marches through those ill-odored quagmires of deceit. The more he allowed his imagination to dwell upon the picture, the fiercer grew his longing to possess it. Also, he knew well enough that to marry a woman like Ida de la Molle would be the greatest blessing that could happen to him, for she would of necessity lift him up above himself. She had no money, it was true, but that was a very minor matter to him; but she had birth and breeding and beauty, and that presence which commands homage. And so it came to pass that he fell deeply and yet more deeply in love with Ida, and that as he did so his connection with Mrs. Quest (although we have seen him but yesterday offering, in a passing fit of tenderness and remorse, to run away with her) became more and more irksome to him. And now, as he drove leisurely back to Boisingham, he felt that he had imperilled all his hopes by a rash indulgence in his trading instincts.

Presently the road he was following took a turn, and revealed a sight that did not tend to improve his already irritable mood. Just here the roadway was bordered by a deep bank covered with trees, which sloped down to the valley of the Ell, at this time of the year looking its loveliest in the soft autumn lights. And here, seated on a slope of turf beneath the shadow of a yellowing chestnut-tree, in such a position as to get a view of the green valley and flashing river, where cattle red and white stood chewing the still luxuriant aftermath, was none other than Ida herself, and, what was more, Ida accompanied by Colonel Quaritch. They were seated on camp-stools, and in front of each of them was an easel. Clearly they were painting together, for, even as Edward gazed the colonel rose, came up close behind his companion's stool, made a ring of his thumb and first finger, gazed critically through it at the lady's performance, and then sadly shook his head and made some remark, whereupon Ida turned round and commenced an animated discussion.

"Hang me," said Edward to himself, "if she has not taken up with that confounded old military frump. Painting together! Ah, I know what that means. Well, I should have thought that if there was one man more than another whom she would have disliked, it would have been that battered-looking colonel." He pulled up his horse and reflected for a moment, then handed the reins to his servant, jumped out, and, climbing through a gap in the fence, walked up to the

tree where the pair were sitting. So engrossed were they in
their argument that they neither saw nor heard him.

" It's nonsense, Colonel Quaritch, perfect nonsense, if you
will forgive me for saying so," Ida was saying with warmth.
" It is all very well for you to complain that my trees are a
blur, and the castle nothing but a splotch, but I am looking
at the water, and if I am looking at the water, it is quite impossible that I should see the trees and the cows otherwise
than·I have rendered them on the canvas. True art is to
paint what the painter sees and as he sees it."

Colonel Quaritch shook his head and sighed.

" The cant of the impressionist school," he said, sadly ;
" on the contrary, the business of the artist is to paint what
he knows to be there ;" and he gazed complacently at his own
canvas, which had the appearance of a spirited drawing of a
fortified place, or of the contents of a child's Noah's ark, so
stiff, so solid, so formidable were its outlines, trees, and
animals.

Ida shrugged her shoulders, laughed merrily, and turned
round to find herself face to face with Edward Cossey. She
started back, and her face hardened ; then she stretched out
her hand, and said, " How do you do ?" in her very coldest tones.

" How do you do, Miss De la Molle ?" he said, assuming as
unconcerned an air as he could, and bowing stiffly to Harold
Quaritch, who returned the bow and went back to his canvas,
which was placed a few paces off.

" I saw you painting," went on Edward Cossey, in a low
tone, " so I thought I would come and tell you that I have
settled that matter with Mr. De la Molle."

" Oh, indeed," answered Ida, hitting viciously at a wasp with
her paint-brush.   " Well, I hope that you will find the investment a satisfactory one.   And now, if you please, do not let
us talk any more about money, because I am quite tired of
the subject."   Then, raising her voice, she went on, " Come
here, Colonel Quaritch, and Mr. Cossey shall judge between
us," and she pointed to her picture.

Edward glanced at the colonel with no amiable air, " I know
nothing about art," he said, " and I am afraid I must be getting on. Good-morning," and, taking off his hat to Ida, he
turned and went.

"Umph!" said the colonel, looking after him with a quizzical expression, "that gentleman seems rather short in his temper. Wants knocking about the world a bit, I should say. But I beg your pardon, I suppose that he is a friend of yours, Miss De la Molle?"

"He is an acquaintance of mine," answered Ida, with emphasis.

CHAPTER XIV.

THE TIGER SHOWS HER CLAWS.

AFTER this very chilling reception at the hands of the object of his affection, Edward Cossey, as may be imagined, continued his drive in an even worse temper than before. He reached his rooms, had some luncheon, and then, in pursuance of a previous engagement, went over to the Oaks to see Mrs. Quest.

He found her waiting for him in the drawing-room. She was standing at the window with her hands behind her, a favorite attitude of hers. As soon as the door was shut, she turned, came up to him, and grasped his hand affectionately between her own.

"It is an age since I have seen you, Edward," she said, "one whole day. Really, when I do not see you, I do not live, I only exist."

He freed himself from her clasp with a quick movement. "Really, Belle," he said, impatiently, "you might be a little more careful than to go through that sort of performance in front of an open window—especially as the gardener must have seen the whole thing."

"I don't care much if he did," she said, defiantly. "What does it matter? My husband is certainly not in a position to make a fuss about other people."

"What does it matter?" he said, stamping his foot. "What does it *not* matter? If you have no care for your good name, do you suppose that I am indifferent to mine."

Mrs. Quest opened her large violet eyes to the fullest extent, and a curious light was reflected from them.

"You have grown wonderfully careful all of a sudden, Edward," she said, meaningly.

"What is the use of my being careful when you are so reckless? I tell you what it is, Belle, we are talked of all over this gossiping town, and I don't like it; and, what is more, once and for all, I won't have it. If you will not be more careful I will break with you altogether, and that is the long and short of it."

"Where have you been this morning?" she asked, in the same ominously calm voice.

"I have been to Honham Castle on a matter of business."

"Oh, and yesterday you were there on a matter of pleasure. Now, did you happen to see Ida in the course of your business?"

"Yes," he answered, looking her full in the face, "I did see her; what about it?"

"By appointment, I suppose."

"No, not by appointment. Have you done your catechism?"

"Yes; and now I am going to preach a homily on it. I see through you perfectly, Edward. You are getting tired of me, and you want to be rid of me. I tell you plainly that you are not going the right way to work about it. No woman, especially if she be in my—unfortunate position, can tamely bear to see herself discarded for another. Certainly I cannot, and I caution you — I caution you to be careful, because when I think of such a thing I am not quite myself," and suddenly, and without the slightest warning (for her face had been hard and cold as stone) she burst into a flood of tears.

Now Edward Cossey, being but a man, was somewhat broken down at this sight. Of course he did his best to console her, though with no great results, for she was still sobbing bitterly, when suddenly there came a knock at the door. Mrs. Quest turned her face towards the wall and pretended to be reading a letter, and he tried to look as unconcerned as possible.

"A telegram for you, sir," said the girl, with a sharp glance at her mistress. "The telegraph boy brought it on here, when he found that you were not at home, because he said he would be sure to find you here; and please, sir, he hopes that you will give him sixpence for bringing it round, as he thought it might be important."

Edward felt in his pocket and gave the girl a shilling, telling her to say that there was no answer. As soon as she was gone he opened the telegram and started. It was from his sister in London, and ran as follows:

"Come up to town at once. Father has had a stroke of paralysis. Shall expect you by the seven o'clock train."

"What is it?" said Mrs. Quest, noting the alarm on his face.

"Why, my father is very ill. He has had a stroke of paralysis, and I must go to town by the next train."

"Shall you be long away?"

"I do not know. How can I tell? Good-by, Belle. I am sorry that we should have had this scene just as I am going, but I can't help it."

"Oh, Edward," she said, catching him by the arm and turning her tear-stained face up towards his own, "you are not angry with me, are you? Do not let us part in anger. How can I help being jealous when I love you so? Tell me that you do not hate me, or I shall be wretched all the time that you are away."

"No, no, of course not; but I must say that I wish that you would not make such shocking scenes—good-by."

"Good-by," she answered, as she gave him her shaking hands. "Good-by, my dear. If only you knew what I feel here," she pointed to her breast, "you would make excuses for me." Almost before she had finished her sentence he was gone. She stood near the door, listening to his retreating footsteps, till they had quite died away, and then flung herself in the chair and rested her head upon her hands. "I shall lose him," she said to herself in the bitterness of her heart. "I know I shall. What chance have I against her? He already cares for Ida a great deal more than he does for me; in the end he will break from me and marry her some time. Oh, I had rather see him dead, and myself too."

Half an hour later Mr. Quest came in.

"Where is Cossey?" he asked.

"Mr. Cossey's father has had a stroke of paralysis, and he has gone up to London to look after him."

"Oh!" said Mr. Quest. "Well, if the old gentleman dies, your friend will be one of the wealthiest men in England."

"Well, so much the better for him. I am sure money is a great blessing. It protects one from so much."

"Yes," said Mr. Quest, with emphasis, "so much the better for him, and all connected with him. Why have you been crying? Because Cossey has gone away—or have you quarrelled with him?"

"How do you know that I have been crying? If I have, it's my affair. At any rate, my tears are my own."

"Certainly they are; I do not wish to interfere with your crying; cry when you like. It will be lucky for Cossey if that old father of his dies just now, because he wants money."

"What does he want money for?"

"Because he has undertaken to pay off the mortgages on the Castle estates."

"Why has he done that, as an investment?"

"No, it is a rotten investment. I believe that he has done it because he is in love with Miss De la Molle, and is naturally anxious to ingratiate himself with her. Don't you know that? I thought perhaps that was what you had been crying about?"

"It is not true," she answered, her lips quivering with pain.

Mr. Quest laughed gently. "I think you must have lost your power of observation, which used to be sufficiently keen. However, of course, it does not matter to you. It will, in many ways, be a most suitable marriage, and I am sure they will make a very handsome couple."

She made no answer, and turned her back to hide the workings of her face. For a few moments her husband stood looking at her, with a gentle smile playing on his refined features. Then remarking that he must go round to the office, but would be back in time for tea, he went, reflecting with satisfaction that he had given his wife something to think about which would be scarcely to her taste.

As for Belle Quest, she waited till the door had closed, and then turned round towards it and spoke aloud, as though she were addressing her vanished husband.

"I hate you," she said, with bitter emphasis. "I hate you. You have ruined my life, and now you torment me as though I were a lost soul. Oh, I wish I were dead! I wish I were dead."

On reaching his office, Mr. Quest found two letters for him, one of which had just arrived by the afternoon post. The first was addressed in the squire's handwriting and signed with his big seal, and the other bore a superscription the sight of which made him turn momentarily faint. Taking up this last with a visible effort, he opened it. It ran as follows:

"DEAR BILL,—No answer this morning. I hope you ain't up to any of your tricks about the tin, because I won't stand it, and that's all. I told you that I had dropped all my oof, not that I had much out of you this year, only five hundred, and a beggarly twenty pound on my birthday, and what I make at the Birmingham—four pound ten a week, and hard work for that. I'm cleaned out, and that's all about it. Only just now a brute of a fellow came in with a summons for rates, and I told him that my friend, that means you, Bill dear, was going to come down handsome in a day or two. He would not believe it—just as though he knew what a mean lot you were—so I told him to bundle out double quick, or I'd heave the coal-shoot at his head; and he went, you bet, but he'll be back before long with the summons. I say the coal-shoot, for there ain't no coals in it, and I can't afford any money to get a bit of fire to warm my bones with. Then there's the landlord says he'll distrain for the rent, unless it's paid up in double-quick time. And so the long and short of it is, that if I don't get about five hundred quid out of you in the course of next week, I'll know the reason why. And I'll just be plain with you, Bill, my old boy. If I don't see the color of that money by this day week, why, I tell you what I am going to do. I'm going to take a little country air; my complexion wants it, and I think Boisingham would suit first-rate. In fact, I shall come down and pay you a visit, old boy, so perhaps you'll ask the lovely Mrs. Quest to get a room ready for me; and when I get down there, if I don't tell all the old respectables a thing or two about their beloved lawyer, and generally make them sit up and see stars, why, I aint I. And now there's the straight tip for you from your affectionate 'Tiger.' But remember she'd always rather purr than growl. It's only when the cash don't come down that her back goes up. All a question of money, my boy, like everything else in this wicked world.
                     "Your beloved   EDITH."

By the time that Mr. Quest had finished reading this precious effusion, the cold sweat was standing in beads on his forehead.

"Great heavens!" he said, "this woman will destroy me. What a devil! And she'd be as good as her word unless I found her the money. I must go up to town at once. I wonder how she got that idea into her head. It makes me shudder to think of such a thing," and he dropped his face upon his hands and groaned in the bitterness of his heart.

"It is hard," he thought to himself; "here I have for years and years been striving and toiling and laboring to become a respectable and respected member of society, and always this old folly haunts my steps and drags me down, and, by Heaven, I believe that it will destroy me after all." With a sigh he lifted his head, and, taking a sheet of paper, wrote on it, "I have received your letter, and will come and see you to-morrow or the next day." This letter he placed in an envelope, which he directed to the high-sounding name of Mrs. D'Aubigné, Stanley St., Pimlico—and put it in his pocket.

Then with another sigh he took up the squire's letter, and glanced through it. Its length was considerable, but in substance it announced his acceptance of the arrangement proposed by Mr. Edward Cossey, and requested that he would prepare the necessary deeds to be submitted to his lawyers. Mr. Quest read the letter absently enough, and threw it down with a little laugh.

"What a queer world it is," he said to himself, "and what a ludicrous side it has to it all! Here is Cossey advancing money to get a hold over Ida de la Molle, whom he means to marry if he can, and who is probably playing her own hand. Here is Belle madly in love with Cossey, who will break her heart. Here am I in love with Belle, who hates me, and playing everybody's game in order to advance my own, and become a venerated member of a society I am superior to. Here is the squire blundering about like a walrus in a horse-pond, and fancying everything is being conducted for his sole advantage, and that all the world revolves round Honham Castle. And then here at the end of the chain is this female harpy, Edith Jones, otherwise D'Aubigné, *alias* the Tiger, gnawing at my vitals and holding my fortunes in her hand.

"Bah! it is a queer world and full of combinations, but the worst of it is that plot as we will the solution of them does not rest with us, no—not with us."

CHAPTER XV.

This is a troublesome world enough, but thanks to that mitigating fate which now and again interferes to our advantage, there do come to most of us times and periods of our existence which, if they do not quite fulfil all the conditions of ideal happiness, yet go near enough to that end to permit in after-days of our imagining that they did so. I say to most of us, but in doing so I allude chiefly to those classes commonly known as the "upper," by which is understood those who have enough bread to put into their mouths and clothes to warm them; those, too, who are not the present subjects of remorseless and hideous ailments, who are not daily agonized by the sight of their famished offspring; who are not doomed to beat out their lives against the madhouse bars, or to see their hearts' beloved and their most cherished hope wither towards that cold space from whence no message comes. For such unfortunates, and for their million-numbered kin upon the globe—the victims of war, famine, slave-trade, oppression, usury, over-population, and the curse of competition, the rays of light must be few indeed; few and far between, only just enough to save them from utter hopelessness. And even to the favored ones, the well-warmed and well-fed, who are to a great extent lifted by fortune or by their native strength and wit above the degradations of the world, this light of happiness is but as the gleam of stars, uncertain, fitful, and continually lost in clouds. Only the utterly selfish or the utterly ignorant can be happy with the happiness of savages or children, however prosperous their own affairs, for to the rest, those who think and have hearts to feel, and imagination to realize, and a redeeming human sympathy to be touched, the mere weight of the world's misery pressing round them like an atmosphere, the mere echoes of the groans of the dying

and the cries of the children are sufficient, and more than
sufficient, to dull, ay, to destroy, the promise of their joys.
But, still, even to this finer sort there do come rare periods
of almost complete happiness—little summers in the tempestu-
ous climate of our years, green-fringed wells of water in our
desert, pure northern lights breaking in upon our gloom.
And strange as it may seem, these breadths of happy days,
when the old questions cease to torment, and a man can trust
in Providence and without one qualifying thought bless the
day that he was born, are very frequently connected with
the passion that is known as love ; that mysterious symbol of
our double nature, that strange tree of life which, with its
roots sucking their strength from the dust heap of humanity,
yet springs aloft above our highest level, and bears its blooms
in the very face of heaven.

Why it is and what it means we shall never know for certain, but it does suggest, itself, that as the greatest terror of
our being lies in the utter loneliness, the unspeakable identity,
and unchanging self-completeness of every living soul, so the
greatest hope and the intensest natural yearning of our hearts
go out towards that passion which in its fire-heats has the
strength, if only for a little while, to melt down the barriers of
our individuality, and give to the soul something of the power
for which it yearns of losing its sense of solitude in converse
with its kind.   For alone we are from infancy to death !—we,
for the most part, grow not more near together but rather
wider apart with the widening years.   Where go the sympathies between the parent and the child, and where is the close
old love of brother for his brother ?

The invisible fates are continually wrapping us round and
round with the winding-sheets of our solitude, and none may
know all our heart save He who made it.   We are set upon
the world as the stars are set upon the sky, and though in following our fated orbits we pass and repass, and each shine out
on each, yet are we the same lonely lights, rolling along
obedient to laws we cannot understand, through those great
spaces of which none may mark the limit.

Only, as says the poet in words of truth and beauty :

> " Only but this is rare—
> When a beloved hand is laid in ours,

When, jaded with the rush and glare
Of the interminable hours,
Our eyes can in another's eyes read clear;
When our world-deafened ear
Is by the tones of a loved voice caressed,
A bolt is shot back somewhere in our breast,
And a lost pulse of feeling stirs again—
What we mean we say and what we would we know.

"And then he thinks he knows
The hills where his life rose
And the sea whereunto it goes."

Some such Indian summer of delight and forgetfulness of
trouble, and the tragic conditions of our days, was now opening to Harold Quaritch and Ida de la Molle. Every day or
almost every day they met and went upon their painting ex-
peditions and argued the point of the validity or otherwise of
the impressionist doctrine of art. Not that of all this painting came anything very wonderful, although in the evening the
colonel in the silence of his chamber would take out his can-
vases and contemplate their rigid proportions with singular
pride and satisfaction. It was a little weakness of his to think
that he could paint, and one of which he was somewhat tenacious. He was, like many another, a man who could do a
number of things exceedingly well and one thing very badly,
and yet had more faith in that one bad thing than in all the
good.

And still, strange to say, although he affected to believe so
firmly in his own style of art and hold Ida's in such cheap regard, it was a little painting of the latter's that was most dear
to him, and which was most often put upon his easel for purposes of solitary admiration. It was one of those very impressionist productions that faded away in the distance and
full of soft gray tints, such as his soul loathed, and had a tree
with a blot of brown color on it, and altogether (though as a
matter of fact a clever thing enough) from his point of view
of art utterly " anathema." This little picture in oils faintly
shadowed out himself sitting at his easel, working in the soft
gray of the autumn evening, and Ida had painted it and given
it to him, and that was why he admired it so much. For to
speak the truth our friend the colonel was going, going fast—

sinking out of sight of his former self into the depths of the love that possessed his soul.

He was a very simple-minded and a pure man. Strange as it may appear, since that first unhappy business of his youth, of which he had never been heard to speak, no living woman had been anything to him. Therefore, instead of becoming further vulgarized and hardened by association with all the odds and ends of womankind that a man travelling about the globe comes in contact with, generally not greatly to his improvement, his faith had had time to grow up stronger even than before, and he once more looked upon woman as a young man looks before he has had experience of the world, as a being to be venerated and almost worshipped, as something better, brighter, purer than himself, hardly to be won, and when won to be worn like a jewel prized at once for value and for beauty.

Now this is a dangerous state of mind for a man of three or four and forty to fall into, because it is a soft state, and this is a world in which the softest are apt to get the worst of it, and at four-and-forty a man, of course, should be hard enough to get the better of other people, as indeed he generally is.

When Harold Quaritch, after all that long interval of years, first set eyes again upon Ida's face, he felt a curious change come over him. All the vague ideas and more or less poetical aspirations which for five long years had gathered themselves round about that memory took shape and form, and though as yet he would not quite confess it, in his heart he knew that he loved her. And as the days went on, and he came to know her better, he grew to love her more and more, till, at last, his whole heart went out towards his late-found treasure, and she grew to him to be more than life, more than aught had been, or could be. Blue and happy were those days which they spent in painting and talking, as they wandered about the Honham Castle grounds. By degrees Ida's slight but perceptible hardness of manner wore away, and she stood out what she was, one of the sweetest and most natural women in England, and, with it all, a woman having brains and force of character.

Soon he discovered that her life had been anything but an

easy one. The constant anxiety about money and her father's affairs had worn her down and hardened her till, as she said, she began to feel as though she had no heart left. Then, too, he heard all her trouble about her dead and only brother James, how dearly she had loved him, and what a sore trouble he had been with his extravagant ways and his continual demands for money, which had to be met somehow or other. At last came the crushing blow of his death, and with it the certainty of the extinction of the male line of the De la Molles, and she said that for a while she had believed her father would never hold up his head again. But his vitality was equal to the shock, and after a while the debts began to come in, which, although he was not legally bound to do so, her father would insist upon meeting to the last farthing, for the honor of the family and out of respect for his son's memory, and there was more trouble about money, that had gone on and on, always getting worse as the agricultural depression deepened, till things had reached their present position. All this she told him bit by bit, keeping back from him only the last development of the drama and the part that Edward Cossey had played in it, and sad enough it made him to think of that ancient house of De la Molle vanishing into the night of ruin.

Also, she told him something of her own life, how companionless it had been since her brother went into the army, for she had no real friends about Honham, and not even an acquaintance of her own tastes, which, without being gushingly so, were decidedly artistic and intellectual. "I should have liked," she said, "to have tried to do something in the world. I dare say that I should have failed, for I know that very few women meet with a success that is worth having. But still I should have liked to try, for I am not afraid of work. But the current of my life is against it, and the only thing that is open to me is to try and make both ends meet upon an income that is always growing smaller, and to save my father, poor old dear, from as much worry as I can."

"Don't think that I am complaining," she went on, hurriedly, "or that I want to rush into pleasure-seeking, because I don't—a little of that goes a long way with me. Besides, I know that I have many things to be thankful for. Few women have such a kind father as I have, though we do quarrel at times, and of course we cannot have everything our own way in this world, and I dare say that I do not make the best of things. Still, at times, it does seem a little hard to have to lead such a narrow life, just when I feel that I could work in a wide one."

Harold looked up in her face, and saw that a tear was gathering in her dark eyes, and in his heart he registered a vow that if, by any means, it ever lay within his power to improve her lot, he would give everything he had to do it. But all he said was:

" Don't be downhearted, Miss De la Molle. Things change in a wonderful way, and often they mend when they look worst. You know," he went on, a little nervously, " I am an old-fashioned sort of individual, and I believe in Providence and all that sort of thing, you see, and that things generally come pretty straight in the long run, if people deserve it."

Ida shook her head a little doubtfully and sighed.

" Perhaps," she said, " but I suppose that we do not deserve it. Anyhow, our good-fortune is a long while coming," and the conversation dropped.

Still, her friend's strong belief in the efficacy of Providence, and generally his masculine sturdiness, did cheer her up considerably. Even the strongest women, if they have any element that can be called feminine left in them, want somebody of the other sex to lean on, and Ida was no exception to the rule. Besides, if Ida's society had charms for Colonel Quaritch, his society had almost if not quite as much charm for her. It may be remembered that on the night that they first met she had spoken to herself of him as the kind of man whom she would like to marry. The thought was a passing one, and it may be safely said that she had not since entertained any serious idea of marriage in connection with Colonel Quaritch. The only person whom there seemed the slightest probability of her marrying was Edward Cossey, and the mere thought of this was enough to make the whole idea of matrimony repugnant to her.

But this notwithstanding, day by day she found Harold Quaritch's society more congenial. Herself by nature, and also to a certain degree by education, a cultured woman, she rejoiced to find in him an entirely kindred spirit. For beneath his somewhat rugged and unpromising appearance Harold Quaritch hid a nature of considerable richness. Few of those who associated with him would have believed that the man had a side to his nature which was almost poetic, or that he was a ripe and finished scholar, and, what is more, not devoid of a certain dry humor. Then he had travelled far, and seen much of men and manners, gathering up all sorts of quaint odds and ends of information. But, perhaps, above these accomplishments, it was the man's transparent honesty and simple-mindedness, his love for what was true and noble, and his contempt and scorn for what was mean and base, which, unwittingly peeping out through his conversation, attracted her more than all the rest. Ida was no more a young girl to be caught by a handsome face or dazzled by a superficial show of mind. She was a thoughtful, ripened woman, quick to perceive, and with the rare talent of judgment wherewith to weigh the proceeds of her perception, and in plain, middle-aged Colonel Quaritch she found a very perfect gentleman, and valued him accordingly.

And so day grew into day in that lovely autumn-tide, and Edward Cossey was away in London, and Quest had ceased from troubling, and journeying together through the sweet shadows of companionship, by slow but sure degrees they drew near to the sunlit plain of love. For it is not common, indeed it is so uncommon as to draw near to the impossible, that a man and woman between whom there stands no natural impediment can halt for very long in those shadowed ways ; there is throughout all nature an impulse that pushes ever onward towards completion, and from completion to fruition. Liking leads to sympathy, and sympathy points the path to love, and then love demands its own. This is the order of affairs, and down its well-trodden road these two were quickly travelling.

George the wily saw it, and winked his eye with solemn meaning. The squire also saw something of it, not being wanting in knowledge of the world, and after much cogitation and many long walks he elected to leave matters alone for the present. He liked Colonel Quaritch, and he thought it would be a good thing for Ida to get married, though the idea of parting from her troubled his heart sorely. Whether or no it would be desirable from his point of view that she should marry the colonel was a point on which he had not, at any rate as yet, fully made up his mind. Sometimes he thought it would, and sometimes the reverse. Then, at times, vague ideas suggested by Edward Cossey's behavior about the loan would come to puzzle him. But as yet he was so much in the dark that he could come to no absolute decision, so with unaccustomed wisdom for so headstrong and precipitate a man, he determined to refrain from interference, and for the present, at any rate, to let events take their natural course.

CHAPTER XVI.

THE HOUSE WITH THE RED PILLARS.

Two days after his receipt of the second letter from the "Tiger," Mr. Quest announced to his wife that he was going to London on business connected with the bank, and expected to be away for a couple of nights.

She laughed straight out. "Really, William," she said, "you are a most consummate actor. I wonder that you think it worth while to keep up the farce with me. Well, I hope that Edith is not going to be very expensive this time, because we don't seem to be too rich just now, and you see there is no more of my money for her to have."

Mr. Quest winced visibly beneath this bitter satire, which his wife uttered with a smile of infantile innocence playing upon her face, but he made no reply. She knew too much. Only in his heart he wondered what fate she would mete out to him if ever she got possession of the whole truth, and the thought made him tremble. It seemed to him that the owner of that baby face could be terribly merciless in her vengeance, and that those soft white hands would close round the throat of a man she hated, and utterly destroy him. Now, if never before, he realized that between him and this woman there must be enmity, and a struggle to the death; and yet, strangely enough, he still loved her!

Mr. Quest reached London about three o'clock, and his first act was to drive to Cossey & Son's, where he was informed that old Mr. Cossey was much better, and having heard that he was coming to town had sent to say that he particularly wished to see him, especially about the Honham Castle estates. Accordingly, Mr. Quest drove on to the old gentleman's mansion in Grosvenor Street, where he asked for Mr. Edward Cossey. The footman said that Mr. Edward was upstairs, and showed him into a study while he went to tell him

of the arrival of his visitor. Mr. Quest glanced round the
luxuriantly furnished room, which he saw was occupied by
Edward himself, for some letters directed in his handwriting
lay upon the desk, and a velveteen lounging-coat that Mr.
Quest recognized as belonging to him was hanging over the
back of a chair. Mr. Quest's eye, wandering over this coat,
was presently caught by the corner of a torn flap of an envelope which projected from one of the pockets. It was of
a peculiar bluish tinge, in fact, of a hue which was much affected by his wife. Listening for a moment, to hear if anybody was coming, he stepped to the coat and extracted the
letter. It *was* in his wife's handwriting, so he took the liberty of hastily transferring it to his own pocket. In another
minute Edward Cossey entered, and the two men shook hands.

"How do you do, Quest?" said Edward. "I think that
the old man is going to pull through this bout. He is helpless but keen as a knife, and has all the important matters
from the bank referred to him. I believe that he will last a
year yet, but he will scarcely allow me out of his sight. He
preaches away about business the whole day long, and says
that he wants to communicate the fruits of his experience to
me before it is too late. He wishes to see you, so, if you
will, you had better come up."

Accordingly, they went up-stairs to a large and luxurious
bedroom on the first floor, where the stricken man lay upon
a patent couch.

When Mr. Quest and Edward Cossey entered, a lady, old
Mr. Cossey's eldest daughter, put down a paper out of which
she had been reading the money article aloud, and, rising,
informed her father that Mr. Quest had come.

"Mr. Quest?" said the old man, in a thin voice. "Ah,
yes, I want to see Mr. Quest very much. Go away, now,
Anna, you can come back by and by ; business before pleasure
—most instructive, though, that sudden fall in American rail-
ways. But I thought it would come, and I got Cossey & Son
clear of them," and he sniffed with satisfaction, and looked
as though he would have rubbed his hands if he had not been
physically incapacitated from so doing.

Mr. Quest came forward to where the invalid lay. He was
a gaunt old man, with white hair and a pallid face, which

looked almost ghastly in contrast to his black velvet skull-cap. So far as Mr. Quest could see, he appeared to be almost totally paralyzed, with the exception of his head, neck, and left arm, which he could still move a little. His black eyes, however, were full of life and intelligence, and roamed about the room without ceasing.

"How do you do, Mr. Quest?" he said; "sorry that I can't shake hands with you, but you see I have been stricken down, though my brain is clear enough, clearer than ever it was, I think. And I ain't going to die yet—don't think that I am, because I ain't. I may live two years more—the doctor says that I am sure to live one at least. A lot of money can be made in a year if you keep your eyes open. Once I made a hundred and twenty thousand for Cossey & Son in one year; and I may do it again before I die. I may make a lot of money, ah, a lot of money!" and his voice went off into a kind of thin scream that was not pleasant to listen to.

"I am sure I hope you will, sir," said Mr. Quest, politely.

"Thank you; take that for good luck, you know. Well, well, Mr. Quest, things haven't done so bad down in your part of the world; not at all bad considering the times. I thought we should have had to sell that old De la Molle up, but I hear that he is going to pay us off. Can't imagine who has been fool enough to lend him the money. A client of yours, eh? Well, he'll lose it, I expect, and serve him right for his pains. But I am not sorry, for it is unpleasant for a house like ours to have to sell an old client up. Not that his account is worth much, nothing at all—more trouble than profit —or we should not have done it. He's no better than a bankrupt, and the insolvency court is the best place for him. The world is to the rich and the fulness thereof. There's an insolvency court specially provided for De la Molle and his like—empty old windbags with long-sounding names; let him go there and make room for the men who have made money— hee! hee! hee!" And once more his voice went off into a sort of scream.

Here Mr. Quest, who had had about enough of this sort of thing, changed the conversation by commencing to comment on various business transactions which he had been conducting on behalf of the house. The old man listened with the

greatest interest, his keen black eyes attentively fixed upon
the speaker's face, till at last Mr. Quest happened to mention that, among others, a certain Colonel Quaritch had opened
an account with their branch of the bank.

"Quaritch?" said the old man, eagerly, "I know that
name. Was he ever in the 105th foot?"

"Yes," said Mr. Quest, who knew everything about everybody; "he was an ensign in that regiment during the Indian
Mutiny, where he was badly wounded when still quite young,
and got the Victoria Cross. I found it all out the other day."

"That's the man; that's the man," said old Mr. Cossey,
jerking his head in an excited manner. He's a blackguard;
I tell you he's a blackguard; he jilted my wife's sister. She
was twenty years younger than my wife—jilted her a week
before her marriage, and would never give a reason, and she
went mad and is in a madhouse now. I should like to have
the ruining of him for it. I should like to drive him into the
poor-house."

Mr. Quest and Edward looked at each other, and the old
man let his head fall back exhausted.

"Now good-by, Mr. Quest; they'll give you a bit of dinner
down-stairs," he said at length. "I'm getting tired, and I
want to hear the rest of that money article. You've done
very well for Cossey & Son, and Cossey & Son will do well
for you, for we always pay by results; that's the way to get
good work and make a lot of money. Mind, Edward, if ever
you get a chance don't forget to pay that blackguard Quaritch out pound for pound, and twice as much again for compound interest—hee! hee! hee!"

"The old gentleman keeps his head for business pretty
well," said Mr. Quest to Edward Cossey as soon as they were
well outside the door.

"Keeps his head?" answered Edward; "I should just think
he did. He's a regular shark now, that's what he is. I really believe that if he knew I had found that thirty thousand
for old De la Molle he would cut me off with a shilling."
Here Mr. Quest pricked up his ears. "And he's close, too,"
he went on, "so close that it is almost impossible to get anything out of him. I am not particular, but upon my word I
think that it is rather disgusting to see an old man with one

foot in the grave hanging on to his moneybags as though he expected to float to heaven on them."

"By the way," said Edward, as they entered the study, "that's queer about that fellow Quaritch, isn't it? I never liked the look of him, with his pious air."

"Very queer, Mr. Cossey," said Quest; "but, do you know, I almost think that there must be some mistake? I do not believe that Colonel Quaritch is the man to do things of that sort without a very good reason. However, nobody can tell, and it is a long while ago."

"A long while ago or not, I mean to let him know my opinion of him when I get back to Boisingham," said Edward, viciously.

"By Jove, it's twenty minutes past six, and in this establishment we dine at the pleasant hour of half-past. Won't you come and wash your hands."

Mr. Quest got a very good dinner, and, contrary to his custom, he drank the best part of a bottle of old port after it. He had an unpleasant business to face that evening, and felt as though his nerves required bracing. About ten o'clock he took his leave, and getting into a hansom bade the cabman drive to Stanley Street, Pimlico, where he arrived in due course. Having dismissed his cab, he walked slowly down the street till he reached a small house with red pillars to the doorway. Here he rang the bell. The door was opened by a middle-aged woman with a cunning face and a simper. Mr. Quest knew her well. Nominally the Tiger's servant, she was really her jackal, and in return for the intelligence she lent to the chase received her portion of the prey.

"Is Mrs. D'Aubigné at home, Ellen?" he said.

"No, sir," she answered, with a simper, "but she will be back from the music-hall before long. She does not appear in the second part. But please come in, sir; you are quite a stranger here, and I am sure that Mrs. D'Aubigné will be very glad to see you, for she have been dreadfully pressed for money of late, poor dear; nobody knows the trouble that I have had with those sharks of tradesmen."

By this time they were up-stairs in the drawing-room, and Ellen had turned the gas up. The room was well furnished in a certain gaudy style, which included a good deal of gilt

and plate glass. Evidently, however, it had not been tidied
since the Tiger had left it, for there on the table were cards
thrown this way and that amidst an array of empty soda-water bottles, glasses with dregs of brandy in them, and other
débris, such as the ends of cigars and cigarettes, and a little
copper and silver money. On the sofa, too, lay a gorgeous
tea-gown resplendent with pink satin, also a pair of gold em-
broidered slippers, not over small, and an odd *gant de Suéde*,
with such an extraordinary number of buttons that it almost
looked like the cast-off skin of a brown snake.

"I see that your mistress has been having company, Ellen,"
he said, coldly.

"Yes, sir, just a few lady friends in to cheer her up a bit,"
answered the woman, with her abominable simper; "poor
dear, she do get that low with you away so much, and no
wonder; and then all these money troubles, and she night by
night working hard for her living. Often and often have I
seen her crying over it all—"

"Ah," said he, breaking in upon her eloquence, "I suppose
that the lady friends smoke cigars. Well, clear away this
mess and leave me—stop, give me a brandy-and-soda first.
I will wait for your mistress."

The woman stopped talking and did as she was bid, for
there was a look in Mr. Quest's eye which she did not quite
like. So having placed the brandy and soda-water before
him she left him to his own reflections.

Apparently they were not very pleasant ones. He walked
round the room, which was reeking of patchouli or some such
compound, well mixed with the odor of stale cigar smoke,
looking absently at the gee-gaw ornaments. On the mantelpiece were some photographs, and among them, to his disgust,
he saw one of himself. With something as near an oath as
he ever indulged in, he seized it, and setting fire to it over the
gas, waited till the flames began to scorch his fingers, and
then flung it, still flaming, down into the grate. Then he
looked at himself in the glass over the mantelpiece—the room
was full of mirrors—and laughed bitterly at the incongruity
of his gentlemanlike, respectable, and even refined appearance,
in that vulgar, gaudy, vicious-looking room.

Suddenly he bethought him of the letter in his wife's handwriting which he had stolen from the pocket of Edward Cossey's coat. He drew it out, and, throwing the tea-gown and the interminable glove off the sofa, sat down and commenced to read it. It was, as he had expected, a love-letter, a wildly passionate love-letter, breathing language which in places almost touched the beauty of poetry, vows of undying affection that were throughout redeemed from vulgarity and even from silliness by their utter earnestness and self-abandonment. Had the letter been one written under happier circumstances and innocent of offence against morality, it would have been a beautiful letter, for passion at its highest has always a beauty of its own.

He read it through and then carefully folded it and restored it to his pocket. "The woman has a heart," he said to himself; "no one can doubt it. And yet I could never touch it, though God knows however much I wronged her I loved her, yes, and love her now. Well, it is a good bit of evidence, if ever I dare to use it. It is a game of bluff between me and her, and I expect that in the end the boldest player will win."

He rose from the sofa—the atmosphere of the place stifled him—and going to the window he threw it open and stepped out on to the balcony. It was a lovely moonlight night, though chilly, and for London the street was a quiet one.

Taking a chair, he sat down there upon the balcony and began to think. His heart was softened by misery, and his mind fell into a tender groove. He thought of his long-dead mother, whom he had dearly loved, and of how he used to say his prayers to her, and of how she sang hymns to him on Sunday evenings. Her death had seemed to choke all the beauty out of his being at the time, and yet now he thanked God that she was dead. And then he thought of the accursed woman who had been his ruin, and of how she had entered into his life and corrupted and destroyed him. Next there rose up before him a vision of Belle—Belle as he had first seen her, a maid of seventeen, the only child of that drunken old village doctor, now also long since dead—and of how the sight of her had for a while stayed the corruption of his heart, because he grew to love her. And then he married Belle by foul means, and the woman rose up in his path again, and he learned that his wife hated him with all the energy of her passionate heart. Then came degradation after degradation, and the abandonment of principle after principle, replaced only by a fierce craving for respectability and rest, a long, long struggle which ever ended in new lapses from the right, till at length he saw himself a hardened schemer, remorselessly pursued by a fury from whom there was no escape. And yet he knew that under other circumstances he might have been a good and happy man—leading an honorable life. But now all hope had gone, that which he was he must be till the end. He leaned his head upon the stone railing in front of him and wept; yes, wept in the anguish of his soul, praying to God for deliverance from the burden of his sins, and yet well knowing that he had none to hope for. For his chance was gone and his fate fixed.

CHAPTER XVII.

THE TIGRESS IN HER DEN.

PRESENTLY a hansom-cab came rattling down the street and pulled up at the door.

"Now for it," said Mr. Quest to himself, as he metaphorically shook himself together.

Next minute he heard a voice which he knew only too well, a loud high voice, say from the cab, "Well, open the door, stupid, can't you?"

"Certainly, my lady fair," replied another voice—a coarse, somewhat husky male voice—"adored Edithia, in one moment."

"Come, stow that rot and let me out," replied the adored Edithia, sharply; and in another moment a large man in evening clothes, a horribly vulgar, carnal-looking man, with red cheeks and a hanging under lip, emerged into the lamplight and turned to hand the lady out. As he did so the woman Ellen advanced from the doorway, and going to the cab door whispered something to its occupant.

"Hullo, Johnnie," said that lady, as she descended from the cab, so loudly that Mr. Quest on the balcony could hear every word, "you must be off; Mr. D'Aubigné has turned up, and perhaps he won't think three good company, so you had just best take this cab back again, my son, and that will save me the trouble of paying it. Come, cut."

"D'Aubigné," growled the flashy man with an oath, "what do I care about D'Aubigné? Advance, D'Aubigné, and all's well! You needn't be jealous of me, I'm a married man, I am——"

"Now stop that noise and be off. He's a lawyer and he might not freeze on to you: don't you understand?"

"Well, I'm a lawyer, too, and a pretty sharp one—*arcades ambo*," said Johnnie, with a coarse laugh; "and I tell you what it is, Edith, it ain't good enough to cart a fellow down into this howling wilderness and then send him away without even a drink; lend us another fiver at any rate. It ain't good enough, I say."

"Good enough or not you'll have to go, and you don't get any fivers out of me to-night. Now pack sharp, or I'll know the reason why," and she pointed towards the cab in a fashion that seemed to cow her companion, for without another word he turned and got into it.

"Where to, sir?" said the cabman.

"Oh, to hell or the Haymarket, it's all one," he growled, flinging himself back into the corner. In another moment the cab had turned, and he was gone, muttering curses as he went.

The woman, who was none other than Mrs. D'Aubigné, *alias* Edith Jones, *alias* the Tiger, turned and entered the house, accompanied by her servant, Ellen, and presently Mr. Quest heard the rustle of her satin dress upon the stairs. He stepped back into the darkness of the balcony and waited. She opened the door, entered, and closed it behind her, and then, a little dazzled by the light, stood for some seconds looking about for her visitor. She was a thin, tall woman, who might have been any age between forty and fifty, with the wrecks of a very fine agile-looking figure. Her face, which was plentifully bedaubed with paint and powder, was sharp, fierce, and handsome, and crowned with a mane of false yellow hair. Her eyes were cold and blue, her lips thin, and rather drawn, so as to show a double line of large and gleaming teeth. She was dressed in a rich and hideous tight-fitting gown of yellow satin, barred with black, and on her arms were long bright yellow gloves. She moved lightly and silently, and looked round her with a long searching gaze like that of a cat, and her general appearance conveyed an idea of hunger and wicked ferocity. Such was the outward appearance of the Tiger, and of a truth it justified her name. "Why, where the dickens has he got to?" she said aloud; "I wonder if he has given me the slip?"

"Here I am, Edith," said Mr. Quest, quietly, as he stepped from the balcony into the room.

"Oh, there you are, are you?" she said, "hiding away in the

dark—just like your nasty, mean ways. Well, my long-lost one, so you have come home at last, and brought the tin with you. Well, give us a kiss," and she advanced on him with her long arms outspread.

Mr. Quest shivered visibly, and, stretching out his hand, stopped her from coming near him.

"No, thank you," he said; "I don't like paint."

The taunt stopped her, and for a moment an evil light shone in her cold eyes.

"No wonder I have to paint," she said, "when I am so worn out with poverty and hard work—not like the lovely Mrs. Q., who has nothing to do all day except spend the money that I ought to have. I'll tell you what it is, my fine fellow, you had better be careful, or I'll have that pretty cuckoo out of her soft nest, and pluck her borrowed feathers off her, like the monkey did to the parrot."

"Perhaps you had better stop that talk, and come to business. I am in no mood for this sort of thing, Edith," and he turned round, shut the window, and drew the blind.

"Oh, all right; I'm agreeable, I'm sure. Stop a bit, though —I must have a brandy-and-soda first. I am as dry as a lime-kiln, and so would you be if you had to sing comic songs at a music-hall for a living. There, that's better," and she put down the empty glass and threw herself on to the sofa. "Now then, tune up as much as you like. How much tin have you brought?"

Mr. Quest sat down by the table, and then, as though suddenly struck by a thought, rose again, and, going to the door, opened it and looked out into the passage. There was nobody there, so he shut the door again, locked it, and then under cover of drawing the curtain which hung over it, slipped the key into his pocket.

"What are you at there?" said the woman, suspiciously.

"I was just looking to see that Ellen was not at the key-hole, that's all. It would not be the first time that I have caught her there."

"Just like your nasty low ways again," she said. "You've got some game on. I'll be bound that you have got some game on."

Mr. Quest seated himself again, and without taking any notice of this last remark began the conversation.

"I have brought you two hundred and fifty pounds," he said.

"Two hundred and fifty pounds!" she said, jumping up with a savage laugh. "No, my boy, you don't get off for that if I know it. Why, I owe all that this moment."

"You had better sit down and be quiet," he said, "or you will not get two hundred and fifty pence. In your own interest I recommend you to sit down."

There was something about the man's voice and manner that scared the female savage before him, fierce as she was, and she sat down.

"Listen," he went on, "you are continually complaining of poverty; I come to your house—your house, mind you, not your rooms, and I find the *débris* of a card-party lying about. I see champagne bottles freshly opened there in the corner. I see a dressing-gown on the sofa that must have cost twenty or thirty pounds. I hear some brute associate of yours out in the street asking you to lend him another 'fiver.' You complain of poverty and you have had over four hundred pounds from me this year alone, and I know that you can earn twelve pounds a week at the music-hall, and not five, as you say. No, do not trouble to lie to me, for I have made inquiries."

"Spying again," said the woman, with a sneer.

"Yes, spying, if you like; but there it is. And now to the point—I am not going on supplying you with money at this rate. I cannot do it, and I will not do it. I am going to give you two hundred and fifty pounds now, and as much every year, and not one farthing more."

Once more she sat up. "You must be mad," she said, in a tone that sounded more like a snarl than a human voice. "Are you such a fool as to believe that I will be put off with two hundred and fifty pounds a year—I, your legal wife? I'll have you in the dock first, in the dock for bigamy."

"Yes," he answered, "I do believe it, for a reason that I shall give you presently. But first I want to go through our joint history, very briefly, just to justify myself, if you like. Five-and-twenty years ago, or was it six-and-twenty, I was a boy of eighteen and you were a woman of twenty, a housemaid in my mother's house, and you made love to me. Then my mother was called away to nurse my brother who died at

school at Portsmouth, and I fell sick with scarlet fever, and
you nursed me through it—it would have been kinder if you
had poisoned me—and in my weak state you got a great hold
over my mind, and I became attached to you, and you were
handsome in those days.   Then you dared me to marry you,
and partly out of bravado, partly from affection, I took out a
license, to do which I made a false declaration that I was over
age, and gave a false name of the parishes in which we re-
sided.   Next day, half tipsy and not knowing what I did, I
went through the form of marriage with you, and a few days
afterwards my mother returned, observed that we were unduly
intimate, and dismissed you.   You went without a word as to
our marriage, which we both looked on as a farce, and for
years I lost sight of you.   Fifteen years afterwards, when I
had almost forgotten this adventure of my youth, I became
acquainted with a young lady with whom I fell in love, and
whose fortune, though not large, was enough to help me considerably in my profession as a country lawyer, in which I was
doing well.   I thought that you were dead, or that, if you
lived, the fact of my having made the false declaration of age
and locality would be enough to invalidate the marriage, as
would certainly have been the case if I had also made a false
declaration of names ; and my impulses and interests prompt-
ing me to take the risk, I married that lady.   Then it was that
you hunted me down, and then for the first time I did what I
ought to have done before, and took the best legal opinions
as to the validity of the former marriage, which, to my horror,
I found was undoubtedly a binding one.   You also took opinions and came to the same conclusion.   Since then the history
has been a simple one.   Out of my wife's fortune of ten thousand pounds I paid you no less than seven thousand as hush-
money, on your undertaking to leave the country for America,
and never return here again.   I should have done better to
face it out, but I feared to lose my position and practice.   You
left and wrote to me that you too had married in Chicago, but
in eighteen months you returned, having squandered every farthing of the money, when I found that the story of your marriage was an impudent lie."

"Yes," she put in, with a laugh, "and a rare time I had with
that seven thousand, too."

"You returned and demanded more blackmail, and I had no choice but to give and give and give. In eleven years you had something over twenty-three thousand pounds from me, and you continually demand more. I believe that you will admit that that is a truthful statement of the case," and he paused.

"Oh, yes," she said, "I am not going to dispute that, but what then? I am your wife, and you have committed bigamy; and if you don't go on paying me I'll have you in jail, and that's all about it, old boy. You can't get out of it any way, you nasty mean brute," she went on, raising her voice and drawing up her thin lips so as to show the white teeth beneath. "So you thought that you were going to play it down low on me in that fashion, did you? Well, you've just made a little mistake for once in your life, and I'll tell you what it is, you shall smart for it. I'll teach you what it is to leave your lawful wife to starve while you go and live with another woman in luxury. You can't help yourself; I can ruin you if I like. Supposing I go to a magistrate and ask for a warrant? What can you do to keep me quiet?"

Suddenly the virago stopped as though she were shot, and her fierce countenance froze into an appearance of terror, as well it might. Mr. Quest, who had been sitting listening to her with his hand over his eyes, had risen, and his face was as the face of a fiend, alight with an intense and quiet fury which seemed to be burning inwardly. On the mantelpiece lay a sharp-pointed Goorka knife, which one of Mrs. D'Aubigné's admirers, who had travelled, had presented to her. It was an awful-looking weapon, and keen-edged as a razor. This he had taken up and held in his right hand, and with it he was advancing towards her lying on the sofa.

"If you make a sound I will kill you at once," he said, speaking in a low and husky voice.

She had been paralyzed with terror, for like most bullies, male and female, she was a great coward, but the sound of his voice roused her, and the first note of a harsh screech had already issued from her lips, when he sprang upon her, and, placing the sharp point of the knife against her throat, pricked her with it. "Be quiet," he said, "or you are a dead woman."

She stopped screaming and lay there, her face twitching, and her eyes bright with terror.

"Now, listen," he said, in the same husky voice. "You incarnate fiend, you asked me just now how I could keep you quiet. I will tell you: I can keep you quiet by running this knife up to the hilt in your throat," and once more he pricked her with its point. "It would be murder," he went on, "but I do not care for that. You and others between you have not made my life so pleasant for me that I am especially anxious to preserve it. Now, listen. I will give you the two hundred and fifty pounds that I have brought, and you shall have the two hundred and fifty a year. But if you ever again attempt to extort more, or if you molest me, either by spreading stories against my character or by means of legal prosecution, or in any other way, I swear by the Almighty that I will murder you. I may have to kill myself afterwards—I don't care if I do, provided I kill you first. Do you understand me?—you tiger, as you call yourself. If I have to hunt you down as they do tigers, I will come up with you at last, and *kill* you. You have driven me to it, and, by Heaven, I will! Come, speak up, and tell me that you understand, or I may change my mind and do it now," and once more he touched her with the knife.

She rolled off the sofa on to the floor and lay there, writhing in abject terror, looking in the shadow of the table, where her long, lithe form was twisting about in its robe of yellow barred with black, more like one of the great cats from which she took her name than a human being. "Spare me," she gasped, "spare me—I don't want to die. I swear that I will never meddle with you again."

"I don't want your oaths, woman," answered the stern form bending over her with the knife. "A liar you have been from your youth up, and a liar you will be to the end. Do you understand what I have said?"

"Yes, yes, I understand. Ah! put away that knife, I can't bear it! It makes me sick."

"Very well, then, get up."

She tried to rise, but her knees would not support her, so she sat upon the floor.

"Now," said Mr. Quest, replacing the knife upon the mantelpiece, "here is your money," and he flung a bag of notes and gold into her lap, at which she clutched eagerly and almost automatically. " The two hundred and fifty pounds will be paid on the first of January in each year, and not one farthing more will you get from me. Remember what I tell you; try to molest me by word or act, and you are a dead woman; I forbid you even to write to me. Now go to the devil in your own way," and without another word he took up his hat and umbrella, walked to the door, unlocked it and went, leaving the Tiger huddled together upon the floor.

For half an hour or more the woman remained thus, the bag of money in her hand. Then she struggled to her feet, her face livid and her body shaking.

"Ugh!" she said, " I'm as weak as a cat. I thought he meant to do it that time, and he will too, for sixpence. He's got me there. I am afraid to die. I can't bear to die. It is better to lose the money than to die. Besides, if I blow on him he'll be put in chokey and I sha'n't be able to get anything out of him, and when he comes out he'll do for me." And then, losing her temper, she shook her fist in the air and broke out into a flood of language such as would neither be pretty to hear nor good to repeat.

Mr. Quest was a man of judgment. At last he had realized that in one way, and one only, can a wild beast be tamed, and that is by terror.

CHAPTER XVIII.

WHAT SOME HAVE FOUND SO SWEET.

TIME went on. Mr. Quest had been back at Boisingham for ten days or more, and was in better spirits than Belle (we can no longer call her his wife) had seen him in for years. Indeed, he felt as though ten years had been lifted off his back. He had taken a great and terrible decision, and had acted upon it, and it had been successful, for he knew that his evil genius was so thoroughly terrified that for a long while at least he would be free from her persecutions. But with Belle his relations remained as strained as ever.

Now that the reader is in the secret of Mr. Quest's life, it will perhaps help him to understand the apparent strangeness of his conduct with reference to his wife and Edward Cossey. It is quite true that Belle did not know the full extent of her husband's guilt. She did not know that he was not her husband, but she did know that nearly all of her little fortune had been paid over to another woman, and that woman a common, vulgar woman, as one of Edith's letters which had fallen into her hands by chance very clearly showed her. Therefore, had he attempted to expose her proceedings or even to control her actions, she had in her hand an effective weapon of defence wherewith she could and would have given blow for blow. This state of affairs of necessity forced each party to preserve an armed neutrality towards the other, while they waited for a suitable opportunity to assert themselves. Not that their objects were quite the same. Belle merely wished to be free of her husband, whom she had always disliked, and whom she now positively hated with that curious hatred which women occasionally conceive towards those to whom they are legally bound, when they have been bad enough or unfortunate enough to fall in love with somebody else. He, on the contrary, had that desire for revenge upon her which even the gentler stamp

of man is apt to conceive towards one who, herself the object
of his strong affection, daily and hourly repels and repays it
with scorn and infidelity. He did love her truly, she was the
one living thing in all his bitter, lonely life to whom his heart
had gone out. True, he put pressure on her to marry him, or,
what comes to the same thing, allowed and encouraged her
drunken old father to do so. But he had loved her and still
loved her, and yet she mocked at him, and in the face of that
fact about the money—her money—which he had paid away
to the other woman, a fact which it was impossible for him to
explain except by the admission of guilt which would be his
ruin, what was he to urge to convince her of this, even had
she been open to conviction? But it was bitter to him, bitter
beyond all conception, to have this, the one joy of his life,
snatched from him. He threw himself with ardor into the
pursuit after wealth and dignity of position, partly because he
had a legitimate desire for these things, and partly to assuage
the constant irritation of his mind, but to no purpose. These
two spectres of his existence, his tiger wife and the fair woman
who was his wife in name, constantly marched side by side
before him, blotting out the beauty from every scene and sour-
ing the sweetness of every joy. But if in his pain he thirsted
for revenge upon Belle, who would have none of him, how
much more did he desire to be avenged upon Edward Cossey,
who, as it were, had in sheer wantonness robbed him of the
one good thing he had. It made him mad to think that this
man, to whom he knew himself to be in every way superior,
should have had the power thus to injure him, and he longed
to pay him back measure for measure, and through *his* heart's
affections to strike him as mortal a blow as he had himself
received.

Mr. Quest was no doubt a bad man, his whole life was a
fraud, he was selfish and unscrupulous in his schemes and re-
lentless in their execution; but whatever may have been the
measure of his iniquities, he was not doomed to wait for another world to have them meted out to him again. His life,
indeed, was full of miseries, the more keenly felt because of
the high pitch and capacity of his nature, and perhaps the
sharpest of them all was the sickening knowledge that had it
not been for that one fatal error of his boyhood, that one false

step down the steep of Avernus, he might have been a good
and even a great man.

Just now, however, his load was a little lightened, and he
was able to devote himself to his money-making, and to the
weaving of the web that was to destroy his rival, Edward Cossey, with a mind a little less preoccupied with other cares.

Meanwhile, things at the Castle were going very pleasantly
for everybody. The squire was as happy in attending to the
various details connected with the transfer of the mortgages
as though he had been lending thirty thousand pounds instead
of borrowing it. The great George was happy in the unaccustomed flow of borrowed cash, that enabled him to treat
Janter with a lofty scorn not unmingled with pity, which was
as balm to his harassed soul, and also to transact an enormous
amount of business in his own peculiar way, with men up trees
and otherwise, for had he not to stock the Moat Farm, and was
not Michaelmas at hand?

Ida, too, was happy, happier than she had been since her
brother's death, for reasons that have already been hinted at.
Besides, Mr. Edward Cossey was out of the way, and that to
Ida was a very great thing, for his presence to her was what
a policeman is to a ticket-of-leave man—a most unpleasant and
suggestive sight. She fully realized the meaning and extent
of the bargain into which she had entered to save her father
and her house, and there lay upon her the deep shadow of evil
that was to come. Every time she saw her father bustling
about with his business letters and his parchments, every time
the universal George arrived with an air of melancholy satisfaction and a long list of the farming stock and implements
he had bought at some neighboring Michaelmas sale, the
shadow deepened, and she heard the clanking of her chains.
Therefore she was the more thankful for her respite.

Harold Quaritch was happy too, though in a somewhat rest-
less and peculiar way. Mrs. Jobson (the old lady who attended
to his wants at Molehill, with the help of a gardener and a simple village maid, her niece, who smashed all the crockery and
nearly drove the colonel mad by banging the doors, shifting
his papers, and even dusting his trays of Roman coins) actually
confided to some friends in the village that she thought the
poor dear gentleman was going mad. When questioned on

what she based this belief, she replied that he would walk up and down the oak-panelled dining-room by the hour together; that then, when he got tired of that exercise, whereby, said Mrs. Jobson, he had already worn a groove in the new Turkey carpet, he would take out a "rokey" (foggy) looking bit of a picture, and set it upon a chair and stare at it through his fingers, shaking his head and muttering all the while. Then— further and conclusive proof of a yielding intellect—he would get a half-sheet of paper with some writing on it and put it on the mantelpiece and stare at that. Next he would turn it upside down and stare at it so, then sideways, then all ways, then he would hold it before a looking-glass and stare at the looking-glass, and so on. When asked how she knew all this, she confessed that Jane had seen it through the keyhole, not once, but often.

Of course, as the practised and discerning reader will clearly understand, this meant only that when walking and wearing out the carpet the colonel was thinking of Ida; when contemplating the painting that she had given him, he was admiring her work and trying to reconcile his admiration with his own conscience and his somewhat peculiar views of art, and that when glaring at the paper, he was vainly endeavoring to make head or tail of the message written to his son on the night before his execution by Sir James de la Molle in the reign of Charles I., and confidently believed by Ida to contain a key to the whereabouts of the treasure he was supposed to have secreted.

Of course the tale of this worthy soul, Mrs. Jobson, did not lose in the telling, and when it reached Ida's ears, which it did at last through the medium of George, for, in addition to his numberless other functions, George was the sole authorized purveyor of the village and country news, it read that Colonel Quaritch had gone raving mad.

Ten minutes afterwards this raving lunatic arrived at the Castle in his dress clothes and his right mind, whereon Ida promptly repeated her thrilling history, somewhat to the subsequent discomfort of Mrs. Jobson and Jane.

No one, as somebody once said with equal truth and profundity, knows what a minute may bring forth, much less, therefore, does anybody know what an evening of say two hundred and forty minutes may produce. For instance, Harold Quaritch—though by this time he had gone so far as to freely admit to himself that he was utterly and hopelessly in love with Ida, in love with her with that settled and determined passion which sometimes strikes a man or woman in middle age—certainly did not know that before the evening was out he would have declared his devotion with results that shall be made clear in their decent order. When he put on his dress clothes to come up to dinner, he had no more intention of proposing to Ida than he had of not taking them off when he went to bed. His love was deep enough and steady enough, but perhaps it did not possess that wild impetuosity which carries people so far in their youth, sometimes indeed a great deal further than their reason approves. It was essentially a middle-aged devotion, and bore the same resemblance to the picturesque passion of five-and-twenty that a snow-fed torrent does to a navigable river. The one rushes and roars and sweeps away the bridges and devastates happy homes, while the other bears upon its placid breast the argosies of peace and plenty, and is generally serviceable to the necessities of man. But for all that, there is something attractive about torrents. There is a grandeur in that first rush of passion which results from the sudden melting of the snows of the heart's purity and faith and high unstained devotion.

But both torrents and navigable rivers are liable to one common fate, they may fall over precipices, and when that happens even the latter cease to be navigable for a space. And that was what was about to happen to our friend the colonel.

To begin with, he had dined well, and whatever ardent twenty-three may think of so gross and material a fact, it is certainly true that if a man is in love before dinner, he is five-and-twenty per cent. more in love after it.

Well, Harold Quaritch had dined, and he had a pleasant as well as a good dinner. The squire, who of late had been cheerful as a cricket, was in his best form, and told long stories with an infinitesimal point. In anybody else's mouth these stories would have been wearisome to a degree, but there was a gusto, an originality, and a kind of Tudor-period flavor about the old gentleman which made his worst and longest story acceptable in any society. The colonel himself, too, had come out in a most unusual way. He had a fund of dry humor in him which he rarely produced, but, when he did produce it, it was of a most satisfactory order. On this particular night it was all on view, greatly to the satisfaction of Ida, who was a witty as well as a clever woman. And so it came to pass that the dinner was a very pleasant one.

Harold and the squire were still sitting over their wine, and the latter was for the fifth time giving to the former a full and particular account of how his deceased aunt, Mrs. Massey, had been persuaded by a learned antiquarian to convert, or rather restore, Dead Man's Mount into its supposed primitive condition of an ancient British dwelling, and of the extraordinary expression of her face when the bill came in, when suddenly the servant announced that George was waiting to see him.

The old gentleman grumbled a great deal, but finally got up and departed to enjoy himself for the next hour or so in talking about things in general with his retainer, leaving his guest to find his way to the drawing-room.

When the colonel reached the room, he found Ida seated at the piano, singing. She heard him shut the door, looked round, nodded prettily, and then went on with her singing. He came and sat down on a low chair some two paces from her, placing himself in such a position that he could see her face, which indeed he always found a wonderfully pleasant object of contemplation. Ida was playing without music; the only light in the room was that of a low lamp with a red fringe to it. Therefore he could not see very much, being only with difficulty able to trace the outlines of her features; but if the shadow thus robbed him, it on the other hand lent her a beauty of its own, clothing her face with an atmosphere of wonderful softness which it did not always possess in the glare of day. The colonel, indeed (we must remember that he was in love and that it was after dinner), became quite poetical (internally of course) about it, and in his heart compared her first to St. Cecilia at her organ, and then to the Angel of the Twilight. He had never seen her look so lovely. At her worst she was a handsome and noble-looking woman, but now the shadow from without, and, though he knew nothing of that, the shadow from her heart within also, aided, maybe, by the music's swell, had softened and purified her face till it did indeed look almost like an angel's. It is strong, powerful faces that are capable of the most tenderness, not the soft and pretty ones ; and even in a plain person, when such a face is in this way seen, it gathers a peculiar beauty of its own. But Ida was not a plain person, so on the whole it is scarcely to be wondered at that a certain effect was produced upon Harold Quaritch.

Ida, to outward appearance at any rate, all unconscious of what was passing in her admirer's mind, went on singing almost without a break. She had a good memory and a sweet voice, and really liked music for its own sake, so it was no great effort for her to do so.

Presently she came to a song from Tennyson's "Maud," the tender and beautiful words whereof will be familiar to most of the readers of her story. It began—

"O let the solid ground
Not fail beneath my feet,
Before my heart has found
What some have found so sweet."

The song is a lovely one, and it did not suffer from her rendering, and the effect produced upon Harold by it was of a most peculiar nature. All his past life seemed to heave and break beneath the magic of the music and the magic of the singer, as a northern field of ice breaks up beneath the outburst of the summer sun. It broke up, and sank, and vanished into the depths of his nature, those dread, unmeasured depths that roll and murmur in the vastness of each human heart as the sea rolls beneath its cloak of ice ; that roll and murmur here, and set towards a shore of which we have no chart or knowledge. The past was gone, the frozen years had melted, and once more the sweet, strong air of youth blew across his heart, and once more there was blue sky above, wherein the angels sailed. Under the influence of that song the barrier of self broke down, and his being went out to meet her being, and all the possibilities of life seemed to breathe afresh.

He sat and listened, and, as he listened, trembled in his agitation, till the sweet echoes of the music died upon the quiet air. They died, and were gathered into the emptiness which receives and records all things, the oath and the prayer, the melody and the scream of agony, the shout of triumph and the wail of woe, and left him broken.

She turned to him, smiling faintly, for the song had moved her also, and he felt that he must speak.

"That is a beautiful song," he said; "sing it again if you do not mind."

She made no answer, but once more sang

> "O let the solid ground
> Not fail beneath my feet,
> Before my heart has found
> What some have found so sweet,"

and then suddenly broke off.

"Why are you looking at me?" she said. "I can feel you looking at me and you make me nervous."

He bent towards her and looked her in the eyes.

"I love you, Ida," he said, "I love you with all my heart," and he stopped suddenly.

She turned quite pale, even in that light he could see her pallor, and her hands fell heavily on the keys.

The echo of the crashing notes rolled round the room and died slowly away—but still she said nothing.

CHAPTER XIX.

IN PAWN.

At last she spoke, apparently with a great effort.

"It is stifling in here," she said, "let us go out;" and she rose, took up a shawl that lay beside her on a chair, and stepped through a French window into the garden. It was a lovely autumn night, and the air was still as death, with just a touch of frost in it.

Ida threw the shawl over her shoulders, and, followed by Harold, walked on through the garden, till she came to the edge of the moat, where there was a seat. Here she sat down and fixed her eyes upon the hoary old battlements of the gateway, clad in their solemn robe of moonlight.

Harold looked at her and felt that if he had anything to say the time had come for him to say it, and that she had brought him here in order that she might be able to listen undisturbed. So he began again, and told her that he loved her dearly. "I am some seventeen years older than you," he went on, "and I suppose that the most active part of my life lies in the past; and I don't know if, putting other things aside, you would care to marry so old a man, especially as I am not rich. Indeed, I feel it presumptuous on my part, seeing what you are and what I am, to ask you to do so. And yet, Ida, I believe that if you could care for me, that, with God's blessing, we should be very happy together. I have led a lonely life, and have had little to do with women—once, many years ago, I was engaged, and the matter ended painfully, and that is all. But ever since I first saw your face in the drift five years and more ago, it has haunted me and been with me, and then I came to live here and I have learned to love you, Heaven only knows how much, and I should be ashamed to try to put it into words, for they would sound foolish. All my life is wrapped up in you, and I feel as though, should you see me no more, I should never be a happy man again," and he paused and looked anxiously at her face, which was set and drawn as though with pain.

"I cannot say 'yes,' Colonel Quaritch," she answered, at length, in a tone that puzzled him, it was so tender and so unfitted to the words.

"I suppose," he stammered—"I suppose that you do not care for me? Of course, I have no right to expect that you would."

"As I have said that I cannot say 'yes,' Colonel Quaritch, do you not think that I had better leave that question unanswered?" she replied in the same soft notes, which seemed to draw the heart out of him.

"I do not understand," he went on. "Why?"

"Why?" she broke in with a bitter little laugh; "shall I tell you why? Because I am *in pawn*. Look," she went on, pointing to the stately towers and the broad lands beyond. "You see this place. *I* am security for it, I *myself* in my own person. Had it not been for me it would have been sold over our heads after having descended in our family for all these centuries, put upon the market and sold for what it would fetch, and my old father would have been turned out to die, for it would have killed him. So you see I did what unfortunate women have often been driven to do, I sold myself body and soul; and I got a good price too—thirty thousand pounds," and suddenly she burst into a flood of tears and began to sob as though her heart would break.

For a moment Harold Quaritch looked on bewildered, not in the least understanding what Ida meant, and then he followed the impulse common to mankind in similar circumstances and took her in his arms. She did not resent the movement, indeed she scarcely seemed to notice it, though, to tell the truth, for a moment or two, which to the colonel seemed the happiest of his life, her head rested on his shoulder.

Almost instantly, however, she raised it, freed herself from his embrace, and ceased weeping.

"As I have told you so much," she said, "I suppose that I had better tell you everything. I know that whatever the temptation," and she laid great stress upon the words, "under no conceivable circumstances—indeed, even if you believed that you were serving me in so doing—I can rely upon you never to reveal to anybody, and above all to my father, what I now tell you," and she paused and looked up at him with eyes in which the tears still swam.

"Of course, you can rely upon me," he said.

"Very well. I am sure that I shall never have to reproach you with the words. I will tell you. I have virtually promised to marry Mr. Edward Cossey, should he at any time be in a position to claim fulfilment of the promise, on condition of his taking up the mortgages on Honham, which he has done."

Harold Quaritch took a step back and looked at her in horrified astonishment.

"*What?*" he asked.

"Yes, yes," she answered, hastily, putting up her hand as though to shield herself from a blow. "I know what you mean; but do not think too hardly of me if you can help it. It was not for myself. I would rather work for my living with my hands than take a price, for there is no other word for it. It was for my father, and my family too. I could not bear to think of the old place going to the hammer, and I did it all in a minute without consideration; but," and she set her face, "even as things are, I believe I should do it again, because I think that no woman has a right to destroy her family in order to please herself. If one of the two must go, let it be her. But don't think hardly of me for it," she added almost pleadingly, "that is, if you can help it."

"I am not thinking of you," he answered, grimly; "by Heaven I honor you for what you have done, for however much I may disagree with the act, it is a noble one. I am thinking of the man who could drive such a bargain with any woman. You say that you have promised to marry him should he ever be in a position to claim it. What do you mean by that? As you have told me so much you may as well tell me the rest."

He spoke clearly and with a voice of authority, but his bearing did not seem to jar upon Ida.

"I meant," she answered, humbly, "that I believe — of course I do not know if I am right—I believe that Mr. Cossey is in some way entangled with a lady, in short with Mrs.

Quest, and that the question of whether or no he comes forward again depends upon her."

" Upon my word," said the colonel—" upon my word the thing gets worse and worse. I never heard anything like it; and for money too. The thing is beyond me."

" At any rate," she answered, " there it is. And now, Colonel Quaritch, one word before I go in. It is difficult for me to speak without saying too much or too little, but I do want you to understand how honored and how grateful I feel for what you have told me to-night—I am so little worthy of all you have given me, and, to be honest, I cannot feel as pained about it as I ought to feel. It is feminine vanity, you know, nothing else. I am sure that you will not press me to say more."

" No," he answered, " no. I think that I understand the position. But, Ida, there is one thing that I must ask—you will forgive me if I am wrong in doing so, but all this is very sad for me. If in the end circumstances should alter, as I pray Heaven that they may, or if Mr. Cossey's previous entanglements should prove too much for him, will you marry me, Ida ?"

She thought for a moment, and then rising from the seat, gave him her hand and said, simply,

" Yes, I *will* marry you."

He made no answer, but, lifting her hand, touched it gently with his lips.

" Meanwhile," she went on, " I have your promise, and I am sure that you will not betray it, come what may."

" No," he said, " I will not betray it."

And they went in.

In the drawing-room they found the squire puzzling over a sheet of paper, on which were scrawled some of George's accounts in figures, which at first sight bore about as much resemblance to Egyptian hieroglyphics as they did to those in use to-day.

" Hullo !" he said, " there you are. Where on earth have you been ?"

" We have been looking at the Castle in the moonlight," answered Ida, coolly. " It is beautiful."

" Um—ah," said the squire, dryly, " I have no doubt that

it is beautiful, but isn't the grass rather damp? Well, look here," and he held up the sheet of hieroglyphics, " perhaps you can add this up, Ida, for it is more than I can. George has bought stock and all sorts of things at the sale to-day, and here is his account; three hundred and seventy-two pounds he makes it, but I make it four hundred and twenty, and hang me if I can find out which is right. It is most important that these accounts should be kept straight. Most important, and I cannot get this stupid fellow to do it."

Ida took the sheet of paper and added it up, with the result that she discovered both totals to be wrong. Harold, watching her, could not help wondering at the nerve of the woman who, after going through such a scene as that which had just occurred, could deliberately add up long rows of badly written figures.

And this money which her father was expending so cheerfully was part of the price for which she had bound herself.

With a sigh he rose and said good-night, and went home with feelings almost too mixed to admit of accurate description. He had taken a great step in his life, and to a certain extent that step had succeeded. He had not altogether built his hopes upon sand, for from what Ida had said, and still more from what she had tacitly admitted, it was necessarily clear to him that she did more or less regard him as a man would wish to be regarded by a woman whom he dearly loved. This was a great deal, more indeed than he had dared to believe, but then, as is usually the case in this imperfect world, where things but too often seem to be carefully arranged at sixes and sevens, came the other side of the shield. Of what use to him was it to have won this sweet woman's love, of what use to have this pure water of lawful happiness put to his lips in the desert land of his lonely life, in order to see the cup that held it shattered at a blow? To him the story of the money loan—in consideration of which, as it were, Ida had put herself in pawn, as the Egyptians used to put the mummies of their fathers in pawn—was almost incredible. To a person of his simple and honorable nature it seemed a preposterous and unheard-of thing that any man calling himself a gentleman should find it possible to sink so low as to take such advantage of a woman's dire necessity and honor-

able desire to save her father from misery and her race from
ruin, and to extract from her a promise of marriage in consideration of the value received. Putting aside his overwhelming personal interest in the matter, it made his blood boil to
think that such a thing could be. And yet it was, and, what
was more, he believed he knew Ida well enough to be convinced that she would not shirk the bargain. If Edward
Cossey came forward to claim his bond it would be paid down
to the last farthing. It was a question of thirty thousand
pounds ; the happiness of his life and of Ida's depended upon
a sum of money. If the money were forthcoming, Cossey
could not claim his flesh and blood. But where was it to
come from. He himself was worth perhaps ten thousand
pounds, or with the commutation value of his pension, possibly twelve, and he had not the means of raising a farthing
more. He thought the position over till he was tired of
thinking, and then with a heavy heart, and yet with a strange
glow of happiness shining through his grief, like sunlight
through a gray sky, at last he went to sleep and dreamed that
Ida had gone from him, and that he was once more utterly
alone in the world.

But if he had cause for trouble, how much more was it so
with Ida ! Poor woman ! under her somewhat cold and stately exterior she had a deep and at times a passionate nature.
For some weeks she had been growing strangely attached to
Harold Quaritch, and now she knew that she loved him, so
that there was no one thing that she desired more in this wide
world than to become his wife. And yet she was bound,
bound by a sense of honor and a sense too of money received,
to stay at the beck and call of a man she detested, and if at
any time it pleased him to throw down the handkerchief, to
be there to pick it up and hold it to her heart. It was bad
enough to have had this hanging over her head when she was
herself more or less in a passive condition, and therefore to a
certain extent reckless as to her future ; but now that her
heart was alight with the holy flame of a good woman's love,
now that her whole nature rebelled and cried out aloud against
the sacrilege involved, it was both revolting and terrible.

And yet so far as she could see there was no great probability of escape. She was a shrewd and observant woman,

and could gauge Mr. Cossey's condition of mind towards her
with more or less accuracy.   Also she did not think it in the
least likely that, having spent thirty thousand pounds to advance his object, he would be content to let his advantage
drop.   Such a course would be repellent to his trading instincts.   She knew in her heart that the hour was not far off
when he would claim his own, and that, unless some accident
occurred to prevent it, it was practically certain that she would
be called upon to fulfil her pledge, and while loving another
man to become the wife of Edward Cossey.

CHAPTER XX.

"GOOD-BY TO YOU, EDWARD."

IT was on the day following the one upon which Harold proposed to Ida, that Edward Cossey returned to Boisingham. His father had so far recovered from his attack as to be at last prevailed upon to allow his departure, being chiefly moved thereto by the supposition that Cossey & Son's branch establishments were suffering from his son's absence.

"Well," he said, in his high, piercing voice, "business is business, and must be attended to, so perhaps you had better go. They talk about the fleeting character of things, but there is one thing that never changes, and that is money. Money is immortal; men may come and men may go, but money goes on forever. Hee! hee! money is the honey-pot, and men are the flies; and some get their fill and some stick their wings, but the honey is always there, so never mind the flies. No, never mind me; you go and look after the honey, Edward. Money—honey, honey—money, they rhyme, don't they? And look here, by the way, if you get a chance—and the world is full of chances to men who have plenty of money—mind you don't forget to pay out that half-pay colonel—what's his name?—Quaritch. He played our family a dirty trick, and there's your poor Aunt Julia in a lunatic asylum to this moment, and a constant source of expense to us."

And so Edward bade his estimable parent farewell and departed. Nor in truth did he require any admonition from Mr. Cossey senior to make him anxious to do Colonel Quaritch an ill turn if the opportunity should serve. Mrs. Quest, in her numerous affectionate letters, had more than once, possibly for reasons of her own, given him a full and vivid *résumé* of the local gossip about the colonel and Ida, who were, she said, according to common report, engaged to be married. Now, absence had not by any means cooled Edward's devo-

tion to Miss De la Molle, which was a sincere one enough in
its own way.   On the contrary, the longer he was away from
her the more his passion grew, and with it a vigorous under-
growth of jealousy.   He had, it is true, Ida's implied promise
that she would marry him, if he chose to ask her, but on this
he put no great reliance.   Hence his hurry to return to Boisingham.

Leaving London by an afternoon train, he reached Boisingham about half-past six, and, in pursuance of an arrangement
already made, went to dine with the Quests.   When he reached
the house he found Belle alone in the drawing-room, for her
husband, having come in late, was still dressing, but somewhat to his relief he had no opportunity of private conversation with her, for a servant was in the room, attending to the
fire, which would not burn.   The dinner passed off quietly
enough, though there was an ominous look about the lady's
face which he, being familiar with these signs of the feminine
weather, did not altogether like.   After dinner, however, Mr.
Quest excused himself, saying that he had promised to attend
a local concert in aid of the funds for the restoration of the
damaged pinnacle of the parish church, and he was left alone
with the lady.

Then it was that all her pent-up passion broke out.   She
overwhelmed him with her affection, she told him that her
life had been a blank while he was away, she reproached him
with the scarcity and coldness of his letters, and generally
went on in a way with which he was but too well accustomed,
and, if the truth must be told, heartily tired.   His mood was
an irritable one, and to-night the whole thing wearied him beyond bearing.

"Come, Belle," he said, at last, "for goodness sake be a
little more rational.   You are getting too old for this sort of
tomfoolery, you know."

She sprang up and faced him, her eyes flashing and her
breast heaving with jealous anger.   "What do you mean?"
she said.   "Are you tired of me?"

"I did not say that," he answered, "but as you have started
the subject I must tell you that I think all this has gone far
enough.   Unless it is stopped I believe we shall both be
ruined.   I am sure that your husband is becoming suspicious,

and as I have told you again and again, if once the business gets to my father's ears he will disinherit me."

Belle stood quite still till he had finished. She had assumed her favorite attitude and crossed her arms behind her back, and her sweet childish face was calm and very white.

"What is the good of making excuses and telling me what is not true, Edward?" she said. "One never hears a man who loves a woman talk like that; prudence comes with weariness, and men grow virtuous when there is nothing more to gain. You *are* tired of me. I have seen it a long time, but like a poor blind fool I have tried not to believe it. It is not a great reward to a woman who has given her whole life to a man, but perhaps it is as much as she can expect, for I do not want to be unjust to you. I am the most to blame, because a woman need never take a false step except of her own free will."

"Well, well," he said, impatiently, "what of it?"

"Only this, Edward. I have still a little pride left, and if you are tired of me, why—*go*."

He tried hard to prevent it, but do what he would, a look of relief struggled into his face. She saw it, and it made her wild with jealous anger.

"You need not look so happy, Edward: it is scarcely decent; and, besides, you have not heard all that I have to say. I know what all this arises from. You are in love with Ida de la Molle. Now, *there* I draw the line. You may leave me if you like, but you shall not marry Ida while I am alive to prevent it. That is more than I can bear. Besides, like a wise woman, she has fallen in love with Colonel Quaritch, who is worth two of you, Edward Cossey."

"I do not believe it," he answered, "and what right have you to say that I am in love with Miss De la Molle? And if I am in love with her, how can you prevent me from marrying her if I choose?"

"Try, and you will see," she answered, with a little laugh. "And now, as the curtain has dropped, and it is all over between us, why the best thing that we can do is to put out the lights and go to bed," and she laughed again and courtesied with much assumed playfulness. "Good-night, Mr. Cossey; good-night, and good-by."

He held out his hand. "Come, Belle," he said, "don't let us part like this."

She shook her head, and once more put her arms behind her. "No," she answered, "I will not take your hand. Of my own free will I will never touch it again : for to me it is like the hand of the dead. Good-by, once more ; good-by to you, Edward, and to all the happiness that I ever had. I built up all my life upon my love for you, and you have shattered it like glass. I do not reproach you ; you have followed after your nature and I must follow after mine, and in time all things will come right—in the grave. I shall not trouble you any more, provided that you do not try to marry Ida, for that I will not bear. And now go, for I am very tired," and, turning, she rang the bell for the servant to show him out.

In another minute he was gone. She listened till she heard the front door close behind him, and then she gave way to her grief, and, flinging herself upon the sofa, covered her face with her hands and sobbed and moaned bitterly, weeping for the past, and weeping, too, for the long, desolate years that were to come. Poor woman! do not let us judge her too hardly, for, whatever was the measure of her sin, it had assuredly found her out, as our sins always do find us out in the end. She had loved this man with a passion which has no parallel in the hearts of well-ordered and well-brought-up women. She had never really lived till this fatal passion took possession of her ; and now that its object had deserted her, her heart felt as though it had died within her. In that short half-hour she suffered more than many women do in their whole lives ; but the paroxysm passed, and she rose pale and trembling, with set teeth and blazing eyes.

"He had better be careful," she said to herself ; "he may go, but if he tries to marry Ida I will keep my word—yes, for her sake as well as his."

When Edward Cossey came to consider the position, which he did seriously on the following morning, he did not find it very satisfactory. To begin with, he was not altogether a heartless man, and such a scene as that which he had passed through on the previous evening was in itself quite enough to upset his nerves. At one time, at any rate, he had been much attached to Mrs. Quest ; he had never borne her any violent affection, that had all been on her side, but still he had been fond of her, and if he could have done so, would probably have married her. Even now he was attached to her, and would have been glad to remain her friend, if she would have allowed it. But then came the time when her heroics commenced to weary him, and he on his side began to fall in love with Ida de la Molle,·and as he drew back so she came forward, till at length he was worn out, and things culminated as has been described. He was sorry for her, too, knowing how deeply she was attached to him, though it is probable that he did not in the least realize the extent to which she suffered, for neither men nor women who have, intentionally or otherwise, been the cause of intense mental anguish to one of the opposite sex, ever do quite realize this. They, not unnaturally, measure the trouble by the depth of their own, and are therefore very apt to come to erroneous conclusions. Of course, we are now speaking of cases where all the real passion is on one side, and indifference or comparative indifference on the other; for where it is mutual the grief will, in natures of equal depth, be mutual also.

At any rate, Edward Cossey was quite sensitive enough to feel the parting with Mrs. Quest acutely, and perhaps he felt the manner of it even more than the fact of the separation. Then came another consideration. He was, it is true, free from his entanglement, which was in itself an enormous relief, but the freedom was of a conditional nature. Belle had threatened trouble in the most decisive tones should he attempt to carry out his secret purpose, which she had not been slow to divine, of marrying Ida. From some occult reason, at least to him it seemed occult, the idea of this alliance was peculiarly distasteful to her, though no doubt the true explanation was that she believed, and not inaccurately, that it was in order to bring it about that he was bent upon deserting her. The question with him was, would she or would she not attempt to put her threat into execution. It certainly seemed to him difficult to imagine what steps she could take to that end, seeing that any such steps would necessarily involve her own exposure, and that too when there was nothing to gain, and when all hopes of thereby securing him for herself had passed away. Nor did he seriously believe that she would attempt anything of the sort. It is one thing for a woman to make such threats in the acute agony of her jealousy, and quite another for her to carry them out in cold blood. Looking at the matter from a man's point of view, it seemed to him extremely improbable that, when the occasion came, she would attempt such a move. He forgot how much more violently, when once it has taken possession of her being, the storm of passion sweeps through such a woman's heart than through a man's, and how utterly reckless to all consequence the former sometimes becomes. For there are women for whom all things melt in that white heat of anguished jealousy—honor, duty, conscience, and the restraint of religion, and of these Belle Quest was one.

But of this he was not aware, and though he recognized a risk, he saw in it no sufficient reason to make him stay his hand. For day by day the strong desire to make Ida his wife had grown upon him, till at last it possessed him body and soul. For a long while the intent had been smouldering in . his breast, and the tale that he now heard, to the effect that Colonel Quaritch had been beforehand with him, had blown it to a flame. Ida was ever present in his thoughts ; even at night he could not be rid of her, for when he slept her vision, dark-eyed and beautiful, came stealing down his dreams. She was his heaven, and if by any ladder known to man he might climb thereto, thither would he climb. And so he set his teeth and vowed that, Mrs. Quest or no Mrs. Quest, he would set his fortune upon the hazard of the die, ay, and win it, even if he loaded the dice.

While he was still thinking thus, standing at his window and gazing out on to the market-place of the quiet little town, he suddenly saw Ida herself driving up in her pony carriage. It was a wet and windy day, and the rain was on her cheek, and the wind tossed a little lock of her brown hair. The cob was pulling, and her proud face was set, as she concentrated her energies upon holding him. Never to Edward Cossey had she looked more beautiful. His heart beat fast at the sight of her, and whatever doubts might have lingered in his mind vanished. Yes, he would claim her promise and marry her.

Presently the pony carriage pulled up at his door, and the boy who was sitting behind got down and rang the bell. He stepped back from the window, wondering what it could be.

"Will you please give that note to Mr. Cossey," said Ida, as the door opened, "and ask him to send an answer?" and she was gone.

The note was from the squire, sealed with his big seal (the squire always sealed his letters in the old-fashioned way), and contained an invitation to himself to shoot on the morrow. "George wants me to do a little partridge driving," it ended, "and to brush through one or two of the small covers. There will only be Colonel Quaritch besides yourself and George, but I hope that you will have a fair rough day. If I don't hear from you I shall suppose that you are coming, so don't trouble to write."

"Oh, yes, I will go," said Edward. "Confound that Quaritch. At any rate, I can show him how to shoot, and, what is more, I will have it out with him about my aunt."

CHAPTER XXI.

THE COLONEL GOES OUT SHOOTING.

THE next morning was fine and still, one of those lovely autumn days of which we get four or five in the course of a season. After breakfast Harold Quaritch strolled down his garden, stood himself against a gate to the right of Dead Man's Mount, and looked at the scene. All about him, their foliage yellowing to its fall, were the giant oaks, which were the pride of the country side, and so quiet was the air that not a leaf upon them stirred. The only sounds that reached his ears were the tapping of the nuthatches, as they sought their food in the rough crannies of the bark, and the occasional falling of a rich, ripe acorn from its lofty place on to the frosted grass beneath. The sunshine shone bright, but with a chastened heat, the squirrels scrambled up the oaks, and high in the blue air the rooks pursued their path. It was a beautiful morning, for summer is never more sweet than on its death-bed, and yet it filled him with solemn thoughts. How many autumns had those old trees seen, and how many would they still see long after his eyes had lost their sight. And if they were old, how old was the Dead Man's Mount there to his left? Old, indeed, for he had discovered it was mentioned in Doomsday Book by that name. And what was it? a boundary hill, a natural formation, or, as its name implied, a funeral barrow? He had half a mind to dig one day and find out, that is, if he could get anybody to dig for him, for the people about Honham were so firmly convinced that Dead Man's Mount was haunted, a reputation that it had had from time immemorial, that nothing would have persuaded them to touch it.

He contemplated the great mound carefully without coming to any conclusion, and then looked at his watch. It was a quarter to ten, time for him to start for the Castle for his day's shooting; so he got his gun and cartridges, and in due course arrived at the Castle, to find George and several myrmidons, in the shape of beaters and boys, already standing in the yard.

"Please, colonel, the squire hopes you'll go in and have a glass of something before you start," said George; so accordingly he went, not to "have a glass of something," but on the chance of seeing Ida. In the vestibule he found the old gentleman busily engaged in writing an enormous letter.

"Hullo, colonel," he halloaed, without getting up, "glad to see you. Excuse me for a few moments, will you? I want to get this off my mind. Here, Ida! Ida! Ida!" he shouted; "here's Colonel Quaritch."

"Good gracious, father," said that young lady, arriving in a hurry, "you are bringing the house down!" and then she turned round and greeted Harold. It was the first time that they had met since the eventful evening described a chapter or two back, so the occasion might be considered a little awkward; at any rate, he felt it so.

"How do you do, Colonel Quaritch?" she said, quite simply, giving him her hand. There was nothing in the words, and yet he felt that he was very welcome. For when a woman really loves there is about her an atmosphere of softness and tender meaning which cannot be mistaken. Sometimes it is only perceptible to the favored individual himself; but more generally is to be discerned by any person of ordinary shrewdness. A very short course of observation in general society will convince the reader of the justice of this observation, and when once he gets to know the signs of the weather he will probably light upon more love affairs than were ever meant for his investigation.

This softness, or atmospheric influence, or subdued glow of affection radiating from a light within, was clearly enough visible in Ida that morning, and certainly it made our friend the colonel unspeakably happy to see it.

"Are you fond of shooting?" she asked, presently.

"Yes, very, and have been all my life."

"Are you a good shot?" she asked again.

"I call that a rude question," he answered, smiling.

"Yes, it is, but I want to know."

"Well," said Harold, "I suppose that I am pretty fair; that is, at rough shooting; I have never had much practice at driven birds and that kind of sport."

"I am glad of that."

"Why, it does not much matter. One goes out shooting for the sport of the thing."

"Yes, I know, but Mr. Edward Cossey"—and she shrank visibly as she uttered the name—"is coming, and he is a *very* good shot, and *very* conceited about it. I want you to beat him if you can; will you try?"

"Well," said Harold, "I don't at all like shooting against a man. It is not sportsmanlike, you know; and, besides, if Mr. Cossey is a crack shot, I dare say that I shall be nowhere, but I shall shoot as well as I can."

"Do you know, it is very feminine, but I would give anything to see you beat him," and she nodded and laughed, whereupon Harold Quaritch vowed in his heart that, if it in him lay, he would not disappoint her.

At that moment Edward Cossey's fast trotting horse drew up at the door with a prodigious crunching of gravel, and Edward himself entered, looking very handsome and rather pale. He was admirably dressed; that is to say, his shooting-clothes were beautifully made and very new-looking, and so were his boots, and so was his hat, and so were his hammerless guns, of which he brought a pair. There exists a certain class of sportsmen who always appear to have just walked out of a sporting-tailor's shop, and to this class Edward Cossey belonged. Everything about him was of the best and newest and most expensive kind possible; even his guns were just down from Purdey's, and the best that could be had for love or money, having cost exactly a hundred and forty guineas the pair. Indeed, he presented a curious contrast to his rival. The colonel had certainly nothing new-looking about *him*— an old tweed coat, an old hat with a piece of gut still twined round it, a sadly-frayed bag full of brown cartridges, and, last of all, an old gun with all the brown worn off the barrels, original cost £17 10s. And yet there was no possibility of making any mistake as to which of the two looked more of a gentleman, or, indeed, more of a sportsman.

Edward Cossey shook hands with Ida, but when the colonel

was advancing to give him his hand he turned and spoke to the squire, who had at length finished his letter, so that no greeting passed between them. At the time Harold did not know if this move was or was not accidental.

Presently they started, Edward Cossey attended by his man with the second gun.

"Hullo, Cossey!" sang out the squire after him, "it isn't much use your bringing two guns for this sort of work. 1 don't preserve much here, you know, at least not now. You will only get a dozen cock pheasants and a few brace of partridges."

"Oh, thank you," he answered, "I always like to have a second gun in case I should want it. It's no trouble, you know."

"All right," said the squire; "Ida and I will come down with the luncheon to the spinney. Good-by."

After crossing the moat Edward Cossey walked by himself, followed by his man and a very fine retriever, and the colonel talked to George, who was informing him that Mr. Cossey was a "pretty shot, he was, but rather snappy over it," till they came to a field of white turnips.

"Now, gentlemen, if you please," said George, "we will walk through these here turnips. I put two coveys of birds in here myself, and it's rare good 'lay' for them; so I think that we had better see if they will let us come up to them."

Accordingly they started down the field, the colonel on the right, George in the middle, and Edward Cossey on the left.

Before they had gone ten yards an old Frenchman got up in the front of one of the beaters and wheeled round past Edward, who cut him over in first-rate style.

From that one bird the colonel could see that the man was a quick and clever shot. Presently, however, a leash of English birds rose rather awkwardly at about forty paces straight in front of Edward Cossey, and Harold noticed that he left them alone, never attempting to fire at them. The fact was that he was one of those shooters who never take a hard shot if they can avoid it, being always in terror lest they should miss it, and so reduce their average.

Then George, who was a very fair shot of the "poking" order, fired both barrels and got a bird, and Edward Cossey got another. It was not till they were getting to the end of the last beat that Harold got a chance of letting off his gun. Suddenly, however, a brace of old birds sprang up out of the turnips in front of him at about thirty yards, as swiftly as though they had been ejected from a mortar, and made off one to the right and one to the left, both of them rising shots. He got the right-hand bird, and then, turning, killed the other also, when it was more than fifty yards away.

The colonel felt satisfied, for the shots were very good. Mr. Cossey opened his eyes, and wondered if it was a fluke, and George ejaculated, "Well, that's a master one."

After this they pursued their course, picking up another two brace of birds on the way to the outlying cover, a wood of about twenty acres, through which they were to brush. It was a good holding wood for pheasants, but lay on the outside of the Honham estate, where they were liable to be poached by the farmers whose land marched, so George enjoined them particularly not to let anything go.

Into the details of the sport that followed we need not enter, beyond saying that the colonel, to his huge delight, never shot better in his life. Indeed, with the exception of one rabbit and a hen pheasant that flopped up right beneath his feet, he scarcely missed anything, though he took the shots as they came. Edward Cossey also shot well, and with one exception missed nothing, but then he never took a difficult shot if he could avoid it. The exception was a woodcock which rose in front of George, who was walking down an outside belt with the beaters. He had two barrels at it and missed it, and on it came among the tree-tops, past where Edward Cossey was standing, about half-way down the belt, giving him a difficult chance with the first barrel and a clear one with the second. Bang! bang! and on came the woodcock, flying low, but at tremendous speed, straight at the colonel's head, a most puzzling shot. However, he fired, and to his joy (and what joy is there like to the joy of a sportsman who has just killed a woodcock which everybody has been popping at?) down it came with a thump almost at his feet.

This was their last beat before lunch, which was now to be seen approaching down a lane in a donkey-cart convoyed by Ida and the squire. The latter was advancing in stages of about ten paces, and at every stage he stopped to utter a most fearful roar by way of warning all and sundry that they were not to shoot in his direction. Edward gave his gun to his bearer and at once walked out to join them, but the colonel went with George to look after two running cocks which he had down, for he was an old-fashioned sportsman, and hated not picking up his game. After some difficulty they found one of the cocks in the hedgerow, but the other they could not find, so reluctantly they gave up the search. When they got to the lane they found the luncheon ready, while one of the beaters was laying out the game for the squire to inspect. There were fourteen pheasants, four brace and a half of partridges, a hare, three rabbits, and a woodcock.

"Hullo," said the squire, "who shot the woodcock?"

"Well, sir," said George, "we all had a pull at him, but the colonel wiped our eyes."

"Oh, Mr. Cossey," said Ida, in affected surprise, "why I thought you never missed *anything.*"

"Everybody misses sometimes," answered that gentleman, looking uncommonly sulky. "I shall do better this afternoon when it comes to the driven partridges."

"I don't believe you will," went on Ida, laughing maliciously. "I bet you a pair of gloves that Colonel Quaritch will shoot more driven partridges than you do."

"Done," said Edward Cossey, sharply.

"Now, do you hear that, Colonel Quaritch?" went on Ida. "I have bet Mr. Cossey a pair of gloves that you will kill more partridges this afternoon than he will, so I hope you won't make me lose them."

"Goodness gracious!" said the colonel, in much alarm. "Why, the last partridge driving that I had was on the slopes of some mountains in Afghanistan. I dare say that I sha'n't hit a haystack. Besides," he said, with some irritation, "I don't like being put up to shoot against people."

"Oh, of course," said Edward, loftily, "if Colonel Quaritch does not like to take it up, there's an end of it."

"Well," said the colonel, "if you put it in that way I don't mind trying, but I have only one gun and you have two."

"Oh, that will be all right," said Ida to the colonel. "You shall have George's gun; he never tries to shoot when they drive partridges, because he cannot hit them. He goes with the beaters. It is a very good gun."

The colonel took up the gun and examined it. It was of about the same bend and length as his own, but of a better quality, having been once the property of James de la Molle.

"Yes," he said, "but then I haven't got a bearer."

"Never mind. I'll do that; I know all about it. I always used to hold my brother's second gun when we drove partridges, because he said I was so much quicker than the men. Look," and she took the gun and rested one knee on the turf, "First position, second position, third position. We used to have regular drills at it," and she sighed.

The colonel laughed heartily, for it was a curious thing to see this stately woman handling a gun with all the skill and quickness of a practised shot. Besides, as the bearer idea involved a whole afternoon of Ida's society, he certainly was not inclined to negative it. But Edward Cossey did not smile, on the contrary he positively scowled with jealousy, and was about to make some remark when Ida held up her finger.

"Hush!" she said, "here comes my father" (the squire had been counting the game); "he hates bets, so you mustn't say anything about our match."

Luncheon went off pretty well, though Edward Cossey did not contribute much to the general conversation. When it was done the squire announced that he was going to walk to the other end of the estate, whereon Ida said that she should stop and see something of the shooting, and the fun began.

CHAPTER XXII.

THE END OF THE MATCH.

They began the afternoon with several small drives, but on the whole the birds went very badly. They broke back, went off to one side or the other, and generally misbehaved themselves. In the first drive the colonel and Edward Cossey got a bird each. In the second drive the latter got three birds, firing five shots, and his antagonist only got a hare and a pheasant that jumped out of a ditch, neither of which, of course, counted anything. Only one brace of birds came his way at all, but, if the truth must be told, he was talking to Ida at the moment and did not see them till too late.

Then came a longer drive when the birds were pretty plentiful. The colonel got one, a low-lying Frenchman, which he killed as he topped the fence, and after that for the life of him he could not touch a feather. Every sportsman knows what a fatal thing it is to begin to miss and then get nervous, and that was what happened to the colonel. Continually there came distant cries of " Mark! mark! over!" followed by the apparition of half a dozen brown balls showing clear against the gray autumn sky and sweeping down towards him like lightning. Whiz in front, overhead, and behind; bang, bang, bang, again went the second gun, and they were away—vanished, gone, leaving nothing but a memory behind them.

The colonel swore beneath his breath, and Ida, kneeling at his side, groaned audibly; but it was of no use, and presently the drive was done, and there he was with one wretched French partridge to show for it.

Ida said nothing, but she looked volumes, and if ever a man felt humiliated, Harold Quaritch was that man. She had set her heart upon his winning the match, and he was making an exhibition of himself that might have caused a schoolboy to blush.

Only Edward Cossey smiled grimly as he told his bearer to give the two and a half brace which he had shot to George.

"Last drive this next, gentlemen," said that universal functionary as he surveyed the colonel's one Frenchman, and then, glancing sadly at the telltale pile of empty cartridge cases, added, " You'll have to shoot up, colonel, this time, if you are going to win them gloves for Miss Ida. Mr. Cossey has knocked up four brace and a half, and you have only got a brace. Look you here, sir," he went on, in a portentous whisper, "keep forrard of them, well forrard, fire ahead, and down they'll come. You're a better shot than he is a long way ; you could give him ' birds,' sir, that you could, and beat him."

Harold said nothing. He was sorely tempted to make excuses, as any man would have been, and he might with truth have urged that he was not accustomed to partridge driving, and that one of the guns was new to him. But he resisted manfully and said never a word.

George placed the two guns, and then went off to join the beaters. It was a capital spot for a drive, for on each side were young larch plantations, sloping down towards them like a V, the guns being at the narrow end, and level with the ends of the plantations, which were at this spot about a hundred and twenty yards apart. In front was a large stretch of open fields, lying in such a fashion that the birds were bound to fly straight over the guns, and between the gap at the end of the V-shaped covers.

They had to wait a long while, for the beat was of considerable extent, and this they did in silence, till presently a couple of single birds appeared coming down the wind, for a stiffish breeze had sprung up like lightning. One went to the left over Edward Cossey's head, and he shot it very neatly, but the other, catching sight of Harold's hat beneath the fence, which was not a very high one, swerved and crossed, an almost impossible shot, nearer sixty than fifty yards from him.

"Now," said Ida, and he fired, and to his joy down came the bird with a thud, bounding full two feet into the air with the force of its impact, being, indeed, shot through the head.

"That's better," said Ida, as she handed him the second gun.

Another moment and a covey came over, high up. He fired both barrels and got a right and left, and, snatching the second gun, sent another barrel after them, hitting a third bird, which did not fall. And then a noble enthusiasm and certainty possessed him, and he knew that he should miss no more. Nor did he. With two almost impossible exceptions he dropped every bird that drive. But his crowning glory, a thing whereof he still often dreams, was yet to come.

He had killed four brace of partridge and fired twelve times, when at last the beaters made their appearance about two hundred yards away at the farther end of rather dirty barley stubble.

"I think that is the lot," he said; "I'm afraid that you have lost your gloves, Ida."

Scarcely were the words out of his mouth when there was a yell of "Mark!" and a strong covey of birds appeared swooping down with the wind right on to him.

On they came, scattered and rather "stringy," and Harold gripped his gun and drew a deep breath, while Ida, kneeling at his side, her lips apart, and her beautiful eyes wide open, watched their advent through a space in the hedge. Lovely enough she looked to charm the heart out of any man, if a man out partridge driving could descend to such frivolity, which we hold to be impossible.

Now is the moment. The leading brace are something over fifty yards away, and he knows full well that if there is to be a chance left for the second gun he must shoot before they are five yards nearer.

"Bang," down comes the old cock bird; "bang," and his mate follows him, falling with a smash into the fence.

Quick as light Ida takes the empty gun with one hand and passes him the cocked and loaded one with the other. "Bang." Another bird topples head-first out of the thinned covey. They are nearly sixty yards away now. "Bang" again, and oh, joy and wonder! the last bird turns right over backwards, and falls dead as a stone some seventy paces from the muzzle of the gun.

He had killed four birds out of a single driven covey, which, as shooters well know, is a feat not often done even by the best driving shots.

"Bravo!" said Ida; "I was sure that you could shoot if you chose."

"Yes," he answered, "it was pretty good work;" and he commenced collecting the birds, for by this time the beaters were across the field. They were all dead, not a runner in the lot, and there were exactly six brace of them. Just as he picked up the last George arrived, followed by Edward Cossey.

"Well, I never," said the former, while something resembling a smile stole over his melancholy countenance; "that's the masterest bit of shooting that I ever did see. Lord Walsingham couldn't beat that himself—fourteen shots and twelve birds picked up. Why," and he turned to Edward, "bless me, sir, if I don't believe the colonel has won them gloves for Miss Ida after all. Let's see, sir, you got two brace this last drive and one the first, and a leash the second, and two brace and a half the third, six and a half brace in all. And the colonel, yes, he has seven brace, one bird to the good."

"There, Mr. Cossey," said Ida, smiling sweetly. "I have won my gloves. Mind you don't forget to pay them?"

"Oh, I will not forget, Miss De la Molle," said he, smiling also, but not too prettily.

"I suppose," he said, addressing the colonel, "that that last covey twisted up and you browned them?"

"No," he answered, quietly, "all four were clear shots."

Mr. Cossey smiled again, an incredulous smile, which somehow sent Harold Quaritch's blood leaping through his veins more quickly than was good for him, and turned away to hide his vexation. He would rather have lost a thousand pounds than that his adversary should have got that extra bird; for not only was he a jealous shot, but he knew perfectly well that Ida was anxious that he should lose, and desired above all things to see him humiliated. And then he, the smartest shot within ten miles round, to be beaten by a middle-aged soldier shooting with a strange gun, and totally unaccustomed to driving? Why, the story would be told over the country. His anger was so great when he thought of it, that, afraid of making himself ridiculous, he set off with his bearer towards the Castle without another word, leaving the others to follow.

Ida looked after him and smiled. "He is so conceited," she said; "he cannot bear to be beaten at anything."

"I think that you are rather hard on him," said the colonel, for the joke had an unpleasant side which jarred on him.

"At any rate," she answered, with a little stamp, "it is not for you to say so. If you disliked him as much as I do you would be hard on him, too. Besides, I dare say that his turn is coming."

The colonel winced, as well he might; but looking at her handsome face, set just now like steel, at the thought of what the future might bring forth, he reflected that if Edward Cossey's turn did come, he was by no means sure that the ultimate triumph would rest with him. Ida de la Molle, to whatever extent her sense of honor and money indebtedness might carry her, was no butterfly to be broken on a wheel, but a woman whose dislike and anger, or, worse still, whose cold, unvarying disdain, was a thing from which the boldest-hearted man might shrink aghast.

Nothing more was said on the subject, and they began to talk, though somewhat constrainedly, about indifferent matters. They were both aware that it was a farce, and that they were playing a part, for beneath the external ice of formalities the river of their devotion ran whither they knew not. All that had been made clear a few nights back, but what will you have? Necessity, overriding their desires, compelled them along the path of self-denial, and, like wise folk, they recognized the fact; for there is nothing more painful in the world than the outburst of hopeless passion.

And so they talked about painting and shooting and what not, till they reached the gray old castle towers. Here Harold wanted to bid her good-by, but she persuaded him to come in and have some tea, saying that her father would like to say good-night to him.

Accordingly he went into the vestibule, where there was a light, for it was getting dusk; and here he found the squire and Mr. Cossey. As soon as he entered, Edward Cossey rose, said good-night to the squire and Ida, and then passed towards the door, where the colonel was standing, rubbing the mud off his shooting-boots. As he came, Harold, being slightly ashamed of the business of the shooting-match, and very sorry to have humiliated a man who prided himself so much upon his skill in a particular branch of sport, held out his hand, and said, in a friendly tone,

"Good-night, Mr. Cossey. Next time that we are out shooting together I expect I shall be nowhere. It was an awful fluke of mine killing those four birds."

But Edward Cossey took no notice of the friendly words or outstretched hand, but came straight on as though he intended to walk past him.

The colonel was wondering what it was best to do, for it was impossible to mistake the meaning of the oversight, when the squire, who was sometimes very quick to notice things, spoke in a loud and decided tone.

"Mr. Cossey," he said, "Colonel Quaritch is offering you his hand."

"I observe that he is," he answered, setting his handsome face, "but I do not wish to take Colonel Quaritch's hand."

Then came a moment's silence, which the squire again broke.

"When a gentleman in my house refuses to take the hand of another gentleman," he said, very quietly, "I think that I have a right to ask the reason for his conduct, which, unless that reason is a very sufficient one, is almost as much a slight upon me as upon him."

"I think that Colonel Quaritch must know the reason, and will not press me to explain," said Edward Cossey.

"I know of no reason," replied the colonel, sternly, "unless indeed it is that I have been so unfortunate as to get the best of Mr. Cossey in a friendly shooting-match."

"Colonel Quaritch must know well that such is not the reason to which I allude," said Edward. "If he consults his conscience he will probably discover a better one."

Ida and her father looked at each other in surprise, while the colonel, by a half-involuntary movement, stepped between his accuser and the door; and Ida noticed that his face was white with anger.

"You have made a very serious implication against me, Mr. Cossey," he said, in a cold, clear voice. "Before you leave this room you will be so good as to explain it in the presence of those before whom it has been made."

"Certainly, if you wish it," he answered, with something

like a sneer. "The reason why I refuse to take your hand, Colonel Quaritch, is that you have been guilty of conduct which proves to me that you are not a gentleman, and, therefore, not a person with whom I desire to be on friendly terms. Shall I go on?"

"Most certainly you will go on," answered the colonel.

"Very well. The conduct to which I refer is that you were once engaged to my aunt, Julia Heston ; that within three days of the time of the marriage you deserted and jilted her in a most cruel way, as a consequence of which she went mad, and is to this moment an inmate of an asylum."

Ida gave an exclamation of astonishment, and the colonel started and colored up, while the squire, looking at him curiously, waited to hear what he had to say.

"It is perfectly true, Mr. Cossey," he answered, "that I was engaged twenty years ago to be married to Miss Julia Heston, though I now for the first time learn that she was your aunt. It is also quite true that that engagement was broken off, under most painful circumstances, within three days of the time fixed for the marriage. What those circumstances were I am not at liberty to say, for the simple reason that I gave my word not to do so, but this I will say, that they were not to my discredit, though you may not be aware of that fact. But as you are one of the family, Mr. Cossey, my tongue is not tied, and I will do myself the honor of calling upon you to-morrow and explaining them to you. After that," he added, significantly, "I shall require you to apologize to me as publicly as you have accused me."

"You may require, but whether I shall comply is another matter," said Edward Cossey, and he passed out.

"I am very sorry, Mr. De la Molle," said the colonel, as soon as he had gone, "more sorry than I can say, that I should have been the cause of this most unpleasant scene. I also feel that I am placed in a very false position, and until I produce Mr. Cossey's written apology that position must to some extent continue. If I fail to obtain that apology, I shall have to consider what course to take. In the meanwhile I can only ask you to suspend your judgment."

CHAPTER XXIII.

THE BLOW FALLS.

On the following morning, about ten o'clock, while Edward Cossey was still at breakfast, a dog-cart drew up at his door, and out of it stepped Colonel Quaritch.

"Now for the row," said he to himself. "I hope that the governor was right in his tale, that's all. Perhaps it would have been wiser to say nothing till I had made more sure," and he poured out some more tea a little nervously, for in the colonel he had, he felt, an adversary not to be despised.

Presently the door opened, and "Colonel Quaritch" was announced. He rose and bowed a salutation, which the colonel, whose face bore a particularly grim expression, did not return.

"Will you take a chair?" he said, as soon as the servant had left, and without speaking the colonel took one—and presently began the conversation.

"Last night, Mr. Cossey," he said, "you thought proper to publicly bring a charge against me which, if it were true, would go a long way towards showing that I was not a fit person to associate with those before whom it was brought."

"Yes," said Edward, coolly.

"Before making any remarks on your conduct in bringing such a charge, which I give you credit for believing to be true, I propose to show to you that it is a false charge," went on the colonel, quietly. "The story is a very simple one, and so sad that nothing short of necessity would force me to tell it. I was, when quite young, engaged to your aunt, Miss Heston, to whom I was much attached, and who was then twenty years of age, and though I had little besides my profession, she had some money, and we were going to be married. The circumstances under which the marriage was broken off were as follows: Three days before the wedding was to take place, I went unexpectedly to the house, and was told by the servant that Miss Heston was up-stairs in her sitting-room. I went up-stairs to the room, which I knew well, knocked, and got no answer. Then I walked into the room, and this is what I saw. Your aunt was lying on the sofa in her wedding-dress (that is, in half of it, for she had only the skirt on), as I first thought, asleep. I went up to her, and saw that by her side was a brandy-bottle, half empty. In her hand also was a glass containing raw brandy. While I was wondering what it could mean, she woke up, got off the sofa, and began to stagger round the room, and I saw that she was intoxicated."

"It's a lie!" said Edward, excitedly.

"Be careful what you say, sir," answered the colonel, "and wait to say it till I have done."

"As soon as I realized what was the matter, I left the room again, and going down to your grandfather's study, where he was engaged in writing a sermon, I asked him to come up-stairs, as I was afraid that his daughter was not well. He came and saw, and the sight threw him off his balance, for he broke out into a torrent of explanations and excuses, from which in time I extracted the following facts: It appeared that ever since she was a child, Miss Heston had been ad-dicted to drinking-fits, and that it was on account of this con-stitutional weakness, which was of course concealed from me, that she had been allowed to engage herself to a penniless subaltern. It appeared, too, that the habit was hereditary, for her mother had died from the effects of drink, and one of her aunts had become mad from it.

"I went away and thought the matter over, and came to the conclusion that under these circumstances it would be im-possible for me, much as I was attached to her, to marry her, because, even if I were willing to do so, I had no right to run the risk of bringing children into the world who might in-herit the curse. Having come to this determination, which it cost me much to do, I wrote and communicated it to your grandfather, and the marriage was broken off."

"I do not believe it, I do not believe a word of it," said Edward, jumping up. "You jilted her and drove her mad, and now you are trying to shelter yourself behind a tissue of falsehood."

" Are you acquainted with your grandfather's handwriting ?" asked the colonel, quietly.

" Yes."

" Is that it ?" he went on, producing a yellow-looking letter, and showing it to him.

" I believe so—at least it looks like it."

" Then read the letter."

Edward obeyed. It was one written in answer to that of Harold Quaritch to his betrothed's father, and admitted in the clearest terms the justice of the step that he had taken. Further, it begged him, for the sake of Julia and the family at large, never to mention the cause of his defection to any one outside the family.

" Are you satisfied, Mr. Cossey ? I have other letters if you wish to see them."

Edward made no reply, and the colonel went on : " I gave the promise that your grandfather asked for, and in spite of the remarks that were freely made upon my behavior, I kept it, as it was my duty to do. You, Mr. Cossey, are the first person to whom the story has been told. And now that you have thought fit to make accusations against me which are without foundation, I must ask you to retract them as fully as you made them. I have prepared a letter which you will be so good as to sign," and he handed him a note addressed to the squire. It ran,

" DEAR MR. DE LA MOLLE,—I beg in the fullest and most ample manner possible to retract the charges which I made yesterday evening against Colonel Quaritch, in the presence of yourself and Miss De la Molle. I find that those charges were unfounded, and I hereby apologize to Colonel Quaritch for having made them."

" And supposing that I refuse to sign," said Edward, sulkily.

" I do not think," answered the colonel, " that you will refuse."

Edward looked at Colonel Quaritch, and the colonel looked at Edward.

" Well," said the colonel, " please understand that I mean you should sign that letter, and, indeed, seeing how absolutely you are in the wrong, I do not think that you can hesitate to do so."

Then, very slowly and unwillingly, Edward Cossey took up a pen, affixed his signature to the letter, blotted it, and pushed it from him.

The colonel folded it up, placed it in an envelope which he had ready, and put it in his pocket.

"Now, Mr. Cossey," he said, "I will wish you good-morning. Another time I should recommend you to be more careful, both in the facts and the manner of your accusations," and with a slight bow he left the room.

"Curse the fellow," thought Edward to himself as the front door closed, "he had me there—I was forced to sign. Well, I will be even with him about Ida, at any rate. I will propose to her this very day, Belle or no Belle, and if she won't have me I will call the money in, and smash the whole thing up"—and his handsome face bore a very evil look as he thought it.

That very afternoon he started, in accordance with this design, to pay a visit at the Castle. The squire was out, but Miss De la Molle was at home, the servant said, and accordingly he was ushered into the drawing-room, where Ida was working, for it was a wet and windy afternoon.

She rose to greet him coldly enough, and he sat down, and then came a pause which she did not seem inclined to break.

At last he spoke. "Did the squire get my letter, Miss De la Molle?" he asked.

"Yes," she answered, rather icily. "Colonel Quaritch sent it up."

"I am very sorry," he added, confusedly, "that I should have put myself in such a false position. I hope that you will give me credit for having believed my accusation when I made it."

"Such accusations should not be lightly made, Mr. Cossey," was her answer, and, as though to turn the subject, she rose and rang the bell for tea.

It came, and the bustle connected with it prevented any further conversation for a while. At length, however, it subsided, and once more Edward found himself alone with Ida. He looked at her and felt afraid. The woman was of a different clay to himself, and he knew it—he loved her, but he did not understand her in the least. However, if the thing

was to be done at all it must be done now, so, with a desperate effort, he screwed himself up to the point.

"Miss De la Molle," he said, and Ida, knowing full surely
what was coming, felt her heart jump within her bosom, and
then stand still.

"Miss De la Molle," he went on, "perhaps you will remember a conversation that we had some weeks ago in the
conservatory?"

"Yes," she said, "I remember—about the money."

"About the money and other things," he said, gathering
courage. "I hinted to you then that I hoped in certain con-
tingencies to be allowed to make my addresses to you, and I
think that you understood me."

"I understood you perfectly," answered Ida, her pale face
set like ice, "and I gave you to understand that in the event
of your lending my father the money, I should hold myself
bound to—to listen to what you had to say."

"Oh, curse the money!" broke in Edward. "It is not a
question of money with me, Ida, it is not, indeed. I love you
with all my heart. I have loved you ever since I saw you.
It was because I was jealous of him that I made a fool of myself last night, with Colonel Quaritch. I should have asked
you to marry me long ago only there were obstacles in the
way. I love you, Ida; there never was a woman like you—
never."

She listened with the same set face. Obviously he was in
earnest, but his earnestness did not move her; it scarcely even
flattered her pride. She disliked the man intensely, and nothing that he could say or do would lessen that dislike by one
jot—probably, indeed, it would only intensify it.

Presently he stopped and stood beside her, his breast heaving, and his face broken with emotion, and tried to take her
hand.

She withdrew it sharply, for his touch was unpleasant to
her.

"I do not think that there is any need for all this," she
said, coldly. "I gave a conditional promise. You have fulfilled your share of the bargain, and I am prepared to fulfil
mine in due course."

So far as her words went, Edward could find no fault with

their meaning, and yet he felt more like a man who has been abruptly and finally refused than one declared chosen. He stood still and looked at her.

"I think it right to tell you, however," she went on, in the same measured tones, "that if I marry you it will be from motives of duty, and not from motives of affection. I have no love to give you, and I do not wish for yours. I do not know if you will be satisfied with this. If you are not, you had better give up the idea," and she, for the first time, looked up at him with more anxiety in her face than she would have cared to show.

But if she hoped that her coldness would repel him, she was destined to be disappointed. On the contrary, like water thrown on burning oil, it only inflamed him the more.

"The love will come, Ida," he said, and once more he tried to take her hand.

"No, Mr. Cossey," she said, in a voice that checked him, "I am sorry to have to speak so plainly, but till I marry I am my own mistress. Pray understand me."

"As you like," he said, drawing back from her, sulkily. "I am so fond of you that I will marry you on any terms, and that is the truth. I have one thing to ask of you, Ida, and that is that you will keep our engagement secret for the present, and get your father (I suppose I must speak to him) to do the same. I have reasons," he went on, by way of explanation, "for not wishing it to become known."

"I do not see why I should keep it secret," she said, "but it does not matter to me."

"The fact is," he explained, "my father is a very curious man, and I doubt if he would like my engagement, because he thinks I ought to marry a great deal of money."

"Oh, indeed," answered Ida. She had believed, as was indeed the case, that there were other reasons not unconnected with Mrs. Quest, on account of which he was anxious to keep the engagement secret. "By the way," she went on, "I am sorry to have to talk of business, but this is a business matter, is it not? I suppose it is understood that, in the event of our marriage, the mortgage you hold over this place will not be enforced against my father."

"Of course not," he answered. "Look here, Ida, I will

give you those mortgage bonds as a wedding-present, and
you can put them in the fire; and I will make a good settle-
ment on you."

"Thank you," she said, "but I do not require any settle-
ment on myself; I had rather none was made; but I consent
to the engagement only on the express condition that the
mortgages shall be cancelled before marriage, and as the property will ultimately come to me, this is not much to ask. And
now one more thing, Mr. Cossey: I should like to know
when you wish this marriage to take place; not at once, I
presume."

"I should wish it to take place to-morrow," he said, with
an attempt at a laugh; "but I suppose that, between one
thing and another, it can't come off at once. Shall we say
this time six months—that will be in May?"

"Very good," said Ida, "this day, six months, I shall be
prepared to become your wife, Mr. Cossey. I believe it is,"
she added, with a flash of bitter sarcasm, "the time usually
allowed for the redemption of a mortgage."

"You say very hard things," he answered, wincing.

"Do I? I dare say. I am hard by nature. I wonder that
you can wish to marry me."

"I wish it beyond everything in the world," he answered,
earnestly. "You can never know how much. By the way,
I know I was foolish about Colonel Quaritch; but, Ida, I
cannot bear to see that man near you. I hope you will drop
his acquaintance as much as possible now."

Once more Ida's face set like a flint. "I am not your wife
yet, Mr. Cossey," she said; "when I am you will have a right
to dictate to me as to whom I shall associate with. At present you have no such right, and if it pleases me to associate
with Colonel Quaritch I shall do so. If you disapprove of
my conduct, the remedy is simple—you can break off the
engagement."

He rose, absolutely crushed, for Ida was by far the stronger
of the two, and, besides, his passion gave her an unfair advantage over him. Without attempting any reply, he held out
his hand and said good-night, for he was afraid to attempt
any demonstration of affection, adding that he would come
to see her father in the morning.

She touched his outstretched hand with her fingers, and then, fearing lest he should change his mind, promptly rang the bell.

In another minute the door had closed behind him, and she was left alone.

CHAPTER XXIV.

"GOOD-BY, MY DEAR, GOOD-BY."

WHEN Edward Cossey had gone, Ida rose and put her hands to her head. So the blow had fallen and the deed was done, and she was engaged to be married to Edward Cossey. And Harold Quaritch! Well, there must be an end to that. It was hard, too—only a woman could know how hard. Ida was not a person with a long record of love affairs. Once, when she was twenty, she had had a proposal which she had refused, and that was all. So it happened that when she became attached to Colonel Quaritch she had found her heart for the first time, and, for a woman, somewhat late in life. Consequently her feeling was all the more profound, and so indeed was her grief at being forced not only to put it away, but to give herself to another man who was not agreeable to her. She was not a violent or ill-regulated woman like Mrs. Quest. She looked facts in the face, recognized their meaning, and bowed before their inexorable logic. It seemed to her almost impossible that she could hope to avoid this marriage, and, if that proved to be so, she might be relied upon to make the best of it. Scandal would, under any circumstances, never find a word to say against Ida, for she was not a person who would attempt to console herself for an unhappy marriage. But it was bitter, bitter as gall, to be thus forced to turn aside from her happiness—for she well knew that with Harold Quaritch her life would be very happy—and fit her shoulders to this heavy yoke. Well, she had saved the place to her father by it, and also to her descendants, if she had any, and that was all that could be said for it.

She thought and thought, wishing in the bitterness of her heart that she had never been born to come to such a heavy day, till at last she could think no more. The air of the room seemed to stifle her, though it was by no means overheated. She went to the window and looked out. It was a wild, wet evening, and the wind was driving the rain before it in sheets. In the west the lurid light of the sinking sun stained the clouds blood-red, and broke in flying arrows of ominous light upon the driving storm.

But bad as the weather was, it attracted Ida. When the heart is heavy and torn by conflicting passions, it seems to answer to the calling of the storm, and to long to lose its petty troubling in the turmoil of the rushing world. Nature has many moods of which our own are but the echo and reflection, and she can be companionable when all human sympathy must fail. For she is our mother from whom we come, to whom we go, and her arms are ever open to clasp the children who can hear her voices. Drawn thereto by an impulse which she could not have analyzed, Ida went up-stairs, put on a thick pair of boots, a mackintosh, and an old hat, and sallied out into the wind and wet. It was blowing big guns, and as the rain whirled down the drops struck upon her face like spray. She crossed the bridge, and went out into the park land beyond. The air was full of dead leaves, and the grass rustled with them, for this was the first wind since the frost. The great boughs of the oaks rattled and groaned above her, and high overhead, among the sullen clouds, a flight of wind-tossed rooks were being blown this way and that.

Ida bent her tall frame against the rain and gale, and fought her way through it. At first she had no clear idea as to where she was going, but gradually, perhaps from custom, she took the path that ran across the fields to Honham Church. It was a beautiful old church, and had originally been built by the Boissey family, and enlarged (particularly as regards the tower, which was one of the finest in the country) by the widow of one of the De la Molles, whose husband had fallen at Agincourt, as a memorial forever. There, upon the porch, were carved the "hawks" of the De la Molles, wreathed round with palms of victory; and there, too, within the chancel, hung the warrior's helmet and his dinted shield.

Nor was he alone, for all around lay the dust of the illustrious dead, come after the toil and struggle of their stormy lives to rest within the walls of the old church. Some of them had monuments of alabaster, where they lay in effigy, their heads pillowed upon that of a conquered Saracen; some had monuments of oak and brass, and some had no monuments at all, for the Puritans had ruthlessly destroyed them. But they were nearly all there, some twenty generations of the bearers of an ancient name, for even those of them who had perished on the scaffold had been borne here for burial. The whole place was eloquent of the dead and of the mournful lesson of mortality. From century to century the bearers of that name had walked in these fields, and lived in yonder castle, and looked upon the familiar swell of yonder ground and the silver flash of yonder river, and now their dust was gathered here and all the turmoil of their lives was lost in the silence of their narrow tomb.

Ida loved the spot, hallowed to her not only by the altar of her faith, but the human associations that clung around and clothed it as the ivy clothed its walls. Here she had been christened, and here among her ancestors she hoped to be buried also. Here as a girl she used to creep in awed silence with her brother James, and look through the window when the full moon was up, at the white figures stretched in their marble silence within. Here, too, she had sat for Sunday after Sunday for more than twenty years, and stared at the quaint Latin inscriptions cut on marble slabs, which recorded the almost superhuman virtues of the departed De la Molles of the seventeenth and eighteenth centuries, her own immediate ancestors. The place was familiar to her whole life; she had scarcely a recollection with which it was not in some way connected; it was not wonderful, therefore, that she loved it, and that in the trouble of her mind her feet shaped their course towards it.

Presently she was there in the churchyard, and, taking her stand under the shelter of a line of Scotch firs, through which the gale sobbed and sang, leaned against a side gate and looked. The scene was desolate enough; the rain dropped from the roof on to the sodden graves beneath, and ran in thin sheets down the flint facing of the tower; the dead leaves whirled and rattled in and about the empty porch, and over all shot one red and angry arrow from the sinking sun. She stood in the wind and rain, and gazed at the old church that had seen the end of so many sorrows more bitter than her own, and the wreck of so many summers, till the darkness began to close round her like a pall, while the wind sang the requiem of her hopes. She was not of a desponding or pessimistic character, but in that bitter hour she found it in her heart to wish, as most people have done at one time or another in their lives, that the tragedy were over and the curtain had fallen, and that she lay beneath those dripping sods without sight or hearing, without hope or dread. It seemed to her that the hereafter must indeed be terrible if it outweighs the sorrows of the here.

And there, poor woman, she thought of the long years between her and rest, and, leaning her head against the gate-post, she began to cry bitterly in the gloom.

Presently she stopped crying, with a start, and looked up, for she felt that she was no longer alone. Her instincts had not deceived her, for there, not more than two paces from her, in the shadow of the fir-tree, was the figure of a man. Just then he took a step to the left, which brought his figure against the sky, and Ida's heart stood still, for she saw who it was now. It was Harold Quaritch, the man over whose loss she had been weeping.

" It's deuced odd," she heard him say, for she was to leeward of him, " but I could have sworn that I heard somebody sobbing ; I suppose it was the wind."

Ida's first idea was flight, and she made a movement for that purpose, and in doing so tripped over a stick and nearly fell.

In a minute he was by her side. She was caught, and perhaps she was not altogether sorry, especially as she had tried to get away.

" Who is it ? what's the matter ?" said the colonel, lighting a fusee under her nose. It was one of those flaming fusees, and burned with a blue light, showing Ida's tall figure and her beautiful face all stained with grief and tears, her wet mackintosh, and the gate-post against which she had been leaning—everything.

" Why, Ida," he said, in amaze, " what are you doing here, crying too ?"

" I'm not crying," she said, with a sob ; " it's the rain has made my face wet."

Just then the light burned out and he dropped it.

"What is it, dear, what is it?" he said, in great distress, for the sight of her alone in the wet and dark, in tears, moved him beyond himself, and indeed he would have been no man if it had not.

She tried to answer, but, poor thing, she could not, and in another minute, to tell the honest truth, she had exchanged the gate-post for Harold's broad shoulder, and was finishing her "cry" there.

Now, to see a young and pretty woman weeping (more especially if she happens to be weeping in your arms) is a very trying thing. It is trying even if you don't happen to be in love with her at all. But if you are in love with her, however little, it is dreadful; whereas, if, as in the present case, you happen to worship her, more, perhaps, than it is good to worship any fallible human creature, then the sight is positively overpowering. And so, indeed, it proved in the present instance. The colonel could not bear it, but lifting her head from his shoulder, he kissed her sweet face again and again. Now nature has generally a remedy for most ills, if only the physician knows where to look for it, and there is no doubt that this sort of treatment has before now proved efficacious in many similar cases. At any rate it answered here, for presently Ida grew quieter.

"Don't," she said, feebly—a phrase common to the sex in such circumstances from duchesses to milkmaids, and one full of human nature.

"What is it, darling?" he said, "what is the matter?"

"Leave go of me, I will tell you," she answered.

He obeyed, though with some unwillingness, for the situation was not without its charms.

She hunted for her handkerchief and wiped her eyes, and then at last she spoke—

"I am engaged to be married," she said, in a low voice, "to Mr. Cossey."

Then, for about the first time in his life, Harold Quaritch swore violently in the presence of a lady.

"Oh, —— it all," he said.

She took no notice of the strength of the language, perhaps indeed she re-echoed it in some feminine equivalent.

"It is true," she said, with a sigh. "I knew that it would come, those dreadful things always do—and it was not my fault—I am sure that you will always remember that. I had to do it; he advanced the money on the express condition, and even if I could pay back the money, I suppose that I should be bound to carry out the bargain. It is not the money that he wants, but his bond."

"Curse him for an infernal Shylock," said Harold again, and he groaned in his bitterness and jealousy.

"Is there nothing to be done?" he asked, presently, in a harsh voice, for he was very hard hit.

"Nothing," she answered, sadly. "I do not see what can help us, unless the man died," she said; "and that is not likely. Harold," she went on, addressing him for the first time in her life by his Christian name, for she felt that after crying upon a man's shoulder it is ridiculous to scruple about calling him by his name—"Harold, there is no help for it. I did it myself, remember, because, as I told you, I do not think that any one woman has a right to place her individual happiness before the welfare of her family. And I am only sorry," she added, her voice breaking a little, "that what I have done should bring suffering upon you."

He groaned again, but said nothing.

"We must try to forget," she went on, wildly. "Oh no! no! I know that it is not possible that we should forget. You won't forget me, Harold, will you? And though it must be all over between us, we must never speak like this again— never. You will always know that I have not forgotten you, will you not, but that I think of you always."

"There is no fear of my forgetting," he said, "and I am selfish enough to hope that you will think of me at times, dear."

"Yes, indeed I will. We all have our burdens to bear. It is a hard world, and we must bear them. And it will all be the same in the end, in just a few years. I dare say these dead people here have felt the same, and how quiet they are. And, perhaps, there may be something beyond, where things are not so. Who can say? You won't go away from this place, Harold, will you? Not until I am married, at any rate; perhaps you had better go then. Say that you won't go till then, and you will let me see you sometimes; it is such a comfort to see you."

"I should have gone, certainly," he said; "to New Zealand, probably, but if you wish it I will stop for the present."

"Thank you; and now good-by, my dear, good-by. No, don't come with me, I can find my own way home. And, now, why do you wait. Good-by, good-by forever in this way. Yes, kiss me once, and swear that you will never forget me. Marry if you wish to; but don't forget me, Harold. Forgive me for speaking so plainly, but I speak as one about to die to you, and I wish things to be clear."

"I shall never marry and I shall never forget you," he answered. "Good-by, my love, good-by."

In another minute she had vanished into the storm and rain, out of sight, and out of his life, but not out of his heart.

And he, too, turned and went his way into the wild and lonely night.

An hour afterwards Ida came down into the drawing-room dressed for dinner, looking rather pale, but otherwise quite herself. Presently the old squire arrived. He had been attending a magistrates' meeting in a neighboring town, and had only just got home.

"Why, Ida," he said, "I could not find you anywhere. I met George as I was driving from Boisingham, and he told me that he saw you walking through the park."

"Did he?" she answered, indifferently. "Yes, I have been out. It was so stuffy in-doors. Father," she went on, with a change of tone, "I have something to tell you. I am engaged to be married."

He looked at her curiously, and then said, quietly—the squire was always quiet in any matter of real emergency— "Indeed, my dear, that is a serious matter. However, speaking off-hand, I think that, notwithstanding the disparity of age, Quaritch—"

"No, no," she said, wincing visibly, "I am not engaged to Colonel Quaritch, I am engaged to Mr. Cossey."

"Oh," he said, "oh, indeed! I thought from what I saw, that—that—"

At this moment the servant announced dinner.

"Well, never mind about it now, father," she said; "I am tired, and want my dinner. Mr. Cossey is coming to see you to-morrow, and we can talk about it afterwards."

And though the squire thought about it a good deal, he made no further allusion to the subject that night.

CHAPTER XXV.

THE SQUIRE GIVES HIS CONSENT.

EDWARD COSSEY did not come away from the scene of his engagement in a very happy or triumphant tone of mind. Ida's bitter words stung like whips, and he understood, as she clearly meant he should understand, that it was only in consideration of the money advanced that she had consented to become his wife. Now, however satisfactory it may be to be rich enough to purchase your heart's desire in this fashion, it is not altogether soothing to the pride of a nineteenth-century man to be continually reminded by the thought that he is a buyer in the market, and nothing but a buyer. Of course, he saw clearly enough that there was an object in all this; he saw that Ida, by making obvious her dislike, wished to disgust him with his bargain, and escape from an alliance of which the prospect was hateful to her. But he had no intention of being so easily discouraged. In the first place his passion for the woman was as a devouring flame, eating ever at his heart. In that at any rate he was sincere; he did love her so far as his nature was capable of love, or at any rate he had the keenest desire to make her his wife. A delicate-minded man would probably have shrunk from forcing himself upon a woman under parallel circumstances; but Edward Cossey did not happen to fall into that category, and as a matter of fact such men are rare. Few even among the gentler classes are there who, where women are concerned, will allow delicacy to weigh against their passion or their interest.

Another thing that he took into count was that Ida would probably get over her dislike. He was a close observer of women, in a cynical and half-contemptuous way, and he remarked, or thought that he remarked, a curious tendency among them to submit with comparative complacency to the inevitable whenever it happened to coincide with their material advantage. Women, he argued, have not, as a class, outgrown the recollections of their primitive condition when their partners for life were chosen for them by lot as the chance of battle. They still recognize the claims of the wealthiest or strongest, and their love of luxury and ease is so keen that if the nest they lie in is only soft enough, they will not grieve long over the fact that it was not of their own choosing. Arguing from these premises, therefore, he came to the conclusion that Ida would soon get over her repugnance to marrying him, when she found how many comforts and good things marriage with so rich a man would place at her disposal, and would learn to look on him with affection and gratitude as the author of her gilded ease, if for no other reason. And so, indeed, she might have done had she been of another and very common stamp. But, unfortunately for his reasoning, there are members of her sex who are by nature of an order of mind superior to these considerations, and who realize that they have but one life to live, and that the highest form of happiness is *not* dependent upon money or money's worth, but rather upon the indulgence of mental aspirations and those affections which, when genuine, draw nearer to holiness than anything else about us. Such a woman, more especially if she be already possessed with an affection for another man, does not easily become reconciled to her lot, however quietly she may endure it, and such a woman was Ida de la Molle.

Edward Cossey, on returning to Boisingham on the evening of his engagement, at once wrote and posted a note to the squire, saying that he would call on him on the following morning on a matter of business. Accordingly, about half-past ten o'clock he arrived, and was shown into the vestibule, where he found the old gentleman standing with his back to the fire and plunged in reflection.

"Well, Mr. De la Molle," said Edward, rather nervously, as soon as he had shaken hands, "I do not know if Ida has spoken to you about what took place between us yesterday."

"Yes," he said—"yes, she told me something to the effect that she had accepted a proposal of marriage from you, subject to my consent, of course; but really the whole thing is so sudden that I have hardly had time to consider it."

"It is very simple," said Edward; "I am deeply attached

to your daughter, and I have been so fortunate as to be accepted by her. Should you give your consent to the marriage, I may as well say at once that I wish to make the most liberal money arrangements in my power. I will make Ida a present of the mortgage bonds that I hold over this property, and she may put them in the fire. Further, I will covenant on the death of my father, which cannot now be long delayed, to settle two hundred thousand pounds upon her absolutely. Also, I shall be prepared to agree that if I have a son, and he should wish to do so, he shall take the name of De la Molle."

"I am sure," said the squire, turning round to hide his natural gratification at these proposals, "your offers on the subject of settlements are of a most liberal order, and of course, so far as I am concerned, Ida will have this place, which may one day be again more valuable than it is now."

"I am glad that they meet with your approval," said Edward; "and now there is one more thing I want to ask you, Mr. De la Molle, and which I hope, if you will give your consent to the marriage, you will not raise any objection to. That is, that our engagement should not be announced at present. The fact is," he went on, hurriedly, "my father is a very peculiar man, and has a great idea of my marrying somebody with a large fortune. Also his state of health is so uncertain that there is no possibility of knowing how he will take anything. Indeed, he is dying; the doctors told me that he might go off any day, and that he cannot last for another three months. If the engagement is announced to him now, at the best I shall have a great deal of trouble, and at the worst he might, if he happened to take a fancy against it, make me suffer in his will."

"Umph!" said the squire; "I don't quite like the idea of a projected marriage with my daughter, Miss De la Molle of Honham Castle, being hushed up as though there were something discreditable about it, but still there may be peculiar circumstances in the case that would justify me in consenting to that course. You are both old enough to know your own minds, and the match would be as advantageous to you as it could be to us, for even nowadays a family, and I may even say personal appearance, still go for something where matrimony is concerned. I have reason to know that your father is a peculiar man, very peculiar. Yes, on the whole, though I don't like hole-and-corner affairs, I shall have no objection to the engagement not being announced for the next month or two."

"Thank you for considering me so much," said Edward, with a sigh of relief. "Then am I to understand that you give your consent to our engagement?"

The squire reflected for a moment. Everything seemed quite straight, and yet he suspected crookedness. His latent distrust of the man, which had not been decreased by the scene of two nights before—for he never could bring himself to like Edward Cossey—arose in force and made him hesitate when there was no visible ground for hesitation. He had, as has been said, an instinctive insight into character that was almost feminine in its intensity, and it was lifting a warning finger before him now.

"I don't quite know what to say," he replied, at length. "The whole affair is so sudden—and, to tell you the truth, I thought that Ida had bestowed her affections in another direction."

Edward's face darkened. "I thought so too," he answered, "until, yesterday, I was so happy as to be undeceived. I ought to tell you, by the way," he went on, running away from the covert falsehood in his last words as quickly as he could, "how much I regret that I was the cause of that scene with Colonel Quaritch, more especially as I find that there is an explanation of the story against him. The fact is, I was foolish enough to be put out because he beat me out shooting, and also because, well I—I was jealous of him."

"Ah, yes," said the squire, rather coldly, "a most unfortunate affair. Of course, I don't know what the particulars of the matter were, and it is no affair of mine, but, speaking generally, I should say never bring an accusation of that sort against a man at all unless you are driven to it, and if you do bring it, be quite certain of your ground. However, that is neither here nor there. Well, about this engagement. Ida is old enough to judge for herself, and seems to have made up her mind; so, as I know no reason to the contrary, and as the business arrangements proposed are all that I could wish, I cannot see that I have any ground for withholding my consent. So all I can say, sir, is that I hope that you will make my daughter a good husband, and that you will both be happy. Ida is a high-spirited woman, and in some ways a very peculiar woman; but, in my opinion, she is greatly above the average of her sex, as I have known it, and provided you have her affection, and don't attempt to drive her, she will go through thick and thin for you. But I dare say you would like to see her. Oh, by the way, I forgot; she has got a dreadful headache this morning, and is stopping in bed. It isn't much in her line, but I dare say that she is a little upset. Perhaps you would like to come up to dinner to-night."

This proposition Edward, knowing full well that Ida's headache was a device to rid herself of the necessity of seeing him, accepted with gratitude and departed.

As soon as he was gone, Ida herself came down.

"Well, my dear," said the squire, cheerfully, "I have just had the pleasure of seeing Edward Cossey, and I have told him that, as you seemed to wish it,—"

Here Ida made a movement of impatience, but remembered herself and said nothing.

"That as you seemed to wish that it should be so, I had no ground of objection to your engagement. I may as well tell you that the proposals that he makes as regards settlements are of the most liberal nature."

"Are they?" answered Ida, indifferently. "Is Mr. Cossey coming here to dinner?"

"Yes; I asked him. I thought that you would like to see him."

"Well, then, I wish you had not," she answered, with animation, "because there is nothing for dinner except some cold beef. Really, father, it is very thoughtless of you;" and she stamped her foot and went off in a huff, leaving the squire full of reflection.

"I wonder what it all means?" he said to himself. "She can't care about the man much or she would not make that fuss about his being asked to dinner. She isn't the sort of woman to be caught by the money, I should think. Well, I know nothing about it; it is no affair of mine, and I can only take things as I find them."

And then he fell to reflecting that the marriage was an extraordinary stroke of luck for the family. Here they were at the last gasp, mortgaged up to the eyes, when suddenly fortune, in the shape of an, on the whole, perfectly unobjectionable young man, appears, takes up the mortgages, proposes settlements to the tune of hundreds of thousands, and even offers to perpetuate the old family name in the person of his son, should he have one. Such a state of affairs could not but be gratifying to any man, however unworldly, and the squire was not altogether unworldly. That is, he had a keen sense of the dignity of his social position and his family, and it had all his life been his chief and laudable desire to be sufficiently provided with the goods of this world to raise the De la Molles to the position which they had occupied in former centuries. Hitherto, however, the tendency of events had been all the other way—the house was a sinking one, and but the other day its ancient roof had nearly fallen about their ears. Now, however, as though by magic, the prospect changed. On Ida's marriage all the mortgages, those heavy accumulations of years of growing expenditure and narrowing means, would roll off the back of the estate, and the De la Molles of Honham Castle would once more take the place in the country to which they were undoubtedly entitled.

It is not wonderful that the prospect proved a pleasing one to him, or that his head was filled with visions of splendors to come.

As it chanced, on that very morning it was necessary for Mr. Quest to pay the old gentleman a visit in order to obtain his signature to a lease of a bakery in Boisingham, which, together with two or three other houses, belonged to the estate.

He arrived just as the squire was in the full flow of his meditations, and it would not have needed a man of Mr. Quest's penetration and powers of observation to discover that he had something on his mind which he was longing for an opportunity to talk about.

The squire signed the lease without paying the slightest attention to Mr. Quest's explanations, and then suddenly asked him when the first interest on the recently effected mortgages came due.

The lawyer mentioned an approaching date.

"Ah," said the squire, "then it will have to be met, but it does not matter, it will be for the last time."

Mr. Quest pricked up his ears and looked at him.

"The fact is, Quest," he went on, by way of explanation, "that there are—well—family arrangements pending which will put an end to these embarrassments in a natural and a proper way."

"Indeed," said Mr. Quest, "I am very glad to hear it."

"Yes, yes," said the squire, "unfortunately I am under some restraint in speaking about the matter at present, or I should like to ask your opinion, for which, as you know, I have a great respect. Really, though, I do not know why I should not consult my lawyer on a matter of business. I only consented not to trumpet the thing about."

"Lawyers are confidential agents," said Mr. Quest, quietly.

"Of course they are. Of course, and it is their business to hold their tongues. I may rely upon your discretion, may I not?"

"Certainly," said Mr. Quest.

"Well, the matter is this: Mr. Edward Cossey is engaged to Miss De la Molle. He has just been here to obtain my consent, which, of course, I have not withheld, as I know nothing against the young man—nothing at all. The only stipulation that he made is, I think, a reasonable one under the circumstances, namely, that the engagement is to be kept quiet for a little while on account of the condition of his father's health. He says that he is an unreasonable man, and that he might take a prejudice against it."

During this announcement Mr. Quest had remained perfectly quiet, his face showing no signs of excitement, only his eyes shone with a curious light.

"Indeed," he said, "this is very interesting news."

"Yes," said the squire. "That is what I meant by saying that there would be no necessity to make any arrangements for the future payment of interest, for Cossey has informed me that he proposes to put the mortgage bonds in the fire before his marriage."

"Indeed," said Mr. Quest; "well, he could hardly do less, could he? Altogether, I think you ought to be congratulated, Mr. De la Molle. It is not often that a man gets such a chance of clearing the encumbrances off a property. And now I am very sorry, but I must be getting home, as I promised my wife to be back for luncheon. As the thing is to be kept quiet, I suppose that it would be premature for me to offer my congratulations to Miss De la Molle."

"Yes, yes, don't say anything about it at present. Well, good-by."

CHAPTER XXVI.

MR. QUEST got into his dog-cart and drove homewards, full of feelings which it would be difficult to describe.

The hour of his revenge was at hand. He had played his cards and he had won the game, and fortune with it, and his enemy lay in the hollow of his hand. He looked behind him at the proud towers of the castle, reflecting as he did so that in all probability they would belong to him before another year was over his head. At one time he had earnestly longed to possess this place, but now this was not so much the object of his desire. What he wanted now was the money. With thirty thousand pounds in his hand he would, together with what he had, be a rich man, and he had already laid his plans for the future. Of the Tiger he had heard nothing lately. She was cowed, but he well knew that it was only for a while. By and by her rapacity would get the better of her fear and she would recommence her persecutions. This being so, he came to a determination—he would put the world between them. Once let him have this money in his hand and he would start his life afresh in some new country; he was not too old for it, and he would be a rich man, and then perhaps he might get rid of the cares which had rendered so much of his life valueless. If Belle would go with him, well and good —if not, he could not help it. If she did go, there must be a reconciliation first, for he could not tolerate the life they lived any longer.

In due course he reached the Oaks and went in. Luncheon was on the table, at which Belle was sitting. She was, as usual, dressed in black, and beautiful to look on; but her round babyish face was pale and pinched, and there were black lines beneath her eyes.

"I did not know that you were coming back to luncheon," she said; "I am afraid there is not much to eat."

" Yes," he said, " I finished my business up at the Castle, so I thought I might as well come home. By the way, Belle, I have a bit of news for you."

" What is it ?" she asked, looking up sharply, for something in his tone attracted her attention and awoke her fears.

" Your friend, Edward Cossey, is going to be married to Ida de la Molle."

She blanched till she looked like death itself, and put her hands to her heart as though she had been stabbed.

" The squire told me so himself," he went on, keeping his eyes remorselessly fixed upon her face.

She leaned forward, and he thought she was going to faint, but she did not. By a supreme effort she recovered herself and drank a glass of sherry which was standing by her side.

" I expected it," she said, in a low voice.

" You mean that you dreaded it," answered Mr. Quest, quietly. He rose and locked the door and then came and stood close to her and spoke.

" Listen, Belle. I know all about your affair with Edward Cossey. I have proofs of it, but I have forborne to use them, because I saw that in the end he would weary of you and desert you for some other woman, and that would be my best revenge upon you. You have all along been nothing but his toy, the light woman with whom he amused his leisure hours."

She put her hands back over her heart, but said never a word, and he went on.

" Belle, I did wrong to marry you when you did not want to marry me, but, being married, you have done wrong to be unfaithful to your vows. I have been rewarded by your infidelity, and your infidelity has been rewarded by desertion. Now I have a proposal to make to you, and if you are wise you will accept it. Let us set the one wrong against the other ; let both be forgotten. Forgive me, and I will forgive you, and let us make peace—if not now, then in a little while, when your heart is not so sore, and go right away from Edward Cossey and Ida de la Molle, and Honham and Boisingham, into some new part of the world where we can begin life again and try to forget the past."

She looked up at him and shook her head mournfully, and

twice she tried to speak and twice she failed. The third time her words came.

"You do not understand me," she said. "You are very kind and I am very grateful to you, but you do not understand me. I cannot get over things so easily as I know most women can; what I have done I never can undo. I do not blame him altogether, it was as much or more my fault than his, but having once loved him I cannot go back to you or any other man. If you like I will go on living with you as we live, and I will try to make you comfortable, but I can say no more."

"Think again, Belle," he said, almost pleadingly; "I dare say that you have never given me credit for much tenderness of heart, and I know that you have as much against me as I have against you. But I have always loved you, and I love you now, really and truly love you, and I will make you a good husband if you will let me."

"You are very good," she said, "but it cannot be. Get rid of me if you like, and marry somebody else. I am ready to take the penalty of what I have done."

"Once more, Belle, I beg you to consider. Do you know what kind of man this is for whom you are giving up your life? Not only has he deserted you, but do you know how he has got hold of Ida de la Molle? He has, as I know well, *bought* her, I tell you he has bought her as much as though he had gone into the open market and paid down a price for her. The other day Cossey & Son were going to foreclose upon the Honham estates, which would have ruined the old gentleman. Well, what did your young man do? He went to the girl, who hates him, by the way, and is in love with Colonel Quaritch, and said to her, 'If you will promise to marry me when I ask you, I will find the thirty thousand pounds and take up the mortgages.' And on those terms she agreed to marry him. And now he has got rid of you and he claims her promise. That is the history. I wonder that your pride will bear such a thing. By Heaven, I would kill the man!"

She looked up at him curiously. "Would you?" she said; "it is not a bad idea. I dare say it is all true. He is worthless. Why does one fall in love with worthless people? Well, there is an end of it; or a beginning of the end. As I have sown, so must I reap;" and she got up, and, unlocking the door, left the room.

"Yes," he said, aloud, when she had gone, "there is a beginning of the end. Upon my word, what between one thing and another, unlucky devil as I am, I had rather stand in my own shoes than in Edward Cossey's."

Belle went to her room and sat thinking, or rather brooding, sullenly. Then she put on her bonnet and cloak and started out, taking the road that ran past Honham Castle. She had not gone a hundred yards before she found herself face to face with Edward Cossey himself. He was coming out of a gunsmith's shop, where he had been ordering some cartridges.

"How do you do, Belle?" he said, coloring up and lifting his hat.

"How do you do, Mr. Cossey?" she answered, coming to a stop and looking him straight in the face.

"Where are you going?" he asked, not knowing what to say.

"I am going to walk up to the Castle to call on Miss De la Molle."

"I don't think that you will find her. She is in bed with a headache.

"Oh! So you have been up there this morning?"

"Yes, I had to see the squire about some business."

"Indeed!" Then, looking him in the eyes again, "Are you engaged to be married to Ida?"

He colored up; he could not prevent himself from doing so.

"No," he answered; "what makes you ask such a question?"

"I don't know," she said, laughing a little, "feminine curiosity, I suppose. I thought that you might be. Good-by," and she went on, leaving Edward Cossey to the enjoyment of a very peculiar set of sensations.

"What a coward!" said Belle to herself. "He does not even dare to tell me the truth."

Nearly an hour later she arrived at the Castle, and, asking for Ida, was shown into the drawing-room, where she found her sitting, reading.

Ida rose to greet her, not without warmth, for the two

women, although they were at the opposite poles of character, had a friendly feeling for each other.

In this way they were both strong, and strength always recognizes and respects strength.

"Have you walked up?" asked Ida.

"Yes, I walked on the chance of finding you. I wanted to speak to you."

"Yes?" said Ida; "what is it?"

"This. Forgive me, but are you engaged to be married to Edward Cossey?"

Ida looked at her in a slow, stately kind of way, which seemed to ask by what right she came to question her. At least, so Belle read it.

"I know that I have no right to ask such a question," she said, with humility, "and, of course, you need not answer it, but I have a reason for asking."

"Well," said Ida, "I was requested by Mr. Cossey to keep the matter secret, but he appears to have divulged it. Yes, I am engaged to be married to him."

Belle's beautiful face turned a shade paler, if that was possible, and her eyes hardened.

"Do you wonder I ask you this?" she said. "I will tell you, though probably when I have done so you will never speak to me again. I am Edward Cossey's discarded mistress," and she laughed bitterly enough.

Ida shrank a little and colored, as a pure and high-minded woman naturally does when she is for the first time suddenly brought into actual contact with impurity and passion.

"I know," went on Belle, "that I must seem a shameful thing to you; but, Ida, good and cold and stately as you are, pray God that you may never be thrown into temptation; pray God that you may never be married almost by force to a man whom you hate, and then suddenly know what a thing it is to fall in love, and for the first time feel your life awake."

"Hush," said Ida, gently, "what right have I to judge you."

"I loved him," went on Belle, "I loved him passionately, and for a little while it was as though heaven had opened its gates; for he used to care for me a little, and I think he would have taken me away and married me afterwards, but I would not hear of it, because I knew it would ruin him. He offered to once, and I refused, and within three hours of that I believe that he was bargaining for you. Well, and then it was the old story, that he fell more and more in love with you, and of course I had no hold upon him."

"Yes," said Ida, moving impatiently, "but why do you tell me all this. It is very painful, and I had rather not hear it."

"Why do I tell you? I tell you because I do not wish you to marry Edward Cossey. I tell you because I wish him to feel a little of what I have to feel, and because I have said he should *not* marry you."

"I wish that you could prevent it," said Ida, with a sudden outburst. "I am sure you are quite welcome to Mr. Cossey so far as I am concerned, for I detest him, and I cannot imagine how any woman could ever have done otherwise."

"Thank you," said Belle; "but I have done with Mr. Cossey, and I think I hate him too. I know that I did hate him when I met him in the street just now, and he told me that he was not engaged to you. You say that you detest him, why then do you marry him; you are a free woman?"

"Do you want to know?" said Ida, wheeling round and looking her visitor full in the face. "I am going to marry him for the same reason that you say caused you to marry—because I must. I am going to marry him because he lent me money on condition that I promised to marry him, and as I have taken the money, I must give him his price, even if it breaks my heart. You think that you are wretched; how do you know that I am not fifty times as wretched. Your lot is to lose your lover, mine is to have one forced upon me and endure him all my life. The worst of your pain is over, all mine is to come."

"Why? why?" broke in Belle. "What is such a promise as that? He cannot force you to marry him, and it is better for a woman to die than to have to marry a man she hates, especially," she added, meaningly, "if she happens to love another man. Be advised by me, I know what it is."

"Yes," said Ida, "no doubt it is better to die, but death is not so easy. As for the promise, you do not seem to understand that no gentleman or lady can break a promise in consideration of which they have received money. Whatever he has done, and whatever he is, I must marry Mr. Cossey, so I do not think that we need discuss the subject any more."

Belle sat silent for a moment or more, and then, rising, said that she must go. " I have warned you," she added, " although to warn you I have had to put myself at your mercy. You can tell the story and destroy me if you like. I do not much care if you do. Women such as I get reckless."

" You must understand me very little, Mrs. Quest " (it had always been Belle before, and she winced at the changed name), " if you think me capable of such conduct. You have nothing to fear from me."

She held out her hand, but in her humility and shame Belle went without taking it, and through the angry sunset light walked slowly back to Boisingham ; and as she walked there was a look upon her face that Edward Cossey would scarcely have cared to see.

CHAPTER XXVII.

MR. QUEST HAS HIS INNINGS.

ALL that afternoon and far into the evening Mr. Quest was employed in drafting, and with his own hand engrossing on parchment certain deeds, to the proper execution of which he seemed to find constant reference necessary to a tin box of papers which was labelled " Honham Castle Estates."

By eleven that night everything was finished, and, having carefully collected and docketed his papers, he put the tin box away and went home to bed.

Next morning, about ten o'clock, Edward Cossey was sitting at breakfast in no happy frame of mind. He had gone up to the Castle to dinner on the previous evening, but it cannot be said that he had enjoyed himself. Ida was there, looking very handsome in her evening dress, but she was cold as a stone and unapproachable as a statue. She scarcely spoke to him, indeed, except in answer to some direct remark, reserving all her conversation for her father, who seemed to have caught the contagion of restraint, and was, for him, unusually silent and depressed.

But once or twice he found her looking at him, and then there was upon her face a mingled expression of contempt and irrepressible aversion which chilled him to the marrow.

These qualities towards him were indeed so much more plainly developed than they had been before, that at last a conviction, which he had at first rejected as incredible, forced itself into his mind. That conviction was, that Belle must have disbelieved his denial of the engagement, and in her eagerness for revenge have told Ida the whole story. The thought made him feel faint and sick, but there was but one thing to be done, and that was to face it out. Once, when the squire's back was turned, he ventured to attempt some little tenderness in which the word " dear " occurred, but Ida did not seem to hear it, and looked straight over his head into space, and this he felt was trying. So trying did he find the whole entertainment indeed, that about half-past nine he rose and came away, saying that he had some bank papers which must be attended to that night.

Now most men would, in all human probability, have been dismayed by this state of affairs into relinquishing an attempt at matrimony which it was evident could only be carried through in the face of the quiet but none the less vigorous dislike and contempt of the other contracting party. But this was not so with Edward Cossey. Ida's coldness exercised upon his tenacious and obstinate mind much the same effect that may be supposed to be produced upon the benighted seeker for the North Pole by a frozen ocean of icebergs. Like the explorer, he was convinced that if once he could get over those cold and frowning heights he would find a smiling and sunny land beyond, and perchance many other delights, and, like the explorer again, he was, metaphorically, ready to die in the effort. For, to tell the truth, he loved and desired her more every day, till now his passion dominated his physical being and his mental judgment, so that whatever loss was entailed, whatever obstacles arose, he was determined to endure and overcome them, if by so doing he might gain his end.

He was reflecting upon all this on the morning in question when Mr. Quest, looking very cool and composed and gentlemanlike, was shown into his room, much as Colonel Quaritch had been shown in two mornings before.

"How do you do, Quest?" he said, in a from-high-to-low kind of tone, which he was in the habit of adopting towards his official subordinates. "Sit down. What is it?"

"It is some business, Mr. Cossey," the lawyer answered, in his usual quiet tones.

"Honham Castle mortgages again, I suppose," growled he; "I only hope that you don't want any more money on that account at present, that's all, because I can't raise another penny while the governor lives, for they don't entail cash and bank shares, you know; and though my credit's pretty good, I am not far from the bottom of it."

"Well," said Mr. Quest, with a faint smile, "it has to do

with the Honham Castle mortgages; but as I have a good deal to say, perhaps we had better wait till the things are cleared away."

"All right. Just ring the bell, will you, and take a cigarette."

Mr. Quest smiled again and rang the bell, but did not take the cigarette. When the breakfast things had been removed he took a chair, and, placing it on the farther side of the table in such a position that the light, which was to his back, struck full upon Edward Cossey's face, commenced to deliberately untie and sort his bundle of papers. Presently he came to the one he wanted. It was not an original letter, but a copy. "Will you kindly read this, Mr. Cossey?" he said, quietly, as he pushed the letter towards him across the table.

Edward finished lighting his cigarette, and then took the letter up and glanced at it carelessly. At the first line, however, his expression changed to one of absolute horror, his face blanched, the perspiration sprang out upon his forehead, and the cigarette dropped from his fingers to the carpet, where it lay smouldering. And no wonder, for the letter was a copy of one of Belle's most passionate epistles to himself. He had never been able to restrain her from writing these compromising letters. Indeed, this one was the very one that some little time before Mr. Quest had abstracted from the pocket of his lounging-coat in his room in London.

He read on for a little way, and then put the letter down upon the table. There was no need for him to go on, it was all in the same strain.

"You will observe, Mr. Cossey, that this is a copy," said Mr. Quest, "but if you like you can inspect the original document."

He made no answer.

"Now," went on Mr. Quest, handing him a second paper, "here is the copy of another letter, of which the original is in your handwriting."

Edward glanced at it. It was an intercepted letter of his own, dated about a year before, and its contents, though not of so passionate a nature as the other, were still of a sufficiently incriminating character.

He put it down upon the table by the side of the first, and waited for Mr. Quest to go on.

"I have other evidence," said his visitor, presently, "but you are probably sufficiently versed in such matters to know that these letters alone are almost enough for my purpose, which is to commence a suit for divorce against my wife, in which you will, of course, in accordance with the provisions of the act, be joined as corespondent. Indeed, I have already drawn up a letter of instruction to my London agents, directing them to take the preliminary steps," and he pushed a third paper towards him.

Edward Cossey turned his back to his tormentor, and, resting his head upon his hand, tried to think.

"Mr. Quest," he said, presently, in a hoarse voice, "without admitting anything, there are reasons which would make it ruinous to me if such an action were commenced at present."

"Yes," he answered, "there are. In the first place there is no knowing what view your father would take of the matter, and how his view would affect your future interests, and in the second your engagement to Miss De la Molle, upon which your heart is so strongly set, would certainly be broken off."

"How do you know that I am engaged?" asked Edward, in surprise.

"It does not matter how I know it," said the lawyer; "I do know it, so it will be useless for you to deny it. As you remark, this suit will probably be your ruin in every way, and therefore it is, as you will easily understand, a good moment for a man who wants his revenge to choose it."

"Without admitting anything," answered Edward Cossey, "I wish to ask you a question. Is there no way out of this? Supposing that I have done you a wrong; wrong admits of compensation."

"Yes, it does, Mr. Cossey, and I have thought of that. Everybody has his price in this world, and I have mine, but the compensation for such a wrong must be a heavy one."

"At what price will you agree to stay the action forever?" he asked.

"The price that I will take to stay the action is the transfer, into my name, of the mortgages you hold over the Honham Castle estates," answered Mr. Quest, quietly.

"Great heavens!" said Edward, "why that is a matter of thirty thousand pounds."

"I know it is, and I know also that it is worth your while to pay thirty thousand pounds to save yourself from exposure, the chance of disinheritance, and the certainty of the loss of the woman whom you want to marry. So well do I know it that I have prepared the necessary deeds for your signature, and here they are. Listen, sir," he went on, sternly; "refuse to accept my terms, and by to-night's post I shall send this letter of instructions. Also I shall send to Mr. Cossey, senior, and to Mr. De la Molle, copies of these two precious epistles," and he pointed to the incriminating documents, "and a copy of the letter to my agents, and where will you be then? Consent, and I will bind myself not to proceed in any way or form. Now, make your choice."

"But I cannot; even if I will, I cannot," said he, almost wringing his hands in his perplexity. "It was on condition of my taking up those mortgages that Ida consented to become engaged to me, and I have promised that I will cancel them on our wedding. Will you not take money instead?"

"Yes," answered Mr. Quest, "I would take money. A little time ago I would not have taken it, because I wanted that property, but I have changed my ideas. But, as you yourself said, your credit is strained to the utmost, and while your father is alive you will not find it possible to raise another thirty thousand pounds. Besides, if this matter is to be settled at all, it must be settled now. I will not wait while you make attempts to raise the money."

"But about the mortgages? I promised to keep them. What shall I say to Ida?"

"Say? Say nothing. You can meet them if you like after your father's death. Refuse if you like, but if you refuse you will be mad. Thirty thousand pounds will be nothing to you, but exposure will be ruin. Have you made up your mind. You must take my offer or leave it. Sign the documents and I will put the originals of those two letters into your hands; refuse, and I will take my steps."

Edward Cossey thought for a moment and then said, "I will sign. Let me see the papers."

Mr. Quest turned aside to hide the expression of triumph

which flitted across his face, and then handed him the deeds.
They were elaborately drawn, for he was a skilful legal
draughtsman, quite as skilful as many a leading chancery con-
veyancer, but the substance of them was that the mortgages
transferred to him by the said Edward Cossey, in and for the
consideration that he, the said William M. Quest, consented
to abandon forever a pending action for divorce againt his
wife, Belle Quest, whereto the said Edward Cossey was to be
joined as corespondent.

"You will observe," said Mr. Quest, "that if you attempt
to contest the validity of this assignment, which you certainly
could not do with any prospect of success, the attempt will
recoil upon your own head, because the whole scandal will
then transpire. We shall require some witnesses, so, with
your permission, I will ring the bell and ask the landlady and
your servant to step up. They need know nothing of the
contents of the papers," and he did so.

"Stop," said Edward, presently. "Where are the original
letters?"

"Here," answered Mr. Quest, producing them from an inner pocket, and showing them to him from a distance.
"When the landlady comes up I will give them to her to
hold in this envelope, directing her to hand them to you
when the deeds are signed and witnessed. She will only
think that it is part of the ceremony."

Presently the man-servant and the landlady arrived, and
Mr. Quest, in his most matter-of-fact way, explained to them
that they were required to witness some documents, and at the
same time handed the letters to the woman, saying that she
was to give them to Mr. Cossey when they had all done signing.

Then Edward Cossey signed, and, placing his thumb on the
familiar wafer, delivered the various documents as his act and
deed, and the witnesses, with much preparation and effort, affixed their awkward signatures in the places pointed out to
them, and in a few minutes the thing was done, and Mr. Quest
was a richer man by thirty thousand pounds than when he
had got up that morning.

"Now give Mr. Cossey the packet, Mrs. Jeffries," he said,
as he blotted the signatures, "and then you can go," and she
did so and went.

When the witnesses had gone Edward looked at the letters, and then with a savage oath flung them into the fire and watched them burn.

"Good-morning, Mr. Cossey," said Mr. Quest, as he prepared to depart with the deeds. "You have now bought your experience and had to pay dearly for it; but, upon my word, when I think of all you owe me I wonder at myself for letting you off at so small a price."

When he had gone, Edward Cossey gave way to his feelings in language more forcible than polite, and what they were may be more easily imagined than described. For now, in addition to all the money that he had lost, and the painful exposure to which he had been subjected, he was face to face with a new difficulty. Either he must make a clean breast of it to Ida about the mortgages being no longer in his hands, or he must pretend that he still had them. In the first alternative, the consideration upon which Ida had agreed to marry him came to nothing. Moreover, she was thereby released from her promise, and he was well aware that under these circumstances she would certainly break off the engagement. In the second, he would be acting a lie, and the lie would sooner or later be discovered, and what then? Well, if it was after marriage, what would it matter? To a woman of gentle birth there is only one thing more irretrievable than marriage, and that is death. Anyhow, he had suffered so much for the sake of this woman that he did not mean to give her up now. He must meet the mortgages after marriage, that was all.

Facilis descensus averni. When a man of the character of Edward Cossey, or indeed of any character, allows his passions to lead him into a course of deceit, he does not find it easy to check his wild career. From dishonor to dishonor shall he go, till at length, in due season, he reaps as he has sown.

CHAPTER XXVIII.

HOW GEORGE TREATED JOHNNIE.

SOME two or three days before the scene described in the last chapter, the faithful George had suddenly announced his desire to visit London.

" What," said the squire in astonishment, for George had never been known to go out of his own county before. " Why, what on earth are you going to do in London ?"

" Well, squire," answered his retainer, looking marvellously knowing, " I don't rightly know, but there's a cheap train goes up to this here exhibition on the Tuesday morning and comes back on the Thursday evening. Ten shillings both ways, that's the fare, and I see in the *Chronicle*, I do, that there's a wonderful show of these new-fangled self-tying and delivering reapers, sich as they use so over sea in America, and I've a fancy to see them and have a holiday look round London town. So as there ain't not northing particler a-doing, if you hain't got anything to say agin it, I think I'll go, squire."

" All right," said the squire ; " are you going to take your wife with you ?"

" Why no, squire, I said that I wanted to go for a holiday, and that ain't no holiday to take the missus too," and George chuckled in a manner that evidently meant volumes.

And so it came to pass that on the afternoon of the day of the transfer of the mortgages from Edward Cossey to Mr. Quest, the great George found himself wandering vaguely about the vast expanse of the Colinderies, and not enjoying himself in the least. He had been recommended by some travelled individual in Boisingham to a certain lodging near Liverpool Street Station, which he found with the help of a friendly porter. Thence he set out for the exhibition, but, being of a prudent mind, thought that he would do well to save his money and walk the distance. So he walked and

walked till he was tired, and then, after an earnest consultation with a policeman, he took a 'bus, which an hour later
landed him—at the Royal Oak. His further adventures we
need not pursue; suffice it to say that, having started from
his lodging at three, it was past seven o'clock at night when
he finally reached the exhibition, more thoroughly wearied
than though he had done a good day's harvesting.

Here he wandered for a while in continual dread of having
his pocket picked, seeking reaping-machines and discovering
none, till at length he found himself in the gardens, where
the electric light display was in full swing. Soon wearying
of this, for it was a cold, damp night, he made a difficult path
to a buffet inside the building, where he sat down at a little
table, and devoured some very unpleasant-looking cold beef.
Here slumber overcame him, for his weariness was great, and
he dozed.

Presently, through the muffled roar and hum of voices,
which echoed in his sleep-dulled ears, he caught the sound
of a familiar name, which woke him up "all of a heap," as he
afterwards said. The name was "Quest." Without moving
his body, he opened his eyes. At the very next table to his
own were seated two people, a man and a woman. He looked
at the latter first. She was clad in yellow, and was very tall
and thin and fierce-looking, so fierce-looking that George involuntarily jerked his head back and brought it with painful
force in contact with the wall. It was the Tiger herself, and
her companion was the coarse, dreadful-looking man called
Johnnie, whom she had sent away in the cab on the night of
Mr. Quest's visit.

"Oh," Johnnie was saying, "so Quest is the covey's name,
is it, and he lives in a city called Boisingham, does he? Is
he an oof bird?" (rich).

"Rather," answered the Tiger, "if only one can make the
money trickle, but he's a nasty mean one, he is. Look here,
not a penny, not a stiver have I got to bless myself with, and
I daren't ask him for any more not till January. And how
am I going to live till January? I got the sack from the
music-hall last week because I was a bit jolly, and old Thomp-
son, the conductor, wanted to drop ten per cent. on my salary
because he said I didn't draw as I used to, and that I was

getting old and ugly. So I just caught him one with the handle of my brollie that made him see stars, and the beast had me up for assault, and it was forty shillings and costs. And now I can't get another billet any way, and I've got a bill of sale over the furniture, and I've sold all my jewels down to my ticker, or at least most of them, and there's that brute," and her voice rose to a subdued scream, " living like a fighting cock, and rolling in 'oof' while his poor wife is left to starve."

" 'Wife.' Oh, yes, we know all about that," said the gentleman called Johnnie.

A look of doubt and cunning passed across the woman's face. Evidently she feared that she had said too much. " Well, it's as good a name as another," she said. " Oh, don't I wish that I could get a grip of him ; I'd wring him," and she twisted her long bony hands as washerwomen do when they wring a cloth.

" I'd back you to," said Johnnie. " And now, adored Edithia, I've had enough of this blooming show, and I'm off. Perhaps I shall look in down Pimlico way this evening. Ta-ta."

" Well, you may as well stand a liquor first," said the adored one. " I'm pretty dry, I can tell you."

" Certainly, with pleasure ; I will order one. Waiter, a brandy-and-soda for this lady—*six* of brandy, if you please ; she's very delicate and wants support."

The waiter grinned and brought the drink, and the man Johnnie turned round as though to pay him, but really he departed without doing so.

George watched him go, and then looked again at the lady, whose appearance seemed to fascinate him.

" Well, if that ain't a master one," he said to himself ; " and she called herself his wife, she did, and then drew up like a slug's horns. Hang me if I don't stick to her till I find out a bit more of the tale."

Thus ruminated George, who, be it observed, was no fool, and who had a hearty dislike and mistrust of Mr. Quest. While he was wondering how he was to go to work, an unexpected opportunity occurred. The Tiger had finished her brandy-and-soda, and was preparing to leave, when the waiter swooped down upon her.

" Money please, miss," he said.

" Money !" she said, " why, you're paid."

" Come, none of that," said the waiter ; " I want a shilling
for the brandy-and-soda."

" A shilling, do you ? Then you'll have to want, you cheat-
ing white-faced rascal you ; my friend paid you before he
went away."

" Oh, we've had too much of that game," said the waiter,
beckoning to a constable, to whom, in spite of the ' fair Edithia's ' very vigorous and pointed protestations, he was pro-
ceeding to give her in charge, for it appeared that she had
only twopence about her. This was George's opportunity,
and he interfered.

" I think, marm," he said, " that the fat gent with you was
a playing of a little game. He only pretended to pay the
waiter."

" Playing a little game, was he ?" gasped the infuriated
Tiger. " If I don't play a little game on him when I get a
chance my name is not Edith d'Aubigné, the nasty mean
beast—the—"

" Permit me, marm," said George, putting a shilling on the
table, which the waiter took and departed with, satisfied. " I
can't bear to see a real lady like you in difficulty."

" Well, you are a gentleman, you are," she said.

" Not at all, marm. That's my way. And now, marm,
won't you have another ?"

No objection was raised by the lady, who had another, with
the result that she became, if not exactly tipsy, at any rate not
far from it.

Shortly after this the building was cleared, and George
found himself standing in Exhibition Road with the woman
on his arm.

" You're going to give me a lift home, ain't you ?" she said.

" Yes, marm, for sure I am," said George, sighing, as he
thought of the cab-fare.

Accordingly they got into a hansom, and Mrs. d'Aubigné
having given the address in Pimlico, of which George instantly made a mental note, they started.

" Come in and have a drink," she said, when they arrived ;
and accordingly he paid the cab—half a crown it cost him—

and was ushered by the woman, with a simper, into the gilded drawing-room.

Here the Tiger had another brandy-and-soda, after which George thought that she was about in a fit state for him to prosecute his inquiries.

"Wonderful place this London, marm; I niver was up here afore and had no idea that I should find folks so friendly. As I was a saying to my friend Laryer Quest down at Boisingham yesterday—"

"Hullo, what's that?" she said. "Do you know the old man?"

"If you mean Laryer Quest, why, in course I do, and Mrs. Quest too. Ah, she's a pretty one, she is."

Here the lady burst into a flood of incoherent abuse which tired her so much that she had a fourth brandy-and-soda; George mixed it for her, and he mixed it strong.

"Is he rich?" she asked, as she put down the glass.

"What, Laryer Quest? Well, I should say that he is about the warmest man in our part of the county."

"And here am I starving," burst out the horrible woman with a flood of drunken tears. "Starving, without a shilling to pay for a cab or a drink, while my wedded husband lives in luxury with another woman. You tell him that I won't stand it; you tell him that if he don't find a 'thou.' pretty quick, I'll let him know the reason why."

"I don't quite understand, marm," said George; "there's a lady down in Boisingham as is the real Mrs. Quest."

"It's a lie!" she shrieked, "it's a lie! he married me before he married her. I could have him in the dock to-morrow, and I would, too, if I wasn't afraid of him, and that's a fact."

"Come, marm, come," said George, "draw it mild from that tap."

"You won't believe me, won't you?" said the woman, on whom the liquor was now beginning to take its full effect; "then I'll show you," and she staggered to a desk, unlocked it, and took from it a folded paper, which she opened.

It was a marriage license, or purported so to be; but George, who was not too quick at his reading, had only time to note the name Quest, and the church, St. Bartholomew's,

Hackney, when she snatched it away from him and locked it up again.

"There," she said, "it isn't any business of yours. What right have you to come prying into the affairs of a poor lone woman?" and she sat down upon the sofa beside him, threw her long arm round his neck, rested her painted face upon his shoulder, and began to weep the tears of intoxication.

"Well, blow me!" said George to himself, "if this ain't a master one! I wonder what my old missus would say if she saw me in this fix. I say, marm—"

But at that moment the door opened, and in came Johnnie, who had evidently also been employing the interval in refreshing himself, for he rolled like a ship in a sea.

"Well," he said, "and who the deuce are you? Come, get out of this, you Methody parson-faced clodhopper, you. Fairest Edithia, what means this?"

By this time the fairest Edithia had realized who her visitor was, and the trick whereby he had left her to pay for the brandy-and-soda recurring to her mind, she sprang up and began to express her opinion of Johnnie in violent and libellous language. He replied, in appropriate terms, as people whose healths are proposed always do, according to the newspaper reports, and fast and furious grew the fun. At length, however, it seemed to occur to Johnnie that he, George, was in some way responsible for this state of affairs, for without word or warning he hit him on the nose—which proved too much for George's Christian forbearance.

"You would, you fat lubber! would you?" he said, and sprang at him.

Now Johnnie was big and fat, but Johnnie was rather drunk, and George was tough and exceedingly strong. In almost less time than it takes to write it he had the abominable Johnnie by the scruff of the neck, and had, with a mighty jerk, hauled him over the sofa so that he lay face downwards thereon. By the door, quite convenient to his hand, stood George's ground-ash stick, a peculiarly good and well-grown one, which he had cut himself in Honham wood. He seized it. "Now, my lad," he said, "I'll teach you how we do the trick where I come from," and he laid on without mercy. Whack! whack! whack! went the ground-ash on Johnnie's tight clothes. He yelled and swore and struggled in the grip of the sturdy countryman, but it was of no use, the ash came down like fate; never was a Johnnie so bastinadoed before.

"Give it the brute, give it him," shrilled the fair Edithia, bethinking her of her wrongs; and he did till he was tired.

"Now, Johnnie," he said, at last, "I'm thinking I've pretty well whacked you dead. Perhaps you'll be more careful how you handle your betters by and by," and seizing his hat he ran down the stairs without seeing anybody, and, slipping into the street, crossed over and listened.

They were at it again. Seeing her enemy prostrate, the Tiger had fallen on him, apparently with the fire-irons, to judge from the noise.

Just then a policeman came hurrying up.

"I say, governor," said George, "the folk in that there house with the red pillars do fare to be a murdering of each other."

The policeman listened to the din and then made for the house, and, profiting by his absence, George retreated as fast as he could, his melancholy countenance shining with a sober satisfaction.

CHAPTER XXIX.

EDWARD MEETS WITH AN ACCIDENT.

THIS is not a very cheerful world at the best of times, though no doubt we ought to pretend that humanity at large is as happy as it is represented to be, in let us say the Christmas number of an illustrated paper. How well we can imagine the thoughtful inhabitant of this country in the year A.D. 7500, or thereabouts, disinterring from the crumbling remains of one of Griffith's safes a Christmas number of the *Illustrated London News*. The archaic letters would no doubt be unintelligible to him, but he would look at the pictures with much the same interest that we regard bushmen's drawings or the primitive clay figures of Peru, and though his whole artistic seventy-sixth-century soul would be revolted at the crudeness of the coloring, surely he would moralize thus : " Oh, happy race of primitive men, how I, the child of light and civilization, envy you your long-forgotten days ! Here in these rude drawings, which in themselves reveal the extraordinary capacity for pleasure possessed by the early races, who could look upon them and gather gratification from the sight, may we trace your joyous career from the cradle to the grave. Here is your figure as a babe, at whose appearance everybody seems delighted, even those of your race whose inheritance will be thereby diminished—and here, a merry lad, you revel in the school which those of our age find so wearisome ; there, grown more old, you stand at the altar of a beautiful but exploded faith, which the world discarded three thousand years ago—a faith that told of hope and peace beyond the grave—and by you stands your blushing bride. No hard fate, no considerations of means, no worldly-mindedness, come to snatch you from her arms as now they daily do. With her you spend your peaceful days, and here at last we see you old but surrounded by love and tender kindness, and almost looking

forward to that grave which you, happy in your delusions, believed would be but the gate of glory. Oh, happy race of
simple-minded men, what a commentary upon our fevered,
avaricious, pleasure-seeking age is this rude scroll of primitive
art !"

So will some unborn *laudator temporis acti* speak in some
dim century to be, when our sorrows have faded and are not.

And yet, though we do not put a record of them in our
Christmas numbers, troubles are as troubles have been and
will continually be ; for, however happy the lot of individuals,
it is not a cheerful world in which we have been called to live.
At any rate so thought Harold Quaritch that night after the
farewell scene with Ida in the churchyard, and so he continued
to think for some time to come. A man's life is always more
or less of a continual struggle ; he is a swimmer upon an adverse sea, and to live at all he must keep his limbs in motion.
If he grows faint-hearted or weary and no longer strives, for
a little while he floats, and then at last, morally or physically,
he vanishes. We struggle for our livelihoods, and for all that
makes life worth living in the material sense, and not the less
are we called upon to struggle with an army of spiritual woes
and fears, which now we vanquish and now are vanquished
by. Every man of refinement, and a good many women, will
be able to recall periods in his or her existence when life has
seemed not only valueless but hateful, when our small suc-
cesses, such as they are, dwindled away and vanished in the
gulf of our many failures, when our hopes and aspirations
faded like a little sunset cloud, and we were surrounded by
black and lonely mental night, from which even the Star of
Faith had passed. Such a time had come to Harold Quaritch
now. His days had not, on the whole, been happy days ; but
he was a good and earnest man, with that touching faith in
Providence which is given to some among us, and which had
brought with it the reward of an even thankful spirit. And
then, out of the twilight of his contentment the hope of happiness had arisen like the Angel of the Dawn, and suddenly
life became beautiful to him. And now it had passed : the
woman whom he deeply loved, and who loved him back again,
had gone from his reach and left him desolate—gone from his
reach, not into the grave, but to the arms of another man.

Our race is called upon to face many troubles—sickness, poverty, and death—but it is doubtful if Evil holds another arrow as sharp as that which pierced him now. He was no longer young, it is true, and, therefore, did not feel that intense agony of disappointed passion, that sickening sense of utter loss, which in such circumstances sometimes settle on the young. But if in youth we feel more sharply and with a keener sympathy of the imagination, we have at least more strength to bear, and hope does not altogether die. For we know that we shall live it down, or if we do not know it then, we *do* live it down. Very likely, indeed, there comes a time when we look back upon our sorrow and he or she who caused it with wonder, yes even with scorn and bitter laughter. But it is not so when the blow falls in later life. It may not hurt so much at the time, it may seem to have been struck with the bludgeon of Fate rather than with her keen dividing sword, but the effect is more lasting, and for the rest of our days we are numb and cold, and Time has no salve to heal us.

These things Harold realized most clearly in the heavy days that followed that churchyard separation.

He took his punishment like a brave man indeed, and went about his daily occupations with a steadfast face, but this bold behavior did not lessen its weight. He had promised not to go away till Ida was married, and he would keep the promise, but in his heart he wondered how he would be able to bear the sight of her. What would it be to see her, to touch her hand, to hear the rustle of her dress and the music of her beloved voice, and to realize again and yet again that all these things were not for him, that they had passed from him into the ownership of another man?

On the day following that upon which Edward Cossey had been terrified into transferring the Honham mortgages to Mr. Quest the colonel went out shooting. He had on the previous day become the possessor of a new hammerless gun by a well-known London maker, of which he stood in considerable need. He had treated himself to this gun when he came into his aunt's little fortune, but it was only just completed. The weapon was a beautiful one, and at any other time it would have filled his sportman's heart with joy. Even as it was, when he put it together and balanced it and took imaginary

shots at blackbirds in the garden, he for a little while forgot
his sorrows, for the sorrow must indeed be heavy which a new
hammerless gun by such a maker cannot do something towards lightening. So on the next morning he took this gun
and proceeded to the marshes by the river, where, he was
credibly informed, several wisps of snipe had been seen, to
attempt to shoot some of them and put the new weapon to
the test.

It was on this same morning that Edward Cossey got a letter which disturbed him not a little. It was from Belle Quest,
and ran thus:

"DEAR MR. COSSEY,—Will you come over and see me this afternoon
about three o'clock? I shall *expect* you, so I am sure you will not disappoint me.   B. Q."

For a long while he hesitated what to do. Belle Quest was
at the present juncture the very last person whom he wished
to see. His nerves were shaken and he feared a scene, but
on the other hand he did not know what danger might threaten
him if he did not go. Quest had got his price, and he knew
that he had nothing more to fear from him; but a jealous
woman has no price, and if he did not humor her it might, he
felt, be at a risk which he could not estimate. Also he was
nervously anxious to give no further cause for gossip. A sudden outward and visible cessation of his intimacy with the
Quests in a little country town like Boisingham, where all his
movements were known, might, he thought, give rise to sur-
mises and suspicion. So, albeit with a faint heart, he determined to go.

Accordingly, at three o'clock precisely he was shown into
the drawing-room at the Oaks. Mrs. Quest was not there;
indeed, he waited for ten minutes before she came in, dressed,
as usual, in black. She was very pale, so pale that the blue
veins on her forehead showed distinctly through her ivory
skin, and there was a curious intensity about her manner
which frightened him. She was very quiet, unnaturally so,
indeed; but her quiet was of the ominous nature of the silence
before the storm, and when she spoke her words were keen
and quick and vivid.

She did not shake hands with him, but sat down and looked

at him, slowly fanning herself with a painted ivory fan which
she took up from the table.

"You sent for me, Belle, and here I am," he said, breaking
the silence.

Then she spoke. "You told me the other day," she said,
"that you were not engaged to be married to Ida de la Molle.
It was not true. You are engaged to be married to her."

"Who said so?" he asked, defiantly. "Quest, I suppose?"

"I have it on a better authority," she answered. "I have
it from Miss De la Molle herself. Now listen, Edward Cossey.
When I let you go, I made a condition, and that condition
was that you should not marry Ida de la Molle. Do you still
intend to marry her?"

"You had it from Ida?" he said, disregarding her question;
"then you must have spoken to Ida—you must have told her
everything. I suspected as much from her manner the other
night. You—"

"Then it is true," she broke in, coldly. "It is true, and in
addition to your other failings, Edward, you are a coward and
a liar."

"What is it to you what I am or what I am not?" he answered, savagely. "What business is it of yours? You have
no hold over me, and no claim upon me. As it is, I have suffered enough at your hands and those of your accursed husband. I have had to pay him thirty thousand pounds, do you
know that? But of course you know it. No doubt the whole
thing is a plant, and you will share the spoil."

"Ah!" she said, drawing a long breath.

"And now look here," he went on. "Once and for all, I
will not be interfered with by you. I *am* engaged to marry
Ida de la Molle, and whether you wish it or no I shall marry
her. And one more thing. I will not allow you to associate
with Ida. Do you understand me? I will not allow it."

She had been holding the fan before her face while he
spoke. Now she lowered it and looked at him. Her face
was paler than ever, paler than death, if that be possible, but
in her eyes there shone a light like the light of a flame.

"Why not?" she said, quietly.

"Why not?" he answered, savagely. "I wonder that you
think it necessary to ask such a question; but as you do, I will

tell you why. Because Ida is the lady whom I am going to marry, and I do not choose that she should associate with a woman who has been my *mistress*."

"*Ah!*" she said again, "I understand now."

At that moment a diversion occurred. The drawing-room looked on to the garden, and at the end of the garden was a door which opened on to another street.

Through this door had come Colonel Quaritch, accompanied by Mr. Quest, the former with his gun under his arm. They had walked up the garden, and were almost at the French window when Edward Cossey saw them. "Control yourself," he said, in a low voice, "here is your husband."

Mr. Quest advanced and knocked at the window, which his wife opened. When he saw Edward Cossey he hesitated a little, and then nodded to him, while the colonel came forward, and, placing his gun by the wall, entered the room, shook hands with Mrs. Quest, and bowed coldly to Edward Cossey.

"I met the colonel, Belle," said Mr. Quest, "coming here with the benevolent intention of giving you some snipe, so I brought him up by the short way."

"That is very kind of you, Colonel Quaritch," said she, with a sweet smile (for she had the sweetest smile imaginable).

He looked at her. There was something about her face which attracted his attention, something unusual.

"What are you looking at?" she asked.

"You," he said, bluntly, for they were out of hearing of the other two. "If I were poetically minded I should say that you looked like the Tragic Muse."

"Do I?" she answered, bursting out laughing. "Well, that is curious, because I feel like Comedy herself."

"There is something wrong with that woman," thought the colonel to himself as he extracted two couple of snipe from his capacious coat-tails. "I wonder what it is."

Just then Mr. Quest and Edward Cossey passed out into the garden talking.

"Here are the snipe, Mrs. Quest," he said. "I have had rather good luck. I killed four couple and missed two couple more; but then I had a new gun, and one can never shoot so well with a new gun."

"Oh, thank you," she said. "Do pull out the 'painters' for me. I like to put them in my riding-hat, and I never can find them myself."

"Very well," he answered, "but I must go into the garden to do it; there is not light enough here. It gets dark so soon now."

Accordingly he stepped out through the window, and began to hunt for the pretty little feathers which are found at the angle of a snipe's wing.

"Is that the new gun, Colonel Quaritch?" said Mrs. Quest, presently; "what a beautiful one!"

"Be careful," he said, "I haven't taken the cartridges out."

If he had been looking at her, which at the moment he was not, Harold would have seen her stagger and catch at the wall for support. Then he would have seen an awful and malevolent light of sudden determination pass across her face.

"All right," she said, "I know all about guns. My father used to shoot, and I always cleaned his gun," and she took the weapon up and began to examine the engraving on the locks.

"What is this?" she said, pointing to a little slide above the locks on which the word "safe" was engraved in gold letters.

"Oh, that's the safety bolt," he said. "When you see the word 'safe,' the locks are barred and the gun won't go off. You have to push the bolt forward before you can fire."

"So," she said, carelessly, and suiting the action to the word.

"Yes, so, but please be careful; the gun is loaded."

"Yes, I'll be careful," she answered. "Well, it is a very pretty gun, and so light that I believe I could shoot with it myself."

Meanwhile Edward Cossey and Mr. Quest, who were walking towards them, had separated, Mr. Quest going to the right across the lawn to pick up a glove which had dropped upon the grass, while Edward Cossey slowly sauntered towards them. When he was about nine paces off, he too halted, and, stooping a little, looked abstractedly at a white Japanese chrysanthemum which was still in bloom. Mrs. Quest turned, as the colonel thought, to put the gun back against the wall. He would have offered to take it from her, but at the moment

both his hands were occupied in extracting one of the " painters " from a snipe. The next thing that he was aware of was
a loud explosion, followed by an exclamation, or rather a cry,
from Mrs. Quest. He dropped the snipe and looked up, just
in time to see the gun, which had leaped from her hands with
the recoil, strike against the wall of the house and fall to the
ground. Instantly, whether by instinct or by chance, he never
knew, he glanced towards the place where Edward Cossey was
standing, and saw that his face was streaming with blood, and
that his right arm hung helpless by his side. Even as he
looked he saw him put his uninjured hand to his head, and,
without a word or a sound, sink down on the gravel path.

For a second there was silence, and the blue smoke from
the gun hung heavily upon the damp autumn air. In the
midst of it stood Belle Quest like one transfixed, her lips
apart, her blue eyes opened wide, and the stamp of terror—or
was it guilt—upon her pallid face.

All this he saw in a flash, and then ran to the bleeding heap
upon the gravel.

He reached it almost simultaneously with Mr. Quest, and
together they turned the body over. But still Belle stood
there enveloped in the heavy smoke.

Presently, however, her trance left her, and she ran up,
flung herself upon her knees, and looked at her former lover,
whose face and head were now a mass of blood.

" He is dead," she wailed ; " he is dead, and I have killed
him. Oh, Edward ! Edward !"

Mr. Quest turned on her savagely ; so savagely that one
might almost have thought that he feared lest in her agony
she should say something further.

" Stop that," he said, seizing her arm, " and go for the doctor, for if he is not dead he will soon bleed to death."

With an effort she rose, put her hand to her forehead, and
then ran like the wind down the garden and through the little
door.

CHAPTER XXX.

HAROLD TAKES THE NEWS.

MR. QUEST and Harold bore the bleeding man—whether he was senseless or dead they knew not—into the house, and laid him on the sofa. Then, having despatched a servant to seek a second doctor in case the one already gone for was out, they set to work to cut the clothes from his neck and arm and do what they could, and that was little enough, towards stanching the bleeding. It soon, however, became evident that Cossey had only got the outside portion of the charge of No. 7, that is to say, that he had been struck by about a hundred pellets out of the three hundred or so which would go to the ordinary ounce and an eighth. Had he received the whole charge he must, at that distance, have been instantly killed. As it was, the point of the shoulder was riddled, and so, to a somewhat smaller extent, was the back of his neck and the region of the right ear. One or two outside pellets had also struck the head higher up, and the skin and muscles along the back were torn by the passage of the shot.

"By Jove," said Mr. Quest, "I think he is done for."

The colonel nodded. He had some experience of shot wounds, and the present was not of a nature to encourage hope of the patient's survival.

"How did it happen?" asked Mr. Quest, presently, as he mopped up the streaming blood with a sponge.

"It was an accident," groaned the colonel. "Your wife was looking at my new gun. I told her that it was loaded, and that she must be careful, and I thought she had put it down. The next thing that I heard was the report. It is all my cursed fault for leaving the cartridges in."

"Ah," said Mr. Quest. "She always thought that she understood guns. It is a shocking accident."

Just then one of the doctors came running up the lawn

carrying a box of instruments, and followed by Belle Quest; and in another minute was at work. He was a quick and skilful surgeon, and having announced that the patient was not dead, at once set to work to tie one of the smaller arteries in the throat, which had been pierced, and through which Edward Cossey was rapidly bleeding to death. By the time that this was done, the other doctor, an older man, put in an appearance, and together they made a rapid examination of the injuries.

Belle stood by holding a basin of water. She did not speak, and on her face was that same fixed look of horror which Harold had observed after the discharge of the gun.

When the examination was finished, the two doctors whispered together for a few seconds.

"Will he live?" asked Mr. Quest.

"We cannot say," answered the older doctor. "We do not think it probable that he will. It will depend upon the extent of his injuries, and whether or no they have extended to the spine. If he does live he will probably be paralyzed to some extent, and he will certainly lose the hearing of the right ear."

When she heard this, Belle sank down upon a chair overwhelmed, and then the two doctors, assisted by Harold, set to work to carry Edward Cossey into another room, which had been rapidly prepared, leaving Mr. Quest alone with his wife.

He came and stood in front of her and looked her in the face, and then laughed.

"Upon my word," he said, "we men are bad enough, but you women beat us in wickedness."

"What do you mean?" she said, faintly.

"I mean that you are a murderess, Belle," he said, solemnly. "And you are a bungler, too. You could not hold the gun straight."

"I deny it," she said, "the gun went off—"

"Yes," he said, "you are wise to make no admissions; they might be used in evidence against you. Let me counsel you to make no admissions. But now look here. I suppose that this man will have to lie in this house until he recovers or dies, and that you will help to nurse him. Well, I will have none of your murderous work going on here. Do you hear

me? You are not to complete at leisure what you have begun
in haste."

"What do you take me for?" she asked, with some return
of spirit; "do you think I would injure a wounded man?"

"I do not know," he answered, with a shrug, "and as for
what I take you for, I take you for a woman whose passion
has made her mad," and he turned and left the room.

When they had got Edward Cossey, dead or alive—and he
looked more like death than life—up to the room prepared for
him, the colonel, seeing that he could be of no further use,
left him with a view of going at once to the castle.

On his way out he looked into the drawing-room, and there
was Mrs. Quest, still sitting on the chair and gazing blankly
before her. Pitying her, he entered. "Come, cheer up, Mrs.
Quest," he said, "they hope that he will live."

She made no answer.

"It was an awful accident, but I am almost as culpable as
you, for I left the cartridges in the gun. Anyhow, God's will
be done."

"God's will," she said, looking up, and then once more relapsed into silence.

He turned to go, when suddenly she rose and caught him
by the arm.

"Will he die?" she said, almost fiercely. "Tell me what
you think—not what the doctors say—you have seen lots of
wounded men and know better than they do. Tell me the
truth."

"I cannot say," he answered, shaking his head.

Apparently she interpreted his answer as yes. At any rate
she covered her face with her hands.

"What would you do, Colonel Quaritch, if you had killed
the only thing you loved in the whole world?" she asked, presently. "Oh, what am I saying? I am off my head. Leave
me and go tell Ida; it will be good news for Ida."

Accordingly, having picked up his gun from the spot where
it had fallen from the hands of Mrs. Quest, he departed for
the Castle.

And then it was that, for the first time, there flashed upon
his mind the extraordinary importance of this dreadful accident in its bearing upon his own affairs. If Cossey died he

could not marry Ida, that was clear. That was what Mrs.
Quest must have meant when she said that it would be good
news for Ida. But how did she know anything about Ida's
engagement to Edward Cossey? And, by Jove! what did
the woman mean when she asked what he would do if he had
"killed the only thing he loved in the world"? Cossey must
be the "only thing she loved," and now he thought of it,
when she believed that he was dead she called him "Edward,
Edward."

Now Harold Quaritch was as simple and unsuspicious a man
as it would be easy to find, but he was no fool. He had
moved about the world, and on various occasions come in contact with cases of this sort, as most other men have done. He
knew that when a woman, in a moment of distress, calls a man
by his Christian name, it is because she is in the habit of
thinking of him and speaking to him by that name. Not that
there was much in that by itself, but in public she called him
"Mr. Cossey." "Edward," clearly then, was the "only thing
she loved," and Edward was secretly engaged to Ida, and Mrs.
Quest knew it.

Now, when a man has the fortune, or rather the misfortune,
to be the only thing a married woman ever loved, and when
that married woman is aware of the fact of his devotion for
and engagement to somebody else, it is obvious, he reflected,
that in nine cases out of ten the knowledge will excite strong
feelings in her breast, feelings, indeed, which in some natures
would amount almost to madness.

When he had first seen Mrs. Quest that afternoon she and
Cossey were alone together, and he had noticed something unusual about her, something unnatural and intense. Indeed, he
had, he remembered, told her that she looked like the Tragic
Muse. Could it be that the look was the look of a woman
maddened by insult and jealousy, who was meditating some
fearful crime? *How did that gun go off?* He did not see it,
and he thanked God that he did not, for somehow we are not
always as anxious to bring our fellow-creatures to justice as
we might be, especially when they happen to be young and
lovely women. How did it go off? She understood guns;
he could see that from the way she handled it. Was it likely
that it exploded of itself, or owing to an accidental touch of

the trigger? It was possible, but not likely. Still, such things had been known to happen, and it would be impossible to prove that it had not happened in this case. If it were an attempted murder it was very cleverly managed, because nobody could prove that it was not accidental. But could it be possible that that soft, beautiful, baby-faced woman could have, on the spur of the moment, taken advantage of his loaded gun to wreak her passion and her wrongs upon her faithless lover? Well, the face is no mirror of the quality of the soul within, and it was possible. Further than that it did not seem to him to be his business to inquire.

By this time he was at the Castle. The squire was out, but Ida was in, and he was shown into the drawing-room while the servant went to seek her. Presently he heard her dress rustle upon the stairs, and the sound of it sent the blood to his heart, for where is the music that is more sweet than the rustling of the dress of the woman whom we love.

She came in and shook hands with him.

"Why, what is the matter?" she said, noticing the disturbed expression on his face.

"Well," he said, "there has been an accident—a very bad accident."

"Who?" she said. "Not my father?"

"No, no; Mr. Cossey."

"Oh," she said, with a sigh of relief. "Why did you frighten me so?"

The colonel smiled grimly at this unconscious exhibition of the relative state of her affections.

"What has happened to him?" asked Ida, this time with a suitable expression of concern.

"He has been accidentally shot."

"Who by?"

"Mrs. Quest."

"Then she did it on purpose—I mean—is he dead?"

"No, but I believe he will die."

They looked at each other, and each read in the eyes of the other the thought which passed through their minds. If Edward Cossey died they would be free to marry. So clearly did they read it that Ida actually interpreted it in words.

"You must not think that," she said; "it is very wrong."

8—Vol. 8

"It is wrong," answered the colonel, apparently in no way surprised at her interpretation of his thoughts, "but unfortunately human nature is human nature."

Then he went on to tell her all about it. Ida made no comment, that is, after those first words, "She did it on purpose," which burst from her in her astonishment. She felt, and he felt too, that the question as to how that gun went off was one which was best left uninquired into by them. No doubt, if the man died, there would be an inquest, and the whole matter would be investigated. Meanwhile one thing was certain, Edward Cossey, whom she was engaged to, was shot and likely to die.

Presently, while they were still talking, the squire came in from his walk, and to him also the story was told, and to judge from the expression of his face he thought it a serious one enough. If Edward Cossey died, the mortgages over the Honham property would, as he thought of course, pass to his heir, who, unless he had made a will, which was not probable, would be his father, old Mr. Cossey, the banker, from whom Mr. De la Molle well knew he had little mercy to expect. This was serious enough, and what was still more serious was that all the bright prospects in which he had for some days been basking, of the re-establishment of his family upon a securer basis than it had occupied for generations, would vanish like a vision. Now, he was not more worldly-minded than other men, but he did most fondly cherish the natural desire to see the family fortunes once more in the ascendant. The projected marriage between his daughter and Edward Cossey would have most fully brought this about, and, however much he might in his secret heart distrust the man himself and doubt whether the match was really acceptable to Ida, he could not view its collapse with indifference. While they were still talking the dressing-bell rang, and Harold rose to go.

"Stop and dine, won't you, Quaritch?" said the squire.

Harold hesitated and looked at Ida. She made no movement, but her eyes said "Stay," and he sighed and yielded. Dinner was rather a melancholy feast, for the squire was preoccupied with his own thoughts, and Ida had not much to say, while, so far as the colonel was concerned, the recollection of the tragedy which he had witnessed that afternoon, and of all the dreadful details with which it was accompanied, was not conducive to appetite.

As soon as dinner was over the squire announced that he would walk into Boisingham to inquire how the wounded man was getting on, and shortly afterwards he started, leaving his daughter and the colonel alone.

They went into the drawing-room and talked about indifferent things. No word of love passed between them; no word, indeed, that could bear even an affectionate significance, and yet every sentence they said carried a message with it, and was as heavy with unuttered passion as a bee with honey. For they loved each other dearly, and love is a thing that cannot be concealed by lovers from each other. Like the air impalpable, it is like the air surrounding, and to those who breathe it necessary and real.

It was happiness to him merely to sit beside her and hear her speak, and watch the changes of her face, and the lamplight playing upon her hair, and it was happiness to her to know that he was sitting there and watching. For the most beautiful thing about deep affection is its accompanying sense of perfect companionship and rest, a sense that nothing else in this life can give, and which, like a lifting cloud, reveals a glimpse of the white peaks of that heavenly peace that we cannot hope to tread in our stormy journey through the world.

And so the evening wore away, till at last they heard the squire's loud voice talking to somebody outside. Presently he entered.

"How is he?" asked Harold. "Will he live?"

"They cannot say," was the answer. "But two great doctors have been telegraphed for from London, and will be down to-morrow."

CHAPTER XXXI.

IDA RECANTS.

THE two great doctors came, and the two great doctors pocketed their hundred-guinea fee, and went, but neither the one nor the other, nor eke the twain, would commit themselves to a fixed opinion as to Edward Cossey's chances of life or death. However, one of them picked out a number of shot from the wounded man, and a number more he left in because he could not pick them out, and they both agreed that the treatment of their humble local brethren was all that could be desired, and so far as they were concerned there was an end of it.

A week had passed, and Edward Cossey, nursed night and day by Belle Quest, still hovered between life and death.

It was a Thursday, and Harold had walked up to the Castle to give the squire the latest news of the wounded man. While he was in the vestibule telling what he had to tell to Mr. De la Molle and Ida, a man whom he recognized as one of Mr. Quest's clerks rang the bell. He was shown in, and handed the squire a fully addressed brief envelope, which, he said, he had been told to deliver by Mr. Quest, and, saying that there was no answer, bowed himself out.

As soon as he was gone the envelope was opened by Mr. De la Molle, who took from it two legal documents which he went on to read. Suddenly the first dropped from his hand, and with an exclamation he snatched at the second.

" What is it, father ?" asked Ida.

" What is it ? Why it's just this. Edward Cossey has transferred the mortgages over this property to Quest, the lawyer, and Quest has served a notice on me calling in the money," and he began to walk up and down the room in a state of great agitation.

"I don't quite understand," said Ida, her breast heaving, and with a curious light shining in her eyes.

"Don't you?" said her father; "then perhaps you will read that," and he pushed the papers to her. As he did so another letter which he had not observed fell out of them.

At this point Harold rose to go.

"Don't go, Quaritch, don't go," said the squire. "I shall be glad of your advice, and I am sure that what you hear will not go any further."

At the same time Ida motioned him to stay, and, though somewhat unwilling, he did so.

"DEAR SIR [began the squire, reading the letter aloud],—Enclosed you will find the usual formal notices calling in the sum of thirty thousand pounds recently advanced upon mortgage of the Honham Castle estates, by Edward Cossey, Esq. These mortgages have passed into my possession for value received, and it is now my desire to realize them. I most deeply regret being forced to press an old client, but my circumstances are such that I am obliged so to do. If I can in any way facilitate your efforts to raise the money I shall be very glad to do so, but in the event of the money not being forthcoming at the end of the six months' notice, the ordinary steps will be taken to realize by foreclosure.

"I am, dear sir, yours truly,
"W. QUEST.

"James de la Molle, Esq., J. P."

"I see now," said Ida; "Mr. Cossey has no further hold on the mortgages or on the property."

"That's it," said the squire; "he has transferred them to that rascally lawyer. And yet he told me—I can't understand it, I really can't."

At this point the colonel insisted upon departing, saying that he would call in again in the evening to see if he could be of any assistance. When he was gone Ida spoke in a cold, determined voice.

"Mr. Cossey told me that when we married he would put those mortgages in the fire. It now seems that the mortgages were not his to dispose of, or else that he has since transferred them to Mr. Quest without informing us."

"Yes, I suppose so," said the squire.

"Very well," said Ida. "And now, father, I will tell you something. I engaged myself—or, to be more accurate, I promised to engage myself—to Edward Cossey, on the condi-

tion that he would take up these mortgages when Cossey &
Son were threatening to foreclose, or whatever it is called."

"Good heavens!" said her astonished father, "what an
idea!"

"I did it," went on Ida, "and he took up the mortgages,
and in due course he claimed my promise, and I became engaged to marry him, though that engagement was most repugnant to me. You will see that, having persuaded him to advance the money, I could not refuse to carry out my share of
the bargain."

"Well," said the squire, "this is all new to me."

"Yes," she answered, "and I should never have told you
of it, had it not been for this sudden change in the position
of affairs. What I did, I did to save our family from ruin.
But now it seems that Mr. Cossey has played us false, and
that we are to be ruined after all. Therefore, the condition
upon which I promised to marry him has not been carried out,
and my promise falls to the ground."

"You mean that, supposing he lives, you will not marry
Edward Cossey."

"Yes, I do mean it."

The squire thought for a minute. "This is a very serious
step, Ida," he said. "I don't mean that I think that the man
has behaved well; but still he may have given up the mortgages to Quest under pressure of some sort, and might be
willing to find the money to meet them."

"I do not care if he finds the money ten times over," said
Ida, "I will not marry him. He has not kept to the letter of
his bond, and I will not keep to mine."

"It is all very well, Ida," said the squire, "and of course
nobody can force you into a distasteful marriage, but I wish
to point out to you one thing. You have your family to think
of as well as yourself. I tell you frankly that I do not believe
that, as times are, it will be possible to raise thirty thousand
pounds to pay off the charges, unless it is by the help of
Edward Cossey. So, if he lives—and as he has lasted so long
I expect that he will live—and you refuse to go on with your
engagement to him, we shall be sold up, and that is all; for
that fellow, Quest, confound him, will show us no mercy."

"I know it, father," answered Ida, "but I cannot and will

not marry him, and I do not think you can expect me to. I got engaged, or rather promised to get engaged to him, because I thought that one woman had no right to put her own happiness before the welfare of an old family like ours, and I would have carried out that engagement at any cost. But since then, to tell you the truth," and she blushed deeply, " not only have I learned to dislike him a great deal more, but I have come to care for some one else who also cares for me, and who therefore has a right to be considered. Think, father, what it means to a woman to sell herself into bodily and mental bondage, when she cares for another man."

" Well, well," said her father, with some irritation, " I am no authority upon matters of sentiment ; they are not in my line, and I know that women have their prejudices. Still you can't expect me to look at the matter in quite the same light as you do. And who is the gentleman—Colonel Quaritch ?"

She nodded her head.

" Oh," said the squire, " I have nothing to say against Quaritch, indeed I like the man, but I suppose that if he has five hundred pounds a year, that is every sixpence he can count on."

" I had rather marry him upon five hundred a year than Edward Cossey upon fifty thousand."

" Ah, yes, I have heard women talk like that before, though, perhaps, they think differently afterwards. Of course I have no right to obtrude myself, but when you are comfortably married, what is going to become of Honham I should like to know, and incidentally of me ?"

" I don't know, father, dear," she answered, her eyes filling with tears ; " we must trust to Providence, I suppose. I know you think me very selfish," she went on, catching him by the arm, " but, oh, father, there are things that are worse than death to women, or at least to some women. I almost think that I would rather die than marry Edward Cossey, though I would have gone through with it if he had kept his word."

" No, no," said her father. " I can't wonder at it, and certainly I do not ask you to marry a man you dislike. But still it is hard upon me to have all this trouble at my age, and the old place coming to the hammer too. It is enough to make a man wish that his troubles were over altogether.

However, we must take things as we find them, and we
find them pretty rough. Quaritch said he was coming back
this evening, didn't he? I suppose there will not be any
public engagement at present, will there? And look here, Ida,
I don't want him to come talking to me about it. I have got
enough things of my own to think of without bothering my
head about your love affairs. Pray let the thing be for the
present. And now I am going out to see that fellow George,
who hasn't been here since he came back from London, and a
nice bit of news it will be that I shall have to tell him."

When her father had gone Ida did a thing she had not
done for some time, she wept a little. All her fine intentions
of self-denial had broken down, and she felt humiliated at
the fact. She had intended to sacrifice herself upon the altar
of her duty, and to make herself the wedded wife of a man
who was repugnant to her, and now, on the first opportunity,
she had thrown up the contract on a quibble, a point of law
as it were. Nature had been too strong for her, as it often is
for people with deep feelings; she could not do it, no, not to
save Honham from the hammer. When she had promised
that she would engage herself to Edward Cossey she had not
been in love with Colonel Quaritch; now she was, and the
difference between the two states was considerable. Still the
fall was a humiliating one to her pride, and, what is more, she
felt that her father was disappointed in her. Of course she
could not expect him at his age (when looked at through the
mist of years all sentiment appears more or less foolish) to
enter into her private feelings. She knew very well that age
strips men of those finer sympathies and sensibilities which
clothe them in youth, much as the winter frost and wind strips
the delicate foliage from the trees. For to them the music of
the world is dead. Love has vanished with the summer dews,
and in its place are cutting blasts and snows and sere memories rustling like fallen leaves about their feet. As we grow
old we are apt to grow away from beauty, and what is high
and pure; our hearts harden by contact with the hard world;
we examine love and find, or think we find, that it is naught
but a variety of lust; friendship, and think it self-interest;
religion, and name it superstition. The facts of life alone remain clear and desirable. We know that money means power,

and we turn our face to Mammon, and if he smiles upon us we are content to let our finer visions go where our youth has gone:

> " Trailing clouds of glory do we come
> From God who is our home."

So says the poet, but, alas! the clouds soon melt into the gray air of the world, and so any of us, before our course is finished, forget that they ever were. And yet which is the shadow of the truth: those dreams and hopes and aspirations of our younger life, or the grimy corruption with which the world cakes our souls?

She knew that she could not expect her father to sympathize with her; she knew that to his judgment, circumstances being the same, and both suitors being equally sound in wind and limb, the choice of one of them should be a matter to be decided by the exterior consideration of wealth and general convenience. For men, and especially old men, who are interested in the matter, putting aside their contempt of "sentiment," little understand the preferences of women. Since the world began women have been an article of commerce, and in their hearts many men look upon them as an article of commerce still, creatures incapable of any real feeling (except, of course, the natural maternal instinct), and quite ready to accommodate themselves to any master which fate gives them. It is, however, only fair to say that they also sometimes reach that conclusion by study from the life rather than by the inherited tradition.

However, Ida had made her choice, made it suddenly, but none the less had made it. It lay between her father's interest and the interest of the family at large, and her own honor as a woman—for the mere empty ceremony of marriage which satisfies the world cannot make dishonor an honorable thing. She had made her choice, and the readers of her history must judge if that choice were right or wrong.

After dinner Harold came again, as he had promised. The squire was not in the drawing-room when he was shown in.

Ida rose to greet him with a sweet and happy smile upon her face, for, in the presence of her lover, all her doubts and troubles vanished like a mist.

" I have a bit of good news for you," said he, trying to look as though he were rejoiced to give it. Edward Cossey has taken a wonderful turn for the better. They say that he will certainly recover."

"Oh," she answered, coloring a little, "and now I have a bit of news for you, Colonel Quaritch. My engagement with Mr. Edward Cossey is at an end. I shall not marry him."

"Are you sure?" said Harold, with a gasp.

"Quite sure; I have made up my mind," and she held out her hand, as though to seal her words.

He took it and kissed it. "Thank God, Ida," he said.

"Yes," she answered, "thank God;" and at that moment the squire came in, looking very miserable and depressed, and of course nothing more was said about the matter.

CHAPTER XXXII.

GEORGE PROPHESIES AGAIN.

Six weeks have passed, and in that time several things have happened. In the first place the miserly old banker, Edward Cossey's father, had died, his death having been accelerated by the shock of his son's accident. On his will being opened, it was found that property and money to no less a value than six hundred thousand pounds passed under it to Edward absolutely, the only condition attached being that he should continue in the house of Cossey & Son and leave a certain share of his fortune in the business.

Edward Cossey had also, thanks chiefly to Belle's tender nursing, almost recovered; with one exception—he was, and would be for life, stone deaf in the right ear. The paralysis which the doctors had feared had not shown itself. One of the first questions when he became convalescent was addressed to Belle Quest.

He had, as in a dream, always seen her sweet face hanging over him, and dimly known that she was ministering to him.

"Have you nursed me ever since the accident, Belle?" he said.

"Yes," she answered.

"It is very good of you, considering all things," he murmured. "I wonder that you did not let me die."

And she turned her face to the wall and said never a word, nor did any further conversation on these matters pass between them.

Then as his strength came back so did his passion for Ida de la Molle revive. He was not allowed to write or even receive letters, and with this explanation of her silence he was fain to content himself. But the squire, he was told, often called to inquire after him, and once or twice Ida came with him.

At length a time came, it was two days after he had been told of his father's death, when he was pronounced fit to be moved into his own rooms, and to receive his correspondence as usual.

The move was effected without any difficulty, and here Belle bade him good-by. Even as she did so George drove his fat pony up to the door, and, getting down, delivered a letter to the landlady, with particular instructions that it was to be delivered into Mr. Cossey's own hands. As she passed, Belle saw that it was addressed in the squire's handwriting.

When it was delivered to him Edward Cossey opened it with eagerness. It contained an enclosure in Ida's writing, and this he read first. It ran as follows:

"DEAR MR. COSSEY,—I am told that you are now able to read letters, so I hasten to write to you. First of all, let me tell you how thankful I am that you are in a fair way to complete recovery from your dreadful accident. And now I must tell you what I fear will be almost as painful to you to read as it is for me to write, namely, that the engagement between us is at an end. To put the matter frankly, you will remember that I rightly or wrongly became engaged to you on a certain condition. That engagement has not been fulfilled, for Mr. Quest, to whom the mortgages on my father's property have been transferred by you, is pressing for their payment. Consequently the obligation on my part is at an end, and with it the engagement must end also, for I grieve to tell you that it is not one which my personal inclination will induce me to carry out. Wishing you a speedy and complete recovery, and every happiness and prosperity in your future life, believe me, dear Mr. Cossey,
          "Very truly yours,   IDA DE LA MOLLE."

He put this uncompromising and crushing epistle down, and nervously glanced at the squire's, which was very short. It began:

"MY DEAR COSSEY,—Ida has shown me the enclosed letter. I think that you did unwisely when you entered into what must be called a money bargain for my daughter's hand. Whether, under all the circumstances, she does either well or wisely to repudiate the engagement after it has once been entered into, is not for me to judge. She is a free agent, and has of course a right to dispose of her life as she thinks fit. This being so, I have, of course, no option but to endorse her decision, so far as I have anything to do with the matter. It is a decision which I for some reasons regret, but which I am quite powerless to alter.
     "Believe me, with kind regards, truly yours,   JAMES DE LA MOLLE."

Edward Cossey turned his face to the wall and indulged in such meditations as the occasion gave rise to, and they were bitter enough. He was as bent upon this marriage as he had ever been, more so in fact, now that his father was out of the way. He knew that Ida disliked him, he had known that all along, but he had trusted to time and marriage to overcome the dislike. And now that accursed Quest had brought about the ruin of his hopes. Ida had seen her chance of escape, and had, like a bold woman, seized upon it. There was one ray of hope, and one only. He knew that the money would not be forthcoming to pay off the mortgages. He could see, too, from the tone of the squire's letter, that he did not altogether approve of his daughter's decision. And his father was dead. Like Cæsar, he was the master of many legions, or rather of much money, which is as good as legions. Money can make most paths smooth to the feet of the traveller, and why not this? After much thought he came to a conclusion. He would not trust his chance to paper, he would plead his cause in person. So he wrote a short note to the squire acknowledging Ida's and his letter, and saying that he hoped to come and see them as soon as ever the doctor would allow him out of doors.

Meanwhile George, having delivered his letter, had proceeded upon another errand. Pulling up the fat pony in front of Mr. Quest's office, he alighted and entered. Mr. Quest was disengaged, and he was shown straight into the inner office, where the lawyer sat looking more refined and gentleman-like than ever.

"How do you do, George?" he said, cheerily; "sit down; what is it?"

"Well, sir," answered that lugubrious worthy, as he awkwardly took a seat, "the question is, what isn't it? these be rum times, they be; they fare to puzzle a man, they du."

"Yes," said Mr. Quest, balancing a quill pen on his finger, "the times are bad enough."

Then came a pause.

"Dash it all, sir," went on George, presently; "I may as well get it out; I have come to speak to you about the squire's business."

"Yes?" said Mr. Quest.

" Well, sir," went on George, " I'm told that these mortgages have passed into your hands, and that you have called
in the money."

" Yes, that is correct," said Mr. Quest again.

" Well, sir, the fact is that the squire can't get the money.
It can't be had nohow. Nobody won't take the land as security. It might be so much water for all people will look
at it."

" Quite so. Land is in very bad odor as security now."

" And that being so, sir, what is to be done ?"

Mr. Quest shrugged his shoulders. " I do not know. If
the money is not forthcoming, of course I shall, however unwillingly, be forced to take my legal remedy."

" Meaning, sir—"

" Meaning that I shall bring an action for foreclosure and
do what I can with the lands."

George's face darkened.

" And that reads, sir, that the squire and Miss Ida will be
turned out of Honham, where they have been for centuries,
and that you will turn in ?"

" Well, that is what it comes to, George. I am sincerely
sorry to press the squire, but it's a matter of thirty thousand
pounds, and I am not in a position to throw away thirty thousand pounds."

" Sir," said George, rising in indignation, " I don't know how
you came by them there mortgages. There is some things
that laryers know and honest men don't know, and that is one
of them. But it seems that you've got 'em and are going to
use 'em ; and that being so, Mr. Quest, I have summut to say
to you—and that is that no good will come to you from this
move."

" What do you mean by that, George ?" said the lawyer,
sharply.

" Never you mind what I mean, sir. I means what I
say. I means that sometimes people has things in their lives
snugged away where nobody can't see them, things as quiet
as though they was dead and buried, and that ain't dead and
buried ; things so much alive that they fare as though they
were fit to kick the lid off their coffin. That's what I means,
sir, and I means that when folk set to work to do a hard and

wicked thing those dead things sometimes gets up and walks
where they is least wanted, and mayhap if you goes on for to
turn the old squire and Miss Ida out of the Castle—mayhap, sir,
something of that sort will happen to you ; for, mark my word,
sir, there's justice in the world, sir, as mayhap you will find out.
And now, sir, I'll wish you good-morning, and leave you to consider what I've said," and he was gone.

"George," called Mr. Quest after him, rising from his chair,
"George," but George was out of hearing.

"Now what did he mean by that—what the devil did he
mean ?" said Mr. Quest, with a gasp, as he sat down again.
"Surely," he thought, "the man cannot have got hold of anything
about Edith. Impossible, impossible ; if he had he would have
said more, he would not have confined himself to hinting, that
would take a cleverer man ; he would have shown his hand. He
must have been speaking at random to frighten me, I suppose.
By heavens, what a thing it would be if he had got hold of something ! Ruin, absolute ruin ! I'll settle up this business as
soon as I can and leave the country ; I can't stand the strain,
it's like having a sword over one's head. I've half a mind to
leave it in somebody else's hands and go at once. No, for that
would look like running away. It must be all rubbish ; how
could he know anything about it ?"

So shaken was he, however, that though he tried once and
yet again, he found it impossible to settle himself down to work
till he had taken a couple of glasses of sherry from the decan-
ter in the cupboard, and even as he did so he wondered, if the
shadow of the sword disturbed him so much, how he would
be affected if it ever were his lot to face the glimmer of its
naked blade.

No further letter came to Edward Cossey from the Castle,
but, impatient as he was to do so, another fortnight elapsed
before he was able to go up to see Ida and her father. At
last, one fine December morning, he was for the first time since
his accident allowed to take carriage exercise, and his first
drive was to Honham Castle.

When the squire, who was sitting in the vestibule writing
letters, saw a poor, pallid man rolled up in fur, with a white
face scarred with shot-marks, and black rings round his large,
dark eyes, being helped from a closed carriage, he did not know

who it was, and called to Ida, who was passing along the passage, to tell him.

Of course she recognized her admirer instantly, and wished
to leave the room, but her father prevented her.

"You got into this mess," he said, forgetting how and for
whom she got into it, "and now you must get out of it in
your own way."

When Edward, having been assisted into the room, saw Ida
standing there, all the blood in his wasted body seemed to rush
for a few seconds into his pallid face.

"How do you do, Mr. Cossey?" she said.   "I am glad to see
you out, and hope that you are better."

"I beg your pardon, I cannot hear you," he said, turning
round ; "I am stone deaf in my right ear."

A pang of pity shot through her heart.   Edward Cossey
feeble, dejected, and limping from the jaws of death, was a
very different being to Edward Cossey in the full blow of his
youth and health and strength.   Indeed, so much did his condition appeal to her sympathies that, for the first since her mental attitude towards him had been one of entire indifference,
she looked on him without repugnance.

Meanwhile her father had shaken him by the hand, and led
him to an arm-chair before the fire.

Then after a few questions and answers as to his accident
and merciful recovery there came a pause.

At length he broke it.   "I have come to see you both," he
said, with a faint, nervous smile, "about the letters you wrote
me.   If my condition would have allowed it I would have
come before, but it would not."

"Yes," said the squire attentively, while Ida folded her
hands in her lap, and sat still with her eyes fixed upon the fire.

"It seems," he went on, "that the old proverb has applied
to my case as to so many others—being absent I have suffered.
I understand from these letters that my engagement to you,
Ida, is broken off."

She made a motion of assent.

"And that it is to be broken off on the ground that, having
been forced by a combination of circumstances which I cannot
enter into to transfer the mortgages to Mr. Quest, consequently that I broke my bargain with you."

" Yes," said Ida.

" Very well, then ; I come to tell you both that I am ready to find the money to meet those mortgages and pay them off."

" Ah !" said the squire.

" Also that I am ready to do what I offered to do before, and which, as my father is now dead, I am perfectly in a position to do, namely, to settle two hundred thousand pounds absolutely upon Ida, and indeed do anything else that she or you may wish," and he looked at the squire.

" It is no use looking at me for an answer," said he, with some irritation. " I have no voice in the matter."

He turned to Ida, who put her hand before her face and shook her head.

" Perhaps," said Edward, somewhat bitterly, " I should not be far wrong if I said that Colonel Quaritch has more to do with your change of mind than the fact of the transfer of these mortgages."

She dropped her hand and looked him full in the face.

" You are quite right, Mr. Cossey," she said, boldly. " Colonel Quaritch and I are attached to each other, and we hope one day to be married."

" Confound that fellow, Quaritch," growled the squire.

Edward winced visibly at this outspoken statement.

" Ida," he said, " I make one last appeal to you. I am devoted to you with all my heart ; so devoted that though it may seem foolish to say so, especially before your father, I really think that I would rather not have recovered from my accident than that I should have recovered for this. I will give you everything that a woman can want, and my money will make your family what it was centuries ago, the greatest in the country side. I don't pretend to have been a saint—perhaps you may have heard something against me in that way—or to be anything out of the way. I am only an ordinary every-day man, but I am devoted to you. Think, then, before you refuse me altogether."

" I have thought, Mr. Cossey," answered Ida, almost passionately ; " I have thought until I am sick of thinking, and I do not think that it is fair that you should press me like this, especially before my father."

" Then," he said, rising with difficulty, " I have said all that

I have to say, and done all that I can do. I shall still hope that you may change your mind. I shall not yet abandon hope. Good-by."

She touched his hand, and then, the squire offering him his arm, he went down the steps to his carriage.

"I hope, Mr. De la Molle," he said, "that bad as things are for me, if they should take a turn, I shall have your support."

"My dear sir," answered the squire, "I tell you frankly that I wish my daughter would marry you. As I said before I have nothing against you, and it would, for obvious reasons, be desirable. But Ida is not like ordinary women. When she sets her mind upon a thing she sets it like a flint. Things may change, however, and that is all I can say. Yes, if I were you, I should remember that this is a changeable world, and that women are the most changeable things in it."

When the carriage had gone he re-entered the vestibule. Ida, who was going away much disturbed in mind, saw him coming, and knew from the expression of his face that there was going to be trouble. With characteristic courage she turned, determined to face it out.

CHAPTER XXXIII.

THE SQUIRE SPEAKS HIS MIND.

For a minute or more her father fidgeted about, moving his papers backward and forward, but said nothing.

At last he spoke. "You have taken a most serious and painful step, Ida," he said. "Of course you have a right to do as you please; you are of full age, and I cannot expect that you will consider me or your family in your matrimonial engagements, but at the same time I think that it is my duty to point out to you what it is that you are doing. You are refusing one of the finest matches in England in order to marry a broken-down, middle-aged, half-pay colonel, a man who can hardly support you, whose part in life is played, or who is apparently too idle to seek another."

Here Ida's eyes flashed ominously, but she made no comment, being apparently afraid to trust herself to speak.

"You are doing this," went on her father, working himself up as he spoke, "in the face of my wishes, and with the knowledge that your action will bring your family, to say nothing of your father, to utter and irretrievable ruin."

"Surely, father, surely," broke in Ida, almost in a cry, "you would not have me marry one man when I love another. When I made the promise I had not become attached to Colonel Quaritch."

"Love! pshaw!" said her father; "don't talk to me in that sentimental and schoolgirl way; you are too old for it. I am a plain man, and I believe in family affection and in *duty*, Ida. *Love*, as you call it, is only too often another word for self-will and selfishness and other things that we are better without."

"I can understand, father," answered Ida, struggling to keep her temper under this jobation, "that my refusal to marry Mr. Cossey is disagreeable to you for obvious reasons, though it is not so very long ago that you detested him your-self.   But I do not see why an honest woman's affection for another man should be talked of as though there was some-thing shameful about it.   It is all very well to sneer at 'love,' but, after all, a woman is flesh and blood; she is not a chattel or a slave-girl, and marriage is not like anything else; it means, as you must know, many things to a woman.   There is no magic about marriage to make that which is unrighteous righteous, or that which is impure pure."

"There," said her father; "it is no good your lecturing me on marriage, Ida.   If you do not want to marry Cossey I can't force you to.   If you want to ruin me and your family and yourself you must do so.   But there is one thing—while it is over me, which I suppose will not be for much longer, my house is my own, and I will not have that colonel of yours hanging about it, and I shall write to him to say so.   You are your own mistress, and if you choose to walk over to church and marry him you can do so, but it will be done without my consent; which, of course, however, is an unnec-essary formality.   Do you hear me, Ida?"

"If you have quite done, father," she answered, coldly, "I should like to go before I say something which I might be sorry for.   Of course, you can write what you like to Colonel Quaritch, and I shall write to him, too."

Her father made no answer beyond sitting down at his table and grabbing viciously at a pen.   So she left the room, indig-nant, indeed, but with as heavy a heart as any woman could well carry in her breast.

"DEAR SIR [wrote the not altogether unnaturally indignant squire],—I have been informed by my daughter Ida of her entanglement with you. It is one which, for reasons that I need not enter into, is most distasteful to me, as well as, I am sorry to say, ruinous to Ida herself and to her fam-ily.   Ida is of full age, and must, of course, do as she pleases with herself. But I cannot consent to become a party to what I disapprove of so strongly, and this being the case, I must beg you to cease your visits to this house.

"I am, sir, your obedient servant,   JAMES DE LA MOLLE.
"Colonel Quaritch."

Ida, as soon as she had sufficiently recovered herself, also wrote to the colonel.   She told him the whole story, keeping nothing back, and ended her letter thus:

"Never, dear Harold, was a woman in a greater difficulty, and never have I more needed help and advice. You know, and have good reason to know, how hateful this marriage would be to me, loving you as I do entirely and alone, and having no higher desire than to become your wife. But, of course, I see the painfulness of the position. I am not so selfish as my father believes, or says that he believes. I quite understand how great would be the material advantage to my father if I could bring myself to marry Mr. Cossey. You may remember that I told you once that I thought that no woman had a right to prefer her own happiness to the prosperity of her whole family. But, Harold, it is easy to speak this, and very, very hard to act up to it. What am I to do? What am I to do? And yet how can I, in common fairness, ask you to answer that question? God help us both, Harold! Is there no way out of it?"

These letters were both duly received by Harold Quaritch on the following morning, and threw him into a fever of anxiety and doubt. He was a just and reasonable man, and, knowing something of human nature, under the circumstances did not altogether wonder at the squire's violence and irritation. The financial position of the De la Molle family was little, if anything, short of desperate, and he could easily understand how maddening it must be to a man like the squire, who loved Honham, which had for centuries been the habitation of his race, better than he loved anything on earth, to suddenly realize that it must pass away from him and his forever, merely because a woman happened to prefer one man to another, and that man, to his view, the less eligible of the two. So keenly did he realize this, indeed, that he greatly doubted whether or no he was justified in continuing his advances to Ida. Finally, after much thought, he wrote to the squire as follows:

"I have received your letter, and also one from Ida, and I hope you will believe me when I say that I quite understand and sympathize with the motives which evidently led you to write it. I am, unfortunately—although I never regretted it till now—a poor man, whereas my rival suitor is a very rich one. I shall, of course, strictly obey your injunctions; and, moreover, I can assure you that, whatever my own feelings may be in the matter, I shall do nothing, either directly or indirectly, to influence Ida's ultimate decision. She must decide for herself."

To Ida he wrote at length:

"DEAREST IDA [he ended],—I can say nothing more; you must judge for yourself; and I shall accept your decision loyally, whatever it may be. It is unnecessary for me now to tell you how inextricably my happiness in life is interwoven with that decision, but at the same time I do not wish to influence it. It certainly, to my mind, does not seem right that a woman should be driven into sacrificing her whole life to secure any monetary advantage, either for herself or for others; but then the world is full of things that are not right. I can give you no advice, for I do not know what advice I ought to give. I try to put myself out of the question, and to consider you, and you only; but even then I fear that my judgment is not impartial. At any rate, the less we see of each other the better at present, for I do not wish to appear to be taking any undue advantage. If we are destined to pass our lives together, this temporary estrangement will not matter; and if, on the other hand, we are doomed to a life-long separation, the sooner we begin the better. It is a cruel world, and sometimes (as it does now) my heart sinks within me as, from year to year, I struggle on towards a happiness that ever vanishes when I stretch out my hand to clasp it; but, if I feel thus, what must you feel, who have so much more to bear? My dearest love, what can I say to you? I can only say, with you, God help us!"

This letter did not tend to raise Ida's spirits. Evidently her lover saw that there was another side to the question, the side of duty, and was too honest to hide it from her. She had said that she would have nothing to do with Edward Cossey, but she was well aware that the matter was still an open one. What should she do? what ought she to do? Abandon her love, desecrate and defile herself, and save her father and her house, or cling to her love, and leave the rest to chance? It was a cruel position, nor did the lapse of time tend to make it less cruel. Her father went about the place pale and melancholy; all his old jovial manner had vanished beneath the pressure of impending ruin. He treated her with studious and old-fashioned courtesy, but she could see that he was bitterly aggrieved by her conduct, and that the anxiety of his position was telling on his health. If this was the case now, what, she wondered, would happen in the spring, when proceedings were actually taken to sell the place?

One bright, cold morning she was walking with her father through the fields down the footpath that led to the church, and it would have been hard to say which of them looked the paler or more miserable of the two. On the previous day the squire had had an interview with Mr. Quest, and made as much of an appeal, *ad misericordiam*, to him, as his pride would allow, only to find the lawyer very courteous, very regretful, but as hard as adamant. Also that very morning a letter had reached him from London, announcing that the last hope of raising money to meet the mortgages to be paid off had failed.

The path ran along towards the road past a line of oaks. Half-way down this line they came across George, who, with his marking instrument in his hand, was contemplating some of the trees which it was proposed to take down.

"What are you doing there?" said the squire, in a melancholy voice.

"Marking, squire."

"Then you may as well save yourself the trouble, for the place will belong to somebody else before the sap is up in those oaks."

"No, squire, don't you begin to talk like that, for I don't believe it. That ain't a-going to happen."

"Ain't a-going to happen, you stupid fellow! ain't a-going to happen!" answered the squire, with a dreary laugh. "Why, look there!"—he pointed to a dog-cart which had drawn up on the road in such a position that they could see it without its occupants seeing them—"they are taking notes already."

George looked, and so did Ida. Mr. Quest was the driver of the dog-cart, which had pulled up in such a position as to command a view of the Castle, and his companion, in whom George recognized a well-known London auctioneer, who sometimes did business in those parts, was standing up, an open note-book in his hand, alternately looking at the noble towers of the gateway and jotting down memoranda.

"D— him, and so he be," said George, utterly forgetting his manners.

Ida looked up and saw her father's eyes fixed upon her with an expression that seemed to say, "See, you wilful woman, see the ruin that you have brought upon us!"

Ida turned away; she could not bear it, and that very night she came to a determination, which she in due course communicated to Harold, and him alone. That determination was to let things be for the present, upon the chance of something happening by which the dilemma might be solved. But if nothing happened—and, indeed, it did not seem probable to her that anything would happen—then she would sacrifice herself at the last moment. She believed, indeed she knew, that she could always call Edward Cossey back to her if she liked. It was a compromise, and, like all compromises, had an element of weakness; but it gave time, and time to her was like water to the dying.

"Sir," said George, presently, "it's Boisingham Quarter Sessions the day after to-morrow, aint it? (Mr. De la Molle was chairman of Quarter Sessions.)

"Yes, of course it is."

George thought for a minute.

"I'm thinking, squire, that if I arn't wanted that day I want to go up to Lunnon about a bit of business."

"Go up to London," said the squire; "why, what do you want to do there? You were in London the other day."

"Well, squire," he answered, looking inexpressibly sly, "that ain't no matter of nobody's. It's a bit of private affairs."

"Oh, all right," said the squire, his interest dying out. "You are always full of mysteries," and he continued his walk.

But George shook his fist in the direction of the road down which the dog-cart had driven.

"Ah, you devil!" he said, alluding to Mr. Quest, "if I don't make Boisingham, yes, and all England, too hot to hold you, my name ain't George. I'll give you what for, my cuckoo, that I will."

CHAPTER XXXIV.

GEORGE carried out his intention of going to London. The morning following the day when Mr. Quest had driven the auctioneer in the dog-cart to Honham, George might have been seen, an hour before it was light, purchasing a third-class return ticket to Liverpool Street. Arriving there in safety, he partook of a second breakfast, for it was ten o'clock, and then, taking a cab, he had himself driven to the end of that street in Pimlico where he had gone with the fair "Edithia," and where Johnnie had made acquaintance with his ash stick.

Dismissing the cab, he made his way to the house with the red pillars, where he was considerably taken aback, for the place had every appearance of being deserted. There were no blinds to the windows, and on the steps were muddy foot-marks and bits of rag and straw, which seemed to be the litter of a recent removal. Indeed, there on the road were the broad wheel-marks of the van which had carted off the furniture. He started at this sight with dismay. The bird had apparently flown, and left no address, and he had had his trip for nothing.

He pressed upon the electric bell; that is, he did this ultimately. George was not accustomed to electric bells; indeed, he had never seen one before; and after attempting in vain to pull it with his fingers, for he knew that it must be a bell, because there was the word itself written on it, he condescended to try his teeth. Ultimately, however, he discovered how to use it, but without result. Either the battery had been taken away, or it was out of gear. Just as he was wondering what to do next he made a discovery—the door was slightly ajar. He pushed it, and it opened, revealing a dirty hall, stripped of every scrap of furniture. Entering, he shut the door, and walked up stairs to the room where he had fled after thrashing

Johnnie. Here he paused and listened, for he thought he heard somebody in the room; nor was he mistaken, for presently a well-remembered voice shrilled out within.

"Who's skulking about outside there?" said the voice. "If it's one of those bailiffs, he better hook it, for there's nothing left here."

George's countenance positively beamed at the sound.

"Bailiffs, marm?" he sung out through the door; "it ain't no varminty bailiffs; it's a friend, and just when you're wanting one, seemingly. Can I come in?"

"Oh, yes, come in, whoever you are," said the voice. Accordingly he opened the door and entered, and this was what he saw. The room had, like the rest of the house, been stripped of everything, with the exception of a box and a mattress, beside which was an empty bottle and a dirty glass. On the mattress sat the fair Edithia, *alias* Mrs. D'Aubigné, *alias* the Tiger, *alias* Mrs. Quest, and such a sight as she presented George had never seen before. Her fierce face bore traces of recent heavy drinking, and was, moreover, dirty, haggard, and dreadful to look upon; her hair was a frowsy mat, on some patches of which the golden dye had faded, leaving it its natural hue, which was a doubtful gray. She had no collar on, and her linen was open at the neck; on her feet were a filthy pair of white-satin slippers, on her back that same gorgeous pink-satin tea-gown which Mr. Quest had observed on the occasion of his visit, now, however, soiled and torn. Anything more squalid or more repulsive than the whole picture cannot be imagined; and though his stomach was pretty strong, and in the course of his life he had seen many a sight of utter destitution, George literally recoiled from it.

"What's the matter?" said the hag, sharply; "and who the dickens are you? Ah, I know now; you're the chap who whacked Johnnie," and she burst into a hoarse scream of laughter at the recollection. "It was mean of you, though, to hook it and leave me. He pulled me, the devil, and I was fined two pounds by the beak."

"Mean of him, marm, not me; but he was a mean varmint altogether, he was, to go and pull a lady, too; I niver heard of such a thing. But, marm, if I might say so, you seem to be in trouble here," and he took a seat upon the deal-box.

"In trouble? I should think I was in trouble. There's been an execution in the house; that is, there's been three executions—one for rates and taxes, one for a butcher's bill, and one for rent. They all came together, and they fought like wild cats for the duds. That was yesterday, and you see all they have left me; cleaned out everything, down to my new yellow satin, and then asked for more. They wanted to know where my jewelry was, but I did them there, hee, hee!"

"Meaning, marm?"

"Meaning that I hid it—that is, what was left of it—under a board. But that ain't the worst. When I was asleep that devil Ellen, who's had her share of the swag all these years, got to the board and collared the things and bolted with them, and look what she's left me instead!"—and she held up a scrap of paper—"a receipt for five years' wages, and she's had them over and over again. Ah, if ever I get a chance at her!" and she doubled her long hand, and made a motion as of a person scratching. "She's bolted, and left me here to starve. I haven't had a bit since yesterday, nor a drink either, and that's worse. What's to become of me? I'm starving. I shall have to go to the workhouse. Yes, me!" she added, in a scream; "me, who have spent thousands; I shall have to go to a workhouse, like a common woman!"

"It's cruel, marm, cruel!" said the sympathetic George, "and you a lawful, wedded wife 'till death do us part.' But, marm, I saw a public over the way. Now, no offence, but you'll let me just go over and fetch a bite and a sup."

"Well," she answered, hungrily, "you're a gent, you are, though you're a country one. You go, while I just make a little toilet, and as for the drink, why let it be brandy."

"Brandy it shall be," said the gallant George, and departed.

In ten minutes he returned, with a supply of beef patties, some plates and glasses, and a bottle of good, strong British Brown, which, as everybody knows, is a sufficient quantity to make three privates or two blue jackets drunk and incapable.

The woman, who now presented a slightly more respectable appearance, seized the bottle, and pouring about a wineglass and a half of its contents into a tumbler, mixed it with an equal quantity of water, and drank it off at a draught.

"That's better," she said; "and now for a patty. It's a real picnic, this is."

He handed her one, but she could not eat more than half of it, for alcohol destroys the more healthy appetite, and she soon flew back to the brandy bottle.

"Now, marm, that you are a little more comfortable, perhaps you will tell me how you got into this way, and you with a rich husband as I well knows to love and cherish you."

"A husband to love and cherish me?" she said; "why, I have written to him three times to tell him that I'm starving, and never a penny has he given me—and there's no allowance due yet, and when there is they'll take it, for I owe hundreds."

"Well," said George, "I call it cruel—cruel, and he rolling in gold. Thirty thousand pounds he has just made, that I know of. You must be an angel, marm, to stand it, an angel without wings. If it were my husband I'd know the reason why."

"Ay, but I daren't. He'd murder me. He said he would."

George laughed, gently. "Lord! Lord!" he said, "to see how men do play it off upon poor weak women, working on their narves and that like. He kill you. Laryer Quest kill you, and he the biggest coward in Boisingham. But there it is; this is a world of wrong as the parson says, and the poor shorn lambs must jamb their tails down and turn their starns to the wind, and so must you, marm. So it's the worklus you'll be in to-morrow. Well, you'll find it a poor place, the skilly is that rough it do fare to take the skin off your throat, and not a drop of liquor, not even a cup of hot tea, and work too, lots of it—scrubbing, marm, scrubbing."

This vivid picture of miseries to come drew something between a sob and a howl from the woman. There is nothing more horrible to the imagination of such people than the idea of being forced to work. If their notions of a future state of punishment could be got at, they would be found in nine cases out of ten to resolve themselves into a vague conception of hard labor in a hot climate. It was the idea of the scrubbing that particularly affected the Tiger.

"I won't do it," she said, "I'll go to chokey first—"

"Look here, marm," said George, in a persuasive voice, and pushing the brandy bottle towards her, "where's the need for you to go to the workhus or to chokey either—you with a rich husband as is bound by law to support you as becomes a lady; and, marm, mind another thing, a husband as has wickedly deserted you—which how he could do so it ain't for me to say—and is living along of another young party."

She took some more brandy before she answered.

"That's all very well, you duffer," she said; "but how am I to get at him? I tell you I'm afraid of him, and even if I weren't, I haven't a cent to travel with, and if I got there what am I to do?"

"As for being afraid, marm," he answered, "I've told you Laryer Quest is a long-sight more frightened of you than you are of him. Then as for money, why, marm, I'm going down to Boisingham myself by the train that leaves Liverpool Street at half-past one, and that's an hour from now, and it's proud and pleased I should be to take a lady down and be the means of bringing them as has been in holy matrimony together again. And as to what you should do when you gets there, why, you should just walk up with your marriage lines and say, 'You are my husband, and I call on you to cease living in sin and to take me back;' and if he don't, why then you swears an information, and it's a case of warrant for bigamy."

The Tiger chuckled, and then, suddenly seized with suspicion, looked at her visitor sharply.

"What do you want me to blow the gaff for," she said; "you're a leery old hand you are, for all your simple ways, and you've got some game on, I'll take my davey."

"I a game—I?" answered George, an expression of the deepest pain spreading itself over his ugly features. "No, marm—and when one has wanted to help a friend, too. Well, if you think that—and no doubt misfortune has made you suspicious—the best I can do is to bid you good-day, and to wish you well out of your troubles, workhus and all, marm, which I do according," and he rose from his box with much dignity, politely bowed to the hag on the mattress, and then, turning, walked towards the door.

She sprang up with an oath.

"I'll go," she said, "I'll take the change out of him; I'll

teach him to let his lawful wife starve on a beggarly pittance. I don't care if he does try to kill me. I'll ruin him;" and she stamped upon the floor and screamed, " I'll ruin him! I'll ruin him!" presenting such a picture of abandoned evil and wickedness that even George, whose nerves were not finely strung, inwardly shrank from her.

" Ah, marm," he said, "no wonder you're put out. When I think of what you've had to suffer, I own it makes my blood go biling through my veins. But if you are a-coming, perhaps it would be as well to stop cursing and put your hat on, for we have got to catch the train," and he pointed to a headgear chiefly made of somewhat dilapidated peacock feathers, and an ulster which the bailiffs had either overlooked or left through pity.

She put on the hat and cloak, and then going to the hole beneath the board, out of which she said the woman Ellen had stolen her jewelry, she extracted the copy of the certificate of marriage which that lady had not apparently thought worth stealing, and put it in the pocket of her pink silk *peignoir*.

Then George, having first secured the remainder of the bottle of brandy, which he put into his capacious pocket, they started, and, finding a hansom, drove to Liverpool Street. Such a spectacle as the Tiger looked upon the platform George was wont in after-days to declare he never did see. But it can easily be imagined that a fierce, dissolute, hungry-looking woman, with half-dyed hair, who had drunk as much as was good for her, dressed in a hat made of peacock feathers, dirty-white shoes, an ulster with some buttons off, and a gorgeous but filthy pink silk tea-gown, presented a sufficiently curious appearance, especially when contrasted with her companion, the sober and melancholy-looking George, who was arrayed in his pepper-and-salt Sunday suit.

So curious indeed was their aspect that the people loitering about the platform collected round them, and George, who was heartily ashamed of the position, was thankful enough when once the train started. He had from motives of economy taken her a third-class ticket, and at this she grumbled, saying that she was accustomed to travel, like a lady should, first; but he appeased her with the brandy bottle.

All the journey through he talked to her about her wrongs, till at last, what between the liquor and his artful incitements, she was inflamed into a condition of savage fury against Mr. Quest. When once she got to this point he would let her have no more brandy, seeing that she was now ripe for his purpose, which was, of course, to use her to ruin the man who would ruin the house he served.

Mr. Quest, sitting in state as clerk to the magistrates assembled in Quarter Sessions at the session-house at Boisingham, little guessed that the sword at whose shadow he had trembled all these years was even now falling on his head, or that the hand that cut the hair that held it was that of the stupid bumpkin whose warning he had despised.

CHAPTER XXXV.

THE SWORD OF DAMOCLES.

At last the weary journey was over, and to George's intense relief he found himself upon the platform at Boisingham. He was a pretty tough subject, but he felt that a very little more of the company of the fair Edithia would be too much for him. As it happened, the station-master was a particular friend of his, and the astonishment of that worthy when he saw the respectable George in such company cannot be expressed in words.

"Why, George! Well, I never! Is she a furriner?" he ejaculated in astonishment.

"If you mean me, you dirty, wheel-greasing steam-boss, you," said Edithia, who was by now in fine bellicose condition, "I'm no more foreign than you are. Shut your ugly mouth, can't you, or"—and she took a step towards the stout station-master. He retreated, precipitately caught his heel against the threshold of the booking-office, and vanished backward with a crash.

"Steady, marm, steady," said George. "Save it up now, do; and as for you, don't you irritate her none of you, or I won't answer for the consequences, for she's an injured woman she is, and injured women are apt to be dangerous."

As chance would have it, a fly which had brought somebody to the station was still standing there, and into it George bundled his fair charge, telling the driver to go the sessions-house.

"Now, marm," he said, "listen to me; I'm going to take you to the man as has wronged you. He's sitting as clerk to the magistrates. Do you go up and call him your husband. Then he'll tell the policeman to take you away. Then do you sing out for justice—because when people sings out for justice everybody's bound to listen—and say that you want a warrant

against him for bigamy, and show them the marriage certificate. Don't you be put down, and don't you spare him. If
you don't startle him you'll never get anything out of him."

"Spare him?" she snarled; "I'll make him sit up; I'll have
his blood. But look here, if he's put in chokey, where's the
tin to come from?"

"Why, marm," answered George, with splendid mendacity,
"it's the best thing that can happen for you, for if they collar him you get the property, and that's law."

"Oh," she answered, "if I'd known that, he'd have been
collared long ago, I can tell you."

"Come," said George, seeing that they were nearing their
destination. "Have one more nip just to keep your spirits
up," and he produced the brandy bottle, at which she took
a long pull.

"Now," he said, "go for him like a wild cat."

"Never you fear," she said.

They dismounted from the cab and entered the court-house
without attracting any particular notice. The court itself was
crowded, for a case which had excited public interest was
coming to a conclusion. The jury had given their verdict,
and sentence was being pronounced by Mr. De la Molle, the
chairman.

Mr. Quest was sitting at his table below the bench, taking
some notes.

"There's your husband," he whispered; "now do you
draw on."

George's part in the drama was played, and with a sigh of
relief he fell back to watch its final development. He saw
the fierce tall woman slip through the crowd like a snake or
a panther to its prey, and some compunction touched him
when he thought of the prey. He glanced at the elderly respectable-looking gentleman at the table, and reflected that
he, too, was stalking his prey, the old squire and the ancient
house of De la Molle. Then his compunction vanished, and
he rejoiced to think that he would be the means of destroying
a man who, to fill his pockets, did not hesitate to destroy the
family with which his life, and the lives of his forefathers for
many generations, had been interwoven.

By this time the woman had fought her way through the

press, bursting the remaining buttons off her ulster in so doing, and reached the bar which separated the spectators from the space reserved for the officials. On the farther side of the bar was a gangway, then came the table at which Mr. Quest sat. He had been busy writing something all this time, now he rose and passed it to Mr. De la Molle, and then turned to sit down again.

Meanwhile his wife had craned her long, lithe body forward over the bar till her head was almost level with the hither edge of the table. There she stood glaring at him, and her wicked face alive with fury and malice, for the brandy she had drank had caused her to forget her fears.

As Mr. Quest turned, his eye caught the flash of color from the peacock-feather hat. From thence it travelled to the face beneath.

He gave a gasp, and the court seemed to whirl round him. The sword had fallen indeed.

"Well, Billy," whispered the hateful voice, "you see I've come to look you up."

With a desperate effort he recovered himself. A policeman was standing near him. He beckoned to him, and told him to remove the woman, who was drunk. The policeman advanced and touched her on the arm.

"Come, you be off," he said; "you're drunk."

At that moment Mr. De la Molle ceased giving judgment.

"I ain't drunk," said the woman, loud enough to attract the attention of the whole court, which now, for the first time, observed her extraordinary attire, "and I've a right to be in the public court."

"Come on," said the policeman, "the clerk says you're to go."

"The clerk says so, does he?" she answered; "and do you know who the clerk is? I'll tell you all," and she raised her voice to a scream, "he's my husband, my lawful wedded husband, and here's proof of it," and she took the folded certificate from her pocket and flung it so that it fell upon the desk of one of the magistrates.

Mr. Quest sank into his chair, and there was a silence of astonishment through the court.

The squire was the first to recover himself.

" Silence !" he said, addressing her. " Silence! This cannot go on here."

" But I want justice," she shrieked. " I want justice ; I want a warrant against that man for *bigamy.*" (Renewed sensation.) " He's left me to starve ; me, his lawful wife. Look here," and she tore open the pink satin tea-gown, " I haven't enough clothes on me, the bailiffs took all my clothes ; I have suffered his cruelty for years, and borne it, and I can bear it no longer. Justice your worships ; I only ask for justice."

" Be silent, woman," said Mr. De la Molle; " if you have any criminal charge to bring against anybody there is a proper way to make it. Be silent or leave this court."

But she only screamed the more for justice, and loudly detailed fragments of her woes to the eagerly listening crowd.

Then policemen were ordered to remove her, and there followed a most frightful scene. She shrieked and bit and fought in such a fashion that it took four men to drag her to the door of the court, where she dropped exhausted against the wall in the corridor.

" Well," said the observant George to himself, " she has done the trick proper, and no mistake. Couldn't have been better. That's a master one, that is." Then he turned his attention to the stricken man before him. Mr. Quest was sitting in his chair, his face ashen, his eyes wide open, and his hands placed flat on the table before him. When silence had been restored he rose, and turned to the bench, apparently with the intention of addressing the court. But he said nothing, either because he could not find words, or because his courage failed him. There was a moment's intense silence, for every one in the crowded court was watching him, and the sense of it seemed to take what resolution he had left out of him. At any rate, he left the table and hurried from the court. In the passage he found the Tiger, who, surrounded by a little crowd, and with her hat awry, and her clothes half torn from her back, was huddled gasping against the wall.

She saw him and began to speak, but he stopped and faced her. He faced her, grinding his teeth, and with such an awful fire of fury in his eyes that she shrank from him in terror, flattening herself against the wall.

"What did I tell you?" he said, in a choked voice, and then passed on. A few paces down the passage he met one of his own clerks, a sharp fellow enough.

"Here, Jones," he said, "you see that woman there. She has made a charge against me. Watch her. See where she goes to, and find out what she is going to do. Then come and tell me at the office. If you lose sight of her, you lose your place too. Do you understand?"

"Yes, sir," said the astonished clerk, and Mr. Quest was gone.

He made his way direct to the office. It was closed, for he had told his clerks that he should not come back after court, and that they could go at half-past four. He had his key, however, and, entering, lit the gas. Then he went to his safe and sorted some papers, burning a good number of them. Two large documents, however, he put by his side to read. One was his will, the other was endorsed "Statement of the circumstances connected with Edith."

First he looked through his will. It had been made some years ago, and was entirely in favor of his wife, or, rather, of his reputed wife, Belle.

"It may as well stand," he said, aloud; "if anything happens to me, she'll take about ten thousand under it, and that was what she brought me." Taking a pen he went through the document carefully, and wherever the name of "Belle Quest" occurred, he put an X, and inserted these words, "Gennett, commonly known as Belle Quest," Gennett being Belle's maiden name, and initialled the correction. Next he glanced at the statement. It contained a full and fair account of his connection with the woman who had ruined his life. "I may as well leave it," he thought; "some day it will show Belle that I was not quite so bad as I seemed."

He replaced the statement in a brief envelope, sealed and directed it to Belle, and finally marked it, "Not to be opened till my death. W. Quest." Then he put the envelope away in the safe and took up the will for the same purpose. Next it, on the table, lay the deeds executed by Edward Cossey, transferring the Honham mortgages to Mr. Quest in consideration of his abstaining from the commencement of a suit for divorce in which he proposed to join Edward Cossey as corespondent. "Ah!" he thought to himself, "that game is up. Belle is not my legal wife, therefore I cannot commence a suit against her in which Cossey would figure as corespondent, and so the consideration fails. I am sorry for that, for I should have liked him to lose his thirty thousand pounds as well as his wife, but it can't be helped. It was a game of bluff, and now that the bladder has been pricked, I haven't a leg to stand on."

Then, taking a pen, he wrote on a sheet of paper which he inserted in the will,

"DEAR B.,—You must return the Honham mortgages to Mr. Edward Cossey. As you are not my legal wife the consideration upon which he transferred them fails, and you cannot hold them in equity, nor, I suppose, would you wish to do so. W. Q."

Having put all the papers away, he shut the safe at the moment the clerk whom he had deputed to watch the Tiger knocked at the door and entered.

"Well?" said his master.

"Well, sir, I watched the woman. She stopped in the passage for a minute, and then George, Squire De la Molle's man, came out and spoke to her. I got quite close, so as to hear what he said, and he said 'You'd better get out of this.'

"'Where to?' she answered. 'I'm afraid.'

"'Back to London,' he said, and gave her a sovereign, and she got up without a word and slunk off to the station, followed by a mob of people. She's in the refreshment-room now, but George sent word to say that they ought not to serve her with any drink."

"What time does the next train go—7.15, does it not?" said Mr. Quest.

"Yes, sir."

"Well, go back to the station and keep an eye upon that woman, and when the time comes get me a first-class return ticket to London. I shall go up myself and give her in charge there. Here is some money," and he gave him a five-pound note; "and look here, Jones, you need not trouble about the change."

"Thank you, sir, I'm sure," said Jones, to whom, his salary

being a guinea a week, on which he supported a wife and family, a gift of four pounds was sudden wealth.

"Don't thank me, but do as I tell you. I will be down at the station at 7.10. Meet me outside and give me the ticket. That will do."

When Jones had gone Mr. Quest sat down to think.

So it was George who had loosed this woman on him, and that was the meaning of his mysterious warnings. How had he found her? That did not matter—he had found her, and in revenge for the action taken against the De la Molle family he had brought her here to denounce him. It had been cleverly managed too. Mr. Quest reflected to himself that he should never have given the man credit for the brains. Well, that was what came of underrating people.

And so this was the end of all his hopes, ambitions, shifts, and struggles. The story would be in every paper in England before another twenty-four hours were over, headed "*Remarkable occurrence at Boisingham Quarter Sessions.—Alleged bigamy of a solicitor.*" No doubt, too, the treasury would take it up and institute a prosecution. This was the end of his strivings after respectability and the wealth that brings it. He had overreached himself. He had plotted and schemed, and hardened his heart against the De la Molle family, and fate had made use of his success to destroy him. In another few months he had expected to be able to leave this place a wealthy and respected man—and now. He laid his hand upon the table and reviewed his past life—tracing it from year to year, and seeing how the shadow of this accursed woman had haunted him, bringing disgrace and terror and mental agony with it—making his life a misery. And now what was to be done? He was ruined. Let him fly to the utmost parts of the earth, let him burrow in the recesses of the cities of the earth, and his shame would find him out. He was an impostor, a bigamist, one who had seduced an innocent woman into a mock marriage and then taken her fortune to buy the silence of his lawful wife. More, he had threatened to bring an action for divorce against a woman to whom he knew he was not really married, and made it a lever to extort vast sums of money or their value.

What is there that a man in this position can do?

He can do two things—he can revenge himself upon the author of his ruin, and, if he be bold enough, he can put an end to himself and his sorrows at a blow.

Mr. Quest rose and walked to the door. Halting, he turned and looked round the office in that peculiar fashion wherewith the eyes take their adieu. Then, with a sigh, he went.

Reaching his own house, he hesitated whether or no to enter. Had the news reached Belle? If so, how was he to face her? Her hands were not clean, indeed, but at any rate she had no mock marriage in her record, and her dislike of him had been unconcealed throughout. She had never wished to marry him, and never for one single day regarded him otherwise than with aversion.

After reflection he turned and went round by the back way into the garden. The curtains of the French windows were drawn, but it was a wet and windy night, and the draught occasionally lifted the edge of one of them. He crept like a thief up to his own window and looked in. The drawing-room was lighted, and in a low chair by the fire sat Belle. She was, as usual, dressed in black, and to Mr. Quest, who loved her, and who knew that he was about to bid farewell to the sight of her, she looked more lovely now than ever. A book lay open on her knee, and he noticed, not without surprise, that it was a Bible. But she was not reading it, her dimpled chin rested on her hand, and her violet eyes were fixed on vacancy, and even from where he was he thought that he could see the tears in them.

She had heard nothing; he was sure of that from the expression of her face; she was thinking of her own sorrows, not of his shame.

Yes, he would go in.

CHAPTER XXXVI.

HOW THE GAME ENDED.

Mr. QUEST entered the house by a side door, and, having taken off his hat and coat, went into the drawing-room. He had still half an hour to spare before starting to catch the train.

"Well," said Belle, looking up. "Why are you so pale?"

"I have had a trying day," he answered. "What have you been doing?"

"Nothing in particular."

"Reading the Bible, I see."

"How do you know that?" she asked, coloring a little, for she had thrown a newspaper over the book when she heard him coming in. "Yes, I have been reading the Bible. Don't you know that when everything else in life has failed them, women generally take to religion?"

".Or drink," he put in. "Have you seen Mr. Cossey lately?"

"No. Why do you ask that? I thought that we had agreed to drop that subject."

As a matter of fact it had not been alluded to since Edward left the house.

"You know that Miss De la Molle will not marry him after all."

"Yes; I know. She will not marry him because you forced him to give up the mortgages."

"You ought to be much obliged to me. Are you not pleased?"

"No. I no longer care about anything. I am tired of passion and sin and failure. I care for nothing any more."

"It seems that we have both reached the same condition, by different roads."

"You?" she answered, looking up; "at any rate you are not

tired of money, or you would not do what you have done to get it."

" I never cared for money itself," he said.   " I only wanted money that I might be rich, and, therefore, respected."

" And you think any means justifiable so long as you get it ?"

" I thought so.   I do not think so now."

" I don't understand you to-night, William.   It is time for me to go to dress for dinner."

" Don't go just yet.   I'm leaving in a minute."

" Leaving ?   Where for ?"

" London ; I have to go up to-night about some business."

" Indeed ; when are you coming back ?"

" I don't quite know — to-morrow, perhaps.   I wonder, Belle," he went on, his voice shaking a little, " if you will always think as badly of me as you do now."

" I ?" she said, opening her eyes widely ; " who am I that I should judge you.   However bad you may be, I am worse."

" Perhaps there are excuses to be made for both of us," he said ; " perhaps, after all, there is no such thing as free-will, and we are nothing but pawns moved by a higher power. Who knows ?   But I will not keep you any longer.   Good-by.   Belle—"

" Yes."

" May I kiss you before I go ?"

She looked at him in astonishment.   Her first impulse was to refuse.   He had not kissed her for years.   But something in the man's face aroused her.   It was always a refined and melancholy face, but to-night it wore a look which to her seemed almost unearthly.

" Yes, William, if you wish," she said, " but I wonder that you care to."

" Let the dead bury their dead," he answered, and, stooping, he put his arm around her delicate waist, and, drawing her to him, kissed her tenderly, but without passion, on the forehead. " There, good-night," he said, " I wish that I had been a better husband to you.   Good-night," and he was gone.

When he reached his room he flung himself for a few moments face downwards upon his bed, and from the convulsive motion of his back an observer might almost have believed that he was sobbing. When he rose, however, there was no trace of tears or tenderness upon his features. On the contrary, they were stern and set, like the features of one bent upon some terrible endeavor. Going to a drawer, he unlocked it, and took from it a Colt's revolver of the small pattern. It was loaded, but he took the cartridges out and replaced them with fresh ones from a tin box. Then he went down-stairs, put on a large ulster with a high collar, and a soft felt hat, the brim of which he turned down over his face, placed the pistol in the pocket of the ulster, and started.

It was a dreadful night, the wind was blowing a very heavy gale, and between the gusts the rain came down in sheets of driving spray. Nobody was about the streets—the weather was far too bad; and Mr. Quest reached the station without meeting a living soul. Outside the circle of light from the lamp over the doorway he paused, and looked about for the clerk Jones. Presently he saw him walking backwards and forwards under the shelter of a lean-to, and, going up, touched him on the shoulder.

The man jumped and started back.

"Have you got the ticket, Jones?" he asked.

"Lord, sir," said Jones, "I didn't know you in that get-up. Yes, here's the ticket."

"Is the woman there still?"

"Yes, sir; she's taken a ticket, third-class, to town. She has been going on like a wild thing because they would not give her any liquor at the refreshment-bar, till at last she frightened them into letting her have six of brandy. Then she began and told the girl all sorts of tales about you, sir— said she was going back to London because she was afraid that if she stopped here you would murder her—and that you were her lawful husband, and that she would have a warrant out against you, and I don't know what all. I sat by there, and heard her with my own ears."

"Did she—did she, indeed?" said Mr. Quest, with an attempt at a laugh. "Well, she's a common thief and worse, that's what she is, and by this time to-morrow I hope to see her safe in jail. Ah, here comes the train. Good-night, Jones. I can manage for myself now."

"What's his game?" said Jones to himself, as he watched

his master slip on to the platform through a gate instead of going through the booking-office. "Well, I've had four quid out of it, anyway, and it's no affair of mine," and Jones went home to tea.

Meanwhile Mr. Quest was standing on the wet and desolate platform quite away from the lamps, watching the red lights of the approaching train come rushing on through the storm and night. Presently the train drew up. No passengers got out.

"Now, mam, look sharp if you're going," cried the porter, and the woman Edith came out of the refreshment-room.

"There's the third, forward there," said the porter, going to the other end to see about the packing away of the mails.

On she came, passing quite close to Mr. Quest, so close that he could hear her swearing at the incivility of the porter. There was a third-class carriage just opposite, and into this she got. It was one of those carriages which are still often to be seen on provincial lines, in which the partitions do not go up to the roof, and was, if possible, more vilely lighted than usual. Indeed, the light which should have illuminated the after half of it had either never been lit or had gone out. There was not a soul in the whole length of the carriage.

As soon as the Tiger was in Mr. Quest watched his opportunity, and, slipping up to the dark carriage, opened and shut the door as quietly as possible, and took his seat in the gloom.

The engine whistled, there was a cry of "Right, forward!" and they were off.

Presently he saw the woman stand up in her compartment and peep over into the gloom.

"Not a blessed soul," he heard her mutter, "and yet I feel as though that devil Billy was creeping about after me. Ugh! it must be the horrors. I can see the look he gave me now."

A few minutes later the train stopped at a station, but nobody got in, and presently it moved on again. "Any passengers for Effry?" shouted the porter, and there had been no response. If they did not stop at Effry there would be no stoppage for forty minutes. Now was his time. He waited a little till they had got up the speed. The line here ran through miles and miles of fen country, more or less drained by dikes and rivers, but still wild and desolate enough. Over this great flat the storm was sweeping furiously—even drowning in its turmoil the noise of the travelling train.

Very quietly he rose and climbed over the low partition which separated his compartment from that in which the woman was. She was seated in the corner, her head back, so that the feeble light from the lamp fell on it, and her eyes were closed.

He slid himself along the seat till he was opposite her, and then he paused and looked at the fierce, wicked face on which drink and paint and years of evil-thinking and living had left their marks, looked at the talon-like hands and the long yellowish teeth, and the half-dyed hair hanging in tags beneath the gaudy bonnet of peacock feathers, and shuddered. There was his bad genius, there was the creature who had driven him from evil to evil and finally destroyed him. Had it not been for her he might have been a good and respected man, and not what he was now, a fraudulent, ruined outcast. All his life seemed to flash before his inner eye in those few seconds of contemplation, all the long weary years of struggle and crime and deceit. And this was the end of it, and *there* was the cause of it. Well, she should not escape him, he would be revenged upon her at last. There was nothing but death before *him*, she should die too.

He set his teeth and drew the loaded pistol from his pocket and cocked it and lifted it to her breast.

What was the matter with the thing? He had never known the pull of a pistol to be so heavy before.

No it was not *that*. He could not do it. He could not shoot a sleeping woman, devil though she was; he could not kill her in her sleep. His nature rose up against it.

He placed the pistol on his knee, and as he did so she opened her eyes. He saw the look of wonder gather in them and grow to a stare of agonized terror. Her face became rigid like a dead person's, and her lips opened to scream, but no sound came. She could only point to the pistol.

"Make a sound and you are dead," he said, fiercely. "Not that it matters though," he added, as he remembered that the scream must be loud that could be heard in that raging gale.

"What are you going to do?" she gasped at last. "What are you going to do with that pistol. And where do you come from?"

"I come out of the night," he answered, raising the weapon, "out of the night into which you are going."

"You are not going to kill me?" she moaned, turning up her ghastly face. "I can't die. I'm afraid to die. It will hurt, and I've been wicked. Oh, you are not going to kill me, are you?"

"Yes, I am going to kill you," he answered. "I told you months ago that I would kill you if you molested me. You have ruined me now, there is nothing but death left for me, and you shall die too, you fiend."

"Oh, no! no! no! anything but that. I was drunk when I did it; that man brought me there, and they had taken all my things, and I was starving," and she glanced wildly round the empty carriage to see if help could be found, but there was none. She was alone with her fate.

She slipped down upon the floor of the carriage and clasped his knees. Writhing in her terror there upon the ground, in hoarse accents she begged and prayed for mercy.

"You used to kiss me," she said; "you cannot kill a woman you used to kiss years ago. Oh, spare me, spare me!"

He set his lips and placed the muzzle of the pistol against her head, and at the contact she shivered and her teeth began to chatter.

He could not do it. He must let her go, and leave her to her fate. After all, she could hurt him no more, for before another sun had set he would be beyond her reach.

His pistol hand fell against his side and he looked down with loathing not unmixed with pity at the abject human snake which was writhing at his feet.

She caught his eye, and her faculties, sharpened by the imminent peril, read relentment there. For the moment at any rate he was softened. If she could master him now while he was off his guard—he was not a very strong man. But the pistol—

Slowly, still groaning out supplications, she rose to her feet.

"Yes," he said, "be quiet while I think if I can spare you," and he half turned his head away from her. And for a moment nothing was heard but the rush of the gale and the roll of the wheels running over and under bridges.

This was her opportunity. All her natural ferocity arose within her, intensified a hundred times by the instinct of self-protection. With a sudden blow she struck the pistol from his hand, and it fell upon the floor of the carriage. And then, with a frightful yell, she sprang like a wild-cat straight at his throat. So sudden was the attack that the long, lean hands were gripping his windpipe before he knew that it had been made. Back she bore him, though he seized her round the waist. She was the heavier of the two, and back they went, crash against the carriage-door.

It gave! Oh, God, the catch gave! Out together, out with a yell of despair into the night and the raging gale, down together through sixty feet of space into the black river beneath. Down together, deep into the watery depths—down into the abyss of death.

The train rushed on, the wild winds blew, and the night was as the night had been. But there in the black water, though there was never a star to see them, there, locked together in death as they had been locked together in life, the fierce glare of hate and terror yet staring in their glazed eyes, two bodies rolled over and over as they sped silently towards the sea.

CHAPTER XXXVII.

SISTER AGNES.

TEN days had passed. The tragedy of which the forego-
ing is a record had echoed through all the land. Numberless
articles and paragraphs had been written in numberless papers,
and numberless theories had been built upon them. But the
echoes were already commencing to die away. Both the
actors in the dim event were dead, and there was no pending
trial to keep the public interest alive.

The two bodies, still linked in that fierce dying grip, had
been picked up upon a mudbank. An inquest had been held,
at which an open verdict had been returned, and they had
been buried. Other tragedies had occurred, the papers were
filled with the reports of a noted and remarkably full-flavored
divorce case, and the affair of the country lawyer who had
committed bigamy and together with his lawful wife come
to a tragic and mysterious end began to be forgotten.

In Boisingham and its neighborhood much sympathy was
shown with Belle, whom people still called Mrs. Quest, though
she had no title to that name; but she received it coldly and
kept herself secluded.

As soon as her supposed husband's death was beyond a
doubt, Belle had opened his safe (for he had left his keys on
his dressing-table), and found therein his will and other papers, including the mortgage deeds, to which, as Mr. Quest's
endorsement on his will advised her, she had no claim. Nor,
indeed, had her right to them been good in law, would she
have retained them, seeing that they were a price wrung from
her late lover under threat of an action that could not be
brought.

So she made them into a parcel and sent them, together
with a formal note of explanation, to Edward Cossey, greatly
wondering in her heart what course he would take with ref-

erence to them. She was not left long in doubt. The receipt of his deeds was acknowledged, and three days afterwards she heard that a notice calling in the borrowed money had been served upon Mr. De la Molle on behalf of Edward Cossey.

So he had evidently made up his mind not to forego this new advantage which chance threw in his way. Pressure, and pressure alone, could enable him to attain his end, and he was applying it unmercifully. Well, she had done with him now, it did not matter to her; but she could not help faintly wondering at the extraordinary tenacity and hardness of purpose which his action showed. Then she turned her mind to the consideration of another matter, in connection with which her plans were approaching maturity.

It was some days after this, exactly a fortnight from the date of Mr. Quest's death, that Edward Cossey was sitting one afternoon brooding over the fire in his rooms. He had much business awaiting his attention in London, but he would not go to London. He could not tear himself away from Boisingham, and such of the matters as could not be attended to there were left without attention. He was still as determined as ever to marry Ida, more determined if possible, for from constant brooding on the matter he had arrived at a condition approaching monomania. He had been quick to see the advantage resulting to him from Mr. Quest's tragic death and the return of the deeds, and though he knew that Ida would hate him the more for doing it, he instructed his lawyers to call in the money, and make use of every possible legal means to harass and put pressure upon Mr. De la Molle. At the same time he had written privately to the squire, calling his attention to the fact that matters were now once more as they had been at the beginning, but that he was, as before, willing to carry out the arrangements which he had already specified, provided that Ida could be persuaded to consent to marry him. To this Mr. De la Molle, notwithstanding his grief and irritation at the course his would-be son-in-law had taken about the mortgages on the death of Mr. Quest, and the suspicion that he now had as to the original cause of their transfer to the lawyer, had answered courteously enough, saying what he had said before, that he could not force his daughter into a marriage with him, but that if she chose to agree to it he should offer no objection.   And there the matter stood.   Once or twice he had met Ida walking or driving. She had bowed to him coldly, and that was all.   Indeed, he had only one crumb of comfort in his daily bread of disappointment, and that hope deferred which, where a lady is concerned, makes the heart more than normally sick, and that was, that he knew his hated rival, Colonel Quaritch, had been forbidden the castle, and that intercourse between him and Ida was practically at an end.

But he was a dogged and persevering man, and he knew the power of money and the shifts to which people who are made desperate by the want of it can be driven.   He knew, too, that it was no unusual thing for women who were attached to one man to sell themselves to another of their own free will, realizing that love may pass, but wealth (if the settlements are properly drawn) does not.   Therefore he still hoped that with so many circumstances bringing an ever-increasing pressure upon her, Ida's spirit would in time be broken, her resistance would collapse, and he would have his will.   Nor, as the sequel will show, was that hope a baseless one.

As for his infatuation, there was literally no limit to it.   It broke out in all sorts of ways, and was for miles round a matter of public notoriety and gossip.   Over the mantelpiece in his sitting-room was a fresh example of it.   He had by one means and another obtained several photographs of Ida, notably one of her in a court-dress which she had worn two or three years before, when her brother James had insisted upon her being presented.   These photographs he had caused to be enlarged, and had then commissioned a well-known painter to paint from them a full-length life-size portrait of Ida in her court-dress, at the cost of five hundred pounds.   This order had been executed, and the portrait, which, although, as might be expected, the coloring was not entirely satisfactory, was still an effective likeness and a fine piece of work, now hung in a splendid frame over his mantelpiece.

There, on the afternoon in question, he was sitting before the fire, his eyes fixed upon the portrait, of which the outline was beginning to grow dim in the waning December light, when the servant-girl came in and announced that a lady

wanted to speak to him. He asked what her name was, and
the girl said that she did not know, because she had her veil
down, and was wrapped up in a big cloak.

In due course the lady was shown up. He had relapsed
into his reverie, for nothing seemed to interest him much
now unless it had to do with Ida—and he knew that the lady
was not Ida, because the girl said that she was short. As it
happened, he was sitting with his right ear, in which he was
stone deaf, to the door, so that between his infirmity and his
dreams he never heard Belle—for it was she—enter the room.

For a minute or more she stood looking at him as he sat
with his eyes fixed upon the picture, and as she looked an
expression of pity stole across her sweet, pale face.

" I wonder what curse there is laid upon us that we should
be always doomed to seek for what we cannot find," she said
aloud.

He heard her now, and, looking up, saw her standing in the
glow and flicker of the firelight, which played upon her white
face and black-draped form. He started violently, and as he
did so she loosed the heavy cloak that she wore, and the hood
of it fell behind her. But where was the lovely rounded form,
and where the clustering, golden curls? Gone, and in their
place a coarse robe of blue serge, on which hung a crucifix
and the white hood of the nun.

He sprang from his chair with an exclamation, not knowing
if he dreamed or if he really saw the woman who stood there
like a ghost in the firelight.

" Forgive me, Edward," she said, presently, in her sweet,
low voice. " I dare say that this all looks theatrical enough—
but I have put on this dress for two reasons : firstly, because
I have to leave this town in an hour's time ; and, secondly, to
show you that you need not fear that I have come to be im-
portunate. Will you light the candles ?"

He did so mechanically, and then pulled down the blinds.
Meanwhile Belle had seated herself near the table, her face
buried in her hands.

" What is the meaning of all this, Belle ?" he said.

" ' Sister Agnes,' you must call me now," she said, taking
her hands from her face. " The meaning of it is that I have
left the world and entered a sisterhood, which works among

the poor in London, and that I have come to bid you farewell, a last farewell."

He stared at her in amazement. He did not find it easy to connect the idea of this beautiful, passionate, human, loving creature with the cold sanctuary of a sisterhood. He did not know that it is natures like this whose very greatness and intensity is often the cause of their destruction, when they come in adverse contact with laws which are fitted to the average of their race, that are most capable of these strange developments. The man or woman who can really love and endure—and they are rare—can also, when their passion has utterly broken them, turn them to climb the stony paths that lead to love's antipodes.

"Edward," she went on, "you know in what relation we have stood to each other, and all that that relationship means to woman. You know that I have loved you with all my heart, and all my strength, and all my soul; that your voice has been music to me, and your kiss heaven." (Here she trembled and broke down.)

"You know too," she continued, presently, "what has been the end of all this, the shameful end. I am not come to blame you. I do not blame you, for the fault was mine, and if I have anything to forgive I forgive it freely; and whatever memories may still live in my heart I swear I put away all bitterness, and that my most earnest wish is that you may be happy as happiness is to you. The mistake was mine; that is, it would have been mine were we free agents, which we are not. I should have loved my husband, or rather the man whom I thought my husband, for, with all his faults, he was of a different clay to you, Edward."

He looked up, but said nothing.

"I know," she went on, pointing to the picture over the mantelpiece, "that your mind is still set upon her, and that I am nothing, and less than nothing, to you. When I am gone you will scarcely give me a thought. I do not know if you will succeed in your end, and I think that the methods you are adopting are wicked and shameful. But whether you succeed or not, your fate also will be what my fate is—to love a person who is not only indifferent to you, but who positively dislikes you, and reserves all her secret heart for another man, and I know no greater penalty than is to be found in that daily misery."

"You are very consoling," he said, sulkily.

"I only tell you the truth," she answered. "What sort of life do you suppose mine has been that I am so utterly broken, so entirely robbed of hope that I have determined to leave the world and hide myself and my misery in a sisterhood?"

"And now, Edward," she went on after a pause, "I have something to tell you, for I will not go away, if indeed you allow me to go away at all after you have heard it, until I have confessed"—and she leaned forward and looked him full in the face—"*I shot you on purpose, Edward.*"

"What," he said, springing from his chair, "you tried to murder me?"

"Yes, yes; but don't think too hardly of me. I am only flesh and blood, and you drove me mad with jealousy—you taunted me with having been your mistress and said that I was not fit to associate with the lady you were going to marry. It made me mad, and the opportunity offered—the gun was there, and I shot you. God forgive me; I think that I have suffered more than you did. Oh, when day after day I saw you lying there and did not know if you would live or die, I thought that I should have gone mad with remorse and agony."

He listened so far, and then suddenly walked across the room towards the bell. She placed herself between him and it.

"What are you going to do?" she said.

"Going to do? I am going to send for a policeman and give you into custody for attempted murder, that is all."

She caught his arm and looked him in the face. In another second she had loosed it.

"Of course," she said, "you have a right to do that. Ring and send for the policeman, only remember that the whole truth will come out at the trial."

This checked him, and he stood thinking.

"Well," she said, "why don't you ring?"

"I do not ring, " he answered, " because, on the whole, I think I had better let you go. I do not wish to be mixed up with you any more. You have done me mischief enough; you have finished by attempting to murder me. Go, I think that the convent is the best place for you; you are too bad and too dangerous to be left at large."

"Oh!" she said, like one in pain. "Oh! and you are the man for whom I have come to this! O God! it is a cruel world." And she pressed her hands to her heart and stumbled rather than walked to the door.

Reaching it, she turned, and her hands, still pressing the coarse blue gown against her heart, leaned her back against the door.

"Edward," she said, in a strained whisper, for her breath came thick. "Edward—I am going forever—have you no kind word—to say to me?"

He looked at her, a scowl upon his handsome face, and then, by way of answer, he turned upon his heel.

And so, still holding her hands against her poor broken heart, she went out of the house, out of Boisingham, and of the touch and knowledge of the world. These two were, though she knew it not, fated to meet again, once and once only, in after-years, and under circumstances sufficiently tragic; but the story of that meeting does not lie within the scope of this history. To the world Belle was dead, but there is another world of sickness and sorrow and sordid unchanging misery and shame, where the lovely face of Sister Agnes moves to and fro like a ray of God's own light, and there those who would know her must go to seek her.

Poor Belle! Poor, shamed, deserted woman. She was an evil-doer, and the fatality of love and the rush of her quick blood, and the unbalanced vigor of her mind, which might, had she been more happily placed, have led her to all things that are pure and true and of good report, had combined to drag her into shame and misery. But the evil that she did has been paid back to her in full measure, pressed down and running over. Few of us need to wait for a place of punishment to get the due of our follies and our sins. Here we expiate them. They are with us day and night, about our path and about our bed, scourging us with the whips of memory, mocking us with empty longing and the hopelessness of despair. Who can escape the consequence of sin, or even of the misfortune which led to sin? Certainly Belle did not, nor did Mr. Quest, nor even that fierce-hearted harpy who hunted him to his grave.

And so good-by to Belle. May she find peace in its season.

CHAPTER XXXVIII.

MEANWHILE things had been going very ill at the Castle. Edward Cossey's lawyers were carrying out their client's instructions to the letter with a perseverance and ingenuity worthy of a county-court solicitor. Day by day they found some new point upon which to harass the wretched squire. Some share of the first expenses connected with the mortgages had, they said, been improperly thrown upon their client, and they again and again demanded, in language which was almost insolent, the immediate payment of the amount. Then there was three months' interest overdue, and this also they pressed and clamored for, till the old gentleman was nearly driven out of his senses, and as a consequence drove everybody about the place out of theirs.

At last this state of affairs began to tell upon his constitution, which, strong as he was, could not at his age withstand such constant worry. He grew to look years older, his shoulders acquired a stoop, and his memory began to fail him, especially on matters connected with the mortgages and farm accounts. Ida, too, became pale and ill, she caught a heavy cold, which she could not throw off, and her face acquired a permanently pained and yet listless look.

One day, it was on the 15th of December, things came to a climax. When Ida came down to breakfast she found her father busy poring over some more letters from the lawyers.

" What is it now, father ?" she said.

" What is it now ?" he answered, irritably. " Why, it's another claim for £200, that's what it is. I keep telling them to write to my lawyers, but they won't; at least they write to me too. There, I can't make head or tail of it. Look here," and he showed her two sides of a big sheet of paper covered with statements of accounts. " Anyhow, I have not got £200, that's clear. I don't even know where we are going to find the money to pay the three months' interest. I'm worn out, Ida, I'm worn out; that's the long and short of it. There is only one thing left for me to do, and that is to die, and that's the long and short of it. I get so confused with all these figures. I'm an old man now, and all these troubles are too much for me."

"You must not talk like that, father," she answered, not knowing whatever to say, for affairs were indeed desperate.

"Yes, yes, it's all very well to talk so, but facts are stubborn. Our family is ruined, and we must accept it."

"Cannot the money be got anyhow? Is there *nothing* to be done?" she asked, desperately.

"What is the good of asking me that? There is only one thing that can save us, and you know what it is as well as I do. But you are your own mistress. I have no right to put pressure on you. You must please yourself. Meanwhile I think we had better leave this place at once, and go and live in a cottage somewhere, if we can get enough to support us; if not we must starve, I suppose. I cannot keep up appearances any longer."

Ida rose, and with a strange, sad light of resolution shining in her eyes, came to where her father was sitting, and putting her hands upon his shoulders, looked him in the face.

"Father," she said, "do you wish me to marry that man?"

"Wish you to marry him? What do you mean?" he said, not without irritation, and avoiding her gaze. "It is no affair of mine. I don't like the man, if that's what you mean. He is acting like—well, like the cur that he is, in putting on the screw as he is doing; but, of course, that is the way out of it, and the only way, and there you are."

"Father," she said again, "will you give me ten days, that is, until Christmas Day. If nothing happens between this and then I will marry Mr. Edward Cossey."

A sudden light of hope shone in his eyes. She saw it, though he tried to hide it by turning his head away.

"Oh, yes, he answered, "as you wish; settle it one way or the other on Christmas Day, and then we can go out with the new year. You see your brother James is dead and I have no one left to advise me now, and I suppose that I am getting old. At any rate, things seem to be too much for me. Settle it as you like.

Settle it as you like," and he got up, leaving his breakfast half swallowed, and went off to moon aimlessly about the park.

So she made up her mind at last. This was the end of her struggling. She could not let her old father be turned out of house and home to starve, for practically they would starve. She knew her hateful lover well enough to be aware that he would show no mercy. It was a question of the woman or the money, and she was the woman. Either she must let him take her or they must be destroyed; there was no middle course. And in these circumstances there was no room for hesitation. Once more her duty became clear to her. She must give up her life, she must give up her love, she must give up herself. Well, so be it. She was weary of the long endeavor against fortune, now she would yield and let the tide of utter misery sweep over her like a sea—and bear her away till at last it brought her to that oblivion in which perchance all things are as though they had never been.

She had scarcely spoken to her lover, Harold Quaritch, for some weeks. She had, as she understood it, entered into a kind of unspoken agreement with her father not to do so, and that agreement Harold had understood and respected. Since their last letters to each other they had met once or twice casually or at church and interchanged a few indifferent words, though their eyes spoke another story, and touched each other's hands and parted, and that was absolutely all. But now that she had come to this momentous decision she felt that he had a right to learn it, and so once more she wrote to him. She might have gone to see him or told him to meet her, but she would not. For one thing, she did not dare to trust herself on such an errand in his dear company, for another she was too proud, thinking that if her father came to hear of it he might consider that it had a clandestine and underhand appearance.

And so she wrote. With all she said we need not concern ourselves. The letter was a passionate one, more passionate than one would perhaps have expected from a woman of Ida's calm and stately sort. But a mountain may have a heart of fire although it is clad in snows, and so it sometimes is with women who look as cold and unemotional as marble. Besides, it was her last chance—she could write him no more letters, and she had much to say.

"And so I have decided, Harold," she said, after telling him of all her doubts and troubles. "I must do it, there is no help for it, as I think you will see. I have asked for the ten days' respite. Well, I really hardly know why, except that it is a respite. And now what is there left to say to you except good-by? I love you Harold, I make no secret of it, and I shall never love any other. Remember all your life that I love you and have not forgotten you, and never can forget. For people placed as we are there is but one hope—the grave. In the grave earthly considerations fail and earthly contracts end, and here I trust and believe we shall find each other—or at least forgetfulness. My heart is so sore I know not what to say to you, for it is difficult to put all I feel in words. I am overwhelmed and my spirit is broken, and I wish to God that I were dead. Sometimes I cease to believe in a God who can allow his creatures to be so tormented, and give us love only that it may be daily dishonored in our sight; but who am I that I should complain? and, after all, what are our troubles compared to some we know of? Well, it will come to an end at last, and meanwhile pity me and think of me.

"Pity me and think of me, yes, but never see me more. As soon as this engagement is publicly announced go away, the farther the better. Yes, go to New Zealand, as you suggested once before, and in pity of our human weakness never let me see your face again. Perhaps you may write to me sometimes —if my—if Mr. Cossey will allow it. Go there and occupy yourself, it will divert your mind; you are too young a man to lay yourself upon the shelf; mix yourself up in the politics of the place, take to writing, anything, so long as you can absorb yourself. I send you a photograph of myself (I have nothing better) and a ring that, night and day, I have always worn since I was a child. I think that it will fit your little finger, and I hope that you will always wear it in memory of me. And now it is late and I am tired, and what is there more that a woman can say to the man she loves—and whom she must leave forever? Only one word—Good-by. IDA."

When Harold got this letter it fairly broke him down. His hopes had been revived when he thought that all was lost, and now again they were utterly dashed and broken. He could see no way out of it, none at all. He could not quarrel with Ida's decision, shocking as it was, for the simple reason that he knew in his heart that she was acting rightly and even nobly. But, oh, the thought of it made him sick. It is probable that to a man of imagination and deep feeling Hell itself can invent no more hideous torture than that which he must undergo in the position in which Harold Quaritch found himself. To truly love some good woman or some woman whom he thinks good—for it comes to the same thing—to love her more than life, to hold her dearer even than his honor (though few men do ever love a woman thus), to be, like Harold, beloved in turn, and then to know that that woman, that one thing for which he could count the world well lost, and would even sacrifice his hope of heaven, that light that makes his days beautiful, that starry joy set like a diadem upon life's dark brows, has been taken from him by the mockery of fate (not by death, for that he could bear), taken from him, and given —for money or money's worth—to the arms of some other man. It is, perhaps, better that a man should die than that he should pass through such an experience as that which threatened Harold Quaritch now; for, though the man die not, yet will it kill all that is best in him; and whatever triumphs may await him, and whatever women may be ready in the future to pin their favors to his breast, life will never be for him what it might have been, because his lost love took its glory with her. And the moral of this, which we commend to all young men—the softer sex needing, of course, no advice in that direction—is, Never leap into a deeper pit of passion than you can climb out of again; for though the lady who tempts you thereto be fairer than Aphrodite the foam-born, and sweeter than the light, yet, when perchance she has left you, will you find the place where once she was a cold and lonely spot to stay in till the end.

No wonder, then, that he despaired. No wonder, too, there rose up in his breast a great anger and indignation against the man who had brought this last extremity of misery upon them both. He was a just man and could make allowance for his rival's infatuation—which, indeed, Ida being concerned, it was not difficult for him to understand. But he was also, and above all things, a gentleman; and the spectacle of a woman being inexorably driven into a distasteful marriage by money pressure,

put on by the man who wished to gain her, revolted him beyond measure, and, though he was slow to wrath, moved him
to fiery indignation. So much did it move him that he took
a resolution—Mr. Cossey should know his mind about the
matter, and that at once. Ringing the bell, he ordered his
dog-cart, and drove to Edward Cossey's rooms, with the full
intention of giving that gentleman a very unpleasant quarter
of an hour.

Mr. Cossey was in, and fearing lest he should refuse to see
him, the colonel followed the servant up the stairs, and entered
almost as she announced his name. There was a grim and
even formidable look upon his plain but manly face, and something of menace, too, in his formal and soldierly bearing ; nor
did his aspect soften when his eyes fell upon the full-length
picture of Ida over the mantelpiece.

Edward Cossey rose with astonishment and irritation, not
unmixed with nervousness, depicted on his face. The last person whom he wished to see and expected a visit from was Colonel Quaritch, whom in his heart he held in considerable awe.
Besides, he had of late received such a series of unpleasant
visits that it is not wonderful that he began to dread these
interviews.

"Good-day," he said, coldly. "Will you be seated ?"

The colonel bowed his head slightly, but he did not sit down.

"To what am I indebted for the pleasure ?" began Edward
Cossey, with much politeness.

"Last time I was here, Mr. Cossey," said the colonel, in his
deep voice, speaking very deliberately, "I came to give an explanation ; now I come to ask one."

"Indeed !"

"Yes. To come to the point. Miss De la Molle and I are
attached to each other, and there has been between us an understanding that that attachment might end in marriage."

"Oh ! has there ?" said the younger man, with a sneer.

"Yes," answered the colonel, keeping down his rising temper as well as he could. "But now I am told, upon what
appears to be good authority, that you have actually condescended to bring, directly and indirectly, pressure of a
monetary sort to bear upon Miss De la Molle and her father,
in order to force her into a distasteful marriage with you."

"And what the devil business of yours is it, sir," asked
Cossey, "what I have or have not done? Making every allowance for the disappointment of an unsuccessful suitor (for I
presume that you appear in that character)," again he sneered,
"I ask, what business is it of yours?"

"It is every business of mine, Mr. Cossey, because if Miss
De la Molle is forced into this, I shall lose my wife."

"Then you will certainly lose her. Do you suppose that I
am going to consider you? Indeed," he went on, being now
in a towering passion, "I should have thought that, considering the difference between us, of age and fortune, you might
find other reasons than you suggest to account for my being
preferred to you, if I should be so preferred. Ladies are apt
to choose the better man, you know."

"I don't quite know what you mean by the 'better man,'
Mr. Cossey," said the colonel, quietly. "Without wishing to
make any comparisons, I may say that in birth, in breeding,
perhaps even in education and the record of my life, in which
at least I have not disgraced myself, I am fully your equal,
though I admit that you have the advantage of me in money
and in years. However, that is not the point; the point is
that I have had the fortune to be preferred to *you* by the lady
in question, and *not* you to me. I happen to know that you,
and the idea of marriage with you, is as distasteful to Miss
De la Molle as it is to me. This I know from her own lips.
She will only marry you, if she does at all, under the direst
necessity, and to save her father from the ruin you are deliberately bringing upon him."

"Well, Colonel Quaritch," he answered, "have you quite
done lecturing me? If you have, let me tell you, as you seem
anxious to know, that if by any legal means I can marry Ida
de la Molle, I certainly fully intend to marry her; and let me
tell you another thing, that when once I am married to her it
will be the last that you shall see of her, if I can prevent it."

"Thank you for your admissions," said Harold, still more
quietly. "So it seems that it is all true; it seems that you
are using your wealth to harass this unfortunate gentleman
and his daughter, until you drive them into consenting to this
marriage. That being so, I wish to tell you privately what I
shall probably take some opportunity of telling you in public,

namely, that a man who does such things is a *cur*, and worse than a cur, he is a blackguard, and *you* are such a man, Mr. Cossey."

Edward Cossey's face turned perfectly livid with fury, and he drew himself up as though to spring at his adversary's throat.

The colonel held up his hand. "Don't try that on with me," he said. "In the first place it is vulgar, and in the second you have only just recovered from an accident, and are no match for me, though I am forty years old. Listen, our fathers had a way of settling their troubles; I don't approve of that sort of thing as a rule, but in some cases it is salutary. If you think yourself aggrieved, it does not take long to cross the water, Mr. Cossey."

Edward Cossey looked puzzled. "Do you mean to suggest that I should fight a duel with you?" he said.

"To challenge a man to fight a duel," answered the colonel, with deliberation, "is an indictable offence, therefore I make no such challenge. I have made a suggestion; if that suggestion falls in with your views, as," and he bowed, "I hope it may, we might perhaps meet accidentally abroad in a few days' time, when we might talk this matter over further."

"I'll see you hanged first," answered Cossey. "What have I to gain by fighting you, except a very good chance of being shot? I have had enough of being shot as it is, and we will play this game out upon the old lines, until I win it."

"As you like," said Harold. "I have made a suggestion to you which you do not see fit to accept. As to the end of the game, it is not finished yet, and, therefore, it is impossible to say who will win it. Perhaps you will be checkmated after all. In the meanwhile, allow me again to assure you that I consider you both a cur and a blackguard, and to wish you good-morning." And he bowed himself out, leaving Edward Cossey in a condition of concentrated rage which it was not good to look on.

CHAPTER XXXIX.

THE condition of mind which could induce a peaceable Christian-natured individual, who had moreover in the course of his career been mixed up with enough bloodshed to have acquired a thorough horror of it, to offer to fight a duel is difficult to picture. Yet this condition had been reached by Harold Quaritch.

Edward Cossey had wisely enough declined to entertain the idea, but the colonel had been perfectly in earnest about it. Odd as it may appear in the latter end of this nineteenth century, nothing would have given him greater pleasure than to pit his life against that of his unworthy rival. Of course, it was foolish and wrong, but human nature is the same in all ages, and in the last extremity we fall back by instinct on those methods which men have from the beginning adopted to save themselves from intolerable wrong and dishonor, or, be it admitted, to bring the same upon others.

But Cossey utterly declined to fight. As he said, he had had enough of being shot, and so there was an end of it. Indeed, in after-days the colonel frequently looked back upon this episode in his career with shame not unmingled with amusement, reflecting when he did so on the strange potency of that passion which can bring men to seriously entertain the idea of such extravagances.

Well, there was nothing more to be done. He might, it is true, have seen Ida, and working upon her love and natural inclinations have tried to persuade her to cut the knot by marrying him off-hand. Perhaps he would have succeeded, for in such affairs women are apt to find the arguments advanced by their lovers weighty and well worthy of consideration. But he was not the man to adopt such a course. He did the only thing that he could do—answered her letter by

saying that what must be must be. He had learned that on
the day subsequent to his interview with his rival the squire
had written to Edward Cossey informing him that a decided
answer would be given to him on Christmas Day, and that
thereon all vexatious proceedings on the part of that gentleman's lawyers had been stayed for the time. He could now
no longer doubt what that answer would be. There was only
one way out of the trouble, the way that Ida had made up
her mind to adopt.

So he set to work to make his preparations for leaving
Honham and this country for good and all. He wrote to
land agents and put Molehill upon their books to be sold or
let on lease, and also to various influential friends to obtain
introductions to the leading men in New Zealand. But these
matters did not take up all his time, and the rest of it hung
heavily on his hands. He mooned about the place until he
was tired. He tried to occupy himself in his garden, but it
is weary work sowing crops for strange hands to reap, and so
he gave it up.

Somehow the time wore on until at last it was Christmas
Eve ; the eve, too, of the fatal day of Ida's decision. He
dined alone that night as usual, and shortly after dinner some
waits came to the house and began to sing their cheerful
carols outside. The carols did not chime in at all well with
his condition of mind, and he sent five shillings out to them
with a request that they would go away, as he had a headache.

Accordingly they went ; and shortly after their departure
the great gale for which that night is still famous began to
rise. Then he fell to pacing up and down the quaint old oak-
panelled parlor, thinking until his brain ached. The hour was
at hand, the evil was upon him and her whom he loved. Was
there no way out of it, no possible way ? Alas ! there was
but one way and that a golden one, but where was the money
to come from ? He had it not, and as land stood it was impossible to raise it. Ah, if only that great treasure which old
Sir James de la Molle had hid away and died rather than reveal could be brought to light, now in the hour of his house's
sorest need ! But the treasure was very mythical, and if it
had ever really existed it was not now to be found. He went
to his despatch box and took from it the copy he had made

of the entry in the Bible, which had been in Sir James's
pocket when he was murdered in the courtyard. The whole
story was a very strange one. Why did the brave old man
wish that his Bible should be sent to his son, and why did
he write that somewhat peculiar message in it?

Suppose that Ida was right, and that it contained a cipher
or cryptograph which would give a clew to the whereabouts
of the treasure? If so it was obvious that it would be one of
the simplest nature. A man confined by himself in a dun-
geon and under immediate sentence of death would not have
been likely to pause to invent anything complicated. It
would, indeed, be curious that he should have invented anything at all under such circumstances, and when he could have
so little hope that the riddle would be solved. But, on the
other hand, his position was desperate; he was quite surrounded by foes; there was no chance of his being able
to convey the secret in any other way, and he *might* have
done so.

Harold placed the piece of paper upon the mantelpiece,
and sitting down in an arm-chair opposite began to contemplate it earnestly, as indeed he had often done before. In
case the reader should not remember its exact wording it is
repeated here. It ran: " *Do not grieve for me, Edward, my
son, that I am thus suddenly and wickedly done to death by
rebel murderers, for nought happeneth but according to God's
will. And now farewell, Edward, till we shall meet in Heaven.
My moneys have I hid, and on account thereof I die unto this
world, knowing that not one piece shall Cromwell touch. To
whom God shall appoint shall all my treasure be, for nought
can I communicate.*"

Well, Harold stared and stared at this inscription. He read
it forward, backward, crossways, and in every other way, but
absolutely without result. At last, wearied out with misery of
mind and the pursuit of a futile occupation, he dropped off
sound asleep in his chair. That happened about a quarter to
eleven o'clock. The next thing that he knew was that he
suddenly woke up; woke up completely, passing as quickly
from a condition of deep sleep to one of wakefulness as
though he had never shut his eyes. He used to say afterwards that he felt as though somebody had come and aroused

him; it was not like a natural waking. Indeed, so unaccustomed was the sensation, that for a moment the idea flashed
through his brain that he had died in his sleep, and was now
awakening to a new state of existence.

This soon passed, however. Evidently he must have slept
some time, for the lamp was out and the fire dying. He got
up and hunted about in the dark for some matches, which at
last he found. He struck a light, standing exactly opposite
to the bit of paper with the copy of Sir James de la Molle's
dying message on it. This message was neatly copied long-
ways upon a half sheet of large writing-paper, such as the
squire generally used. Its first line ran as it was copied—

"*Do not grieve for me, Edward, my son, that I am thus suddenly and wickedly done.*"

Now, as the match burned up, by some curious chance, connected probably with the darkness and the sudden striking
of the light upon his eyeballs, it came to pass that Harold, happening to glance thereon, was only able to read four letters of
this first line of writing, all the rest seeming to him but as a
blur connecting those four letters. They were—

D...........E.............a...........d,

being respectively the initial letters of the first, the sixth, the
eleventh, and the sixteenth words of the line given above.

The match burned out, and he began to hunt about for another.

" D-E-A-D," he said aloud, repeating the letters almost automatically. " Why it spells '*Dead.*' That is rather curious."

Something about this accidental spelling awakened his interest very sharply—it was an odd coincidence. He lit some
candles, and hurriedly examined the line. The first thing that
struck him was that the four letters which went to make up
the word " dead " were about equidistant in the line of writing. Could it be? He hurriedly counted the words in the
line; there were sixteen of them, that is, after the first; one
of the letters occurred at the commencement of every fifth
word.

This was certainly curious. Trembling with nervousness
he took a pencil and wrote down the initial letter of every
fifth word in the message, thus—

"Do not grieve for me, Edward, my son, that I am thus suddenly and
D   E   a
wickedly done to death by rebel murderers, for nought happeneth but ac-
d   m   a
cording to God's will. And now farewell, Edward, till we shall meet in
n   s
Heaven. My moneys have I hid, and on account thereof I die unto this
m   o   u
world, knowing that not one piece shall Cromwell touch. To whom God
n   t
shall appoint shall all my treasure be, for nought can I communicate."
a   b   c

When he had done he wrote these initials in a line—

DEad mans mount abc

Great heaven! he had hit upon the reading of the riddle.

The answer was, "*Dead Man's Mount*," followed by the mysterious letters A B C.

Breathless with excitement, he checked the letters again to see if by any chance he had made an error. No, it was perfectly correct. "Dead Man's Mount." That was and had been for centuries the name of the curious tumulus or mound in his own back garden, the same that learned antiquarians had discussed the origin of so fiercely, and that his aunt, the late Mrs. Massey, had at the cost of two hundred and fifty pounds erected a mushroom-shaped roof over, in order to prove that the hollow in the top had once been the agreeable country seat of an ancient British family.

Could it then be but a coincidence that after the first word the initial of every fifth word in the message should spell out the name of this remarkable place, or was it so arranged? He sat down to think it over, trembling like a frightened child. Obviously, it was not accident; obviously, the prisoner of more than two centuries ago had, in his helplessness, invented this simple cryptograph in the hope that his son, or, if not his son, some one of his descendants would discover it, and thereby become the master of the hidden wealth. What place would be more likely for the old knight to have chosen to secrete the gold than one that even in those days had the uncanny reputation of being haunted? Who would ever think of looking for modern treasure in the burying-place of the ancient dead? In those days, too, Molehill, or Dead Man's

Mount, belonged to the De la Molle family, who had reac-
quired it on the break-up of the abbey. It was only at the
Restoration, when the Döfferleigh branch came into possession
under the will of the second and last baronet, Sir Edward de
la Molle, who died in exile, that they failed to recover this
portion of the property. And if this was so, and Sir James,
the murdered man, had buried his treasure in the mount, what
did the mysterious letters A B C mean? Were they, perhaps,
directions as to the line to be taken to discover it? Harold
could not imagine, nor, as a matter of fact, did he or anybody
else ever find out this either then or thereafter.

Ida, indeed, used afterwards to laughingly declare that old
Sir James meant to indicate that he considered the whole
thing as plain as A B C, but that was an explanation which
did not commend itself to Harold's practical mind.

CHAPTER XL.

HAROLD glanced at the clock—it was nearly one in the morning—time to go to bed if he were going. But he did not feel inclined to go to bed. If he did, with this great discovery on his mind, he should not sleep. There was another thing; it was Christmas Eve, or rather Christmas Day, the day of Ida's answer. If any succor was to be given at all, it must be given at once, before the fortress had capitulated. Once let the engagement be renewed, and even if the money should subsequently be forthcoming, the difficulties would be doubled. But there; he was building his hopes upon sand, and he knew it. Even supposing that he held in his hand the key to the burial-place of the long-lost treasure, who knew whether it would still be there, or whether rumor had not enormously added to its proportions? He was allowing his hopes and his imagination to carry him away.

Still he could not sleep, and he had a mind to see if anything could be made of it. Going to the gunroom, he put on a pair of shooting-boots, an old coat, and an ulster. Next he provided himself with a dark lantern and the key of the summer-house at the top of Dead Man's Mount, and silently unlocking the back door started out into the garden. The night was very rough, for the great gale was now rising fast, and bitterly cold, so cold that he hesitated for a moment before making up his mind to go on. However, he did go on, and in another two minutes was climbing the steep side of the great tumulus. There was a wan moon in the cold sky— the wind whistled most drearily through the naked boughs of the great oaks which groaned in answer like things in pain. Harold was not a nervous or impressionable man, but the place had a spectral look about it, and he could not help thinking of the evil reputation it had borne for all these ages.

There was scarcely a man in Honham, or in Boisingham either,
who could have been persuaded to stay half an hour by himself on Dead Man's Mount after the sun was well down.
Harold had at different times asked one or two of them what
they saw to be afraid of, and they had answered that it was
not what they saw so much as what they felt. He had laughed
at the time, but now he admitted to himself that he was anything but comfortable, though if he had had to put his feelings into words he could probably not have described them
further than by saying that he had a general sensation of
somebody being behind him. However, he was not going to
be frightened by this nonsense, so, consigning all supersti-
tions to their father the devil, he marched on boldly and unlocked the summer-house door. Now, though this curious
edifice had been designed for a summer-house, and for that
purpose lined throughout with encaustic tiles, nobody as a
matter of fact had ever dreamed of using it to sit in. To begin with, it roofed over a great depression some thirty feet
or more in diameter, for the top of the mount was hollowed
out like one of those wooden cups upon which jugglers catch
balls. But, notwithstanding all the encaustic tiles in the
world, damp will gather in a hollow like this, and the damp
alone was an objection. The real fact was, however, that the
spot had an evil reputation, and even those who were sufficiently well educated to know the folly of this sort of thing
would not willingly have gone there for purposes of enjoyment. So it had suffered the general fate of disused places,
having fallen more or less out of repair and become a recepta-
cle for garden tools, broken cucumber frames and lumber of
various sorts.

Harold got the door open and entered, shutting it behind
him. It was, if anything, more disagreeable in the empty
silence of the wide place, for the space roofed over was considerable, than it had been outside, and the question at once
arose in his mind what was he to do now that he had got
there? If the treasure was there at all, probably it was deep
down in the bowels of the great mound. Well, as he was on
the spot, he thought that he might as well have a dig, though
probably nothing would come of it. In the corner were a
pickaxe and some spades and shovels. Harold got them, ad-

vanced to the centre of the space, and, half laughing at his
own folly, set to work. First, having lit another lantern which
was kept there, he removed with the sharp end of the pickaxe
a large patch of the encaustic tiles exactly in the centre of
the depression. Then, having loosened the soil beneath with
the pick, he took off his ulster and fell to digging with a will.
The soil proved to be very sandy and easy to work. Indeed,
from its appearance, he soon came to the conclusion that it
was not virgin earth, but worked soil, which had been thrown
there. Presently his spade struck against something hard,
he picked it up and held it to the lantern. It proved to be
an ancient spearhead, and near it were some bones, though
whether or no they were human he could not at the time de-
termine. This was very interesting, but it was scarcely what
he wanted, so he dug on manfully until he found himself
chest deep in a kind of grave. He had been digging for an
hour now, and was getting very tired. Cold as it was, the
perspiration poured from him. As he paused for breath
he heard the church clock strike two, and very solemnly it
sounded down the wild ways of the wind-torn winter night.
He dug on a little more, and then seriously thought of giving
up what he was somewhat ashamed of having undertaken.
How was he to account for this great hole to his gardener
on the following morning? Then and there he made up his
mind that he would not account for it. The gardener, in
common with the rest of the village, believed that the place
was haunted. Let him set down the hole to the "spooks"
and their spiritual activity.

Still he dug on at his grave for a little longer. It was by
now becoming a matter of exceeding labor to throw the shovel-
fuls of soil clear of the hole. Then he determined to stop,
and with this view scrambled, not without difficulty, out of
the amateur tomb. Once out, his eyes fell on a stout iron
crowbar which was standing among the other tools, such an
implement as is used to make holes in the earth wherein to
set hurdles and stakes; and it occurred to him that it would
not be a bad idea to drive this crowbar into the bottom of
the grave which he had dug, in order to ascertain if there
were anything within its reach. Accordingly he once more
descended into the hole and began to work with the iron

crow, driving it down with all his strength. When he had got it almost as deep as it would go, that is about three feet, it struck something—something hard—there was no doubt of it. He worked away in great excitement, widening the hole as much as he could.

Yes, it was masonry, or if it were not masonry it was something uncommonly like it. He drew the crow out of the hole, and, seizing the shovel, commenced to dig again with renewed vigor. As he could no longer conveniently throw the soil from the hole, he took a "skep," or leaf basket, which lay handy, and, placing it beside him, put as much of the sandy soil as he could lift into it, and then lifted it and shot it on the edge of the pit. For three quarters of an hour he labored thus most manfully till at last he came down to the stonework. He cleared a patch of it and examined it attentively by the light of the dark lantern. It appeared to be rubble work built in the form of an arch. He struck it with the iron crow and it gave back a hollow sound. There was a cavity of some sort underneath.

His excitement and curiosity redoubled. By great efforts he widened the spot of stone work already laid bare. Luckily the soil, or, rather, sand, was so friable that there was very little exertion required to loosen it. This done, he took the iron crow, and, inserting it beneath a loose flat stone, levered it up. This was a beginning, and, having got rid of the large flat stone, he struck down again and again with all his strength, driving the sharp point of the heavy crow into the rubble work beneath. It began to give; he could hear bits of it falling into the cavity below. There! it went with a crash—more than a square foot of it.

He leaned over the hole at his feet, devoutly hoping that the ground on which he was standing would not give way also, and tried to look down. The next second he threw his head back, coughing and gasping. The foul air rushing up from the cavity or chamber, or whatever it was, had half poisoned him. Then, not without difficulty, he climbed out of the grave and sat down on the pile of sand he had thrown up. Clearly he must let the air in the place sweeten a little. Clearly also he must have assistance if he were to descend into the great hole. He could not undertake that by himself.

He sat there upon the edge of the pit wondering who there was that he could trust. Not his own gardener. To begin with, he would never come near the place at night, and, besides, such people talk. The squire? No, he could not rouse him at this hour; and also, for obvious reasons, they had not met lately. Ah, he had it. George was the man! To begin with, he could be trusted to hold his tongue, and the episode of the production of the real Mrs. Quest had taught the colonel that George was a person of no common powers. He could think, and he could act also.

He threw on his coat, extinguished the large stable lantern, and, having passed out, locked the door of the summer-house, and started down the mount at a trot. The wind had risen steadily during his hours of work, and was now blowing a furious gale. It was about a quarter to four in the morning, and the stars shone brightly in the hard, clean-blown sky. By their light and that of the waning moon he struggled on in the teeth of the raging tempest. As he passed under one of the oaks he heard a mighty crack overhead, and, guessing what it was, ran like a hare. He was none too soon. A circular gust of more than usual fierceness had twisted the top right out of the great tree, and down it came upon the turf with a rending, crashing sound that made his blood turn cold. After this escape he avoided the neighborhood of the groaning trees.

George lived in a neat little farmhouse about a quarter of a mile away. There was a short cut to it across the fields, and this he took, breathlessly fighting his way against the gale, which swept and roared and howled in its splendid might as it came leaping across the ocean from its birthplace in the distances of air. Even the stiff hawthorn fences bowed before its breath, and the tall poplars on the sky-line bent like a rod beneath the first rush of a salmon.

Excited as he was, the immensity and grandeur of the sight and sounds struck upon him with strange and awful force. Never before had he felt so far apart from man and so near to that dread Spirit round whose feet millions of rolling worlds rush on forever, at whose word they are, endure, and are not.

He struggled on until at last he reached the house. It was

quite silent, but in one of the windows a light was burning. No doubt its occupants found it impossible to sleep in that wild gale. The next thing to consider was how to make himself heard. To knock at the door would be useless in that .turmoil. There was only one thing to be done—throw stones at the window. He found a good-sized pebble, and, standing underneath, threw it with such good-will that it went right through the glass, lighting, as he afterwards heard, full upon Mrs. George's sleeping nose, and nearly frightening that good woman, whose nerves were already shaken by the gale, into a fit. Next minute a red nightcap appeared at the window.

" George ! " roared the colonel, in a lull of the gale.

" Who's there ? " came the faint answer.

" Me—Colonel Quaritch. Come down. I want to speak to you."

The head was withdrawn, and a couple of minutes afterwards Harold saw the front door begin to open slowly. He waited till there was space enough and then slipped in, and together they forced it to.

" Stop a bit, sir," said George; " I'll light the lamp," and he did.

Next minute he stepped back in amazement.

" Why, what on arth hev you bin after, sir ? " he said, contemplating Harold's filth-begrimed face and hands and clothes. " Is anything wrong up at the castle, or is the cottage blown down ?"

" No, no," said Harold; " listen. You've heard tell of the treasure that old Sir James de la Molle buried in the times of the Roundheads ?"

" Yes, yes. I've heard tell of that. Hev the gale blown it up ?"

" No; but, by Heaven, I believe that I am in a fair way to find it."

George took another step back, remembering the tales that Mrs. Jobson had told, and not being by any means sure that the colonel was not in a dangerous condition of lunacy.

" Give me a glass of something to drink, water or milk, and I'll tell you. I've been digging all night, and my throat's like a limekiln."

" Digging ; why, where ?"

" Where ?   In Dead Man's Mount."

" In Dead Man's Mount?" said George.   " Well, blow me, if that ain't a funny place to dig at on a night like this;" and, too amazed to say anything more, he went off to get the milk.

Harold drank three glasses without stopping, and then sat down to tell as much of his moving tale as he thought desirable.

CHAPTER XLI.

HOW THE NIGHT WENT.

GEORGE sat opposite to him, his hands on his knees, the red nightcap on his head, and a comical expression of astonishment upon his melancholy countenance.

"Well," he said, when Harold had done, "blow me if that ain't a master one. And yet there's folks who say that there ain't no such thing as Providence — not that there's anything prowided yet — p'raps there ain't nawthing there after all."

"I don't know if there is or not, but I'm going back to see, and I want you to come with me now."

"Now?" said George, rather uneasily. "Why, colonel, that bain't a very nice spot to go digging about in on a night like this. I niver heard no good of that there place—not as I holds by sich talk myself," he added, apologetically.

"Well," said the colonel, "you can do as you like, but I'm going back at once, and going down the hole too; the gas must be out of it by now. There are reasons," he added, "why, if this money is to be found at all, it should be found this morning. To-day is Christmas Day, you know."

"Yes, yes, colonel; I know what you mean. Bless you, I know all about it; the old squire must talk to somebody; if he don't he'd bust, so he talks to me. That Cossey's coming for his answer from Miss Ida this morning. Poor young lady; I saw her yesterday, and she looks like a ghost, she du. Ah, he's a mean one, that Cossey. Laryer Quest warn't in it with him after all. Well, I cooked his goose for him, and I'd give sommut to have a hand in cooking that banker chap's too. You wait a minute, colonel, and I'll come along, gale and ghostesses and all. I only hope it mayn't be after a fool's arrand, that's all," and he retired to put on his boots. Presently he appeared again, his red nightcap still on his head, for he was afraid that the wind would blow a hat off, and carrying an unlighted lantern in his hand.

"Now, colonel, I'm ready, sir, if you be," and they started.

The gale was, if anything, fiercer than ever. Indeed, there had been no such tempest in those parts for years, or, rather, centuries, as the condition of the timber by ten o'clock that morning amply testified.

"This here wind must be like that as the squire tells us on in the time of King Charles, as blew the top of the church tower off on a Christmas night," shouted George; but Harold made no answer, and they fought their way onward without speaking any more, for their voices were almost inaudible. Once the colonel stopped and pointed to the skyline. Of all the row of tall poplars which he had seen bending like whips before the wind as he came along but one remained standing now, and as he pointed that vanished also.

Reaching the summer-house in safety, they entered, and the colonel shut and locked the door behind them. The frail building was literally rocking in the fury of the storm.

"I hope the roof will hold," shouted George, but Harold took no heed. He was thinking of other things. They lit the lanterns, of which they now had three, and the colonel slid down into the great grave he had so industriously dug, motioning George to follow. This that worthy did, not without trepidation. Then they both knelt and stared down through the hole in the masonry, but the light of the lanterns was not strong enough to enable them to make out anything with clearness.

"Well," said George, falling back upon his favorite expression in his amazement, as he drew his nightcapped head from the hole, "if that ain't a master one I niver saw a masterer, that's all. What be you agoing to do now, colonel? Hev you a ladder here?"

"No," answered Harold, "I never thought of that; but I've a good rope; I'll get it."

Scrambling out of the hole, he presently returned with a long coil of stout rope. It belonged to some men who had been recently employed in cutting boughs off such of the oaks as needed attention.

They undid the rope and let the end down to see how

deep the pit was. When they felt that the end lay upon the floor they pulled it up. The depth from the hole to the bottom of the pit appeared to be about sixteen feet, or a trifle more.

Harold took the iron crowbar, and having made the rope fast to it, fixed the bar across the mouth of the aperture. Then he doubled the rope, tied some knots in it, and let it down into the pit, preparatory to climbing down it.

But George was too quick for him. Forgetting his doubts as to the wisdom of groping about Dead Man's Mount at night, in the ardor of his burning curiosity, he took the dark lantern, and, holding it in his teeth, passed his body through the hole in the masonry and cautiously slid down the rope.

"Are you all right?" asked Harold, in a voice tremulous with excitement, for was not his life's fortune trembling on the turn?

"Yes," answered George, in a doubtful voice, and Harold, looking down, could see that he was holding the lantern above his head and staring at something very hard.

Next moment a most awful howl of terror echoed up through the pit, the lantern was dropped upon the ground, and the rope commenced to be agitated with the utmost violence.

In another two seconds George's red nightcap appeared through the hole, followed by a face that was literally livid with terror.

"Let me up for Goad's sake," he gasped, "or he'll hev me by the leg!"

"He! who?" asked the colonel, not without a thrill of superstitious fear, as he dragged the panting man through the hole.

But George would give no answer until he was through the hole and out of the grave. Indeed, had it not been for the colonel's eager entreaties, backed to some extent by actual force, he would have been out of the summer-house and half way down the mount by now.

"What is it?" roared the colonel in the hole to George, who, shivering with terror, was standing on the edge thereof.

"It's a blessed ghost, that's what it is, colonel," answered George, keeping his eyes fixed upon the hole as though he momentarily expected to see the object of his fears emerge.

"Nonsense!" said Harold, doubtfully. "What rubbish you talk! What sort of a ghost?"

"A white un," said George; "all bones like."

"All bones?" answered the colonel; "why, it must be a skeleton."

"I don't say that he ain't," was the answer; "but if he be he's seven foot high, and sitting airing of hisself in a stone bath."

"Oh, rubbish!" said the colonel. "How can a skeleton sit and air himself? He would tumble to bits."

"I don't know, but there he is, and they don't call this place 'Dead Man's Mount' for nawthing."

"Well," said the colonel, argumentatively, "a skeleton is a perfectly harmless thing."

"Yes, if he's dead maybe, sir; but this one's alive; I saw him nod his head at me."

"Look here, George," answered Harold, feeling that if this went on much longer he should lose his nerve altogether, "I'm not going to be scared. Great heavens, what a gust! I'm going down to see for myself."

"Very good, colonel," answered George, "and I'll wait here till you come up again; that is, if you iver du."

Thrice did Harold look at the hole, and thrice, like false Sextus, did he shrink back.

"Come," he shouted, angrily, "don't be an infernal fool; get down here and hand me the lantern."

George obeyed, with evident trepidation. Then Harold got through the hole, and with many an inward tremor, for there is scarcely a man on the earth who is really free from supernatural fears, descended hand over hand. But in so doing he managed to let the lantern fall, and it went out. Now, as the reader will probably admit, this was exceedingly trying. It is not pleasant to be left alone in the dark underground in the company of an unknown "spook." He had some matches, but, what between fear and cold, it was some time before he could get a light. Down in this deep place the rush of the great gale reached his ears like a faint and melancholy sighing, and he heard other tapping noises too, or he thought he did—noises of a creepy and unpleasant nature. Would the matches never light? The chill and deathlike damp of the place struck to his marrow, and the cold sweat poured from his brow. Ah! at last! He kept his eyes steadily fixed upon the lantern till he had lit it and it was burning up brightly. Then, by an effort, he lifted his eyes and looked round him.

And this is what he saw.

There, three or four paces from him, in the centre of the chamber of Death, sat, or rather lay, a figure of Death. It reclined in a stone chest or coffin, like a man in a hip-bath which is too small for him. The bony arms hung down on either side, the bony limbs projecting towards him; the great white skull hung forward over the massive breast-bone. It moved, too, of itself, and as it moved the jaw-bone tapped against the breast and the teeth clacked gently together.

Terror seized him while he looked, and, as George had done, he turned to fly. How could that thing move its head? The head ought to fall off.

Seizing the rope, he jerked it violently in the first effort of mounting.

"Hev he got yew, colonel?" sung out George above; and the sound of a human voice brought him back to his senses.

"No," he answered, as boldly as he could, and then, setting his teeth, turned and tottered straight at the horror in the chest.

He was there now, and, holding the lantern straight against the thing, examined it. It was a skeleton of enormous size, and the skull was fixed to the vertebra with rusty wire.

At this evidence of the handiwork of man his fears almost vanished. Even in that company he could not help remembering that it is scarcely to be supposed that spiritual skeletons carry about wire with which to tie on their skulls.

With a sigh of relief he held up the lantern and looked round. He was standing in a good-sized vault or chamber, built of rubble stone. Some of this rubble had fallen in to his left; but otherwise, though the workmanship showed that it must be of extreme antiquity, the stone lining was still strong and good. He looked upon the floor, and then for the first time perceived that the nodding skeleton before him was not the only one. All round lay remnants of the mighty dead. There they were, stretched out in the form of a circle, of which the stone kist was the centre.* One place in the circle was vacant; evidently it had once been occupied by the giant frame which now sat within the kist. Next he looked at the kist itself. It had all the appearance of one of those rude stone chests in which the very ancient inhabitants of this island buried the ashes of their cremated dead. But, if this was so, whence came the uncremated skeletons?

Perhaps a subsequent race, or tribe, had found the chamber ready prepared, and used it to bury some among them who had fallen in battle. It was impossible to say more, especially as, with one exception, there was nothing buried with the skeletons which would assist to identify their race or age. That exception was a dog. A dog had been placed by one of the bodies. Evidently, from the position of the bones of its master's arms, he had been left to his last sleep with his hand resting on his hound's head.

Bending down, Harold examined the seated skeleton more closely. It was, he discovered, accurately jointed together with strong wire. Clearly this was the work of hands which were born into the world long after the flesh on those mighty bones had crumbled into dust.

But where was the treasure? He saw none. His heart sank as the idea struck him that he had made an interesting archæological discovery, and that was all. Before undertaking a closer search he returned to the hole, and hallooed to George to come down, as there was nothing but some bones to frighten him.

This the worthy George was at length with much difficulty persuaded to do.

When at last he stood beside him in the vault, Harold ex-

---

* At Bungay, in Suffolk, there recently stood a mound or tumulus, on which was built a windmill. Some years ago the windmill was pulled down, and the owner of the ground, wishing to build a house upon the site, set to work to cart away the mound. His astonishment may be conceived when he found in the mound a great number of skeletons arranged in circles. These skeletons were of large size, and a gentleman who saw them informed me that he measured one. It was over seven feet high. The bones were, unhappily, carted away and thrown into a dyke. But no house has been built upon the site of the resting-place of those unknown warriors.—AUTHOR.

plained to him what the place was, and how ridiculous were
his fears, without, however, succeeding in allaying them to any
considerable extent.

And really when one considers the position, shut up as they
were in the bowels of a place which had for centuries owned
the reputation of being haunted, faced by a nodding skeleton
of almost superhuman size, and surrounded by various other
skeletons, all "very fine and large," with the most violent
tempest that had visited the country for years sighing away
outside, it is not wonderful that George was scared.

"Well," he said, his teeth chattering, "if this ain't the
masterest one that iver I did see." But here he stopped,
language was not equal to the expression of his feelings.

Meanwhile Harold, with a heart full of anxiety, was turning the lantern this way and that in the hope of discovering
some traces of Sir James's treasure, but nought could he see.
There, to the left, the masonry had fallen in. He went to it
and pulled aside some of the stones. There was a cavity behind, apparently a passage leading no doubt to the secret entrance to the vault, but he could see nothing in it. Once
more he searched round. There was nothing. Unless the
treasure was buried somewhere, or hidden away in the passage, it was non-existent, that was all.

And yet what was the meaning of that jointed skeleton
sitting in the stone bath? It must have been put there for
some purpose, probably to frighten would-be plunderers away.
Could he be sitting on the money? He rushed to the chest
and looked through the bony legs. No, his pelvis rested on
the stone bottom of the kist.

"Well, George, it seems we're done," said Harold, with a
ghastly attempt at a laugh. "There's no treasure here."

"Maybe its underneath that there stone corn-bin," suggested George, whose teeth were still chattering. "It should
be here, or hereabouts, surely."

This was an idea. Helping himself to the shoulder-blade
of some deceased hero, Harold, using it as a trowel, began to
scoop away the soft sand upon which the stone chest stood.
He scooped and scooped manfully, but he could not come to
the bottom of the kist.

He stepped back and looked at it. It must be one of two

things—either the hollow at the top was but a shallow cutting in a great block of stone, or the kist had a false bottom.

He literally sprang at it, and, seizing the giant skeleton by the spine, jerked it out of the kist, and dropped it in a bristling bony heap on one side. Just as he did so there came a gust of wind so furious that, buried as they were in the earth, they literally felt the mound rock beneath it. Instantly it was followed by a frightful crash overhead.

George collapsed in terror, and for a moment Harold could not for the life of him think what had happened. He ran to the hole and looked up. Straight above him he could see the sky, in which the first cold lights of dawn were quivering. Mrs. Massey's summer-house had been blown bodily away, and the "ancient British Dwelling-Place" was once more as it had been for centuries, open to the sky.

"The summer-house has gone, George," he said. "Thank God that we were not in it, or we should have gone too."

"Oh, Lord, sir," groaned the unhappy George, "this is an awful business. It's like a judgment."

"It might have been if we had been up above instead of safe down here," he answered. "Come, bring that other lantern."

George roused himself, and together they bent over the now empty kist, and examined it closely.

The stone bottom was not of quite the same color as the walls of the kist, and there was a crack across it. Harold felt in his pocket and drew out his knife, which had at the back of it one of those strong iron hooks that are used to extract stones from the hoofs of horses. This hook he worked into the crack, and managed before it broke to pull up a fragment of stone. Then, looking round, he found among the rubbish, where the wall had fallen in, a long, sharp flint. This he inserted in the hole, and they both levered away at it.

Half of the cracked stone came up a few inches, far enough to allow them to get their fingers underneath it. So it *was* a false bottom.

"Catch hold," gasped the colonel, "and pull for your life."

George did as he was bid, and, setting their knees against the hollowed stone, they tugged till their muscles cracked.

"It's a-moving," said George. "Now then, colonel."

20

Next second they both found themselves on the flat of their backs. The stone had given with a run.

Up sprang the colonel like a kitten. The broken stone was standing edgeways in the kist. There was something soft beneath it.

" The light, George," he said, hoarsely.

Beneath the stone were some layers of rotten linen.

Was it a shroud or what?

They pulled the linen out by handfuls. One! two! three! Oh, great Heaven!

There, under the linen, were row on row of shining gold coins set edgeways.

For a moment everything swam before Harold's eyes, and his heart stopped beating. As for George, he muttered something inaudible about it's being a " master one," and collapsed.

With trembling fingers Harold managed to pick out two pieces of gold which had been disturbed by the upheaval of the stone, and held them to the light. He was a skilled numismatologist, and had no difficulty in recognizing them. One was a beautiful three-pound piece of Charles I., and the other a Spur Royal of James I.

That proved it. There was no doubt that this was the treasure hidden by Sir James de la Molle, and he it must have been also who had conceived the idea of putting a false bottom to the kist, and setting up the skeleton to frighten marauders from the treasure, if by any chance one should enter.

For a minute or two the men stood staring at each other over the great treasure which they had unearthed in that dread place, shaking with the reaction of their first excitement, and scarcely able to speak.

" How deep du it go?" said George.

Harold got his knife and loosened some of the top coins, which were very tightly packed, till he could move his hand in them freely. Then he pulled out handful after handful of every sort of gold coin. There was a rose noble of Edward IV.; double sovereigns of Henry VIII.; triple sovereigns and gold crowns of Edward VI.; double rials, rials, and angels of Mary; rose royals, spur royals, angels, large sovereigns, and laurels of James I.; double rials and rials of Elizabeth; three-pound pieces, broads, and half-broads of Charles I., some in greater quantity and some in less, but all were represented. Handful after handful did he pull out, and yet the bottom was not reached. At last he came to it. The layer of gold pieces was about thirty inches thick by three feet six long.

"We must get this into the house, George, before any one is about," gasped the colonel.

"Yes, sir, yes; but how be we agoing to carry it?"

Harold thought for a minute, and then acted thus. Bidding George stay in the vault with the treasure, which he was with difficulty persuaded to do, he climbed the improvised rope ladder, and got in safety through the hole. In his excitement he had forgotten about the summer-house having been carried away by the gale, which was still blowing, though not with so much fury as before, and the wind-swept desolation that met his view as he emerged into the dawning light broke upon him with a shock. The summer-house was clean gone, nothing but a few uprights remained of it; and fifty yards away he thought he could make out the crumpled-up shape of the roof. Nor was that all. Quite a quarter of the great oaks which were the glory of the place were down, or splintered and ruined. But what did he care for the summer-house or the oaks now? Forgetting his exhaustion, he ran down the slope and reached the house, which he entered as softly as he could by the side door. Nobody was about yet, or would be for another hour. It was Christmas Day, and not a pleasant morning to get up on, so the servants would be sure to lie abed. On his way to his bedroom he peeped into the dining-room, where he had fallen asleep on the previous evening. When he had woke up, it may be remembered, he lit a candle. This candle was now flaring itself to death, for he had forgotten to extinguish it, and by its side lay the paper from which he had made the great discovery. There was nothing in it, of course, but somehow the sight impressed him very much. It seemed months since he awoke to find the lamp gone out. How much may happen between the lighting of a candle and its burning away! Smiling at this trite reflection, he blew that light out, and, taking another, went to his room. Here he found a stout hand-bag, with which he made haste to return to the Mount.

"Are you all right, George?" he shouted down the hole.

"Well, colonel, yes, but not sorry to see you back. It's lonesome like down here with these deaders."

"Very well. Look out! There's a bag. Put as much gold in it as you can lift comfortably, and then make it fast to the rope."

Some three minutes passed, and then George announced that the bagful of gold was ready. Harold hauled away, and with a considerable effort brought it to the surface. Then, getting the bag on to his shoulder, he staggered off with it to the house. In his room stood a massive sea-going chest, the companion of his many wanderings. It was about half full of uniforms and old clothes, which he bundled unceremoniously on to the floor. This done, he shot the bagful of shining gold, as bright and uncorrupted now as when it was packed away two and a half centuries ago, into the chest, and returned for another load.

Twenty times did he make this journey. At the tenth something happened.

"Here's a writing, sir, with this lot," shouted George. "It was packed away in the money."

He took the "writing," or rather parchment, out of the mouth of the bag, and put it in his pocket unread.

At last the store, enormous as it was, was exhausted.

"That's the lot, sir," shouted George, as he sent up the twentieth bagful. "If you'll kindly let down that there rope, I'll come up, too."

"All right," said the colonel, "put the skeleton back first."

"Well, sir," answered George, "he looks wonderful comfortable where he lay, he du; so, if you're agreeable, I think I'll let him be."

Harold chuckled, and presently George arrived, covered with filth and perspiration.

"Well, sir," he said, "I never did think that I should get tired of handling gold coins, but it's a rum world, and that's a fact. Well, I nivir, and the summer-house gone, and jist look at thim there oaks. Well, if that beant a master one."

"You never saw a masterer, that's what you were going to say, wasn't it? Well, and take one thing with another, nor

did I, George, if that's any comfort to you.   Now look here,
just cover over this hole with some boards and earth, and
then come in and get some breakfast.   It's eight o'clock and
past, and the gale is blowing itself out.   A merry Christmas
to you, George!" and he held out his hand, covered with cuts
and grime and blood.

George shook it.   "Same to you, colonel, I'm sure.   And a
merry Christmas it is.   God bless you, sir, for what you've
done to-night.   You've saved the old place from that banker
chap, that's what you've done ; and you'll have Miss Ida, and
I'm durned glad on it, that I am.   Lord! won't this make the
squire open his eyes," and the honest fellow brushed away a
tear and fairly capered with joy, his red nightcap waving on
the breeze.

It was a strange and beautiful sight to see the solemn
George capering thus in the midst of that windy desolation.

Harold was too moved to answer, so he shouldered his last
load of treasure and limped off with it to the house.   Mrs.
Jobson and her talkative niece were up now, but they did not
happen to see him, and he reached his room in safety.   He
poured the last bagful of gold into the chest, and smoothed it
down.   It filled it to the brim.   He shut the chest and locked
it, and then as he was, covered with filth and grime, bruised
and bleeding, and his hair flying wildly about his face, he sat
down upon it, and from his heart thanked Heaven for the wonderful thing that had happened to him.

So exhausted was he that he nearly fell asleep as he sat, but,
remembering himself, he rose, and, taking the parchment from
his pocket, he cut the faded silk with which it was tied, and
opened it.

On it was a short inscription in the same crabbed writing
which he had seen in the old Bible that Ida had found.

It ran as follows :

"Seeing that the times be so troublous that no man can be sure of his
own, I, Sir James de la Molle, have brought together all my substance in
money from wheresoever it lay at interest, and have hid the same in this
sepulchre, to which I found the entry by a chance, till such time as peace
come back to this unhappy England.   This have I done on Christmas Day,
in the year of our Lord 1643, having completed the hiding of the gold
while the great gale was blowing.   JAMES DE LA MOLLE."

Thus, on a long-gone Christmas Day, in the hour of a great wind, was the gold hid, and now, on this Christmas Day, when another great wind raged overhead, was it found once more, just in time to save a daughter of the house of De la Molle from a fate as bad as death.

CHAPTER XLII.

IDA GOES TO MEET HER FATE.

MOST people of a certain age and a certain degree of sensitiveness of disposition, in looking back down the vista of their lives, whereon memory's melancholy light plays in fitful flashes like the alternate glow of a censer swung in the twilight of a tomb, can recall some one night of peculiar mental agony. It may have come when first we found ourselves face to face with the chill and hopeless horror of departed life; when, in our soul's despair, we stretched out vain hands and wept, called and no answer came; when we kissed those beloved lips and shrank aghast at contact with their clay, those lips more eloquent now in the rich pomp of their unutterable silence than in the brightest hour of their unsealing. It may have come when our honor and the hope of all our days lay at our feet shattered like a sherd on the hard roadway of the world. It may have come when she, the sweet star of our youth, the pure and holy thing, the type of completed beauty and woman's most perfect measure, she, to whom was given the chalice of our joy, and who held in her white hand the love-begotten germ of all our power, ruthlessly emptied and crushed it, and, as became a star, slid down our horizon's ways to rise upon some other sky. Or it may have come when Brutus stabbed us, or when a child whom we had cherished struck us with a serpent-fang of treachery, and left the icy poison to creep upon our heart. One way or another it has been with most of us, that long night of utter woe, and all will own that it is a ghastly thing to face.

And so Ida de la Molle had found it. The shriek of the great gale rushing on that Christmas Eve round the stout Norman towers was not more strong than the breath of the despair that shook her life. She could not sleep—who could sleep on such a night, the herald of such a morrow? The wail and roar of the wind, the crash of falling trees, and the rattle of flying stones seemed to form a fit accompaniment to the turmoil of her mind.

She rose, and, putting on her dressing-gown, went to the window, and in the dim light watched the trees gigantically tossing in a great struggle for their life. An oak and a birch were within her view. The oak stood the gale out—for a while. Presently there came an awful gust and beat upon it. It would not bend, and the tough roots would not give, so beneath the weight of the breath of its destiny the big tree broke in two like a straw, and its spreading top was whirled into the moat. But the birch gave and bent; it bent till its delicate filaments lay upon the wind like a woman's streaming hair, and the fierceness of the gust wore itself away and spared it.

"See what happens to those who stand up and defy their fate," said Ida to herself, with a bitter laugh. "The birch has the best of it."

Ida rose and closed the shutters; the sight of the storm affected her already strained nerves almost beyond bearing. She began to walk up and down the big room, flitting like a ghost from end to end and back again, and again back. What could she do? What should she do? Her fate was upon her; she could no longer resist the inevitable—she must marry him. And yet her whole soul revolted from the act with an overwhelming fierceness which astonished even herself. She had known two girls who had married people whom they did not like, being at the time, or pretending to be, attached to somebody else, and she had observed that they accommodated themselves to their fate with considerable ease. But it was not so with her; she was fashioned of another clay, and it made her faint to think of what was before her. And yet the prospect was one on which she could expect little sympathy. Her own father, although personally he disliked the man whom she must marry, was clearly filled with amazement that she should prefer Colonel Quaritch, middle-aged, poor, and plain, to Edward Cossey, handsome, young, and rich as Crœsus. He could not comprehend or measure the extraordinary gulf which her passion dug between the two. If, therefore, this was so with her own father, how would it be with the rest of the world?

She paced her bedroom till she was tired, and then, in an access of despair, which was sufficiently distressing in a person of her reserved and stately manner, flung herself, weeping and sobbing, upon her knees, and, resting her aching head upon the bed, prayed as she had never prayed before that this cup might pass from her. She did not know—how should she?— that at that very moment her prayer was being answered, and that her lover was then, even as she prayed, lifting the broken stone and revealing the hoard of ruddy gold.   But so it was; she prayed in despair and agony of mind, and the prayer carried on the wild wings of the night brought a fulfilment with it.   Not in vain were her tears and supplications, for even now the deliverer delved among

> "The dust and awful treasures of the dead,"

and even now the light of her coming happiness was breaking on her tortured night as the first cold gleams of the Christmas morning were breaking over the stormy fury of the void without.

And then, chilled and numb in body and mind, she crept into her bed again and at last lost herself in sleep.

By half-past nine o'clock, when Ida came down to breakfast, the gale had utterly vanished, though its footprints were visible enough in shattered trees, unthatched stacks, and ivy torn in knotty sheets from the old walls it clothed.   It would have been difficult to recognize in the cold and stately lady who stood at the dining-room window, noting the havoc and waiting for her father to come in, the lovely, passionate, dishevelled woman who some few hours before had thrown herself upon her knees praying to God for the succor she could not win from man.   Women, like nature, have many moods, and many countenances to express them.   The hot fit had passed, and the cold fit was on her now.   Her face, except for the dark hollows round the eyes, was white as winter, and her heart was cold as winter's ice.

Presently her father came in.

"What a gale!" he said, "what a gale!   Upon my word I began to think that the old place was coming down about our ears; and the wreck among the trees is dreadful.   I don't think there can have been such a wind since the time of King

Charles I., when the top of the tower was blown clean off the church—you remember I was showing you the entry about it in the registers the other day, the one signed by the parson and old Sir James de la Molle. The boy who has just come up tells me that he hears that poor old Mrs. Massey's summer-house on the top of Dead Man's Mount has been blown away, which is a good riddance for Colonel Quaritch. Why, what's the matter with you? How pale you look."

"The gale kept me awake. I got very little sleep," answered Ida.

"And no wonder. Well, my dear, you haven't wished me a merry Christmas yet. Goodness knows we want one badly enough. There has not been much merriment at Honham of late years."

"A merry Christmas to you, father," she said.

"Thank you, my love, the same to you; you have got most of your Christmases before you, which is more than I have. God bless me, it only seems like yesterday since the big bunch of holly tied to the hook in the ceiling there fell down on the breakfast-table and smashed all the cups, and yet it is more than sixty years ago. Dear me! how angry my poor dear mother was! She never could bear the crockery to be broken —it was a little failing of your grandmother's," and he laughed more heartily than Ida had heard him do for some weeks.

She made no answer, but busied herself about the tea. Presently, glancing up, she saw her father's face change. The worn expression came back upon it, and he lost his buoyant bearing. Evidently a new thought had struck him, and she was in no great doubt as to what it was.

"We had better get on with breakfast," he said. "You know that Cossey is coming up at ten o'clock."

"Ten o'clock?" she said, faintly.

"Yes. I told him ten so that we could go to church afterwards if we wished to. Of course, Ida, I am still in the dark as to what you have made up your mind to do, but whatever it is I thought that he had better once and for all hear your final decision from your own lips. If, however, you feel yourself at liberty to tell it to me as your father, I shall be glad to hear it."

She lifted her head and looked him full in the face, and then paused. He had a cup of tea in his hand, and it was held in the air half-way to his mouth, while his whole face showed the overmastering anxiety with which he was awaiting her reply.

"Make your mind easy, father," she said, "I am going to marry Mr. Cossey."

He put the cup down in such a fashion that he spilled half of the tea, most of it over his own clothes, without even noticing it, and then turned away his face.

"Well," he said, "of course it is not my affair, or, at least, only indirectly so, but I must say, my love, I congratulate you on the decision which you have come to. I quite understand that you have been in some little difficulty about the matter; young women often have been before you, and will be again; but to be frank, Ida, that Quaritch business was not at all suitable, either in age, or fortune, or in anything else. Yes, although Cossey is not everything that one might wish, on the whole I congratulate you heartily."

"Oh, pray don't," broke in Ida, almost in a cry. "Whatever you do, pray don't congratulate me!"

Her father turned round again and looked at her. But Ida's face had already recovered its calm, and he could make nothing of it.

"I don't quite understand you," he said; "these things are generally considered matters for congratulation."

But for all he might say and all that he might urge in his mind to the contrary he did, more or less, understand what her outburst meant. He could not but know that the exclamation was the last outcry of a broken spirit. In his heart he realized then, if he had never clearly realized it before, that this proposed marriage was a thing hateful to his daughter, and his conscience pricked him sorely. And yet—and yet—it was but a woman's fancy—a passing fancy! She would become reconciled to the inevitable as women do, and when her children came she would grow accustomed to her sorrow, and her trouble would be forgotten in their laughter. And if not? Well, it was but one woman's life which would be affected, and the very existence of his race, and the very cradle that had nursed them from century to century were now at stake. Was all this to be at the mercy of a girl's fancy? No! let the individual suffer.

So he argued. And so at his age and in his circumstances most of us would argue also, and, perhaps, considering all things, we should be right. For in this world personal desires must continually give way to the welfare of others. Did they not do so our system of society could not endure.

No more was said upon the subject. Ida made pretence of eating a piece of toast; the squire mopped up the tea upon his clothes, and then drank some more.

Meanwhile the remorseless seconds crept on. It wanted but five minutes to the hour, and the hour would, she well knew, bring the man with it.

The five minutes passed slowly and in silence. Both her father and herself realized the nature of the impending situation, but neither of them spoke of it. Ah! there was the sound of wheels upon the gravel. So it had come.

Ida felt like death itself. Her pulse sank and fluttered; her vital forces seemed to cease their work.

Another two minutes passed, and then the door opened and the parlor-maid came in.

"Mr. Cossey, if you please, sir."

"Oh," said the squire. "Where is he?"

"In the vestibule, sir."

"Very good. Tell him I will be there in a minute."

The maid went.

"Now, Ida," said her father, "I suppose we had better get this business over."

"Yes," she answered, rising; "I am ready."

And, gathering up her energies, she passed out to meet her fate.

CHAPTER XLIII.

GEORGE IS SEEN TO LAUGH.

Ida and her father reached the vestibule to find Edward Cossey standing with his face to the mantelpiece and nervously toying with some curiosities upon it. He was, as usual, dressed with great care, and his face, though pale and worn from the effects of agitation of mind, looked, if anything, handsomer than ever. As soon as he heard them coming, which owing to his partial deafness he did not do till they were quite close to him, he turned round with a start, and a sudden flush of color came upon his pale face.

The squire shook hands with him in a solemn sort of way, like people do when they meet at a funeral, and Ida barely touched his outstretched fingers with her own.

A few random remarks followed about the weather, which really for once in a way was equal to the conversational strain put upon it, but at length these died away and there came an awful pause. It was broken at length by the squire, who, standing with his back to the fire, his eyes fixed upon the wall opposite, after much humming and hawing, delivered himself thus—

"I understand, Mr. Cossey, that you have come to hear my daughter's final decision on the matter of the proposal of marriage which you have made and renewed to her. Now, of course, this is a very important question, very important indeed, and it is one with which I cannot presume even to seem to interfere. Therefore I shall, without comment, leave my daughter to speak for herself—"

"One moment before she does so," he interrupted, drawing indeed but a poor augury of success from Ida's icy looks. "I have come to renew my offer and to take my final answer, and I beg Miss De la Molle to consider how deep and sincere must be that affection which has endured through so many rebuffs. I know, or at the least I fear, that I do not occupy the place in her feelings that I should wish to, but I look to time to change this; at any rate, I am willing to take my chance. As regards money, I repeat the offer that I have already made."

"There, I should not say too much about that," broke in the squire, impatiently.

"Oh, why not?" said Ida, in bitter sarcasm. "Mr. Cossey knows it is one of the best arguments with our sex. I presume that as a preliminary to the renewal of the engagement, the persecution of my father, which is being carried on by your lawyer, will cease?"

"Absolutely."

"And if the engagement is not renewed the money will of course be called in?"

"My lawyers advise that it should be," he answered, sullenly; "but see here, Ida, you may make your own terms about money. Marriage, after all, is practically a matter of bargaining, and I am not going to stand out about the price."

"You are really most generous," went on Ida, in the same bitter tone, the irony of which made her father wince, for he understood her mood better than did her lover. "I only regret that I cannot appreciate the generosity more than I do. But it is at least in my power to give you the return which you deserve. So I can no longer hesitate, but once and for all—"

And she stopped dead, and stared at the glass door as though she saw a ghost. Both her father and Edward Cossey followed the motion of her eyes, and this was what they saw. Up the steps came Colonel Quaritch and George. Both were pale and weary-looking, but the former was at least clean. As for George, this could not be said. His head was still adorned with the red nightcap, his hands were cut and dirty, and on his clothes was an unlimited quantity of encrusted filth.

"What the dickens—" began the squire, and at that moment George, who was leading, knocked at the door.

"You can't come in now," roared the squire; "don't you see that we are engaged?"

"But we must come in, squire, begging your pardon," answered George, with determination, as he opened the door, "we've got that to say as won't keep."

"I tell you that it must keep, sir," said the old gentleman, working himself into a rage. "Am I not to be allowed a moment's privacy in my own house? I wonder at your conduct, Colonel Quaritch, in forcing your presence upon me when I tell you that it is not wanted."

"I am sure that I apologize, Mr. De la Molle," began the colonel, utterly taken aback, "but what I have to say is—"

"The best way that you can apologize is by withdrawing," answered the squire with majesty. "I shall be most happy to hear what you have to say on another occasion."

"Oh, squire, squire, don't be such a fule, begging your pardon for the word," said George, in exasperation. "Don't go a-knocking of your head agin a brick wall."

"Will you be off, sir?" roared his master, in a voice that made the walls shake.

By this time Ida had recovered herself. She seemed to feel that her lover had something to say that concerned her deeply—probably she read it in his eyes.

"Father," she said, raising her voice, "I won't have Colonel Quaritch turned away from the door like that. If you will not admit him I will go outside and hear what it is that he has to say."

In his heart the squire held Ida in some awe. He looked at her, and saw that her eyes were flashing and her breast heaving, and he gave way.

"Oh, very well, since my daughter insists on it, pray come in," and he bowed. "If such an intrusion falls in with your ideas of decency it is not for me to complain."

"I accept your invitation," answered Harold, looking very angry, "because I have something to say which you must hear, and hear at once. No, thank you. I will stand. Now, Mr. De la Molle, it is this, wonderful as it may seem. It has been my fortune to discover the treasure hidden by Sir James de la Molle in the year 1643."

There was a universal gasp of astonishment.

"What!" said the squire. "Why, I thought that the whole thing was a myth."

"No, that it ain't, sir," said George, with a melancholy smile, "cos I've seen it."

Ida had sunk into a chair.

"What is the amount?" she asked, in a low, eager voice.

"I have been unable to calculate exactly, but, speaking roughly, it cannot be much under fifty thousand pounds, estimated on the value of the gold alone. Here is a specimen of it," and Harold pulled out a handful of rials and other coins, and poured them on to the table.

Ida hid her face in her hand, and Edward Cossey, realizing what this most unexpected development of events might mean for him, began to tremble.

"I should not allow myself to be too much elated, Mr. De la Molle," he said, with a sneer, "for even if this tale be true, it is treasure trove, and belongs to the crown."

"Ah," said the squire, "I never thought of that."

"But I have," said the colonel, quietly. "If I remember right, the last of the original De la Molles left a will in which he specially devised this treasure hidden by his father to your ancestor. That this is the identical treasure I am fortunately in a position to prove by this parchment," and he laid the writing that he had found with the gold upon the table.

"Quite right—quite right," said the squire, "that will take it out of the custom."

"Perhaps the Solicitor to the Treasury may hold a different opinion," said Cossey, with another sneer.

Just then Ida took her hand from her face. There was a dewy look about her eyes, and the last ripples of a happy smile lingered round the corners of her mouth.

"Now that we have heard what Colonel Quaritch had to say," she said in her softest voice, and addressing her father, "there is no reason why we should not finish our business with Mr. Cossey."

Here Harold and George turned to go, but she waved them back imperiously, and began speaking before any one could interfere, taking up her speech where she had broken it off when she caught sight of the colonel and George coming up the steps.

"I can no longer hesitate," she said, "but once and for all I decline to marry you, Mr. Cossey, and I hope that I shall never see your face again."

At this announcement the bewildered squire put his hand

to his head. Edward Cossey staggered visibly and rested himself against the table, while George murmured, audibly, " That's a good job."

" Listen," said Ida, rising from her chair, her dark eyes flashing as the thought of all the shame and agony that she had undergone rose up within her mind.

" Listen, Mr. Cossey," and she pointed her finger at him, " this is the history of our connection. Some months ago I was so foolish, taking you for a gentleman, as to ask your help in the matter of the mortgages which your bank was calling in. You then practically made terms that if it should at any time be your wish I should become engaged to you ; and I, having no option, accepted. Then, in the interval, while it was inconvenient to you to enforce your rights, I gave my affection elsewhere. But when you, having deserted the lady who stood in your way—no, do not interrupt me ; I know it, I know it all ; I know it from her own lips—came forward and claimed my promise, I was forced to assent. Then a loophole of escape presented itself and I availed myself of it. What followed ? You again became possessed of power over my father and this place, you insulted the man I loved, you resorted to every expedient that the law would allow to torture my father and myself. You set your lawyers upon us like dogs upon a hare, you held ruin over us and again and again you offered me money, as much money as I wished, if only I would sell myself to you. And then you bided your time, leaving despair to do its work.

" I saw the toils closing round us. I knew that if I did not yield my father would be driven from his home in his old age, and that the place he loved better than his life would pass to strangers—would pass to you. No, father, do not stop me ; I *will* speak my mind.

" And at last I determined that cost what it might I would yield. Whether I could have carried out my determination God only knows. I almost think that I should have killed myself upon my marriage day. I made up my mind. Not five minutes ago the very words were upon my lips that would have sealed my fate, when deliverance came. And now go. I have done with you. Your money shall be paid to you, capital and interest, down to the last farthing. I tender back my price, and knowing you for what you are, I—I despise you. That is all I have to say."

"Well, if that beant a master one," ejaculated George, aloud.

Ida, who had never looked more beautiful than she did in this moment of passion, turned to seat herself, but the tension of her feelings and the torrent of her wrath and eloquence had been too much for her, and she would have fallen had not Harold, who had been listening amazed to this overpowering outburst of nature, ran up and caught her in his arms.

As for Edward Cossey, he had shrunk back involuntarily beneath the volume of her scorn, till he stood with his back against the panelled wall. His face was white as a sheet; despair and fury shone in his large dark eyes. Never had he desired this woman more fiercely than he did now, in the moment when he knew that she had escaped him forever. In a sense he was to be pitied, for passion tore his heart in twain. For a moment he stood thus, and then with a spring rather than a step, he advanced across the room till he was face to face with Harold, who with Ida, half fainting, still in his arms, and her head upon his shoulder, was standing on the farther side of the great open grate.

"—— you," he said, "I owe this to you—you half-pay adventurer," and he lifted his arm as though to strike him.

"Come, none of that," said the squire, speaking for the first time. "I will have no brawling here."

"No," put in George, edging his long form between the two, "and, begging your pardon, sir, don't you go a-calling of better men than yourself adwenturers. At any rate, if the colonel is an adwenturer, he has adventured to some purpose, as is easy to see," and he pointed to Ida lying in his arms.

"Hold your tongue, sir," roared the squire, as usual relieving his feelings on his retainer. "You are always shoving your oar in where it isn't wanted."

"All right, squire, all right," said George the imperturbable; "then his manners shouldn't be sich."

"Do you mean to allow this?" said Cossey, turning fiercely to the old gentleman. "Do you mean to allow this man to marry your daughter for her money?"

"Mr. Cossey," answered the squire, with his politest and most old-fashioned bow, "whatever sympathy I may have felt for you is being rapidly alienated by your manner. I told you that my daughter must speak for herself. She has spoken very clearly, and, in short, I have absolutely nothing to add to her words."

"I tell you what it is," Cossey said, shaking with fury, "I have been tricked and fooled and played with, and so sure as there is a God above us I will have my revenge on you all somehow. The money that this man says that he has found belongs to the queen and not to you, and I will take care that the proper people are informed of it before you can make away with it, and when that is taken from you, if, indeed, the whole thing is not a trick, we will see what will happen to you. I tell you that I will take this property and I will pull this old place you are so fond of down stone by stone and throw it into the moat, and send the plough over the site. I will sell the estate piecemeal and blot it out. I tell you I have been tricked—you encouraged the marriage yourself, you know you did, and you forbade that man the house," and he paused for breath and to collect his words.

Again the squire bowed, and his bow was a study in itself. You do not see such bows nowadays.

"One minute, Mr. Cossey," he said, very quietly, for it was one of his peculiarities to become abnormally quiet in circumstances of real emergency, "and then I think that we may close this painful interview. When first I knew you I did not like you. Afterwards, through various circumstances, I modified my opinion and set my dislike down to prejudice. You are quite right in saying that I encouraged the idea of a marriage between you and my daughter, and also that I forbade the house to Colonel Quaritch. I did so because, to be honest, I saw no other way of avoiding the utter ruin of my family; but perhaps I was wrong in so doing. I hope that you may never be placed in a position which will force you to such a decision. Also at the time, indeed never till this moment, have I quite realized how the matter really stood. I did not understand how strongly my daughter was attached in another direction, perhaps I was unwilling to understand it. Nor did I altogether understand the course of action by

which, it seems, you obtained a promise of marriage from my
daughter in the first instance. I was anxious for the marriage because I believed you to be a better man than you are,
and because I thought that it would place my daughter and
her descendants in a much improved position, and that she
would in time become attached to you. I forbade Colonel
Quaritch the house because I thought that an alliance with
him would be most undesirable for everybody concerned. I
find that in all this I was acting wrongly, and I frankly admit
it. Perhaps as we grow old we grow worldly also, and you
and your agents pressed me very hard, Mr. Cossey. Still I
have always told you that my daughter was a free agent and
must decide for herself, and therefore I owe you no apology
on that score. So much then for the question of your engagement to Miss De la Molle. It is done with.

"And now as regards the threats you make. I shall try to
meet them as occasion arises, and if I cannot do so it will be
my misfortune. But one thing they show me, though I am
sorry to have to say it to any man in a house which I can
still call my own—they show me that my first impressions of
you were the correct ones. *You are not a gentleman*, Mr.
Cossey, and I must beg to decline the honor of your further
acquaintance," and with another bow he opened the vestibule-
door and stood holding the handle in his hand.

Edward Cossey looked round with a stare of rage, and then
muttering one most comprehensive curse he stalked from the
room, and in another minute was driving fast through the ancient gateway.

Poor man! Let us pity him, for he also certainly got his
full due.

George followed him to the outer door and then he did a
thing that nobody had seen him do before, he burst out into
a loud laugh.

"What are you making that noise about?" asked his master, sternly.. "This is no laughing matter."

"*Him!*" replied George, pointing to the retreating dog-
cart—*he's* a-going to pull down the castle and throw it into
the moat and to send the plough over it, is he? *Him*—that
varmint! Why, them old towers will be a-standing there
when his beggarly bones is dust, and when his name ain't no

more a name; and there'll be one of the old blood sitting in
them too.   I knaw it, and I hev allus knawed it.   Come,
squire, though you allus du say how as I'm a fule, what did I
tell yer?   Didn't I tell yer that Prowidence weren't a-going
to let this place go to any laryers or bankers or thim sort.
Why, of course I did.   And now you see.   Not but what it
is all owing to the colonel.   He was the man that found it,
but then God Almighty taught him how to do it.   But he's
a good un, he is; and a gentleman, not like *him*," and he
once more pointed with unutterable scorn to the road down
which Edward Cossey had vanished.

"Now, look here," said the squire, "don't you stand talking here all day about things you don't understand.   That's
the way you waste time.   You be off and look after this gold;
it should not be left alone, you know.   We will come down
presently to Molehill, for I suppose that is where it is.   No,
I can't stop to hear the story now, and besides I want Colonel
Quaritch to tell it to me."

"All right, squire," said George, touching his red nightcap, "I'll be off," and he started.

"George," hallooed his master after him, but George did
not stop.   He had a trick of deafness when the squire was
calling and he wanted to go somewhere else.

"Confound you," roared the old gentleman, "why don't
you stop when I call you?"

This time George brought his long, lank frame to a stand-
still.

"Beg pardon, squire."

"Beg pardon, yes---you're always begging pardon.   Look
here, you had better bring your wife and have dinner in the
servants' hall to-day, and drink a glass of port."

"Thank you, squire," said George, again touching his red
nightcap.

"And look here, George.   Give me your hand, man.   Here's
a merry Christmas to you.   We've gone through some queerish
times about this place together, but now it almost looks as
though we were going to end our days in peace and plenty."

"Same to you, squire, I'm sure, same to you," said George,
pulling off his cap.   "Yes, yes, we've had some bad years,
what with poor Mr. James and that Quest and Cossey (he's

the master varmint of the lot he is), and the bad times and the
Moat Farm and all ; but, bless you, squire, now that there'll be
some ready money and no debts, why, if I don't make out
somehow so that you all get a good living out of the place
I'm a Dutchman. Yes, it's been a bad time and we're getting old ; but there, that's how it is, the sky almost allus clears
towards nightfall. God Almighty has a mind to let one down
easy, I suppose."

"If you would talk a little less about God Almighty, and
come to church a little more, it would be a good thing, as
I've told you before," said the squire ; "but there, go along
with you."

And the honest fellow went.

CHAPTER XLIV.

THE squire turned and entered the house. He generally was fairly noisy in his movements, but on this occasion he was exceptionally so. Possibly he had a reason for it.

On reaching the vestibule he found Harold and Ida standing side by side as though they were being drilled. It was impossible to resist the conclusion that they had suddenly assumed that attitude because it happened to be the first position into which they could conveniently fall.

There was a moment's silence, and then Harold took Ida's hand and led her up to where her father was standing.

"Mr. De la Molle," he said, simply, "once more I ask you for your daughter in marriage. I am quite aware of my many disqualifications, especially those of my age and the smallness of my means; but Ida and myself hope and believe that, under all the circumstances, you will no longer withhold your consent," and he paused.

"Quaritch," answered the squire, "I have already in your presence told Mr. Cossey under what circumstances I was favorably inclined to his proposal, so I need not repeat all that. As regards your means, although they would have been quite insufficient to avert the ruin which threatened us, still you have, I believe, a competence, and owing to your wonderful and most providential discovery the fear of ruin seems to have passed away. It is owing to you that that discovery, which, by the way, I want to hear all about, has been made; had it not been for you it never would have been made at all, and therefore I certainly have no right to say anything more about your means. As regards your age, well, after all, forty-four is not the limit of life, and if Ida does not object to marrying a man of those years, I cannot object to her doing so. With reference to your want of occupation, I think that if you marry Ida this place will, as times are, keep your hands pretty full, especially when you have an obstinate donkey like that fellow George to deal with, for I am getting too old and stupid to look after it myself; and, besides, things are so topsy-turvy that I can't understand them. There is one thing more that I want to say: I forbade you the house. Well, you are a generous-minded man, and it is human to err, and I think that perhaps you will understand my action and not bear me a grudge on that account. Also, I dare say that at the time, and possibly at other times, I said things that I should be sorry for if I could remember what they were, which I can't; and if so, I apologize to you as a gentleman should when he finds himself in the wrong. And now I say, God bless you both, and I hope you will be happy in life together, and so come here, Ida, my love, and give me a kiss. You have been a good daughter all your life, and so Quaritch may be sure that you will be a good wife too."

Ida did as she was bid, and then she went over to her lover and took his hand, and he kissed her on the forehead, and so, after all their troubles, they finally ratified the contract.

And we, who have followed them thus far, and have perhaps been a little moved with their struggles, hopes, and fears, will not surely grudge to re-echo the squire's old-fashioned prayer, "God bless them both."

God bless them both. Long may they live, and happily.

Long may they live, and for very long may their children's children of the race, if not of the name, of De la Molle, pass in and out through the old Norman gateway and past the sturdy Norman towers. The Boisseys, who built them, here had their habitation for six generations. The De la Molles, who wedded the heiress of the Boisseys, lived here for thirteen generations. May the Quaritches, whose ancestor married Ida, heiress of the De la Molles, endure as long!

Surely it is permitted to us to lift a corner of the curtain of futurity and to see, in spirit, Ida Quaritch, stately and beautiful, as we knew her, but of a happier countenance, seated, on some Christmas Eve to come, in the drawing-room of the castle and telling to the children at her knees the wonderful tale of how their father and old George, on this very night, when the great gale blew, long years ago, discovered the ruddy pile of gold, hoarded in that awful storehouse amid the bones of Saxon or Danish heroes, and thus saved her to be their mother. We can surely see the wide and wondering eyes and the fixed faces as for the tenth time they listen to a story before which the joys of Crusoe will grow pale, and hear the eager appeals for confirmation made to the military-looking gentleman, very grizzled now, but grown better-looking with the advancing years, who is standing warming himself before the fire, the best and most beloved husband and father in the whole country-side.

Perhaps there may be a vacant chair, and another tomb among the ranks of the departed De la Molles; perhaps the ancient walls will no longer echo to the sound of the old squire's stentorian voice. And what of that? It is our common lot.

But when he goes the country-side will lose a man of whom they will not see the like again, for the breed is dead or dying; a man whose very prejudices, inconsistencies, and occasional wrong-headed violence will be held, when he is no longer here, to have been endearing qualities. And for manliness, for downright English, godfearing virtues, for love of queen, country, family, and home, they may search in vain to find his equal among the thin-blooded gentility of the cosmopolitan Englishmen of the dawning twentieth century. His faults were many, and at one time he went near to sacrificing his daughter to save his house, but he would not have been the man he was without them.

And so to him, too, farewell. Perhaps he will find himself better placed in the Valhalla of his forefathers, surrounded by those stout old De la Molles whose memory he regarded with so much affection, than here in the Victorian era. For, as has been said elsewhere, the old squire would undoubtedly have looked better in a chain-shirt and a battle-axe than ever he did in a frock-coat, especially with his retainer George armed to the teeth behind him.

They kissed, and it was done; and out from the church tower in the meadows broke with clash and clangor the glad sound of the Christmas Bells. Out it swept over pitle and

fallow, over grove and wood. It floated down the valley of
the Ell, it beat against Dead Man's Mount (henceforth to the
vulgar mind more haunted than ever), and echoed up the castle's Norman towers and down the oak-clad vestibule. Away
over the common went the glad message of Earth's Saviour,
away high into the air, startling the rooks upon their airy
courses, as though the iron notes of the world's rejoicing would
fain float to the throned feet of the World's Everlasting King.

Peace and good-will, ay, and happiness, to the children of
men while their span is, and hope for the beyond, and Heav-
en's blessing on holy love and all good things that are.   This
was what those liquid notes seemed to say to the most happy
pair who stood hand in hand in the vestibule and thought of
all they had escaped and all that they had won.

"Well, Quaritch, if you and Ida have quite done staring at
each other, which isn't very interesting to a third party, perhaps you will not mind telling us how you happened on old
Sir James de la Molle's hoard.

Thus adjured, Harold began his thrilling story, telling the
whole history of the night in detail, and if his hearers had expected to be astonished, certainly their expectations were considerably more than fulfilled.

"Upon my word," said the squire when he had done, "I
think I am beginning to grow superstitious in my old age.
Hang me if I don't believe it was the finger of Providence itself
that pointed out those letters to you. Anyway, I'm off to
see the spoil. Run and get your hat, Ida, my dear, and we
will all go together."

And they went and looked at the chest brimful of red gold,
yes, and passed down, all three of them, into those chill pres-
ences in the bowels of the mount, and, coming thence awed
and silent, sealed up the place forever.

CONCLUSION.

GOOD-BY.

On the following morning such inhabitants of Boisingham as happened to be about were much interested at seeing an ordinary farm tumbrel coming down the main street, and being driven, or rather led, by no less a person than George himself, while behind it walked the well-known form of the old squire, arm-in-arm with Colonel Quaritch.

They were still more interested, however, when the tumbrel drew up at the door of the bank — not Cossey's, but the opposition bank—where, although it was Boxing Day, the manager and the clerk were waiting, apparently for its coming.

But their interest culminated when they perceived that the cart only contained a few flour sacks, and yet that each of these sacks seemed to require three or four men to lift it with any comfort.

Thus was the gold safely housed. Upon being weighed its value was found to be about fifty-three thousand pounds of modern money. As, however, some of the coins were exceedingly rare, and of great value to museums and collectors, this value was considerably increased, and the treasure was ultimately sold for fifty-five thousand two hundred and fifty-four pounds. Only Ida kept back enough of the choicest coins to make a gold waistband or girdle and a necklace for herself, destined no doubt in future days to form the most cherished heirloom of the Quaritch family.

On that same evening the squire and Harold went to London and opened up communications with the Solicitor to the Treasury. Fortunately they were able to refer to the will of Sir Edward de la Molle, the second baronet, in which he specially devised to his cousin, Geoffrey Döfferleigh, and his heirs forever, not only his estates, but his lands, "together with the treasure hid thereon or elsewhere by my late murdered father, Sir James de la Molle." Also they produced the writing which Ida had found in the old Bible, and the parchment discovered by George among the coin. These three documents formed a chain of evidence which even officials interested for the Treasury could not refuse to admit, and in the upshot the crown renounced its claims, and the property in the gold passed to the squire, subject to the payment of the same succession duty which he would have been called upon to meet had he inherited a like sum from a cousin at the present time.

And so it came to pass that when the mortgage money was due it was paid to the last farthing, capital and interest, and Edward Cossey lost his hold upon Honham forever.

As for Edward Cossey himself, we may say one more word about him. In the course of time he got over his violent passion for Ida sufficiently to allow him to make a brilliant marriage with the only daughter of an impecunious peer. She keeps her name and title and he plays the part of the necessary husband. Anyhow, my reader, if it is your glorious fortune to frequent the gilded saloons of the great, you may meet Lady Honoria Tallbit and Mr. Cossey. If you do meet him, however, it may be as well to avoid him, for the events of his life have not been of a nature to improve his temper. This much then of Edward Cossey.

If after leaving the gilded saloons aforesaid you should happen to wander down Piccadilly or the Strand, as the case may be, you may meet another character in this history. You may see a sweet, pale face, still stamped with a child-like roundness and simplicity, but half hidden in the coarse hood of the nun. You may see her, and if you care to follow you may find what is the work wherein she seeks her peace. It would shock you; you would fly from it in horror; but in her work of mercy and loving kindness—and she does it unflinchingly—and among her fellow-nuns there is no one more beloved than Sister Agnes. So good-by to her also.

Harold Quaritch and Ida were married in the spring, and the village children strewed the churchyard path—the same path where in anguish of soul they had met and parted on that dreary winter's night—with primroses and violets.

And there at the old church door, when the wreath is on her brow and the veil about her face, let us bid farewell to Ida and her husband, Harold Quaritch.

THE END.

www.ingramcontent.com/pod-product-compliance
Lightning Source LLC
Chambersburg PA
CBHW022209010726
47493CB00002B/490